MICHELLE COLE

F.A.T. CHANCE

Write World Publishing Group, Inc.
3523 McKinney Avenue
Suite: 373
Dallas, TX 75204

The trademark Write World "we write the books that make the whole world read!"™ is registered in the U.S. Patent and Trademark Office.

Library of Congress Control Number: 2002108468

Cole, Michelle
    F.a.t. chance

ISBN 978-0-9722173-3-0

Manufactured in the United States of America

Published simultaneously in Canada

March 2007

✳✳✳✳✳

In the year 2012, two childhood friends leave the small town of Tunis, Texas, for Los Angeles, with dreams of making it big in Hollywood. *Raven Kensington* is exquisitely-beautiful, with a trademark, Miss America smile. The African-American beauty is enormously-gifted, but knows that discrimination is *still* alive and well in Tinseltown. Raven's determined to make her dreams become reality. Once she arrives in Hollywood, no one denies that she's gorgeous, she's just "not the right race, or size, for Hollywood."

Raven *refuses* to give up. After years of blood, sweat, and tears, she reluctantly accepts a stereotypical role, that turns out to be a *blessing* in disguise.

Rebecca Simms is a blonde, blue-eyed beauty, with a bright smile. By Hollywood's standards, "Becky," is *the* reflection of beauty. However, Becky's size-eight frame isn't thin enough for Tinseltown. After years of struggling in Hollywood, Becky finally receives her big break, and it's an opportunity of a lifetime.

Things are finally looking up for Raven and Becky, until tragedy strikes. One of them will conform to the pressures of Hollywood, and dying to be thin, will cost one of the beauties, her life.

Tony Dash is a movie-star handsome, playboy-billionaire, who has never been committed to any relationship. He attends a movie premiere party in Beverly Hills one night. It is there that he first lays eyes on Raven Kensington. Tony is unable to take his eyes off the stunning-beauty. Raven not only catches Tony's eye, she becomes the first, and only woman, to ever, capture his heart.

Michelle Cole is *masterful*, as she tells this truly-inspiring story, as only she can. It's the story of hopes, dreams, love, friendships, and life's triumphs and tragedies. It's the story of an *extraordinary* woman, who fought for herself, and *for all those*, who want to be treated as the beautiful, individual human beings, that we all are, not treated as colors, or sizes. *F.A.T. CHANCE* is a story, that *speaks*, to *everyone*.

Books by Michelle Cole:

*Lilla Belle the First Stages

From the moment that I became a mother, I vowed to teach her,

guide her, and love her. From the moment I held her in my arms,

I knew I would meet death, before I let her meet harm.

From the moment I looked into her eyes, I beamed with pride,

they looked just like mine. From the moment she spoke her very

first word, it was the most beautiful voice, I had ever heard.

From the moment that she took her first step, overwhelmed with

joy, I cheered and wept. From the moment I saw her watching me,

I led by example, by showing her, how she should be.

~Poem from: "Lilla Belle the First Stages"

For all those who simply wanted a chance, for all those who believed in themselves, and **resisted** the word, **can't**.

For all those who were told, they would never be anything, for all those who were told, they weren't as good as another human being.

For all those who were told, you weren't the right race or color, for all those who knew, you were just as good as any other.

For all those who were told, you weren't the right size or weight, for all those who were told, you don't have a pretty face.

For all those who chose right, instead of wrong, for all those despite the obstacles, stayed strong.

For all those who stood firm and straight, for all those who used love to conquer hate.

For all those who got up and didn't give up, for all those who were told, they would never live up.

For all those ancestors who paved the way for me, for all those who are gone now, and never lived to see.

For all those who didn't pick up the ladder, when they made it to the top, for all those who worked hard, for everything they got.

For all those who didn't break down, for all those who broke through, and despite what others said, you still **believed in you**.

For all those who know, **all things are in God's hands**, for all those who **trust Him**, even if, we don't always understand.

For all those who kept hammering, until the nail went through, this book, is especially, for you.

*m.c.

Chapter 1

It was a warm spring day in March. Twelve-year-old Raven Kensington stood before the sixth grade class reading her book report. She was a gorgeous young girl; she was a vision. Raven had an exquisite face. Her dark, magnetic eyes were framed by long, black lashes. Her dark chocolate skin was flawless. There was a small mole above Raven's lips, on the left side. Her even, white teeth revealed her trademark, Miss America smile. Her raven-black hair was long and wavy. Raven Kensington's beauty was breathtaking! Her eloquent-voice was almost as captivating as her looks.

Tanya Riley, the sixth grade teacher, sat at her desk. She studied the young girl with the beautiful face and attention-getting eyes, with quiet admiration.

Known as "the pretty black girl" by many, Raven was very humble, which made her even more attractive. Raven Kensington wasn't your average girl. There was nothing average about her.

The class sat quietly as Raven read her book report.

Mrs. Riley smiled. She never had to ask the class to be quiet when Raven spoke. It seemed when Raven talked, everyone listened.

The teacher observed her class. The boys were admiring Raven's beauty. Some of the girls were looking at Raven with hate and envy in their eyes. Get used to it, the teacher thought to herself, as if speaking to Raven with her mind. You're going to have to face hate and jealousy, not to mention racial prejudice, for the rest of your life. But somehow, she knew that Raven would be just fine. Tanya Riley sensed an immense inner-strength in the young girl. Tanya had always been an excellent judge of character, and she seriously doubted if she was wrong about Raven Kensington.

When Raven concluded her book report, she received a loud round of applause from her classmates.

"You wanna be a lollipop when you grow up?" Clint Stanton, the class clown, blurted out.

The class roared with laughter. They thought Clint was simply trying to be funny. *Again.*

"Class, settle down, please. Settle down!" said Mrs. Riley. "Let's give our undivided attention to Raven and Clint now. Clint, before Raven responds, it is not *wanna*, it is *want* to."

Clint shrugged his shoulders and nodded.

Mrs. Riley sensed that for once, there was something behind Clint's comment. She just wasn't sure what it was. The teacher was determined to find out, so she sat and listened.

"A *lollipop*? What do you mean? I said I'm going to be an actress," said Raven.

"Raven, I'm not tryin' to be funny! But look at all of the actresses on TV and in the movies. They all look like sticks!"

The class roared with laughter again.

"They have stick bodies and large heads. That's why I call 'em lollipops. Get it? You're no lollipop, Raven. And be grateful that you're not!"

"You're also *not* white!" snapped Susan Porter, a very homely Caucasian girl who disliked Raven. "You becoming an actress? Huh! That will be the day. *Fat chance!*"

"Susan Porter!" Mrs. Riley exclaimed. "Apologize to Raven right this minute. And don't ever make a comment like that in my class again," the teacher warned.

"I'm sorry, Raven," Susan mumbled.

"What does *fat chance* mean?" Clint asked.

Raven looked at Clint. "Fat chance means very unlikely. Susan is saying that it is very unlikely that I will become an actress." Raven looked Susan straight in the eye. "What I can or can't become, is not, up to Susan. It's up to me. It's not her call, or anyone else's call, it's mine. I will tell all of you what I know. It's a very fat chance that Susan Porter is right. Not only will I be an actress, I will be the *best* actress that anyone has ever seen!" Raven's dark eyes were piercing and serious, but as she spoke again, she flashed her trademark smile. "Now, Clint, in response to your comment, no, I am not a *lollipop*, as you call it, nor would I like to be one. I am very satisfied with the body that God has given me. The focus shouldn't be on changing people, but *accepting* them, for who and what they are. There are things that we can change, and there are things that we cannot change. Race and how we look, are two things, that we can't change. And it's something that I wouldn't want to change, because however we are, it is *exactly* how God wanted us to be. He made us. No one is a mistake, a handicap, or an insult. We are all beautiful. I have just as much pride and contentment for being black, as someone else might have for being white, Hispanic, Asian, or whatever race or nationality, he or she might be. Love the package that you are in. Accept and be proud of who you are and how you are. However, the media sends a message, that is just the opposite. One size does not fit all. There are beautiful females in *all* races and in *all* sizes. And shapes," Raven added. "This world is not lily-white, nor is it only made up of the incredible shrinking females who continue to dominate in the media. Hollywood and society need to reflect *reality*. They need to show what is, not how they wish it to be. What we see on TV, in movies, and in magazines, is not a reflection of how the world looks, or how the world is. And from what has been shown over all of these many years, and what is *still* being shown, is that there are incredible injustices going on. *Still*. Society and Hollywood continue to do what they have done for eons. They are still discriminating. Not just with race, but also with size. There are obviously some racist people who are responsible for what we see and don't see in movies and on TV. I have seen many Hollywood powerhouses on TV denying discrimination of any kind. However, it is not what they say, it is what they *do*, continually, that tells the story. Action speaks louder than words. The proof is in the pudding. I stand on the shoulders of those African-Americans who came before me. A Hollywood for *all*, is what I hope to see one day. And hopefully, there will be a day, when actors and actresses are given work, because of their talent, instead of being overlooked, because of their race, and or, their size. There are African-Americans in Hollywood, and there have been for years now, but there should still be a lot more of us, in front of, and behind, the cameras. Another thing that concerns me about the media, is the very dangerous and negative message, that they are sending to many, *especially*, to females. Oftentimes, what we see is what we want to be, especially if it is praised or considered the *in* thing. The message that's sent by the media, is that being thin, is *the* symbol of beauty. You have to be thin, in order to be beautiful. And supposedly, the thinner you are, the better you look. I will use the phrase, the body to *die* for, because many females have died, and many are still dying, trying to look like the teeny-tiny females that are praised and idolized in the media. It's just as dangerous to be too thin, as it is to be overweight. It's certainly important to be healthy, but it's also important to have a healthy mind. The mind is captain of the body, because it's so very powerful. The focus should be on being *healthy*, not thin. You don't have to be thin, in order to be healthy. Nor does one have to be thin, in order to be beautiful. In other words, being thin, does not mean that you are healthy, nor does being thin mean, that you are beautiful. Thin, simply means, thin. And whether you're a size two or a size twenty, be proud of who you are. A woman's worth should not be determined by her weight or whether or not she has a pretty face, but we all know that in the entertainment industry, and even with some employers in the real-world, it is. I am medium size. I am not obese, nor am I skinny. I do realize that by Hollywood's standards, I would be considered fat. If I ever wanted to lose weight, it would be because I wanted to, not because society, or the entertainment industry, thinks I should."

Raven was interrupted by another loud round of applause. When the clapping died, Raven continued. "I have also noticed that the media is easier on males. There seems to be very little pressure, if any, on males, to be thin and handsome. How many homely, potbellied-males do we see on TV and in movies? I have seen quite a few of them."

"Tell 'em Raven!" said Sun-Yoo, a thin Asian girl sitting next to Clint.

Raven looked at Susan Porter. "Susan, I'm going to add to what I have already said, regarding race. Racism, like life in general, will always exist. Here we are in 2006, and it's stronger than ever. Racism doesn't just exist in Hollywood, it's alive and well, in *many* places, such as the workplace, in schools, in stores, in homes, on our highways. We've all heard of DWB, driving while black. Racism even exists in some churches. And in some families, hate and prejudice are taught as family values. I cannot, nor will I let that stop me from making my dreams become reality. I know that because of my race, I will certainly have to work much harder than white actresses."

"You got that right!" said Clint.

"I'm sure everyone in here has seen the cartoon, *Rudolph the Red-Nosed Reindeer*."

The class nodded their heads.

"I thought so," said Raven. "Rudolph is my favorite Christmas cartoon. I'm sure you are all wondering where I'm going with this, but stay with me, please. Rudolph was also discriminated against. *Think* about it. He was a reindeer, just like the other reindeers, but because his nose was a different color, the other reindeers did not want to have anything to do with Rudolph. Sounds familiar? The other reindeers would not get past his nose being a different color. Likewise, we as human beings, or *some* of us, do the exact same thing. Because someone is a different color, creed, nationality, or religion, we don't want to have anything to do with them. Like so many other things, hate and racial prejudice are taught, it's not something anyone is born with. We all have differences, including those who are the same race or nationality. We are all wonderfully-different, yet, in many ways, we are very much the same. How we are alike, is far more important, than how we are different. We all have basically the same needs, joys, and hopes. And regardless of what *anyone* says, *all* men, *are*, created *equal*. But, as many of us know, we are not all treated, equally. However, *no race*, is better than any other race, and *no one*, is better than anyone else!"

"That's right, Raven!" said Rebecca Simms, Raven's best friend.

"You go, girl!" Clint shouted.

"Another thing that the Rudolph cartoon showed was that different is sometimes better. In Rudolph's case, he was the best and the most talented reindeer. He was also the most memorable of all the reindeers. I will not accept how things have always been, and that includes when I go to Hollywood. Race and size may be issues with Hollywood and society, but they are not issues with me! I'm not going to become a *lollipop*, as Clint puts it. Nor do I have *any* desire to be white. I am very content with the package that I came in. *No one* can place limitations on me. Only I can do that. I will never accept anything just because *someone* said so. *Especially*, if it's wrong. The *only* expectations that I need to live up to, are my own."

Raven paused, while her classmates clapped again.

"I'm not motivated or driven by what others do or say, by what's out there, or by how others look. I am a *self*-motivated person, who's driven by what's inside of *me*. I will be a successful actress, without compromising who I am and what I believe in. I don't expect to have an easy ride, but I will not let bigotry, *anything*, or *anyone*, stop me, from doing what I want to do. Being what I want to be. I *don't* need *anyone's* permission to be successful. The *only* person who can stop me, is *me*. There is one thing that I am certain of. What is to be, is up to *me*! Are there any questions?"

Her classmates shook their heads no, as Raven Kensington took her seat.

Susan Porter's face was beet-red. She hadn't expected such a response from Raven.

Mrs. Riley and the class sat stunned. Was this an old wise woman in a twelve-year-old's body?

The teacher shook her head in amazement. Raven's intelligence was uncanny. "That was brilliantly-spoken, Raven!" said the teacher. "Simply, *brilliant.*"

The class clapped loudly, agreeing with the teacher. Raven received a standing ovation.

Raven Kensington was not only beautiful, she was also incredibly-wise. Mrs. Riley knew that beauty and brains weren't always in the same package, but in Raven's case, they were.

"We will finish the other book reports tomorrow. Have a great day, class," said the teacher, just as the bell rang. "Raven! I'd like to speak to you for just a minute, please."

Rebecca looked at her friend and smiled. "I'll wait for you in the hall."

"Okay, Beck." Raven walked over to the teacher's desk. "Yes, Mrs. Riley?"

"I have never been so impressed by any student! Your report and responses were simply incredible! *Oscar*-winning! I could not have said it better myself. Keep up the great work, Raven. And you are certainly correct, don't let race, weight, or *anything* stop you from living your dreams. You are a very beautiful and wise girl. I know that you'll make it, Raven. Follow your heart!" Mrs. Riley smiled. "I'll be reading about a famous actress named Raven Kensington, one day." The teacher gave her favorite student a big hug.

"Thanks, Mrs. Riley!" said Raven. "I'll see you tomorrow."

"'Bye, pretty girl," said Mrs. Riley, still pondering Raven's previous statements. *"Hmmm ... Einstein?"* the teacher laughed to herself. "Sharp cookie, that Raven. *Razor*-sharp!"

Mrs. Riley was born with a silver spoon in her mouth. Her family was rich. And although she was white, she knew, like Raven, that racism was very much alive, even in 2006.

Tanya Riley discussed Raven with other teachers during lunch.

"Raven Kensington? *Kensington*? Which student is that?" asked Ken Webster, a seventh grade science teacher.

Mrs. Riley described Raven.

"Oh! The *pretty* black girl. She has the kind of beauty that a blind man could see. I could see her becoming an actress or model. She's gorgeous!" Ken exclaimed.

The other teachers sat at the table nodding their heads in agreement.

"Ken, there's so much more to Raven Kensington than her looks. She's incredibly-wise. She's also very smart. Raven reads at a high-school level. She pronounces words better than any of us here at this table. Raven has a high IQ. She's one of a kind. In all of my eighteen years of teaching, I have never had a student who impressed me the way she does. I'm sure her parents are very proud of her too. I can only imagine as she gets older, how much more incredible she'll become in wisdom, and looks," said Mrs. Riley.

"She reads at a *high-school level?*" Ken was very impressed.

"Yes, sir. High-school level!" said Mrs. Riley, sounding more like a proud parent. "The principal wanted to promote Raven to the seventh grade, but her parents said no. In some ways I agree with them, but I'm only Raven's teacher, I'm not her mother."

"Wow! I'm impressed!" Ken smiled. "Going back to Raven's dream to become an actress, she certainly has the looks for it. Acting isn't an easy choice for anyone, but I know Miss Kensington will be just fine."

"There's not a doubt in my mind, if *anyone* makes it, Raven Kensington will," said Tanya Riley. That, she was certain of.

The bell rang, signaling the end of lunch.

The students began scrambling to get to class on time. And ironically, the teachers saw Raven and Rebecca, in a deep conversation of their own.

"A real beauty!" said Ken, eyeing Raven.

"Which one?" asked Mrs. Riley, already knowing to whom he was referring.

"Actually both. But I was talking about Raven," said Ken, as he flashed a sheepish-grin.

Tanya Riley laughed. "Somehow, Ken, that doesn't surprise me."

"It shouldn't surprise anyone, Tanya. Raven's a sight for sore eyes," said Ken. "She's very beautiful. Quite a vision."

* * *

At dinner that evening, Tanya told her husband about Raven. "She's incredible, Larry, I always give credit where credit is due."

Tanya Riley sat in her living room after dinner, watching the news.

Her husband insisted on cleaning the kitchen.

"What's the catch?" she asked him.

"Football!"

Tanya shook her head. "I should have known. *Hmmm* ... o-kay, you can watch the big men in tights."

Larry laughed at his wife's description of football athletes.

* * *

The next day, Clint Stanton was called to read his book report.

This should be interesting, thought Mrs. Riley.

The class sat quietly, anticipating what Clint would do or say to make them laugh, this time. He was always making the class laugh.

Clint was a chubby white kid with blond hair and gray eyes. He wasn't bad-looking. He loved being the center of attention. Clint found a way to do that by telling jokes. His grades were very poor though. Clint didn't seem to care, and the sad thing was, neither did his parents.

* * *

Clint read slowly from his paper. "As ... you ... all ... know, we were all 'spose to do a report 'bout what we wan-na be when we grown. I am happy to respond to that. I'm a Toys "R" Us kid, so, I don't wan-na grow up! I mean, I don't *want*, to grow up," said Clint, thinking about Mrs. Riley correcting his English the day before. "I will live with my parents for-ever. I will not help with any bills ei-ther. And, speakin' of weight, you will wait a very *long* time, if you think I'm goin' to lose any weight! I ain't gon-na work either. Well, I may work one job, that of San-ta, once a year. After all, look at my bel-ly, it shakes just like jel-ly." Clint made his stomach move up and down. "From a business aspect, I figure ... I might as well get paid for be-ing fat."

The class roared with laughter.

"See, I don't need a pillow like the skin-ny, skinny fake Santas. My big bel-ly is real." Clint continued to read slowly from his paper. "Those stars, actresses, are lollipops who look like the people in the hunger com-mer-cials that we all see on TV. It is a stick, I mean *sick*, example of beauty. Look-ing like a stick is not my ideal of beauty. Faces drawn in." Clint sucked in his chubby cheeks. "Ribs showin', is simply, disgustin'. Most ... newborn babies weigh more than those chicks. I hope Raven hurrys up and grows up and goes to Hollywood, so that she can set another stan-dard. Get rid of the lollipops!" Clint removed a lollipop from his pocket and waved it at the class, as if to make his point. "Oh, my! If it ain't ... if it ain't a wollipop, ladies and gentlemen! What role are you auditionin' for?" Clint asked, as he pretended to talk to the lollipop that he was holding in his hand.

"Clint Stanton!" said Mrs. Riley.

"I'm almost finished, teacher," said Clint. "Raven, you are *very* beautiful! I hope that when we grown, you'll marry this ol' country white boy!"

The entire class was roaring with laughter.

Mrs. Riley tried hard not to laugh, but she couldn't refrain from laughing at Clint either. "Clint Stanton, read your actual book report, please," said Mrs. Riley, trying to keep a straight face.

"Teacher! This *is* my book report. Another F-, huh?" Clint said, shrugging his shoulders and looking unconcerned. "How 'bout an F+ for effort?"

"We'll discuss your book report after class," said Mrs. Riley.

Clint gave his book report to the teacher, then he sat down at his desk. He smiled and winked at Raven.

Mrs. Riley sat thinking about Clint's parents. The teacher tried many times, discussing Clint's grades and his actions at school with them, but to no avail.

His father, also named Clint, owned several local banks, and his solution was "how much," would the teacher accept to give his Junior a passing grade. "Name your price," the elder Clint told Mrs. Riley.

Speaking with his mother was just as depressing. It wasn't a secret that Myrtle Stanton, Clint's mother, was an alcoholic. In her eyes, "her boy," could do no wrong. How sad, thought the teacher. Poor boy. Mrs. Riley hoped the Stantons would wake up before it was too late, but so far, they were both in a deep sleep.

Rebecca Simms was the last student to read her book report. To family and friends, she was known as "Becky." And like her best friend, Raven, Becky also wanted to become an actress. Rebecca was a very pretty girl. She had sky-blue eyes, long, golden-blonde hair, and a bright smile.

Raven and Rebecca had been best friends since kindergarten. The girls had many things in common. Both were good-looking, both were straight-A students, and both girls shared an immense-passion for acting. Raven and Becky also attended the same church, loved movies, and they would often act out parts and recite famous lines.

Their favorite subjects differed though. Raven's favorite subjects were reading, writing, Spanish, and spelling. She also loved martial arts. Raven had been practicing and studying martial arts since the age of four. She had black belts in jujitsu, kung-fu, and karate.

Rebecca's favorite subject was math, hands down. She was brilliant with numbers. Becky also loved ballet, and she had been taking ballet classes since the age of six.

Everyone knew that Raven and Becky were best friends. In fact, they were like sisters.

"We're best friends for life!" the girls declared to each other at the age of five.

"Until my husband comes," a then-five-year-old Raven told Becky. "Isn't that the way it's supposed to be, Beck?"

"I think so," Becky replied, as she shrugged her shoulders. "I don't know."

Raven looked at her blonde friend. "Don't worry, Beck, you will *always* be dear to me. You're more than my best friend, you're my *sister*, in *every* way that matters!"

"You want to get married when you get bigger?" Becky asked her friend.

Raven smiled. "Yes, Beck, I sure do!"

"What kind of man would you like to marry, Raven?"

Raven looked pensive. "A man who's crazy."

"*Crazy*?" asked Becky, looking puzzled.

"Yes, Beck, crazy … *in love* with me!"

"Tell me something! For a minute there, I thought that you had gone crazy yourself, and completely lost it. What else?"

"Someone who's rich, handsome, and worships the ground that I walk on," said Raven, without batting an eye. "Don't look at me like that, Beck. That's not asking for much. That's not a tall order to fill, is it?"

Becky laughed in answer. Raven Kensington was the sister that she never had. There was never any envy between them. They had always been very supportive of each other. Becky never cringed from all of the many times that everyone complimented Raven on her looks. Nor did it bother Becky, when others pointed out that Raven was the prettiest of the two.

Becky knew that she was also very pretty, although she knew Raven was prettier. In fact, Raven was the prettiest girl that Becky had ever seen, black, white, or otherwise. Raven was more than pretty, she was beautiful. She was also down-to-earth. And that was one of the many things that Becky loved about her best friend. There wasn't anyone like her. But regardless of how incredible Raven Kensington was, Becky didn't think any less of herself, because she was comfortable in her own skin.

The girls often talked about their plans to work in order to save money to go to Hollywood, after they graduated from high school. They didn't want to be like many aspiring actors and actresses, who went to Tinseltown, penniless.

* * *

When the summer of 2010 arrived, Raven and Becky got a job working at McDonald's, because it was within walking distance of their homes. They were both very independent. They had already decided that they would make it on their own, once they left home.

The teenagers were very busy now. In addition to working, they maintained straight-A's in school, went to martial arts and ballet classes, and acted in plays. And somehow, Raven always managed to go to the park, which was clearly, one of her favorite pastimes.

Raven and Becky's manager, Mitch Peters, gave them Sundays off, so they could attend church, and spend that day with their families. Mitch knew how busy Raven and Becky were. He also knew how hard they worked.

Mitch was very nice to Raven and Becky. They were excellent employees. They were always on time, they always worked hard, and they always took pride in their work. They were both honest too. Any employer would have been more than happy to have the girls as employees, thought Mitch. It had been a long time since he had seen two young people, "beauties" at that, work so hard. Mitch also thought that Raven and Becky had increased business. The beauties were always complimented on their looks, especially by many of the male customers. Mitch was convinced that many of them didn't come for the food, but to simply look at, and talk to, Raven and Becky.

Mitch didn't blame them though. They were very beautiful. *Especially*, Raven. Many of the male customers couldn't take their eyes off her. Neither could he, or his boss, Mark Peters, who was of no relation to Mitch. Raven Kensington was *stunningly*-beautiful.

"Is this McDonald's or Models, Inc?" Mark Peters joked on his last restaurant visit. "Where did we find such *beauties*?"

* * *

The two years passed by much too quickly for Mitch. But for Raven and Becky, the years couldn't have flown by fast enough. Neither could wait to graduate and set sail for Tinseltown.

Mitch sat in his office one night watching Raven. She scrubbed the counters, floors, and restrooms, like no other. Funny, Mitch thought to himself, most females who didn't have half her looks, would never clean the way she does. They would be afraid that they might break a nail or something, or think that working at McDonald's, period, was far beneath them. But not Raven. Mitch admired her a great deal. It was very hard not to.

Mitch tried hard to convince Raven to become a manager. She was honest, highly-intelligent, reliable, a quick study, a take-charge person, had great people skills, worked very well under pressure, and she was *so* ...

"Miss Kensington, to my office, please." Mitch decided to page Raven. He wanted to ask her again. She would be graduating the following week.

Raven walked to her boss's office, wondering why he had paged her. "*Miss Kensington*? That sounds serious."

"Did you turn down the management opportunity because of the salary? If so, I would be happy to increase the initial offer," said Mitch, looking hopeful. He sat, staring at his best employee. Looking at Raven, it was hard to keep one's mind on business. She was so gorgeous and sexy, even in a McDonald's uniform and cap. But Raven Kensington could wear rags, and still look stunning. Mitch had always been in awe of Raven's beauty. She would always draw eyes, as well as provoke fantasies. *Always*.

"No, Mr. Peters. It's not the money. I'm going to Los Angeles after I graduate. Becky and I are heading for the hills, Beverly Hills, that is."

Mitch laughed. He also loved Raven's sense of humor. He was going to miss her like crazy. He was going to miss Becky too, but he had a big crush on Raven. And had since day one. "Like many guys, I'm sure," said Mitch, not meaning to speak his thoughts out loud.

"*Like many guys*? What are you talking about, Mr. Peters?"

Mitch's face turned red. "Raven, I'm sorry. My mind was a million miles away. I hate to lose you and Becky. You two are the best employees that I have. That I've ever had. I am going to miss both of you. A lot." Especially you, he wanted to say, but didn't. "Is there *anything* that I could do to change your mind?" Mitch looked at Raven with pleading eyes. "*Anything*?"

"No, Mr. Peters, there isn't. Thank you for the offers though. I'm also going to miss you."

"When you ladies make it big, don't forget about us little people down here in Tunis, Texas!"

"We won't, Mr. Peters," said Raven, flashing her dazzling, trademark smile. "We won't!"

* * *

On *May 28*, 2012, Raven Kensington and Rebecca Simms graduated, with honors! They hugged each other, hugged their families, and hugged all of their classmates.

Raven's older brother, Trey, attended the graduation with his wife and three children. And Angie, the youngest of the three Kensington children, was also there, smiling broadly. No one smiled more than Raven's parents, Charles and Mae Kensington.

Mitch Peters and his family also attended the graduation, along with many of the employees from McDonald's.

Everyone was happy for the graduates, but no one was as happy as the graduates themselves. They tossed their caps in the air with much excitement, cheers, and hopes. They would all soon embark on a new journey. And like life, it was filled with lots of dreams and unknowns.

Charles and Mae Kensington were disappointed, at first, when Raven told them that she was going to Hollywood to be an actress. They knew that it was something their daughter had told them, since she was a little girl, but they both hoped that it was just a passing fancy. Charles and Mae didn't like the Hollywood nightmares that they had heard so much about, not to mention what the media exposed. They also didn't want their very private daughter living in a fish bowl. Nothing they said changed Raven's mind.

"I'm going to be an actress." Raven was adamant. She received academic scholarships from Harvard, Spelman, Yale, Texas A&M, Stanford, Princeton, and Howard. But in spite of the numerous scholarships, Raven still wanted to act.

When Charles and Mae saw how much acting meant to their oldest daughter, they decided that her happiness, was the most important thing. After all, it wasn't what their dreams were, it was what Raven's dreams were. It was her life, and it was hers to live.

"Follow your heart, sweetheart," said her mother. She was going to miss her daughter so much. The thought of not seeing Raven every day, made her mother's heart ache. That beautiful smile, having their usual, heart-to-heart talks, and laughing at something Raven had said, would forever be etched in Mae Kensington's heart. She admired her oldest daughter immensely.

Mae cried on graduation night. She remembered giving birth to her daughter. Raven looked like a baby doll. She had the cutest little round face, gorgeous dark eyes that shined bright, and a head full of curly, raven-black hair. Raven was simply, adorable.

Charles's sister, Ann, who was killed in a car accident, was also crazy about Raven. Ann had given her the nickname, "Bear." *Bear Baby.*

"*Bear?*" Charles asked his sister, looking puzzled.

"Charles, did I stutter? Yes, Bear! Bears are so *cute* and *cuddly*, and so is my niece. She's so cu-utte! She's so adorable ... And look at all of that hair! That's another reason I have nicknamed her Bear."

Ann would always play in Raven's hair. "She has so much hair, she could wear ponytails. There's not a more appropriate name for my little niece." Ann would take baby Raven everywhere, showing her off. "This is *my* baby!" she'd say.

Raven Kensington was *everyone's* baby. Everybody was crazy about her. She was going to be greatly-missed. Mae couldn't seem to stop crying.

Charles Kensington put his arms around his wife, to comfort her.

"Our little Raven has grown up. Where did all of the years go? They came and went way too soon," said Mae.

"Mae! It's going to be okay. Raven's leaving home, she's not *dying*. It's time she spread her wings and flew. And we both know how very independent our daughter is. If anybody can make it, Raven can! I'm not just saying that to make you feel better either. I *mean* that. Raven's very strong, she's very wise. She'll be just fine, Mae, just fine," said Charles. "And she's also very *strong*-willed. Raven has an *ironclad* will, Mae. A strong will will take you further than brains. And our daughter has both. A person's *will*, will get them very far in life." He was going to miss their oldest daughter a lot too. Raven was his favorite. "I'm not thrilled about her going out to sin-land either, but I want her to be happy."

"So do I, Charles," said Mae. "You know, she never gave us an ounce of trouble! And even as a baby, she was so good. Rarely cried. She was a beautiful baby, and now, she's even *more* beautiful as a woman."

"Now Angie on the *other* hand ..." Charles laughed, as he thought of their youngest daughter. She and Raven were complete opposites.

"Angie's a handful," said Mae, laughing through her tears. "Truly a handful. Trey was a good kid. But none of them were like Raven."

Her husband nodded his head in agreement.

"Angie will be fine. She's not a bad kid."

"Is that why your hair is turning gray at the temples, Mrs. Kensington?" her husband joked.

Mae Kensington laughed in answer.

There was a knock on their bedroom door.

"Who goes there?" Charles Kensington asked.

"It's me, Daddy. Raven."

It was two o'clock in the morning. Raven had gone to the huge graduation party thrown for her class at the Hilton. Her parents were usually asleep at that time, but as Raven walked to her bedroom, she could hear them talking, although she couldn't hear what they were saying.

"Come on in, sweetheart," said her father. "We have a bone to pick with you. You think you grown now, huh?"

Raven laughed in answer.

"Coming in *this* house at two in the morning! Your mother and I were discussing what your punishment should be." Charles Kensington looked at his oldest daughter. His love and admiration for Raven was immeasurable. Charles didn't know exactly what it was, but his daughter possessed something very special. It was as if he could sense that, from the moment that he held Raven in his arms, when she was first born. He loved all three of his children, dearly and unconditionally, but he loved his oldest daughter most. He never told anyone, but his wife knew it. Mae knew her husband better than anyone.

"Hol-ly-wood!" Raven sang. "Hol-ly-wood!" Raven sat in the chair beside her parents' bed.

Her father turned on the lamp. "Did my baby have a great time at the party?" Charles asked his daughter.

"Yes, Daddy. I had a great time!" Raven flashed her trademark, Miss America smile, that her father knew, melted the hearts of many, him included.

Mae Kensington studied her oldest daughter, who was now eighteen. Raven had grown even more beautiful over the years. She was the *essence* of beauty. Raven was mesmerizing. Her dark eyes danced. Her mouth smiled. The birthmark was where it had always been since birth, adding even more enhancement to an already exquisitely-beautiful face. Raven's dark chocolate skin was still flawless. Her raven-black hair was still long and wavy. Her eloquent-voice had grown even more captivating over the years. Raven stood, five feet, three inches tall. She had soft, rounded hips, and full breasts. Raven's size-eleven frame was very curvaceous. Her mother continued to study her. Watching Raven, was like looking at the most beautiful portrait.

Besides her breathtaking-beauty, there were other things that Mae loved and admired about her oldest daughter, that were far more important than looks. Raven carried herself like a lady. She was the *epitome* of elegance and class. Raven Kensington was a woman, in the *purest* meaning of the word. And what a woman she was!

Raven sat before her parents. Her long black hair was pulled back in a ponytail. "Mommie, what's wrong? Why are you crying?"

"I'm fine, sweetheart. I was just admiring the incredible woman that you've become. Your father and I were discussing you tonight. We remember, as if it were yesterday, bringing you home from Shannon Hospital. You were beautiful then, and you are even more so now. You're also very beautiful on the inside. One can't say that about all beautiful women either. I hope that you stay that way, sweetheart. We're just going to miss you so much, that's all. Angie and Trey are going to miss you a lot too. They look up to you, you know."

Tears filled Raven's dark eyes. "I'm going to miss all of you too. I love all of you very much. *Remember*, I'm only a phone call away. And whenever I can, I'll come home to visit. You'll can also come visit Becky and me. I'm going to have to work hard and long to make my dreams become reality. I'll call home regularly. But if any of you need me, I'll drop whatever I'm doing, and I'll be here. You do know that? Mommie, Daddy, don't you?" Raven looked at her parents, lovingly. She loved them deeply and dearly.

"Yes, sweetheart, we know," said her father. Charles looked at his beautiful daughter. "I can rest a *little* easier knowing that you can knock a man on his butt, if he gets out of line."

Raven laughed. They both knew that she could do much more than that. Raven had been taking martial arts for fourteen years, she was a very skilled martial artist.

"We mean it, Raven! Call us, anytime. Your father and I both know how you are. Independence is one thing, being *foolish* is another."

"I know, Mommie. I promise, I will call."

"Sure you will, Miss Independent!" said Angie.

"Angie! I should have known you weren't asleep. Come on in, sweetheart. How about a group hug?" said Charles.

The Kensingtons had always been a very close family.

"I can't wait for my sister to become a big movie star!" Angie beamed. "There would certainly be advantages for all of us."

Everyone laughed. They all knew that Angie would use that to date cute guys. Angie had always been boy-crazy. And she had already told everyone that her big sister was going to be a huge star. Like anyone who knew Raven, whatever she set her heart and mind to, she accomplished. Angie looked at Raven, smiling. She was very proud of her big sister. And there wasn't a doubt in Angie's mind, that her sister, would not become the successful actress that she was leaving home to become. As far as Angela Kensington was concerned, it was as good as done.

The foursome talked for several hours, before Charles Kensington yawned. "Okay, my two beautiful daughters. *Good night!* Your mother and I are *old*, we can't hang with you youngsters. Get out of here!" Charles laughed, as he kissed both of his daughters on their foreheads.

   * * *

Raven stayed home three weeks after graduating. She wanted to spend some quality time with her family.

Mae Kensington had long talks with Raven. She told her to be very careful. She knew men. And Mae knew that they would try to bed her daughter.

"Be a *lady*, Raven. That's the one thing I not only want you to do for *Mommie*, but for yourself. You owe some things to yourself, and taking care of yourself, and being a lady, are two of them. You can be gorgeous, and you certainly are, but you don't have to be a slut, or dress like one, to fulfill your dreams. And if *anyone* ever tells you otherwise, they are lying to you. There are so many other things, that I've always talked with all of you kids about. You are a lady with high standards and great morals and values. You're a woman of great integrity. Stand *strong* and firm. Don't compromise *any* of those things, for *anyone*, or *anything*. *Always* be true to yourself. Don't be what people think you should be. *Be who you are.* Be *Raven* ... Raven Kensington!"

Mother and daughter hugged. Afterwards, Raven went to her bedroom to pack. Her dark eyes were filled with tears. She was going to miss her mother a lot. They had always been very close.

* * *

The Kensingtons and Simms threw a big party for Raven and Becky, who received fantastic, much-needed gifts.

Trey and Jeb, their older brothers, paid for a two-week stay at the lavish, Beverly Hills Hotel, as graduation gifts to their sisters. Their brothers knew that this would give Raven and Becky time to look for an apartment in a decent area, find jobs, and live in the lap of luxury with the rich and famous. Raven and Becky were ecstatic!

Charles and Mae Kensington left their daughter speechless with their gift to her. *Twenty thousand dollars*. The Kensingtons started a savings account for each of their children, when they were first born. Each Kensington child would be given their savings when they graduated from high school to use as they so wished. Charles and Mae never told their children about their savings. Trey had kept it a secret, and Raven promised to do the same.

Dax and Sonya Simms gave their daughter *fifteen thousand dollars*.

Becky was overjoyed.

Becky's parents gave Raven a thousand dollars, and Raven's parents gave Becky a matching gift.

Raven and Becky were also given three hundred dollars each in American Express cheques from their former boss, Mitch Peters. The two graduates also received gifts from other family members, church members, and friends. And in addition to the very generous gifts from family and friends, Raven and Becky had also saved money from working over the years. They were not rich, but they were certainly in very good field position.

* * *

The next morning, a cab arrived to take Raven and Becky to Easterwood Field Airport. They decided to say good-bye to everyone at home. Their families took their leaving harder than Raven and Becky thought they would. Everyone cried, even their fathers and brothers. Seeing the girls leave was hard on everyone. It seemed especially difficult for their mothers. It was very hard for Mae and Sonya, watching their "babies" leave home. Finally, with lots of tears, big hugs, and "I love yous," Raven and Becky were whisked off in the cab.

As the cab drove away, Raven and Becky waved to their families until they could no longer see them. They loved their families very much, and they were going to miss them, terribly, but they knew that they had to leave. There was both sadness and excitement as they rode to the airport. They looked at each other and smiled through their tears. They were so excited, it felt like butterflies were in their stomachs. Raven and Becky had dreamt of this day since they were young girls. Their passion for acting had grown even greater over the years.

When they arrived at the airport, Raven and Becky checked in their luggage, then waited to board the plane to Los Angeles. They had already purchased their tickets.

A few hours later, the moment that they had been eagerly waiting for, arrived. Raven and Becky stood up and anxiously boarded their plane. They were finally on their way to Los Angeles, Tinseltown,

Hollywood ... the land of ... big dreams.
* * *

Becky took a nap. Raven was too excited to sleep. She sat in deep thought. Raven thought of where she had been, and where she would be going in life. What was Raven Kensington's destiny?

Raven and Becky had done their homework. They had the contact names, addresses, and phone numbers of every talent agency in the Los Angeles area. They had taken plenty of eight-by-ten glossies, to deliver personally and to mail to agencies. Their resumes and cover letters were also professionally done. They knew that in L.A., it was literally a necessity to have an agent, unlike New York.

Raven and Becky also knew that there were times when there were open-auditions, which was a come-one, come-all opportunity, for those hoping to land roles, without representation. They had also heard of people being discovered on sight.

Raven sat thinking. She knew that people were also handpicked, if a producer, director, or talent agent liked their *look*. And Raven knew exactly what that look was. Who didn't? She was on her way to a Hollywood which wasn't as lily-white as it used to be, but still predominantly-white. In a nutshell, lily-white, rail-thin females, were still the rule. Raven Kensington smiled, perhaps it was the rule for others, but not for her.

Raven and Becky had already decided that they would knock on doors and make countless phone calls, daily, even when they found agents. They were going to be very aggressive and hands-on. Both knew that the entertainment industry was immensely-competitive. They were not going to sit back and wait for their agents to call them. Their goal was to find agents who wouldn't have a problem with that.

Raven had never liked the word discovered. She felt their talent was already there. The only thing that she and her best friend needed was opportunity. They both had exceptional-talent. She and Becky were naturals.
* * *

Raven and Becky were flexible to what they would do. They were going to shoot for commercials, TV, and movies. The one thing that they would not do was porn.

* * *

Hours later, the flight attendant spoke. "Ladies and gentlemen, please place all trays and seats in an upright position, fasten your seat belts, and prepare for landing. Thank you for choosing American Airlines. We hope your flight was enjoyable. We also hope that we will be your airline of choice in the future. Again, thanks for choosing American Airlines!"

The flight attendant seemed friendly, but nervous. Maybe she's new, thought Raven. Raven had always been very aware of her surroundings and what was going on around her. Many Americans became much more aware of what was happening around them, since *September 11, 2001*. That date would forever be etched in the hearts and minds of many.

"Wake up, Sleeping Beauty." Raven nudged Becky.

Becky smiled. "Are we there yet? Will our limo be waiting? Or will we have to fire our chauffeur?"

The two friends laughed.

"We've just landed. The flight went smoothly, thank God."

Becky nodded in answer. She was wide awake now.

"Beck, we're here! We're finally here! Watch out Hollywood!"

"Here we come!" Becky finished, as the plane's wheels hit the runway.

* * *

Raven and Becky turned more than a few heads as they strolled through the airport. Both ladies were the symbol of beauty and elegance. They looked like movie stars. And that was exactly what they had come to the City of Angels to become. They picked up their luggage, bought a map of L.A., then walked outside and hailed a cab.

"Where to?" asked the cab driver, as he placed their luggage in the trunk.

* * *

"The Beverly Hills Hotel," Becky answered.

"Wow, ladies! Beautiful women with *expensive* tastes." The cab driver smiled at Raven and Becky more than once. Too bad all of my customers don't look like these two, he thought to himself.

Raven and Becky sat and chatted as they took in the people and the sights. They both looked ecstatic when they spotted the famous Hollywood Sign, perched high on top of Mount Lee.

The two friends agreed that California was a beautiful place. They loved the scenery, the mountains and the ocean, especially. The cab driver had purposely taken the scenic route. The ride didn't last long enough though. Raven and Becky wanted to see a great deal more. In fact, they planned on touring the entire Los Angeles area, including Malibu, Pacific Palisades, Brentwood, Santa Monica, and all areas in-between.

"Well, ladies, we're here!" said the cab driver.

The minute the cab driver pulled up to the front entrance of the hotel, two well-dressed bellhops came out, greeted them, and immediately removed Raven's and Becky's luggage from the cab.

Raven and Becky thanked the cab driver, gave him a generous tip, then stood admiring the beautifully-elegant building that was before them.

Raven's dark eyes took in everything, as usual. So this is Beverly Hills, Raven thought to herself. *Beverly Hills.*

Raven and Becky walked to the registration area, as the bellhops followed suit.

While the lady at the desk looked up their reservation, the young ladies admired the elegant, meticulously-kept lobby, that was simply lavish.

The two friends smiled. This was certainly living the life. You know that you've made it, when you can live in Beverly Hills.

"Here it is! Raven Kensington and Rebecca Simms. Two weeks' stay. Ladies, you have a non-smoking garden suite, with two queen-size beds, and a gorgeous view of the gardens. Suite 202. It's a lovely suite, ladies! Please don't hesitate to call us, if we can do anything to make your stay more enjoyable. We want your stay to be no less than exceptional. By the way, I'm Lauren. Any questions?"

"Not at this time," said Raven and Becky in unison.

"Here's a key for each of you. Enjoy your stay, ladies!"

After thanking Lauren, Raven and Becky followed the bellhops to their suite. They were glowing. It was hard to believe that they were actually in Beverly Hills. Finally!

When they made it to their suite, Raven tipped the bellhops, and thanked them. "Is this living the life or *what*? I had no idea that our brothers paid for a suite! This isn't a room, this is an apartment!" Raven laughed.

"No kidding!" said Becky. "The elegance is off the hook too."

"C'est une belle suite," said Raven, who was fluent in French and Spanish.

Raven and Becky oohed and aahed as they walked the luxurious suite. They had never seen anything so lavish.

Raven's eyes combed everything, the crown molding, the big, white, leather sofa, the elegantly-dressed beds, and the huge, walk-in closets. The suite was very elegant, with immensely-expensive decor. "No one has to twist my arm," said Raven. "I can certainly get used to this! *My, my, my* ..."

Becky laughed in answer.

Raven walked into the bathroom. It too was superbly-elegant and spacious. The bathroom had a large, garden-size tub, with a separate shower. Raven eyed the double sinks and the marble floor. She could easily see why celebrities often stayed at this hotel, why anyone would stay here, if they could. Raven felt right at home. It was as if she knew that one day, she would have a home that topped this.

Raven thought of her mother. She always saw her mother looking in *Elite Homes* magazines, which featured big, luxurious homes. Raven knew that if her mother could afford it, she would build one in an instant. Raven smiled. She was going to have one of those homes built for her mother. *One day ... Un jour ...*

    * * *

The Kensingtons had a very nice home, and for that, Raven had always been very grateful. But it didn't have the elegance and luxury of The Beverly Hills Hotel or the homes in the magazines. Raven had always referred to them as "big-money homes."

Raven walked out of the bathroom to find Becky looking out the window. Lauren was right, they had a gorgeous view.

Raven stood beside her best friend. "Gorgeous view, isn't it, Beck?"

"It sure is, Sis. Our brothers *definitely* paid a pretty penny for this suite."

"Yes, they sure did, but they know that we'll pay them back tenfold later. Speaking of our brothers, we'd better call home to let our families know that we made it to L.A. safely," said Raven, dialing on her Nokia cell phone.

"You're right," said Becky. "The last thing we want to do is have our families worried about us."

They talked to their families for almost an hour. Everyone was happy that they had made it to L.A., and to the hotel, safely. Mae and Sonya reminded their daughters to "keep in touch."

Raven spotted a complimentary Sunday's paper. "Great! I was going to get a Sunday's paper. We can look for employment, an apartment, and open-auditions."

As they sat on their beds and relaxed, the two friends couldn't stop smiling. This was the place that they had dreamed about since they were in kindergarten.

"Sis?"

"Yes, Beck?"

"You know when the dark-haired bellhop said that they had to assist Mr. Washington, do you think he meant, Washington, as in *Denzel*?"

"That's certainly possible. After all, we are in *star*-city. Swimming pools, movie stars. Ya'll come back now, ya hear?" said Raven.

Becky laughed. "Sis, you're too much!"

Raven turned on the Sony TV, and even that was big. Big money, big things, thought Raven. Raven turned to *CNN* to find out what was going on in the world.

After watching *CNN* for an hour, Raven and Becky decided to tour the hotel. Before leaving their suite, they freshened up their makeup and brushed their hair.

The beauties looked stunning, as they walked the hotel slowly, observing everything and everyone, although careful not to stare.

Raven and Becky blended in perfectly with the clientele, because they looked every bit like movie stars themselves. And as they walked the hotel, they spotted a number of celebrities. Oprah, Nicole Kidman, Star Jones Reynolds, Sandra Bullock, Halle Berry, Bill Cosby, Julia Roberts, Brad Pitt, and Angela Bassett.

They also saw Jonathan, one of the bellhops who had assisted them earlier. "Well hello again, ladies!" said Jonathan. "There's a big celebrity-bash tonight in the Grand Ballroom. I'm used to seeing a lot of celebrities. You beautiful ladies fit right in." Jonathan smiled.

Raven and Becky thanked Jonathan for the compliment.

Raven saw that there was a small park directly across the street from the hotel. She had always loved parks. She went there often, to think, to relax, and to enjoy the beautiful scenery. Raven liked people-watching too, and listening to nature.

"There's *Whoopi*," an excited Becky whispered.

"It sure is, isn't it? Remain calm, Beck. Remember, never let them see you sweat," said Raven. But Raven almost lost it when she saw Shemar Moore.

Now, it was Becky's turn to calm her down. "Ah-ah-ah, remain calm, Sis. *Remember*, never let them see you sweat."

Both of them laughed.

Shemar greeted them with a smile. "Hello, ladies. You'll doing all right?"

"Hello, Shemar. Yes, we are." Raven answered, as if she knew him personally.

* * *

After greeting the two beauties, Shemar walked to the Grand Ballroom, while Raven and Becky continued touring the hotel. Raven had always thought Shemar Moore gorgeous. The first time that she saw him was years ago, when he starred on *Y&R*, a *CBS* soap opera. Shemar appeared to be down-to-earth too, and that, she liked. Raven always hoped that when she did make it, her feet would stay firmly planted on the ground. She hoped and prayed that she would never get beside herself, look down on others, or forget where she came from, as some celebrities did.

Even more important to Raven Kensington than being down-to-earth, was helping people. Raven felt the world would be a much better place, if more people helped others.

After touring the hotel, Raven and Becky walked back to their suite and looked in the newspaper for jobs and an apartment. The sooner they found a job and an apartment, the more time they would have to enjoy their stay at the luxurious hotel. They would also have more time to tour Los Angeles.

They planned to visit all of the places that they had heard about. Places like the Grauman Chinese Theatre, Hollywood's Walk of Fame, Disneyland, Paramount and Universal Studios, Westwood Village ... Their list was long. Raven and Becky were determined to have fun and enjoy life. They knew how precious, and short, life was.

* * *

Later that evening, Becky designed a budget for them. Math was her mastery. Both ladies knew the value of a dollar, and even though people in Beverly Hills had money to burn, they certainly were not there yet. But each knew in their heart of hearts, that one day, they would be. But, for now, they had to live for the moment. And for the moment, they had to use their money wisely and live within their means. Not beyond.

* * *

Raven circled a number of job opportunities and apartments. They were going to get up early to get an early start. After all, the early bird caught the worm, and they had two very important ones to catch. Employment, and a place to live.

Raven wanted them to get a job in one of the stores, or restaurants, that celebrities visited often. This would put them in constant interaction with people in show business. They could also be discovered.

Raven was very pleased to know that Spago was hiring. Spago was a very popular, upscale restaurant that many celebrities frequented.

* * *

Hours later, once their plans were squared away, Raven and Becky ordered dinner.

Becky told Raven that steak was on the menu. She knew that steak was one of Raven's favorite dishes.

Raven laughed.

"What's so funny, Sis?"

"The fact that if I had an agent, he or she would have a heart attack if I ordered steak and a baked potato for dinner. You know that kind of food is forbidden for celebs! I think a light salad with fat-free dressing, a tall glass of water, or a Diet Coke, would be an *ideal*-meal for a movie star," said Raven. "Ideal, for Hollywood."

"That's what you're having?" Becky asked.

Raven laughed again. "If it's the same thing as a sirloin steak, *well-done*, and a baked potato, sure."

Becky laughed hard.

"I am going to eat the same way that I've always eaten. I came to change Hollywood. I didn't come so Hollywood would change me," said Raven. "There is absolutely *nothing*, wrong with me, but there is *a lot*, wrong with Hollywood."

"There's a new sheriff in town," said Becky.

Raven flashed her trademark smile. "Yes, my friend, it sure is. I'm the sheriff, *for all those* …"

Raven was a curvaceous, size eleven. She was healthy and in great shape. Raven exercised regularly. She also looked and felt great, but as she had acknowledged years earlier, by Hollywood's standards, she was still considered fat. But, by Hollywood's *so-called* standards, the majority of people would be considered fat. Anyone was who didn't look like a toothpick. Raven was adamant about what she had said six years earlier, she was not going to become a lollipop. Hollywood and society needed wake-up calls, very badly, and Raven Kensington couldn't wait, to dial their numbers.

* * *

Becky phoned room service to order their dinner. She ordered a cheeseburger and French fries, for herself, and a sirloin steak, with a baked potato, for Raven. Two iced-teas completed their order.

Raven searched the channels to find a good movie.

They decided to watch, *Lifetime*: *"Television for Women."* *Lifetime* always had great movies. Raven and Becky also loved watching, *The Golden Girls* and *City Confidential*.

"Good. The movie's just coming on," said Raven.

"What's it called?" Becky asked.

"For the Love of You." Raven answered. "This should be interesting."

"Very."

* * *

A half-hour later, Jonathan knocked on their door. He had convinced room service to let him take the ladies' dinner to them.

Becky tipped him this time. And both Raven and Becky thanked Jonathan, as they sat down at the table to watch the movie and eat their dinner.

"He likes you." Raven told Becky, when Jonathan left.

"Yeah, right!" said Becky. "Where is this coming from, Miss Cleo?"

"It's coming from Miss Kensington. It's coming from *me*, my instincts. He *does* like you, Beck. I'm not making that up. Trust me."

"He's not handsome. He looks all right," said Becky, who had always preferred to date good-looking guys.

"Your eyes obviously allow you to see some things about people, but the *important* things, are *not* seen with the eyes, *only*, with the heart. Learn to see with your heart, most of all, Beck," said Raven. "A man does not have to have movie-star looks. No man has ever made anyone happy by *looking* good, but a man can make you happy, by *being* good. Is he a good man? A good person? How does he treat you? Does he have good morals and values? Does he love you, *unconditionally*?"

"You're on a roll, Sis! Go on," said Becky.

Raven laughed. "Does he cherish you? Is he faithful, trustworthy, understanding? Is there a bond between the two of you? Chemistry? And, of utmost importance, is he *God-sent*? Should I go on?"

Becky nodded. "Why certainly, Dr. Kensington. Talk fast! I know you're charging me by the minute."

"Are you kidding? I'm charging you by the second!"

Becky laughed.

"You know, Beck, a lot of people miss out on good mates because they can't or won't get past the looks. Grant it, Shemar Moore, he's not, but he's not bad-looking either. He also seems very polite and kind. Again, our eyes obviously see things too, but I can't emphasize enough, how important it is that we see with our hearts, *most* of all," said a very wise Raven. "It's also very obvious that neither of us knows Jonathan at all. You could get to know him though. Then we would know if he is *the one* for my sister, the very beautiful and talented, Rebecca Simms!"

Becky laughed. "You're right again, Dr. Kensington. How much do I owe you?"

Raven laughed in answer.

"Sis, I'm only eighteen! I didn't come to L.A. to fall in love. Not yet anyway. There are *so* many things that I want to do first," said Becky.

* * *

"I know, Beck, I was simply letting you know that he likes you."

Raven and Becky ate their dinner and watched the movie. And as always, it was very enjoyable.

After watching the second movie on *Lifetime*, Raven went to take a hot bubble bath, and Becky phoned room service to inform them that their trays were ready to be picked up. As Becky placed the trays outside the door, Jonathan walked up.

Perfect timing. "Did you ladies enjoy dinner?"

Becky looked at him closely this time. She tried to see if she could pick up on what Raven had told her, but she didn't pick up anything.

"Yes, in fact, we did. The food was superb. Thanks for asking," said Becky.

Becky was about to close the door, when Jonathan commented on her beauty. He then told her that his friend, Ryan, liked Raven. "He's white. Would your friend date a *white* guy?"

"Race doesn't matter to Sis." Becky answered. "That's what I call Raven. She's like a sister to me. We, *are* sisters."

Jonathan smiled. "Good looks run in your family."

Becky knew that race didn't matter to Raven, because after all, they were best friends. In fact, they were like sisters. Becky laughed again when Jonathan told her that Ryan said he was speechless, because of Raven's beauty, which didn't surprise Becky. Her best friend was the essence of beauty.

Jonathan went on. "Ryan says that Raven is exceptionally-beautiful. *Breathtaking*, was his exact word."

Becky laughed. "Are you sure your friend's name isn't Simon?" With all of Jonathan's, "Ryan says," it reminded Becky of the game, Simon Says.

Jonathan laughed at Becky's comment. "No, ma'am. His name is Ryan. Please, don't shoot the messenger. Simon, I mean, Ryan, wouldn't like that. Neither would the messenger."

Jonathan stood watching the very pretty blonde who was standing before him. Then finally, Jonathan confirmed what Raven had told her. "Forget about Ryan. He's on his own. I would like to get to know *you* better. I don't mean in *that* way." Jonathan quickly told Becky. He didn't want her to think that he was referring to sex. "I'm very interested in *you*."

Jonathan didn't know how long Raven and Becky were staying at the hotel. He was very interested in Becky, and he didn't want to take a chance on her leaving, without her knowing that.

Jonathan extended a hand. "Please allow me to *formally*-introduce myself. I'm Jonathan. Jonathan Sparks. You may call me, *John*, if you would like to."

"Pleased to meet you, Jonathan," said Becky. "*John*."

Jonathan and Becky talked until he was paged by the front desk.

When Jonathan left, Becky sat on the sofa smiling, and thinking to herself how nice Jonathan's smile was. She also loved his sea-green eyes. Raven was right, he wasn't bad-looking, thought Becky. But Raven was right, most of all, about the fact that Jonathan liked her.

There she goes again, with those dark, all-seeing eyes of hers. Raven Kensington was a human radar. Becky shook her head. Her best friend never ceased to amaze her. Talking about sixth sense! Becky couldn't wait for Raven to exit the bathroom. She had a lot to tell her. Starting with the fact that she was right. *Again*.

"You're going to turn into a prune!" Becky joked.

Raven laughed. "I'll be one, squeaky-clean, sweet-smellin' prune!"

A short time later, Raven exited the bathroom. She looked clean, fresh, and relaxed.

"I have a lot to tell you when I come out of the shower." Becky told Raven.

"Okay, Beck," said Raven. "I'll be waiting."

Raven preferred baths.

Becky preferred showers.

* * *

Raven stood, looking out the window, enjoying the gorgeous view. She and Becky were finally here, in the City of Angels.

"Beautiful, isn't it?" Becky asked, forty-five minutes later.

Raven nodded her head. Like the hotel, the view was beautiful. "Okay, 'fess up, Beck. What is it that you want to tell me?" said the ever-impatient Raven.

"You were right. Jonathan, *John*, does like me. How did you know that? He was so cool about it. You know, sometimes I don't think you're human." Becky told Raven.

"I'm not going to say I told you so. *Hmmm* ... you're already calling him *John*, instead of *Jonathan*? Boy, Beck, you work fast! So tell me, what exactly happened while I was taking my bubble bath?" Raven teased, as she flashed her trademark smile.

Becky laughed hard, as she threw a pillow at Raven. "There's more, get comfy, Sis." Becky told Raven about Ryan liking her.

Both of them laughed when Becky repeated what Jonathan told her, about why, a usually-talkative Ryan, was speechless.

"Sis, he also wanted to know if you would date a *white* guy."

"I sure would. And as you know, Beck, I have dated white guys before. As long as he's the *right* guy. That's the most important thing to me. I have absolutely *nothing* against interracial couples," said Raven.

"I told him as much myself," said Becky, who knew her best friend extremely well.

Like Becky, romance was the last thing on Raven's mind. She didn't mind dating, but Raven had always made it clear, that she was not interested in a serious relationship at this stage in her life. Raven had enough to think about just trying to make it in sin-land, as her father often called Hollywood, without adding to her pressures.

Making it in Hollywood was certainly not going to be an easy task, but to Raven, that made making it in Hollywood even more appealing.

Raven also knew that barriers and obstacles revealed an individual's strength. Going through, showed what you were made of. It revealed your true character. It could also make you stronger and wiser. However, Raven was still determined that no one else's barriers were going to stop her. The *only* barriers that would, or could stop her, were her own, the ones that she placed on herself.

Raven Kensington had never placed *any* barriers on herself. And she certainly wasn't about to start to now, nor was she going to allow *anyone* else, to place barriers on her.

Chapter 2

"*Earth to my sister*," *said* Becky, who saw that Raven was in deep thought. Vintage Raven, thought Becky, mind always at work.

Raven laughed. "I hear you, Beck."

"Did you pick up that Ryan likes you?"

"No, Beck, I sure didn't. Not too many things get by me, but that certainly did. I thought that I saw a wedding ring on his left hand though. Maybe not. Like you, I'm not interested in a serious relationship of any kind right now. One day, someday, but today is not that day. I'm not saying that I'm not going to date. Dating can be fun. It's just not a priority of mine now. But, I will be the first to say, that the *right* man makes *all* the difference. Getting back to Ryan though, if he is married, he can certainly forget about dating me. I don't do married men. Oops, that didn't sound too good, did it?"

Becky laughed hard in answer.

"I don't *date* married men. I don't, and I won't, go there."

"I don't think he had a ring on, but then again, I was admiring the hotel and all of the celebrities too much to notice Ryan's hands," said Becky, as she looked at the suite, admiringly. "Look at this! It's so very elegant, lavish. Sis, *imagine* having a house like this one day."

Raven's dark eyes lit up. "I thought the same thing myself. I've always loved beautiful and elegant things. I'm going to have a house like this one day. We both are. You'll see, Beck. My mother will too. She's always dreamed of her dream home, per se. And one day, I'm going to build her one. It will also be paid for. She's going to *own* it. I also believe in giving back and helping the less fortunate. *Heart*-work pays off! It's priceless. If more people helped others, the world would be a *much* better place."

"That's true, Sis."

"And for those of us who don't have money to give, we can help people in other ways. Doing volunteer work, acts of kindness, being a friend. Even a simple *hello* could make a big difference in someone's life. Sometimes the smallest things have the greatest impact. I love nice things, and there is nothing wrong with having money, as long as it doesn't have you. Money's not everything. The best things in life are priceless, free. When I do make it, I'll be wearing better shoes, but I'll make sure that others will also be wearing better shoes. It does no good to *get*, if you don't *give*."

Becky nodded in agreement. "That's so very true, Sis. That's one of the many things that I love about you, your enormous heart. Remember, Clint Stanton? You taught him to read better. His grades got better too."

"I'm a firm believer, that if anyone can read, they can learn. Sometimes things aren't always as they seem to be. In Clint's case, I looked behind the laughter. Don't get me wrong, not everyone who's laughing is unhappy. All of us have problems we go through. Problems are a part of life. For everyone. We will never, ever, be able to live problem-free. I wanted to show Clint, that he could be both, smart and funny. He wasn't a straight-A student, but he did come a long way. I will never forget his lollipop theory though. That was good and accurate. It may have sounded funny, but Clint's point is definitely *well*-validated," said Raven.

"I wonder what his plans are. What do you think he'll do with his life?" Becky asked.

Clint said that he wanted to be a farmer, even during their high school years. He also said that he still planned on working as Santa once a year. And, oh yes, according to Clint, he still wanted to marry Raven.

Becky laughed, remembering Clint's very humorous book report when they were in sixth grade. Clint Stanton was definitely a character.

Raven shrugged her shoulders. "I don't know what Mr. Stanton will do. Maybe he will become a farmer. I don't know. Sometimes the ones who we think won't be successful, turn out to be the most successful. I do know one thing though, he's *not* going to marry me."

Raven and Becky laughed at the thought. Whenever Clint would tell Raven that he was going to marry her, she would simply laugh.

Raven knew that Clint's mother would hate that idea. Myrtle Stanton was a bigot if there ever was one. She refused to believe that Raven was the person who taught Clint how to read better. *Why?* Because Raven was black. According to Clint's mother, whites were much smarter than blacks, and whites were also the superior race.

"She's a very beautiful black gal." Clint's mother told Mrs. Riley one day in class. "But being great-looking doesn't make *her* smart. There's just no way that *she* taught my Junior how to read better. No way! She probably can't even read herself."

The class had never seen Mrs. Riley so angry. The teacher told Clint's mother to leave her class, immediately.

Raven and Becky talked for most of the night. They talked about their pasts, but mostly about their dreams and their futures.

And that night, when Raven finally did fall asleep, she dreamt that she was standing onstage, holding, an *Oscar.*

Raven's dream of being a successful actress burned with desire deep inside of her. The desire was in every fiber of her being, and it had been since she was a little girl. It wasn't just enough to be a successful actress, Raven Kensington wanted to be the *best* actress that ever graced Hollywood. And the world.

Raven knew at a young tender age, her being black, and not the Hollywood size, were two of the already difficult obstacles that she would have to knock down. But one thing that Hollywood was certainly going to find out, Raven Kensington, was very hard-hitting, she was a knockout-puncher!

* * *

Rebecca Simms slept in the other bed, also dreaming big dreams.

The young women had come to Hollywood to turn their dreams into reality. They were here now, in the land of swimming pools and movie stars. Raven Kensington and Rebecca Simms had finally arrived in La-la-land, *the land ... of ... dreams ...*

* * *

Mae Kensington said a very special prayer for her oldest daughter and Becky. She stayed awake most of the night, thinking about Raven. Her daughter had always been very confident. Raven was very sure of herself. And she had always had what her mother and grandmother described as, "old folks' sense." Raven was very wise and witty. She was usually several steps ahead of everyone else, even as a little girl. Raven had always been very independent. She was so full of life. So full of energy. Raven had a great sense of humor. She could have easily been a comedienne. Mae couldn't stop thinking about her oldest daughter. Raven had always been different from her other children, in more ways than one. Raven was the only Kensington child who was left-handed. Trey and Angie called her, "Momma." Raven, called her, "Mommie." Tears filled Mae's eyes. Just that morning, Raven had left home, but her absence was already greatly-felt. Mae Kensington smiled through her tears. That was just the kind of person Raven was. You felt her enormous presence, and you also felt her absence. In a *big* way. Mae fell asleep late that night, with Raven, on her mind.

* * *

The next morning, Raven and Becky awoke early to go job-hunting. Raven had written down addresses and phone numbers of places that were hiring in the Los Angeles area. Spago was first on the list. They were hiring immediately.

Raven wore a black Versace suit, with matching shoes. Black was one of her favorite colors. Becky wore a light blue Donna Karan suit, that matched her eyes. Both ladies looked very chic and stunning.

They decided to rent a car for two weeks, especially since the manager at Enterprise Rent-A-Car had given them a great deal. Having a car would enable them to go to more places to search for employment and look for an apartment. And it was certainly cheaper than traveling via cab. Raven and Becky knew that they would catch the bus after the two weeks were over, but for now, renting a car would be the best thing to do. And they could certainly afford it.

* * *

At eight-thirty, Lauren phoned Raven and Becky's suite to tell them that a young man from Enterprise was there to pick them up.

Raven and Becky walked down to the lobby and spotted a very handsome, well-dressed man, standing near the front desk.

The man greeted them with a smile. "Miss Kensington?"

Raven nodded.

"Miss Simms?"

"That's me." Becky answered.

Eric extended a hand. "Pleased to meet both of you. I'm Eric Williams, from Enterprise Rent-A-Car." Eric led the way to their vehicle, a black Chevy Malibu. "Will this car be okay for you ladies?" Eric asked pleasantly.

"Yes, thanks," Raven and Becky spoke in unison.

Eric kept eyeing Raven. He wondered if she had a boyfriend, or if she was married. She looked young, but he knew these days, many people married young. He kept looking at her. Eric thought Raven drop-dead gorgeous. He tried not to stare, but it was very hard not to stare at Raven. She was such a lovely lady. Eric loved her voice too. It was very eloquent, and sultry. He also loved Raven's eyes. Her eyes were mesmerizing. And Eric knew that he would never forget *that* smile, that radiant smile of hers. Raven had the kind of smile that would light up any room. Eric thought her beautiful to a fault.

Rebecca Simms smiled to herself. The effect that her best friend had on people, *males*, especially. Becky called it the "Raven effect." She could tell that the Enterprise guy wasn't any different from the others. Males, young and old, watched Raven. She was such a stunningly-beautiful woman. Men also liked the way Raven moved, she was poetry in motion.

* * *

Becky knew that Raven saw Eric watching her. Not too many things got past Raven Kensington. Her dark, all-seeing eyes were exactly that. Her mother called them "X-ray eyes," because it was as if Raven saw inside of you. And she often did. Few doubted that she didn't.

Becky nudged her friend.

Raven smiled at her. She knew why Becky had nudged her. The two women knew each other very well.

Before Raven and Becky left Enterprise Rent-A-Car, Eric gave them another map of the L.A. area. The map was very detailed.

"You drive, Sis. I'll map out our destinations," said Becky.

"Fair enough. Spago first?" Raven asked.

Becky smiled. "Definitely!"

Eric had written down the directions to Spago. Raven drove there without any problems. Eric's directions were very clear and accurate.

* * *

When they arrived at Spago, they asked for Rob Sneider. He was the manager doing the interviewing and hiring.

"Please have a seat, ladies. I'll bring applications for you ladies to fill out. I'll also tell Mr. Sneider that you're here," said a very friendly waitress, named Donna. "Would either of you care for anything to drink?"

Raven and Becky politely declined.

* * *

A half-hour later, Becky informed Donna that she had completed her application.

"Okay, young lady. Follow me."

Raven gave Becky words of confidence. "You'll do just fine, Beck."

Raven sat and observed the restaurant and the staff. The restaurant was nice and elegant. She and Becky had come at a time when there were very few customers. Raven was sure the manager also preferred it that way. It was the best time to conduct interviews.

* * *

Becky came out of Rob's office fifty-five minutes later, with a slight smile on her face. "Your turn, Sis. Good luck!"

Donna led Raven to Rob's office for her interview.

Rob Sneider greeted Raven with a warm smile and a handshake. He liked her striking good looks and firm handshake, instantly.

Rob observed the beautiful black woman, who sat before him. His gray eyes combed every inch of her. I could look into those gorgeous, bedroom-eyes all day long, thought Rob, who also noticed Raven's well-manicured hands. She's very easy on the eyes. Rob smiled. Very easy. Raven was very stunning to him. Rob interviewed her longer than most. Not only did he enjoy looking at her, but he also enjoyed talking with her. She carried herself very well. She was also highly-intelligent. Raven always looked him in the eye when she spoke to him, and that was one of the many things, that Rob liked about this young beauty. She was different, Rob decided. Very different. To Rob Sneider, Raven Kensington was rare, one of a kind. After two hours, Rob reluctantly ended the interview.

Rob smiled as he shook hands with Raven and thanked her for coming. "You should hear from me in a day or two, Miss Kensington. If not before then."

* * *

Rob sat in his office, thinking about Raven and Becky. He wasn't surprised that the beauties wanted to become actresses. They both had movie-star looks. They would fit right in with his customers. They were both beautiful, classy, and elegant. They were also intelligent.

There was one concern that Rob had. Would these ladies work hard? He had seen, all too often, gorgeous ladies simply prancing around and hardly working. He knew that Raven and Becky wanted full-time employment. He had three full-time positions available.

His full-timers had to be topnotch, hardworking employees. Rob had interviewed many people, and he needed to hire desperately, but he was determined not to hire bodies. No matter how beautiful. He had learned that lesson the hard way, years ago.

According to their applications, they had both worked at a McDonald's in a place that Rob had never heard of. *Tunis*, Texas. They had worked there for two years. Rob wondered what kind of employees they were. He made a note to call and speak with Raven and Becky's former boss, a guy named, Mitch Peters.

Rob was very interested in hiring Raven and Becky. He told his assistant, Scott Barring, to do an immediate background check on them. If their references and background checks came back fine, Rob Sneider had already decided that he would hire them. *Gladly.*

* * *

"Everything okay, Beck?" Raven asked, as they walked to the car.

"I don't know, Sis. I was a little nervous during the interview. I hope he hires us. I know how much both of us want to work there. It's a very nice restaurant, isn't it?"

"Yes, it is. If it's any consolation, I was also nervous. Being nervous is natural. I'm sure you did fine. Rob liked you. He liked both of us. I'll take that as a good sign. They only have three full-time positions available now. But, we'll trust God, we'll be fine. And *if* we don't get this job, I know that He will bless us to get a job," said Raven. "We must be optimists. We are going to get *somebody's* job. And regarding our acting careers, we are going to make it! *Failing*, is not, an option!"

"What would I do without you, Sis? You're such an inspiration to me!" said Becky, feeling better.

"Correction, what would we do without each other? You're also an inspiration to me, Rebecca Simms. We are both each other's rock. And we will always be."

Raven and Becky had always had mutual love and respect for each other, and in every way that mattered; they weren't *like* sisters, they *were*, sisters.

Raven and Becky went to a number of other places. At five-thirty in the afternoon, they were tired and famished. They decided to call it a day.

"Let's go eat!" said Becky. "Can you believe that we haven't eaten all day? Where do you want to go? It doesn't matter to me."

"You won't believe this, Beck, Mickey D's. I have a taste for their Chicken McNuggets. I guess I didn't get enough of McDonald's when we worked there for two years," said Raven.

Becky laughed. "I'll never tire of their famous fries. I saw a McDonald's a few minutes ago. Turn around. I'm sure it's that way," said Becky, pointing.

Raven turned the car around and headed for Mickey D's. To Raven's surprise, there were very few customers. Raven was glad. She wanted to eat at a quiet, peaceful place, especially after having such a busy, active day. Raven just wanted to relax and unwind.

"What's so funny?" Becky asked Raven, as they sat down to eat.

"What's funny is us. We're staying at one of the most lavish hotels in Beverly Hills and eating at McDonald's. Not to say that the rich don't eat at fast-food restaurants, because I'm sure that they do, but ... I might laugh at anything now, Beck, I'm so tired. We woke up at five o'clock this morning. We've been on the go all day. Which job are you hoping that we get?" Raven asked.

"Spago, hands down."

"Me too. I also like the atmosphere. Not to mention the possible connections and being informed about auditions," said Raven. "Ironically, many auditions aren't listed in newspapers. It's probably because many producers and directors want you to have agents."

Becky nodded. "I've also noticed that. I'm not sure why that is."

The two friends ate and talked. Becky told Raven that she found Eric Williams, the manager at Enterprise Rent-A-Car, very charming and handsome.

Raven agreed, but she reminded Becky that she wasn't interested in dating anyone now. "Later." Raven turned the tables. She brought up John, the guy at the hotel who liked Becky. Raven told Becky again, that John seemed like a very nice guy. "However, you always have to get to know the person in order to find out who the *real* person is. And time always reveals that."

"Yes, time always reveals," said Becky. "Getting back to Mr. Eric, I almost told him to close his mouth. I started to say, man, where are your manners? Didn't your momma ever tell you that it's rude to stare at people? Sis, he was staring at you so hard and long, he was about to become cross-eyed."

Raven laughed. "Beck, you are crazy!"

"No, Sis, Eric is the one who went berserk! I'm going to have to keep you locked away. You're causing too many stirs. As *usual*."

* * *

When they drove back to The Beverly Hills Hotel, John's eyes lit up at the sight of Becky. He had been thinking about her all day.

Raven and Becky talked to him for a few minutes, before heading to their suite. John wanted to talk longer, but he sensed that they'd had a long day. He didn't want to push, or seem like a nuisance.

* * *

Rob Sneider sat at his desk, smiling. He had expedited Raven's and Becky's background checks. Both of their background checks came back spotless. And their former boss, Mitch Peters, gave both ladies excellent references. Mitch told Rob that he would not regret hiring the two beauties. Mitch also laid to rest Rob's other concern. Rob had asked Mitch, if the women's close friendship, ever affected their work.

"Never!" said Mitch. "They're both very professional and mature ladies. Don't let the movie-star looks fool you." Mitch wouldn't stop raving about his two former employees.

After hanging up from talking with Mitch, Rob phoned the ladies' hotel suite and left a message on their voice mail, asking them to call him. Rob Sneider was very happy, because the young ladies had impressed him immensely.

* * *

When Raven and Becky entered their suite, the message light on their phone was flashing.

Becky checked the voice mail, to see who had called. "It's Rob! From Spago! He wants us to call him," said an excited Becky.

Raven smiled.

"Do you think this means, what I think it means?" Becky asked.

"Perhaps. But let's not celebrate just yet, Beck. Give Rob a call."

When Becky called Spago, Rob Sneider answered the phone. And just as both ladies hoped, he offered them full-time positions. Rob seemed even more excited than Raven and Becky.

Rob spoke with both of them. They were going to start in ten days. "That's when the next training class begins." Training was extremely important to Rob. He told them to come in at ten o'clock the next morning for orientation. "You'll fill out your new-hire paperwork, tour the restaurant, and be introduced to the staff. I'll also give both of you history packets, that will inform you about Spago's history." Rob congratulated both of them. "I look forward to working with you ladies!"

After speaking with Rob, the two friends hugged. They were ecstatic. They had jobs! Spago also paid pretty well.

Raven and Becky phoned their families to share the wonderful news with them, then they changed clothes and went to one of Raven's favorite places, the park. It was a beautiful day in Beverly Hills.

On their way to the park, they talked about the day's events and what they planned to do after they left Spago the next morning.

"Tonight, we can write down the apartments that I circled on Sunday. We'll apartment-hunt tomorrow," said Raven. "I hope that we find an apartment quickly, because then we'll have practically two weeks left, and we can *really* have a vacation. We can tour L.A., and we can also visit all of the famous landmarks. We'd better have fun while we can. The calm, before the storm."

Becky nodded in agreement. "Oh, yes. We would certainly enjoy the hotel a lot more and enjoy our first few weeks here, having gotten the two biggest primary goals out of the way. A job, and a place to live. One down, Sis."

Raven smiled. "And one, to go."

After walking the entire park, Raven and Becky sat on a bench, admiring the scenery, enjoying the peace and quiet, and talking constantly of their dreams.

Both thought Beverly Hills very beautiful. The place certainly lived up to its image of opulence and *unparalleled*-beauty. Raven and Becky saw many lovely mansions, with fancy, expensive cars parked out front.

"Mark my words, Beck, you're going to live here one day."

"I've always dreamed of living in Beverly Hills."

"And you will, Beck. You *will* live here. One day," said Raven. "You'll see. Malibu, Pacific Palisades, Brentwood, Santa Monica, and Bel Air are also very lavish places," said Raven. "And obviously, all are very pricey. We will live within our means. We can visit, but we *sho' cain't* stay."

Becky laughed. "No, we *sho' cain't* stay, at least not now."

The two friends sat at the park for hours, enjoying each other's company, as always. They had always gotten along very well.

Raven and Becky walked back to the hotel before dark. They knew that crime was everywhere, even in Beverly Hills. No place was Mayberry, the fictional town where Andy Griffith and family lived, on *The Andy Griffith Show*.

* * *

As they walked to their suite, Raven saw John watching Becky. "Beck, John really wants to talk with you. He was practically foaming at the mouth." Raven joked.

Becky laughed. "I'll go talk with him. You coming?"

"You're kidding, right? Beck, the key word here is *you*. He wants to talk with you, not me. You two go get acquainted. Be careful. And don't do anything I wouldn't do. And, please, don't take any *wooden*-nickels."

Becky laughed hard in answer.

John's eyes lit up again when he saw Becky. He had just clocked out. He hoped that she would talk with him.

"Hello again, John," said Becky.

"Hi, Becky. Where you off to?" John asked her.

"Nowhere. I'm just walking the grounds, that's all."

"Mind if I join you?" asked John, looking hopeful.

Becky smiled. "Not at all."

After walking for a while, Becky and John sat by the pool. Becky was glad that she had come down to talk with John. He was very intelligent. She enjoyed talking with him. They learned a great deal about each other from their lengthy conversation.

Becky learned that John was a twenty-year-old single guy, who was currently studying for his MBA. He worked at the hotel full-time and went to UCLA part-time. John lived with his parents in Woodland Hills. He was also an only child. And, as he had stated repeatedly, he was very interested in getting to know Rebecca Simms better.

John learned that Becky, and her best friend, Raven, were aspiring actresses. They both had dreams of making it big in Hollywood. And they were both from Texas. Becky also told John that she was an eighteen-year-old single lady, with no immediate plans for a serious relationship at this time in her life. Becky was very honest with John.

Becky didn't want him, or any other guy, believing that she was ready to marry, settle down, and have kids. Maybe someday. But, for now, she wanted to turn her dreams into reality, first. Like Raven, *making it*, was currently her first priority.

Becky and John shared many common interests. They both loved traveling, reading, math, and music. They were also very passionate about pursuing their dreams. And although John had no interest in acting, he loved going to the movies and meeting many of the celebrities who often stayed at The Beverly Hills Hotel. Some of them were snobbish, but some of them were very nice and down-to-earth, John told Becky. His eyes danced with excitement as he talked with the very attractive blonde sitting beside him.

   * * *

Raven relaxed in the big, garden-size tub, that was filled with hot water and plenty of bubbles. She loved taking long, leisurely bubble baths.

Raven sat in the tub listening to a jazz station that she had found earlier that afternoon. And the music, like the bath, was very soothing. Raven closed her eyes. Dreams continued to fill her head. Dreams that she was going to pursue relentlessly, to turn them into reality.

Raven loved everything about the lavish hotel. She knew that she could easily get used to this kind of luxury. And one day, she would be able to afford to do anything that she wanted to do. She was certain of that!

She had always loved nice things. Except, as her brother Trey, always told her, her nice things, were always expensive. "My sister has expensive tastes. Very expensive tastes. Either you'll become rich, or marry a rich man."

"Maybe both." Raven told her brother. "Who knows?"

Raven bathed, washed and conditioned her hair, then brushed her pearly-whites. Not only did Raven smell good, she also felt good.

   * * *

Becky walked in later, with a big smile on her face.

Raven returned her friend's smile.

Becky didn't have to say a word. Happiness was written all over her face. "John and I had a long talk. We talked about a lot of things. I really enjoyed myself, Sis. I think he did too."

"You *think*, he had a good time? Please, Beck, who are you trying to kid? You know he had a great time! Don't forget to whom you're talking, Missy."

"Yes, Sis, we had a great time. I like John. But I told him that I wasn't interested in anything serious; however, I also told him that I would date. After all, there's no harm in dating."

Raven nodded her head in agreement. Becky was right, there was no harm in dating. One just had to be very cautious in today's times, as with anything.

* * *

John drove home that evening grinning like a little boy on Christmas day. He hadn't been this happy in a long time. He had dated fairly often, but no female excited him the way Rebecca Simms did. John didn't know if anything would become of their new friendship, but he was willing to accept whatever fate dealt them.

When John made it home, he told his parents that he wasn't hungry. John went to his room to study, but he couldn't keep his mind on his books. Becky occupied his mind, totally. "John Boy," as his friends sometimes called him, had been bitten by the lovebug.

John's parents discussed him at dinner. They both thought, accurately, that their son had met a girl. And apparently, he *really* liked this one. They weren't worried about his grades dropping though, because their son was a natural scholar. John made A's with very little effort.

That night, Jonathan had a very pleasant dream. He dreamed that he and Becky had gotten married. And like so many dreams, this one also seemed, very real.

* * *

Becky showered, washed her hair, then brushed her teeth. When she came out of the bathroom, she and Raven watched several movies, then they talked for most of the night.

Becky told Raven that Ryan quit his job earlier that day. "He's having marital problems. Ryan told John that he was going to move back home to Pleasant Hill."

"Pleasant Hill?" Raven asked. "Where is that?"

"John said that it's in the Bay Area. Near a place called Walnut Creek, not too far from Oakland." Becky shrugged. "I told John that you would never have gone out with Ryan. Not because Ryan was white, but because he was *married*, and we don't date married men. We don't *do* them either."

"Beck!"

The two friends laughed.

"You're right about that. I don't date, or *do*, married men. I thought I saw a ring on his left hand."

Becky nodded. "You were right again, Sis. Boy! You don't miss a beat, do you?"

Raven laughed. "I try not to. As far as I'm concerned, Ryan's wedding ring is simply a piece of jewelry to him. I don't know what the problems are in Ryan's marriage, but I do know that cheating is wrong. If he's a man who cheats on his wife, there's no way that a man like that would ever appeal to me. He would also cheat on me. You can tell a lot about a person by the way that they treat their mate, their family, their friends, not to mention the way that they treat *self*. It's not always who you're with, it's who you are. If you're a male who beats women, then it doesn't matter who you're with, you're going to beat her too. If, she lets you. Likewise, if you are married to a male who cheats, he will cheat on whomever he's with. It doesn't matter how great she looks or how good she is, in or out of bed, you are what you are. Even the best marriages have problems, but there's never an excuse to cheat or abuse anyone, physically, emotionally, mentally, or verbally. No excuse! And I've heard some women say that being with a married man is special. I have yet to find out what's special about a used or borrowed product. Not to mention a product that is rotten, to begin with. Females who date or sleep with married men, *scream* bad volumes about themselves. They often think that they're doing something for him that his wife isn't doing, but that couldn't be farther from the truth. The problem lies with the cheater, not the person who's being cheated on. That's why dogs shouldn't get married. Why get married when you know you're going to be screwing everything that moves? My heart goes out to the good wives who love their husbands, and who are devoted and dedicated to those no-good dogs."

"Women cheat too."

"I know that, Beck. Like many things, it often goes both ways. I can't think of the country that kills the man or woman if they are caught being unfaithful." Raven laughed. "If the United States were the same way, there would be very few people left in America."

Becky laughed hard.

"Beck, you know I'm right! Ryan shouldn't be sharing a bed with his wife. Like *all* dogs, he should sleep on the floor."

Becky laughed so hard she cried. Raven was too funny.

"I have never been a selfish person, Beck. I'll share many things with people, but not a man. Not only must I be number one, I better be the *only* one. Too many males today are *anybody's* man. There is a big difference between a man and a male. Very big difference. And likewise, there is a big difference between a female, and a woman."

"You know, Sis, if this acting thing doesn't work out, you could be a very successful comedienne." Becky sat on the sofa looking at Raven. "Are you sure you want to be an actress, or a psychiatrist, or a comedienne, or an attorney, or a ... Who knows? There is no limit with you, Miss Kensington! Beautiful woman of *many* talents. I assured John there was no way that you were going to even consider dating a *married* Ryan, under *any* circumstances."

* * *

The next day, Raven and Becky spent four hours at Spago. They completed paperwork, toured the restaurant, and met most of the staff, just as Rob said they would. They were also paid for their time.

After leaving Spago, they went apartment-hunting. It was time to set their sights on a place to live. One thing was for sure, it would *not*, be in Beverly Hills.

Raven and Becky visited eight apartments, before finding one they both liked. The Summerwood Apartments were very nice, well-maintained, and gated. The apartments were also located in a very nice area. There were nearby stores, a park, which pleased Raven all the more, and right across the street from Summerwood, there was a bus stop. Living across the street from a bus stop was very convenient, especially since they didn't have a car. Raven and Becky could have easily bought a car with the money that they had, but both had decided against it. At least for the time being.

Raven and Becky loved the apartment. They completed an application and left a deposit with Rita Hall, the apartment manager who reminded Becky of Mrs. Claus. Rita told them that she would contact them within forty-eight hours.

* * *

When they drove back to the hotel, Raven told Becky that she was going to go to the park across the street.

"Are you sure you don't want John and me to come with you?"

Raven shook her head no. "No thank you, Beck. I'll be fine."

"You will come back before dark?"

"Beck! Yes, Mother, I will. I know that crime is everywhere, even in *these* hills. I also have my belts."

"*Belts*? Oh yeah, Miss Lee. I've always wondered, does that karate stuff *really* work?" Becky asked, as she pretended to demonstrate some karate moves.

Raven laughed at her friend's demonstrations. "It sure does. It's extremely good to know, especially in these days and times. So, unless someone pulls out a gun, I'll be fine. And by the way, Beck, your *karate* demonstrations need *a lot* of work!"

Becky laughed hard in answer.

"And speaking of martial arts, I have already found another sensei. I'll also practice at home. I want to remain sharp and very skillful."

"Yes, Miss Perfectionist, I know you," said Becky. "Are you sure you don't want me to go with you? I can always chat with John later."

"I'm honored that you'd put me first, but no thanks, my friend. I'll be fine." Raven looked at her blonde friend. "We are always worrying about one another, aren't we?"

"Yes, Sis, but that's what sisters do. Be careful."

"*Always*," said Raven.

* * *

Dressed down, or dressed up, Raven Kensington drew eyes like a magnet. Even dressed in gray sweatpants, a black T-shirt, and black baseball cap, Raven turned heads. She was the kind of woman who made males and females alike, sit up and take notice. Nothing concealed the young woman's staggering-beauty, or her enormous presence. Raven was definitely a force to be reckoned with.

It was obvious to everyone watching her, that Raven was a woman with immense-beauty and class. She was also very distinguished. There was something very powerful about her too. And as Raven walked through the hotel, it wasn't just men watching her admiringly, women were also watching her. Many wondered who she was.

One Caucasian lady with long blonde hair and green eyes sat in the lobby, watching her husband, stare at the young black beauty. Tessa Winters didn't like the look in her husband's eyes. She hated Raven on sight.

The white lady eyed her husband angrily. Here she sat, dressed in a Vera Wang gown, and he seemed taken by *a black gal in sweat-pants*? What was this world coming to? Tessa thought.

But even the elegant and attractive Tessa Winters knew, this was no ordinary woman. This young woman, whoever she was, was extraordinary. Tessa became angry with herself for becoming envious. Why should she be jealous? Jealous of *her*? *Me*? Jealous of *that*?

At forty-five, Tessa Winters had paid thousands of dollars for plastic surgery, she had been in a number of movies, and she had married a rich man who had given her two beautiful children. She had everything. *Or did she*?

Tessa continued to watch Raven. The thought of her being jealous of anyone of color, especially, was ludicrous. At least that's what she tried to tell herself.

And, as if Raven sensed Tessa watching her, she looked her in the eye and flashed her trademark, Miss America smile.

"Bitch!" Tessa whispered under her breath. "Drop dead."

"Gorgeous. Ready to go?" Tessa's husband asked her.

Tessa shot him an angry look. Calvin Winters had watched Raven until she was completely out of sight. And now, thought Tessa, he comes to get me. I took a backseat to *that*? But Tessa's eyes had also been glued to Raven.

"What's the matter, darling? You're looking deathly-pale. Are you ill?" Tessa's husband asked her. Tessa's face was chalk-white.

"Take me home," Tessa snapped. "Now!"

* * *

Raven watched all of the fancy cars and limos that drove by. She wondered who was in the limos with the dark, tinted windows.

Raven thought of the dream that she'd had since she was a little girl. To be a star. A big star! The *biggest* ... in the world.

Raven's family wasn't surprised that she wanted to be an actress. They all knew that she was a natural. They had told her many times that she should be on TV.

Raven felt that she was born to be an actress. It had been a burning desire inside of her for years. Raven Kensington thought of Hollywood. She didn't just want to be a successful actress, Raven wanted to make a difference. In Hollywood, and the world.

Raven continued to think. She always felt that everyone should be included. She had always felt that if anyone were meant to be excluded, they wouldn't exist. We are all here for a reason, thought Raven. Every life has a purpose and value. And everyone should be treated equally and fairly. She had seen, all too often, blacks, other nonwhites, the poor, and larger females, constantly being excluded.

Raven knew that beauty and talent came in *all* sizes, shapes, and colors. She had always been very confident and very comfortable in her own skin. Not only did Raven Kensington know who she was, she loved, who she was. And never once, did Raven wish to be white or petite. She loved herself, her race, her size, and shape, as is, and she was determined to do something about the race and size discrimination that plagued Hollywood, society, and the world.

Besides equality and a level playing field, acceptance and appreciation were two more things that came to Raven's mind. Accept people the way that they are. Accept the package they came in. Love and appreciate, *all* kinds of people, and *all* kinds of beauty.

Raven thought of beauty pageants, especially how they used to be. One would have wondered if there were *any* beautiful black, Hispanic, Asian women, et cetera, because there was a time, for years in fact, that beauty pageants consisted of white females, only. The young beauty continued to think, the Miss America Pageant chose an African-American emcee for the *first* time, in 2002. It was the first time in the pageant's eighty-one year history. *Eighty-one years*. Raven shook her head.

Raven was wise enough to know that invisible "Keep Out" signs for blacks, still existed, in many places, literally. She smiled. *They* might as well say "welcome," because I am coming through! And I am not going to *keep out*, unless, I don't want to come in! Raven flashed her trademark smile.

"What are you flashing that very *pretty* smile for?" Becky asked.

Raven saw Becky walking towards her. She had always been very alert. "Oh … just doin' a little California dreamin'," said Raven. "How is John doing?"

"He's fine," said Becky. "He had to go back to work. I told John that we accepted his touring offer. I think we'll have a lot of fun."

"Yes, *especially* you two," said Raven.

The friends sat and talked at the park for hours, before heading back to the hotel.

* * *

The next day, Rita Hall called to tell Raven and Becky that the apartment was theirs if they still wanted it. They were elated. The apartment was very nice. Raven and Becky immediately went shopping for their new home.

* * *

Raven was also pleased that there was a church near the apartments. It was within walking distance too. Raven planned to go the following Sunday.

Becky declined to go. She believed in God, but she never really liked going to church. She went at home because her parents made her go. Becky believed that one didn't have to go to church to worship God. This was no surprise to Raven. Becky had told Raven about her beliefs years ago. And although Raven didn't agree with her friend, she respected her beliefs. Raven figured as long as Becky didn't practice voodoo, or worship the devil, whether she went to church or not was her business. Hers, and God's.

* * *

On Sunday, Raven almost overslept, because she had stayed up late the previous night. And because she was running late, she took a rare shower. Raven wore a light gray suit, with an elegant, wide-brimmed, matching hat. She tilted the hat to the side and positioned it low over her face, giving her an aura of elegance, power, and unbearable mystery.

Becky sat up in bed, yawning and watching her friend. "Wow! Sis, you look gorgeous as usual. You look like a million bucks!"

"Thanks, Sleeping Beauty. I'll see you later. Get enough sleep for me too," said Raven.

Raven reached the City of Angels Church of Christ in record time. She sat at the back. Her dark eyes took in everything, as usual.

Raven enjoyed the songs by the choir. But most of all, she enjoyed the sermon. It was very moving and inspirational. It seemed as if the pastor was talking directly to her.

When the usher asked visitors to stand, Raven stood up, smiled, and introduced herself. "My name is Raven Kensington. I'm a member of Old Bethlehem Baptist Church in Tunis, Texas. I'm pleased to be here. I enjoyed the songs the choir sang, but most of all, I enjoyed the moving sermon by your pastor. Please keep me in your prayers."

* * *

"Amen!" said the congregation.

"We sure will, Sister Kensington!" said one man very loudly.

"We certainly will keep you in our prayers, young lady," said the pastor, whose name was Flint Daly. "We hope to see you again."

"Amen! Amen!" roared the men. They definitely wanted to see *this* lady again. She was so strikingly-beautiful. They loved the way she looked, the way she moved, and *that* voice ...

Pastor Daly admitted to himself how gorgeous and fine the young woman was. I'm a pastor, but I'm still a man, he thought to himself. Still a man. It's okay to admire another woman's beauty, and *other* things ... As long as I don't act on it. The pastor smiled. He was a married man.

* * *

Raven felt herself getting very nauseous. I have to leave, thought Raven. She didn't want to be remembered as the visitor who vomited in church.

As a deacon was announcing the offering amount, Raven put one finger up and quietly left the church.

After the church service ended, most of the men were looking for her. Raven Kensington, had already left the building.

"Where did *she* go?" one deacon asked Esther Knox, who was the usher.

"The young lady?" Esther asked.

"Yes."

Esther laughed before answering. "She left already."

The deacon wasn't the only man looking for the young mysterious beauty. Some of the men quickly walked outside, hoping to catch Raven before she left. They wanted to look at her, talk to her, and encourage her to come again. Please, do come again, they all wished silently. *Please*, come again.

"*That* sister looked so good, I'm going to have to go to Texas if I can't have her," said a man who looked to be in his thirties. "My! My! My! Why *torture* a man like that? You know what, Sister Knox?"

"What?"

"The devil sent her here to tempt us!"

Esther laughed.

"I'm serious, think about it. But in the name of Jesus, devil, you're a liar! Devil be gone!" The man smiled. "Is *she* coming again?"

Esther laughed hard in answer.

* * *

Raven drove to Walgreens to purchase Pepto-Bismol and 7-Up. She sipped some of the Pepto-Bismol in the car. She needed it to work quickly. Maybe I have food poisoning, Raven thought to herself. They had dined at a seafood restaurant the previous evening. Whatever it was, Raven hoped that it would go away quickly.

Raven had planned on shaking the pastor's hand after the service. But feeling as nauseous as she felt, she wasn't going to take that chance. If it's God's will, I'll see him again next Sunday, thought Raven.

Becky was still in her pajamas when Raven returned to the hotel. When Becky saw the Pepto, she became concerned. "You okay, Sis?"

"I think so. I became very nauseous towards the end of the church service," said Raven.

"How are you feeling now, Sis?" Becky asked.

"Still nauseous."

"I'll fix you a cold glass of 7-Up. Take some more Pepto and lie down. I'll keep a close eye on you. If you start to feel worse, I'll take you to see a doctor."

"Thanks, Dr. Simms. Ice and 7-Up would be nice," said Raven, as she undressed.

Becky canceled her plans with John to keep an eye on her friend, despite Raven's protests.

"I'll be fine, Beck. You don't have to stay here with me. There's room service. I'm not alone."

"I know you're not alone, because I'm here. I am going to stay with you, Sis."

    * * *

Hours later, when Raven awoke, she felt a lot better. "I feel better. Maybe it wasn't food poisoning after all. I don't know what it was, but I'm just happy that I feel like myself again."

"I told you what it was!" Becky laughed. "The pure dee-devil. How was church? Did you like it?"

"Loved it! Pastor Daly preaches right from the Bible, as all pastors should. I'm sure that I'll be visiting again. And as always, I received good and bad stares."

"Typical," said Becky. "Even in God's house. Shame, shame. Christians hatin'. How shameful."

"Going to church has never made anyone a Christian, Beck. Some of the biggest devils are in church. And anyway, where there are people, regardless of where you are, you will have good and bad, no matter what," said Raven wisely. "But I'm not going to church for them. I'm going for *me*. I learned years ago not to let things like that bother me. I'm used to people burning holes in me with their eyes. I try not to worry about things that I can't do anything about."

"If looks could kill, Sis, you'd be a goner," said Becky.

"*If*, but thank God, they can't. Because if they could, we'd *both* be goners, Beck."

"I don't get as many hate and envy stares as you do." Becky told her friend. "In the Bible it says something like, jealousy is crueler than the grave."

Raven nodded. "Yes, that's deep. Jealousy is awful. But like so many other things, it will always exist. In my opinion, it's wasted energy. Whoever you are, however you look, be thankful and grateful, and work with what you got. There's always good, better, best. I'm happy for anyone who succeeds. I admire and compliment others on their looks, intelligence, skills, whatever is applicable," said Raven. "I pray and hope that God keeps me that way."

"Well, unfortunately, Sis, some don't have much to work with."

Raven laughed. "Well, again, my motto is, work with what ya

got. Be it a little, or a lot."

Raven and Becky spent the rest of the day in their suite, resting, relaxing, and talking. The friends always enjoyed their talks. No subject was off limits, they could talk about anything. And they often did.

Becky kept a close eye on Raven. She wanted to make sure that Raven *really* was feeling better. Becky knew how stubborn Raven could be.

* * *

The following week was even busier than the first one. Raven and Becky had their furniture delivered to their new apartment. They also had all of their utilities turned on. They decided on separate phone lines.

* * *

By week's end, Raven and Becky had moved most of their belongings from the hotel to their apartment. They were all set to move in; however, they stayed the full two weeks at the hotel.

And that same week, they got their first taste of Hollywood, by auditioning for parts at an open-audition. It was also a heavy dose of reality, *especially*, for Raven.

* * *

Raven and Becky were very excited, and nervous. They awoke early in the morning to be the first two there. They assumed correctly, that hundreds, maybe even thousands of people, would show up. And show up they did.

Security personnel helped control the massive crowd.

Assistants divided the enormous group into teams, to make it easier for everyone, and to speed things along.

"Raven Kensington!" the producer called. His voice sounded more like a growl to Raven.

"Knock 'em dead, Sis!" Becky told Raven.

"You do the same, Beck!"

The producer eyed Raven. Stenton Baybrook had been a producer for over fifteen years. The chubby white man sat watching

Raven like a hawk. He started to tell her that the part had already been taken, but decided against it. After all, thought Stenton, she might know that Jackson guy, and that other preacher, Sharp somebody. Could this be a set up? Stenton's blue eyes were like ice. He wondered why Raven had even bothered to come. He chuckled to himself. Did she really think she had a chance? The chuckle quickly turned into anger again, as Stenton watched the clock. Allowing *her* to audition was wasting his time, and costing him money.

This was a new TV series, and the few, very small *black* roles had already been filled. They had three parts for *them* in the show. There was the maid for the rich white family, her illegitimate son who was serving life in prison, and the maid's sixteen-year-old nephew, who couldn't read. The three blacks in the show would be rarely seen, and they had less than four lines between them. They want us to give them parts? Well, hopefully I'll receive an award. I have three of them in this show, Stenton thought to himself.

"Read this!" Stenton barked to Raven.

Raven read the man just as easily as she read the script before her. She already knew that he wasn't going to choose her. She had expected this, but it was even worse when it was before you, and you were actually going through it.

Raven read the script exceptionally-well. Her voice and actions were flawless. However, she knew from the way that the producer looked at her, that it didn't matter how good she was, he had already made up his mind, when he saw the color of her skin. He wasn't going to even think of choosing her. And, Raven was right.

"You're definitely not what we're looking for! Thanks for coming in," said Stenton, rudely. He was very cold towards Raven; he acted as if he hated her.

"What exactly are you looking for?" Raven asked. She wanted the producer to tell her, what she already knew. "I am a young woman."

"Look, I don't have time for this! I'm sorry, I forgot, *you'll* are slow. Read … my … lips," said the producer, talking very slowly, "you are *not* what we're looking for! I don't have to give you any explanation. Stop wasting my time! Next!" Stenton barked. "Suzie Kinkely!"

Becky ran towards Raven. She was beaming. "I've been called back for a second audition! I know you were too!" Becky told her friend. Becky knew that Raven was even more talented than she was. Therefore, she had assumed that Raven had also been called back.

"No, Beck, I wasn't."

Becky frowned. "You're kidding, right?"

Raven shook her head no.

"I'm sorry, Sis." Becky didn't need to ask why. She already knew. "If that's the way they are, I'm leaving!" said Becky.

"No, Beck, you're not. I don't want you turning down opportunities because of the bigots in Hollywood. I'm going to make it, and so are you," said Raven with assurance. Raven was hurt and angry, but very determined. And the producer had made her even more so. "When is your second audition?"

"This afternoon. They're eager to make a decision. They are already behind schedule," said Becky. She was excited, but she was very angry about how Raven had been treated. "Let's go home. I'll come back this afternoon."

But that afternoon, Becky didn't go back. She didn't want any part of it. The *it* being the way that the producer had treated her best friend, the woman who was like a sister to her.

* * *

When Raven awoke from her nap, she looked at the clock, then looked at Becky. "Beck! I thought you said the second auditions were this afternoon."

"They were. I just didn't go," said Becky.

Raven sat down beside her best friend. "Oh, *Beck*. You can be as stubborn as me sometimes. You *can't* do this. If you refuse to go through with opportunities that you have, based on discrimination in Hollywood, you will never make it, girl!"

Becky laughed hard.

"I'm *serious*, Beck. I know that you did this because you love me. I already *know* that you love me. I love you too, Beck. I really appreciate what you did, but *please*, promise me that you won't ever do this again." Raven's dark eyes grew serious, as she looked at her best friend. "*Beck?*"

Becky hesitated.

"*Rebecca Simms?*"

"O … kay. I *hate* discrimination, Sis. It's so awful!"

Raven nodded in agreement. She didn't want Becky or anyone else feeling sorry for her. After all, she wasn't the one with the problem.

"Yes, it is awful, Beck. But it doesn't matter how many *no's* I get, I'm *going* to make it! I'm going to keep fighting. I have to! For me, and for all those, who were discriminated against in the past, for all those, who are being discriminated against now, and for all those, who will come after me. If I fight, perhaps it will be better for them. If I give up, Beck, *they* win." Raven flashed her trademark smile. "And besides my friend, you know that I *hate* to lose."

Becky laughed, as she gave Raven a big hug.

* * *

Raven and Becky continued going to open-auditions, because they didn't have agents yet. They had mailed and hand-delivered their eight-by-ten glossies, resumes, and cover letters to every talent agency known to man. They desperately wanted to find agents, but they knew that they still had to work hard, and be hands-on, to find work in Hollywood. So far, they hadn't received any callbacks from agents, or for parts.

* * *

Months later, Raven and Becky arrived early at another open-audition, looking like a million bucks, as usual. It was for a TV sitcom. The producer was a thin, middle-aged man, who seemed a tidbit friendlier than Stenton.

"Rebecca Simms!" Herbert Manfield yelled.

* * *

Raven wished Becky luck. Luck was simply a figure of speech to Raven, because she didn't believe in it. As far as she was concerned, nothing happened by chance or accident. *Nothing.*

Darren Reardon, the show's writer, stared at the young pretty blonde. The only thing that he didn't like about Becky, he decided, was her size. If only she were several sizes smaller. He guessed that she was probably a size eight or nine. The producer and writer agreed; they needed someone very petite.

"Thanks, Rebecca. We'll call you." Darren lied. He was used to lying. It was second nature to him, especially in the business that he was in.

Raven sat, silently-rooting for her best friend. Becky was an awesome actress. Her performances were always riveting.

After Becky's audition was over, she walked slowly towards Raven.

"How did things go?" Raven asked.

"They *didn't*," Becky replied, using Raven's line. Becky knew that the man had lied to her.

"Raven Kensington!" Darren yelled.

Raven read the script, and as always, she delivered a flawless-performance. Darren looked at Raven. Definitely *not*. There were a number of things that he didn't like about Raven. Her race, and her weight. Her butt was too big. She looked to be a size or two larger than the blonde. Darren continued to study Raven. She definitely needed to lose weight to even have a chance, and even then, her chances were still slim-to-none, the writer had concluded. There were very few black roles in Hollywood, Darren thought to himself. Even in the 21st century.

Darren Reardon had been a successful writer in Hollywood for ten years. He seldom wrote parts for blacks in any of his shows. He had already decided that there wouldn't be any maids, prostitutes, thieves, unwed-mothers, or illiterates, in this show either. Darren studied the young black woman. There were things that he liked about Raven though. Her beauty was stunning, undeniable. Her voice was very eloquent, and sexy. She looked like she had money. Darren wondered if Raven was raised by a white family. Her mannerisms, and class, reflected that, the writer thought to himself, as he continued to study Raven.

The director scoped Raven too. Fraiser loved her shapely-body. His eyes were fixated on Raven. He thought her mouth-watering. Fraiser continued to stare at the sultry-beauty. His eyes rested on Raven's full breasts and her curvaceous bottom. Raven had aroused him. Fraiser also thought her immensely-talented, but there was just *no way* that a woman of her race and size would have a chance of making it in Tinseltown. White, *pencil*-thin females, were the rule. They were ideal, not the voluptuous women, like the woman who stood before him. And certainly not black women. Although, he certainly would have preferred Raven over the shapeless-sticks any day. Raven had a lot more delicious items on her plate. Fraiser smiled. What a pity, thought Fraiser. If only ... but, she wasn't. The right race, or size. He knew that some blacks had been successful in Hollywood, but not many. Fraiser could count them on his hands, literally.

"Thanks, Miss Kensington, we'll call you." Fraiser watched Raven walk away. He loved her walk too. He would have loved to get her in bed.

* * *

"This is harder than I thought it was going to be," said Becky, looking frustrated.

"Yes, it is, Beck. Knowing something is one thing, actually experiencing it, going through it, is another." Raven acknowledged. "Yet, we *must*! We knew that it wasn't going to be easy before we came here. Even Clint knew, way back when," said Raven. "Look at the big stars today, many of them were turned down too. *A lot*. But they didn't give up. If they would have given up, they would not be where they are today. We can't, correction, we *won't* give up, Beck!"

* * *

"No, Sis, we *won't* give up!" said Becky.

"We will fight, for our right, to act!" Raven flashed that trademark smile of hers. "You know, Beck, one day, we're going to look back at this and laugh."

"Unfortunately, Sis, that day hasn't come yet," said Becky.

Raven laughed. "Trust me, Beck. Believe you me, it *will*."

* * *

Later that day, John visited Raven and Becky at their new apartment. He loved it. "Very nice, ladies! Very nice," he told them. John was also happy that they had rented a place in a nice neighborhood. It wasn't Beverly Hills, but it was a very nice area, and that was the most important thing.

* * *

Over the next several months, Raven and Becky mastered their positions at Spago, auditioned for parts almost daily, and settled into their new apartment and new city.

After five months of seemingly nonstop auditioning, Raven and Becky finally landed roles, as movie extras.

Over the next several years, Raven and Becky continued to work at Spago and work as movie extras, hoping that something bigger and better would eventually come along. And it did, finally, for Becky. She was called by a talent agent, who wanted to represent her. Walt Miller told Becky that he was very excited after viewing her photos, and that he was very anxious to meet with her. Becky was ecstatic. Raven was very happy for her too.

* * *

While Becky went to meet with Walt Miller, Raven went to another audition. And as always, the two women wished each other luck, as they parted ways.

Raven arrived at the audition early, as usual. She knew that hundreds, if not thousands of *hopefuls*, would show up, with hopes of becoming a star. They always did.

* * *

As soon as Raven walked inside, she was greeted immediately by the janitor, who was an elderly black man with a friendly smile. The man watched the young woman, and like many who saw Raven, he was in awe of her beauty. He kept smiling at Raven. *Boy*, thought the old man, this young woman makes me wish for younger days. He watched Raven, as she signed up for the audition.

Raleigh Brown had worked for MGM for many years. He would often stand and watch the auditions. His kind were very scarce, even in today's times. There were more blacks in Hollywood, but not nearly enough, thought Raleigh. He continued gazing at the young black woman. She was definitely gorgeous. She also carried herself very well. Raleigh loved Raven's voice too. Very unique, the old man thought. She would certainly be a breath of fresh air, very refreshing, for Hollywood.

The old man stood thinking how he would love to see a woman of color, and size, become a successful actress. Most of the black women who did have success were usually thin. This woman was different in more ways than one. She was gorgeous, and she had curves for days. The old man flashed a sly-smile. Raleigh wondered if Raven could act.

He soon got his answer.

Raleigh witnessed Raven's signature, flawless-performance. He watched Raven in sheer amazement. Raleigh rooted silently for the young black woman. He watched the entire audition. And as far as the old man was concerned, the role should be Raven's, not because she was black, but because she had earned it, by being the *best*. Raleigh believed that one needed to earn what they wanted, not be *given*, anything. He also believed in a level playing field, which he knew wasn't a reality, even in current times. The old man shook his head. It was more than sad that after all of these many, many years, *race*, still mattered. And from the looks of things, apparently, it always would.

After Raven finished her performance, the producer told her to "wait around."

Raven was very excited. She had been auditioning, consistently, for years. This was the *first* time that she had been told to "wait around." Raven flashed a hopeful-smile.

Raleigh walked up to Raven. "Great job, young lady!" He offered Raven words of encouragement; he knew that it wasn't easy. Despite how easy Raven made it look. The old man smiled. Raleigh definitely loved Raven's style.

Raven returned the old man's smile, as she thanked him for the words of encouragement, and the compliment.

The females who came to audition were mostly-white. There were some blacks, some Hispanics, and a few Asian women.

The Hispanic women talked in Spanish, amongst one another. They said that no one had a chance except the thin, white women.

Raven spoke to them in Spanish, offering them words of encouragement.

The ladies were very impressed. They asked Raven where she learned the language.

"*Escuela,*" Raven answered.

The ladies smiled. "*Tu eres muy hermosa.*"

"*Gracias,*" said Raven.

The Hispanic ladies didn't make the second cut, but before they left, they wished Raven luck, in Spanish. They were very impressed by the fact that she could speak the language so well.

Hours later, Raven's name was called again. She delivered another flawless-performance; it was even better than the first. The producer, director, and writer watched Raven in awe. They couldn't remember when they had seen an actress with *this* much talent.

"She's awesome!" said two white girls in unison.

"And she's like, *totally*-gorgeous too," said a young blonde.

"Thanks, Miss Kensington, we'll call you," said the writer.

Raven left with mixed feelings. She sensed that the producer and director liked her, but the writer didn't.

When the producer, director, and writer gathered to discuss the auditions at the end of the seemingly-endless day, Raven's name came up. Everyone except the writer agreed that Raven was by far the best. But ...

"But what?!!!" said Craig Huckley, the director. He was livid. Craig wanted the part to be Raven's. Because she had earned it.

"She's fat! She's black! She's ... she's not going to pack theaters!" said Shirley Gainesburg, the writer.

"That's a bunch of bull, and you know it, Shirley!" said Craig, who knew that Shirley was also very envious of Raven. "She's *not* fat! Let's face it, *anyone* who is not a size two or three would be fat by Hollywood's standards, including *you*, Shirley. You're not exactly the poster girl for slimness yourself!" Craig was very angry. He knew that his comments might cost him the job, but he was willing to take the risk. He was speaking the truth. He was tired of it. He had seen far too often, wasted talent, naturals, like Raven, turned away because of ignorance and bigotry. Craig went on. "She's African-American, and so what? What's wrong with that? She *is* very beautiful, she's *immensely*-talented, and she's sexy as hell! Shirley, are you going to stand there and tell me that I'm wrong? Who are you kidding? I want Raven Kensington, not because she's black, but because she is the *best*! I'm very hard to please, and I have *never*, seen *that* kind of talent. Ever! And pack theaters, *trust* me, she will more than pack theaters. Raven Kensington is very bankable. She's a *gold* mine! I'm the director of this movie, and damn it, I want her!"

Shirley had heard enough, she was fuming. "Dammit, Craig! You listen to me. This is *my* movie! I own the rights. I also call the shots for this project! If I have to hire another director, I will! You are a great director, but you're not the only great one out there, Craig. You know, if I didn't know any better, I would say that you wanted to take the black beauty to bed. You act as if you're going to have convulsions if *she* doesn't get this part. She's not right for this part. This part was not written with a black woman in mind, and certainly not one of her size. So there's your answer, Craigie!"

"Not right for the part?" Craig looked at Shirley, his eyes were filled with anger. "If this were, *The Autobiography of Marilyn Monroe*, I would agree that race would certainly matter in that case, but that's *not* the case here! You and the other bigots need to stop making excuses. That line's worn out. 'Not right for the part, not the right color, not the right size, not the right *this* or *that*.' Those are very lame excuses, Shirley! Those dogs don't hunt. There is no excuse, discriminating, is wrong! Explain the *right* look to me. *Human beings* are what it should be about. *Any* human being that comes to audition should have a level playing field. What is this, writing roles for blacks? That's racist! How about writing for *human beings*? We are all individuals. When writers, producers, directors ... start *showing* the actions that I speak, then and only then, will we see the kind of change that we could see in Hollywood. And the world. What you and so many Hollywood powerhouses do, is no different than employment discrimination in the real-world. Instead of hiring the best, you hire who you want to hire, people who look like you and me. They don't have to be the best, they don't even have to be qualified, they just have to be *white*. The color of a person's skin shouldn't be an issue. Race should be meaningless, but it's not. It should be *far* behind us. It should be ancient history, but from the looks of things, discrimination will always exist. And it's very *sickening*, among other things!"

Shirley clapped. "Bravo! Are you running for president of the NACP?"

"It's the *NAACP*, Shirley!" said Craig.

"Whatever! Your speech was fantastic, Craig. Fantastic!"

Everything that Craig said went right over Shirley's head. "*No* Raven Kensington! Do I need to hire another director?" Shirley hated to call Craig's bluff. She wanted him very badly. Craig Huckley was arguably the best director in Hollywood.

Craig glared at Shirley, his eyes were like green ice. "You mentioned earlier that I'm the *best* director. That's why you offered me this job in the first place. Right, Shirley?"

"Yes. You're the best director in Hollywood, Craig. You know that," said Shirley.

Craig shook his head. "You're not interested in the *best*, Shirley. You're interested in *colors*. *If* you were interested in the best, you would hire Raven Kensington. If she were in a white body, you would've hired her instantly. She was by far the *best*, and you know it!"

"Again, do I need to hire another director?" Shirley asked.

"Yes. You damn sure do!" said Craig, as he stormed out of the office.

* * *

Raleigh Brown heard most of the conversation. It was hard not to. Craig and Shirley were screaming at each other. The old man agreed with Craig. Raleigh felt that Raven should have gotten the part too, because she was simply, the best. He shook his head. He hoped the young woman wouldn't give up. He prayed that she would keep fighting. Raleigh knew that with her *immense*-beauty and talent, Raven Kensington, could be a *huge* star.

* * *

Raven smiled on her way home. She felt that she had *finally* landed a role.

She was wrong. Days turned into weeks. The "call" never came. Raven was very disappointed, but she was very happy for Becky. Walt Miller was now her agent.

Becky didn't tell Raven, but she had asked Walt to take a look at Raven's photos. "She's even more beautiful than I am. More talented too." Becky told Walt, pleading for her best friend. Becky didn't feel bad because it was the truth.

It was also the truth, thought Becky, that if Raven were white, who knows where she would be right now? Regardless of how bleak things looked, Becky knew that Raven was going to be a huge star one day. She could feel it. She was very certain of it. "Hang in there, Sis," said Becky, as if Raven could hear her. "You hang in there. Your day *is* going to come. And when it does, Hollywood, watch out!"

Raven hadn't been called by agents either. Many of them had seen her photos, and no one could deny that she was a beauty, but as far as they were concerned, she was the wrong race, and size, for Hollywood.

Walt saw Raven's photos before he phoned Becky. And although he knew that Raven didn't have a chance of making it in Hollywood, her beauty, was staggering. Walt stared at Raven's photos for a *long* time. *Those* eyes, *that* skin, *those* cheekbones, *those* lips ... *That* face ... *She*, was one, exquisitely-beautiful woman.

Everyone in Walt's office agreed that Raven Kensington was stunningly-beautiful. But there was no way that anyone would be able to make money off Raven. And making money, was the bottom line. Very few people, if any, would hire her, for anything.

Walt finally tossed Raven's photos. He was very tempted to keep them for himself, but decided against it.

* * *

Raven *refused* to give up. She went to another open-audition. This time, it was for a made-for-TV movie. Leonard Cartwright, the producer, called Raven in his office, after she had auditioned, unsuccessfully, for a part in the movie.

"Raven, you can make it, but not for commercial or mainstream roles. You have to *compromise*. There aren't many roles for your kind. You have to play by Hollywood's rules, in order to win. You have to play the game, their way. You are very sexy! You can make a *killing* taking off your clothes. Doing B-movies. Porn." Leonard stared at Raven. He could only imagine how she looked without clothes. "I've seen the way that men look at you, Raven. There is *a lot* of money in X-rated films. Anyone who has ever made it, took off their clothes, slept with whomever they had to sleep with. They did *whatever* they had to do, in order to get their big break." Leonard tried hard to convince Raven. He wanted to bed her. Leonard eyed Raven's curvaceous body, deliciously. "You don't have much of a choice. I care about you, that's why I'm being honest with you. There are two strikes against you, Raven. Surface strikes, I'll call 'em. You're African-American, and you're bigger than what Hollywood says you should be. And let's face it, you're not white!"

Leonard's last statement, immediately made Raven think of Susan Porter.

"Leonard, it's good that you said I'm not white, because I'm not *supposed* to be white. And correction, Leonard, being black, is *not* a strike! And, no, I'm not eighty-to-a-hundred pounds soaking wet, nor would I like to be. I've never had a desire to be a bag of bones. I am a very fine woman, with curves. And people of color, and females who aren't toothpicks, are not invisible. We are very *visible*. We are also human beings. *Beautiful*, human beings. It is long, long overdue, that my race and size, be looked at, instead of being, looked over. It is time that we be included, not excluded. Strikes, Leonard? Nothing, and no one, that God made, is a strike, or mistake. If I didn't know any better, I would think that you were talking about baseball, not a human being. Ignorance and bigotry will *never* make me feel that it's awful, or shameful, to be black, or a size eleven. I'm a beautiful black woman. I'm very proud of who, and what, I am. And you, Hollywood, society, nothing, or no one, can, nor will they *ever*, make me think otherwise. I am the *only* one who defines me. I will determine what I can, and can't do. I will determine, how far I can go. I am going to make it, right here in Hollywood, and I'm going to do it *my* way! The barriers that you and so many others here have set up, are not for me; they might as well be invisible. I am coming through! What's to be is up to me, and *me* only. I don't need your permission to be successful, that's my call. I, determine that." Raven stood up. "Take a *good* look at *this* face, and this *voluptuous*, size-eleven frame."

"No one can deny that you're a staggeringly-beautiful woman, Raven. You're one of the most beautiful women that I have *ever* seen. That's not the issue here. Or should I say issues?"

Raven shook her head. Leonard obviously had no idea what she meant. "I said, take a *good* look, because you will, be seeing me again. Maybe *too* much of me. Have a good day, Leonard."

Chapter 3

The ever-so familiar words replayed in Raven's head, repeatedly, as she sat at the park. She had heard them for years now.

"You're gorgeous, but this role wasn't written for a black woman."

"If only you were smaller."

"Would you be willing to show your breasts?"

"Would you be willing to show your butt?"

"Would you French kiss another female?"

"Would you be willing to have sex with me?"

Raven had stood her ground. No, she was not going to lose weight. No, she was not going to take off her clothes. No, she was not going to engage in sex of any kind, and she certainly wasn't going to engage in same-sex relationships. And no, she wasn't going to do any X-rated films either.

Raven knew that she couldn't turn back now. She knew that she couldn't give up. She had to continue to fight, not just for herself, but for all those who were like her, who looked like her, who were her size. She had to keep fighting for all those, who were struggling to make it in Hollywood now, and for all those, who would come after her. If nothing else, she wanted things to be better for them, hopefully, *much* better.

Raven was determined to fight for her dream of what she wanted for herself and others, a Hollywood, for all! Tears fell from her eyes. Her emotions were that of anger and hurt. She *hated* discrimination, and *everything*, that it stood for.

Raven thought about all of the people who were hurt and killed in the past, because of the color of their skin. She cried for those who were *still* being hurt and killed by ignorance, and bigotry.

After crying for hours, Raven felt renewed and reenergized. "I'm *not* going to break down, I'm going to break through. I'm not going to give up, I'm going to *get* up." She kept thinking of Tinseltown, and all of the many times that they had won. There was no way, that they were going to win this time. *No way*. Raven was going to show them, they had just lost one. She flashed her trademark smile. "It's *hard* to stop a train."

* * *

Becky entered the apartment looking for Raven. "Where are you, Sis?" Becky laughed. "I bet she's at the park!" She'd had a much better day. She had landed a TV commercial and she couldn't wait to share the wonderful news with her best friend.

"Sis! There you are," said a very excited Becky. "Guess what?"

"What, Beck? Whatever it is, you're about to explode. Tell me!"

"I have been chosen to do a commercial! It's a hair commercial! They're going to pay me *twelve thousand dollars*!" Becky screamed. "And the more the commercial is played, the more money I'll make from the residuals."

Raven gave Becky a big hug. "That's fantastic, Beck! You know I'm happy for you."

"Sis, how did your day go?"

Raven told Becky all about her conversation with Leonard Cartwright.

"That bastard! How dare he make those remarks. You're very beautiful, Sis. You're also very talented. There's not a doubt in my mind that you're going to make it. I know you very well, Miss Kensington. You're the *best* fighter that I've ever known. None of this should surprise you. Even when we were kids and you wrote that *Yale* book report, you knew how it would be, and you were right. I know that it makes you angry. It makes me angry too. I love you! You're my sister. Stick to your guns. I've been around you *too* long,

Sis. I'm even starting to sound like *you*."

Raven laughed.

"Miss Kensington, you can't *begin* to know how your words of wisdom have helped me over the years."

"Thanks, Beck. You're right though, it does make me angry. Very angry. But I'm going to turn that anger into something positive. I was very angry and hurt after leaving Leonard's office today. I went to one of my favorite places, the park. I feel *a lot* better now," said Raven.

"You know, Sis, Leonard, whatever his last name is, Hollywood, the *whole* world, will one day know who you are. I'll probably be successful, but believe me, you're going to be an international *superstar*. And it's not a matter of *if*, but *when*. Mark my words, Sis. I'm telling you what I *know*." It was something that Becky had always felt. Raven was going to be as big as they come. She was going to be bigger than anyone before her. "There is something else."

"What, Beck?"

"The money that I'm going to make from the commercial is *ours*. My money is your money."

"You know that's mutual, Beck. You're going to make me cry! Thanks, but no thanks. I'll tell you what though, if I start to get low on dough, then I just *might* take you up on that offer. But I'm fine for now. *Thanks* so much, Beck."

"Not a problem," said Becky. "After all, what are sisters for?"

Tears sprung to Raven's dark eyes.

* * *

Raven, and everyone in Tunis, recorded Becky's hair commercial. Everyone was very proud of her. They were very proud of Raven too, and they told her so. "Hang in there, Raven! Your turn will come," everyone told her. "Your turn *will* come!"

* * *

Three months later, a middle-aged Caucasian man approached Raven at Spago. "May I please have a word with you?" the man asked.

Rob walked over to them, he wanted to make sure that everything was okay. Raven didn't look as if she knew the man. Rob was very protective of his employees.

The man extended a hand to Rob. "Hi, sir. I'm Andrew Spellman. I'm a talent scout / agent. I do it all. I own my own company. I am looking for a young lady to do a toothpaste commercial. This young lady is not only beautiful, but her smile is equally-so," the man pointed out. "She's *got*, the look." The look to be a star, the *biggest* one yet, Andy thought to himself. Raven's beauty was breathtaking, and so was her figure. Andrew Spellman pulled out his wallet. He showed his driver's license and business card to Raven and Rob. "You may call and verify if you'd like, sir. Or you, ma'am," said Andrew, looking at Raven.

"Raven, it's up to you, would you like to speak with this man?" her boss asked her.

"Yes, Rob. I'll talk with him, thanks."

Rob looked at Andrew. "Raven, I'll be close by, if you need me." And true to his word, Rob stayed very visible. He trusted no one. If Andy tried anything with Raven, he'd definitely have to go through him, and that wouldn't be easy.

Becky walked over to the table where Raven and Andrew were sitting. "Sis, is everything okay?" she asked her friend.

"Yes, Beck, I'm okay. Everything is fine."

"I'm here if you need me." Becky told Raven.

"Thanks, Beck."

"Wow! It's great to be loved!" Andrew Spellman remarked. "They both love you, young lady. For a moment there, I thought your boss was going to slug me." Andy joked. "I know you're at work, so I'll get right to the point. I've been watching you for several days now. You are very beautiful, Miss Kensington. I'm sure you hear that all the time. You have the kind of beauty, and smile, that could make men forget what they're saying, not to mention, forget what you're saying. You're very captivating and intriguing. You drive men wild when you're fully-clothed, and not very many women can do that. You're also a very *classy*-lady. You carry yourself very well. You have *enormous* presence. I've never been so impressed! Really, Miss Kensington. Young lady, if *anyone* has it, *you* do. You've got it! I want you for this toothpaste commercial. I also think the pay would be worth your while. Is *fifteen thousand dollars* sufficient?" Andrew watched Raven intently. "If you need to think about it, that's fine. I do need an answer by next Friday though. I certainly hope that you take the project. Here's my card. Please give me a call. I hope to hear from you soon. Thanks for your time, pretty lady." Andrew shook Raven's hand, then left.

Andrew Spellman was no dummy, he knew gold when he saw it. He knew how Hollywood was, but he didn't care. He was going to fight tooth and nail for this gorgeous young lady. There wasn't a doubt in Andrew's mind that it wouldn't pay off. In a *big* way too. Andrew was willing to bet all that he owned on that.

Andrew smiled, as he drove back to his office. Raven Kensington was in a class all by herself. Whoever didn't know her name, all of the many agencies, producers, directors, and writers, who had turned her down, whoever it was that didn't bother to give her a second look, had better get ready to stand up and take notice. They were *all* going to know who Raven Kensington was. *They*, and the whole wide world. Andrew Spellman smiled again. He was very certain of that.

* * *

"Raven, *who* was that?"

"*What* did he say?"

"Is that whom I think it was?"

"Inquiring minds want to know!"

Raven smiled. "His name is Andrew Spellman. He's a talent agent. He wants me to do a toothpaste commercial." Raven didn't tell them how much she would get paid to do the commercial. She would only tell Becky that. And that evening, when she and Becky rode the bus home, she did tell her.

"Whew! *Fifteen thousand dollars*? I know you're going to do it, Sis. Aren't you?" Becky asked.

"*Of course* I am! I'll say one thing about Hollywood, it sure pays well!" said Raven, flashing that trademark smile of hers.

"Very well!" Becky agreed.

The two friends went to Morton's to celebrate, as they had done when Becky landed her commercial.

"Sis, you haven't even begun to scratch the surface. I'm serious. I'm not just talking. I will never forget that *awesome* book report that you wrote in sixth grade. It seemed so long ago, but I'll never forget that. Few will. Mrs. Riley was a big fan of yours. She admired you a lot."

"*Neither* of us, has begun to scratch the surface. We're *both* going to make it, Beck," said a very confident Raven. "We both are."

After dinner at Morton's, John and Becky went to the movies. Raven declined to go. She wanted to give the lovebirds a chance to be alone. Raven went out with John and Becky sometimes, but mostly, she would let the two go alone.

Raven also declined the many offers that she received to go out, including offers from men at the church that she still attended. She didn't have anything against dating, she just wasn't interested in dating now. Raven also knew that the right man hadn't come along yet. I'll know when he does, thought Raven, I'll *know*.

* * *

The commercial was a great experience for Raven. Everyone agreed that she was a "natural." The director asked Andrew, whom everyone called "Andy," where this "hidden diamond" had been hiding.

Raven wrapped the commercial with few retakes. Andy enjoyed working with her. Raven was very professional. She reported on the set early, and she gave no less than her very best, which clearly showed on-screen. Even in a toothpaste commercial, Raven sizzled.

After living in L.A. for five years and trying to *make it* in Hollywood, Becky, finally got her big break. *NBC* was looking for a young pretty blonde to star in a new soap opera. One of the producers remembered a very pretty blonde who worked at Spago. Ted Roberts was also certain that he'd seen Becky somewhere before. Perhaps in a commercial, but he couldn't remember. He was certain of one thing, this young lady was exactly who they were looking for. It was as if the part had been written with Rebecca Simms in mind. The soap opera would be called, *Day's Dawn*. Ted offered Becky the part, immediately.

Ted stood, admiring Becky's beauty. "No screen test needed, Miss Simms. Now, about the show. Samantha Matthews, is the *star* of the show." Ted gave Becky full details. "This is *big*, Miss Simms! And so is the money," Ted added, trying to entice Becky. He knew that money spoke volumes. "There's also a *bonus*. How … would you like to drive that black Jaguar parked out front? It's yours, *if* you take this part."

Becky sat, stunned. She couldn't believe what she was hearing. She was ecstatic. Becky had been praying and hoping for this moment most of her life. Finally, thought a still-shocked Becky. It's *finally* happening. To *me*.

"I will have the contract delivered to you. I'll also send one to your agent. I hope that Walt doesn't get angry with me because I spoke with you first. My partner, Mark Ludke, who is also a producer of *Day's Dawn*, is very excited about working with you too. He dines regularly at Spago, so he's already seen you. We will need the contract signed and returned to us within thirty business days. I think that will give you more than enough time to read, review, and ask any questions, should you have any. We will deliver the Jag to your door, upon receipt of the *signed* contract. Fair enough?"

* * *

"Oh, yes! Fair enough," said a still-shocked Becky. This was still very hard to digest. Becky hadn't quite processed all of it yet. She felt numb. *A hundred thousand dollars per month*? And for doing something that she loved. Becky was speechless. Who in their right mind would turn down an offer like this? Becky thought. *Who*?

And if she shined the way they felt she would, Ted told Becky that he and Mark would renegotiate her contract, giving her a hefty raise, after the first season of the show. Ted also told Becky that full details were in the contract, including the Jaguar, being thrown in as a bonus.

"Miss Simms, we really want you for this part! You *are* Samantha Matthews!" Ted held up one finger. "Don't gain *any* weight though."

Becky looked at the producer.

"I'm just kidding."

But Becky knew that he wasn't.

"Congratulations, Miss Simms! We look forward to working with you."

Becky smiled in answer. *Finally*, after five *long* years in L.A., *her* big break, had come. Becky thought of Raven. She felt very strongly that Raven's big break was around the corner. While Becky waited for Raven to come home from Spago, she also thought about Clint's lollipop theory, and boy was he right. And as always, so was Raven.

Becky kept thinking about Raven. "Your turn is coming, Sis. I feel it. And it's coming in a *big* way," Becky said aloud. She was adamant about that. Raven Kensington was going to be a huge star. Bigger than anyone, past or present. Rebecca Simms smiled. She was so very certain of that, in her heart of hearts.

When Raven came home, Becky shared the unbelievable news with her. Raven was elated for her best friend. She told Becky to hire an attorney to read and study the contract. "*Never* use their attorney. *Always* get your own." Raven wisely advised.

Later that evening, Raven, Becky, and John went to Jimmy's to celebrate.

* * *

Three weeks later, Andrew Spellman phoned Raven. "Hello, may I please speak with Raven Kensington?" Andy already knew that the voice on the other end of the phone was definitely Raven Kensington's. No one had a voice like hers. Immensely-*eloquent*, *sultry*, *clarion*.

"This is she."

"Hello, Miss Kensington, Raven, pretty lady, you're *all* of the above. This is Andy, Andrew Spellman."

Raven laughed. "Hi, Andy. How have you been?"

"I've been doing fine. How have you been, pretty lady?" Andy had another part for Raven. The money was very good, but he wasn't sure if she would take the part.

Raven told Andy that she had been doing fine. She hoped he had another job for her. He had almost missed her, she was on her way out to run errands.

"I'll get right to the point, Miss Kensington. I have another role that I would like you to play. The pay is great! *Six-figures*," Andy paused, to see if Raven would say anything, but she remained silent. "It's a movie."

Still silence.

"I don't know if you've heard of Tessa Winters. Anyway, she's the star of the movie. She plays this rich widow. Her husband volunteers to go to war and he gets killed. The part that I, well, that *they*, want you to play, is ... that of ... the maid."

There was still silence on Raven's end.

"Raven? Pretty lady?"

"Yes, Andy, I'm here," said Raven, not at all surprised.

"Raven, before you say anything, there are some things that I want you to *think* about. You may look at this opportunity as an insult, and if so, I can't say that I'd disagree. However, Raven, everyone must start somewhere. I came to you with this part because it will give you *major* exposure! This part will show your beauty and talent to *millions*. It would be a lot more effective than a commercial. Raven, *nothing* could hide your *immense*-beauty or your *unmatched*-talent. No matter what role you played. I have *big* plans for you, *very* big plans! Everyone who is anyone will finally get to see you. *Trust me* on this one, pretty lady. The producers of this movie saw your photos. They also saw your toothpaste commercial. They didn't want you for this role, initially. They thought that you were too pretty and too prim and proper to play this role. I finally convinced them because I know that you can do it, and do it *better* than anyone! I want you to do this because I know what it will do for your career. *Please*, Raven, trust me. I've always been honest with you. You know that I have. You'll make *three hundred thousand dollars* for three weeks' worth of work. It will be very good money, for both of us, but, especially for you, pretty lady. Raven?"

"I'll think about it, Andy," said Raven, reluctantly.

"Thanks, pretty lady. *Please*, take this role. You won't be sorry!"

Andy thought about the immensely-beautiful and classy Raven Kensington. He admired the young woman a great deal. Andy hoped and prayed that Raven would take the part.

Raven sat down on the sofa. She liked Andrew Spellman. He was open, honest, direct, and he cared about his clients. Raven knew that Andy also cared about her. He wasn't greedy, uncaring, sneaky, ruthless, and crooked, like so many in the entertainment industry. And, so far, he hadn't tried to proposition her either.

Raven phoned her mother.

Mae Kensington was very happy to hear from her daughter. She felt her oldest daughter needed to talk.

Raven told her mother about the maid role.

Mae's heart went out to Raven. She knew that her daughter didn't want to take the part. And more importantly, she knew why. *Stereotypes*. Mae didn't blame Raven. *When* would it end?

"Sweetheart, that certainly shouldn't be shocking. Blacks in stereotypical roles are very common. *Still*. It's very sad, but true. I would take it. Andy's right. Who knows? This part that you don't want to take for obvious reasons, may very well turn out to be a *blessing* in disguise. And *everyone*, has to start somewhere. Many of today's biggest stars took parts that they probably didn't want to take, but it got them to where they are today. However, there are exceptions to refusing parts, and I don't need to say what those exceptions are. But I will if you need me to."

"No, ma'am. You don't have to tell me. I know what the exceptions are," said Raven. "You taught me well, Mommie, *very* well."

Mae Kensington smiled, before going on. "This role of a maid, *take* it, Raven, and play it to the hilt. Play it just like you would play it, if it were the *starring* role. *Outshine* the star! Outshine *everyone*! Sometimes we have to throw the chips out there, and let them fall where they may. And, I *think* you'll like where they're going to fall. Show Hollywood what they're missing! Show them what you and I already know. *No one*, can do *anything*, quite like Raven Kensington. I know that it's been very frustrating for you. But *never* give up, sweetheart. Never! You won't be able to change the tune, if you don't keep playing. *Remember*, you can't recover a fumble, unless you're on the field. Sweetheart, *someone* has to show Hollywood, and the world, that you can be *different*, and still be the *very* best, better than *all* the rest. Hollywood needs to be shown that people need to be judged, not by the package that they came in, but by what's *inside* of that package."

"You're right, Mommie."

"Looks play a huge part. But the problem with Hollywood is their nonacceptance of gorgeous black women like you, and nonwhites. I would put you up against *anyone* in looks. Your looks are *breathtaking, staggering*. However, we both know that's not the issue here. But we're not going to worry about that. You're like a train, Raven, they're hard to stop, and so are you! You're *cream*, sweetheart. The cream, *always*, rises to the top."

This was exactly what Raven needed to hear. Her mother was the wisest woman that she knew. Raven missed talking to her mother face-to-face, but *thank God* for telephones, thought Raven.

"Thanks, Mommie! You gave me the shot that I needed," said Raven, flashing that trademark smile of hers.

"Raven, you're an *intensely*-private person. You always have been. But *remember*, never keep things bottled up inside. That's not healthy. We all need someone to talk to, someone to turn to. We're human. *Always* be careful who you talk to, but I know that you will. And although we can't trust everyone, we all need to *trust someone*. You're very wise, wise beyond your years. And wise people usually make wise choices, wise decisions. But, as humans, and regardless of our wisdom or knowledge, we all make mistakes. Learning from them, is key. Remember too, Raven, that God is *always* there. Mommie will always be here for you too, as long as I'm alive. You also have a *great* friend in Becky. Your pastor's another person who you can talk to, or should be able to go to in confidence. Life is not a sprint, it's a marathon. You must, we all *must*, keep running, keep going. And you will. You're very *strong-willed*, Raven. We all get down sometimes, but never stay down. Brush yourself off and try again. You *will* succeed! There isn't a doubt in my mind about that. You have always been very successful in my eyes, because of the *truly*-beautiful and extraordinary human being that you are. I know what you're capable of, and so do you. It's *in* you, sweetheart. And *boy* is it ever! You were born with it. *Knock 'em dead*, baby! I *love* you, Raven. Call me *anytime*, day or night."

"I love you too, Mommie. *Very* much. *Thank you.*"

The wise and inspirational talk from her mother was exactly what Raven needed. She sat in the living room watching, *City Confidential*.

Three hundred thousand dollars! Whoa! Raven never had so much money in her life. She had already decided that she was going to send her mother some money, and buy some things that she wanted. The majority of the money would go into her savings account.

* * *

"*Hmmm* ... I might even buy a car." Raven smiled. "A very nice one!"

Becky had offered to share the Jag, but with the money that they were both going to be making, it made a lot more sense to Raven to buy a car of her very own. If they couldn't afford two cars, that would be different, thought Raven, but they could, and very easily now.

* * *

The next morning, Andy called Raven, talking fast. "Pretty lady, okay, listen, they *really* want you for this part, so much so, that they've added *another* fifty thousand. C'mon, Raven, *please*. I know that it will lead to bigger and better things. I *know* it, pretty lady!" said Andy, passionately. "*Trust* me!" Andrew Spellman was honest. He knew that Raven Kensington was going to be a huge star. He knew that many people had good looks and talent, but never made it in Hollywood. But then again, they weren't Raven Kensington either.

Andy had been thinking about Raven all morning. Raven Kensington took air out of a room. She moved you, without even trying. She was a woman who demanded respect. She *screamed* beauty, elegance, and class. She made everything look so easy. No one had those gorgeous, mesmerizing eyes, those luscious lips, and that dazzling smile that melted your heart. Raven made men fantasize. She made women envious. He had never met anyone like her. She was unique in every sense of the word. She was different in more ways than one. Raven Kensington was a cut well above the rest. She was what Hollywood needed, not to mention, the world.

"*Three hundred and fifty thousand dollars*?" Raven paused. "I need to read the contract first. As long as *everything* is in writing," said Raven, the businesswoman, "I'll do it."

And, oh yes, thought Andrew Spellman, Raven Kensington was also very intelligent. Andy jumped for joy. "You won't be sorry, Raven. You will *not* be sorry! I'll bring the contract to your home, say, this afternoon? Is three o'clock okay with you?" Andy asked.

"Three o'clock is fine. I'll see you then, Andy."

"Good-bye, pretty lady."

"Good-bye, Andy."

After five, seemingly-long years in Los Angeles, things were finally looking up for the two ladies, who had been best friends since they were five. Raven had landed her first movie role, as a maid, and Becky had landed a leading role, that was certain to make her a big soap opera star. Raven couldn't stop smiling.

And, after five years, Raven and Becky were also financially able to quit working at Spago. They thanked Rob for hiring them, and for being such a great boss.

Rob hated to see them go. "Don't you two make yourselves strangers," he told them on their last day at Spago. "We're all going to miss you two, a lot! Good luck in Hollywood! I know that you ladies will do well." Rob gave both beauties big hugs, as he fought back tears. Raven and Becky were everything their former boss said they were. He never once regretted hiring them. Rob knew that many of the customers were also going to miss the beauties.

After leaving Spago, Raven and Becky went home, ordered pizza, and watched movies. It wasn't very often that they actually got to stay home and do absolutely nothing, but it certainly felt good.

When their pizza arrived, they sat at their dining room table eating and talking. Becky sat, studying Raven. She had always admired her beauty. Her best friend was so incredibly-beautiful. Becky had always thought her beautiful when they were little girls, but as Raven got older, she had become even more so.

Becky smiled, remembering when both of them wore ponytails. She remembered Raven's long black hair, and her own, long blonde locks. Raven had always been the sister that she never had. They'd always had mutual love and respect for each other.

"You're looking pensive." Raven noticed how quiet Becky had become.

"I was just thinking about how beautiful you are. On the outside, and on the inside. I was also thinking about our friendship, how close we are. I remember the ponytails that we would wear most of the time when we were little girls."

Raven laughed.

"I was also thinking about how far we have come. We've come a *long* way, Sis, haven't we?"

"Yes, Beck, we sure have. The struggles certainly made us better. And *stronger.* As the sayings go, no struggle, no progress. No pain, no gain. But, we both knew that it would be tough, *especially*, for this sister. Are you going to be doing love scenes on, *Day's Dawn*?"

"I don't know yet. As long as it doesn't involve anything too deep. John's uncle is an attorney. He's going to go through my contract with a fine-tooth comb," said Becky.

"That's great, Beck. However, make sure that *you* comb it too. It's always wise to get *everything* in writing, and always make sure that *you* read and understand the *entire* contract *before* signing *anything. Never* take *anyone's* word for *anything.* You'll also be riding in style, Miss Jag."

"No," said Becky. "*We*, will be riding in style."

Raven smiled. "Thanks, Beck. Maybe I'll borrow your Jag sometimes."

"Maybe you'll borrow it *sometimes*? Come *clean, Miss Three Hundred and Fifty Thousand Dollar Woman* for three weeks' worth of work. Is there something you're not telling me?"

"Well, you know how I *love BMWs*."

Becky nodded.

"I went to the Beverly Hills BMW dealership on Tuesday. The salesman there is going to give me a good deal, if I buy the car out-right. That's if I decide to get it. More than likely I will though. I will pay for it, not pay on it. I've always preferred *owning* over owing, whenever possible. Nine times out of ten, I'm going to buy the car. So both of us will be ridin' in style. We sure have come a long way, Beck. A *mighty* long way."

Becky nodded again. Indeed they had. The two friends talked about the day that they had first arrived in the City of Angels, everything that happened in-between, and where they were now.

When they had first come to Los Angeles, they had each other, their savings, and their families' love and support. And Rob had hired them, almost immediately. Things hadn't gone too badly, they both agreed, not too badly at all.

Their only frustrations were trying to make it in Hollywood. Raven and Becky had gone to countless auditions. They had put their hearts into the roles and were never chosen for any parts.

They were each other's cheerleaders and support systems. It helped a great deal having someone who you could talk to and lean on. It definitely took more than just good looks and talent to succeed in Hollywood, both women agreed, as they continued to talk about their Hollywood experiences.

Raven had been propositioned many times. Quid pro quo.

"How *badly* do you want this part?"

"What are you *willing* to do to get on TV?"

"Are you as *good* in bed as you look to be?"

"Would you be willing to do porn?"

Raven grew sick and tired of hearing those same, *sickening* comments from the lowlife-scum in Hollywood. She had promised herself, and her mother, that she would not go there. And she still hoped and prayed that God would keep her that way. She was determined not to compromise her morals, her values, her principles, her integrity. After all, Raven had told them, she came to Hollywood to become an actress, not a prostitute.

Becky laughed, as she remembered what Raven had told a producer, when he had propositioned her.

"You know," Raven had told the man, "it's funny, but I *never* once said when I was a little girl, *boy* ... I want to be a *whore* when I grow up! If that's what I wanted to be, I could have stayed in Texas. You can be that anywhere."

The producer's face had turned crimson-red, and he'd sat at his desk, speechless.

    * * *

"*Enough* about the past for now, Miss Ultimate Driving Machine. Congrats! You deserve the best. We *both* do. What color are you going to get?" Becky asked.

"Red."

"That color suits you. Very eye-catching, powerful."

"And your Jag? It's black, right?" Raven asked Becky.

"Yes."

"You know how I *love* black too. I've seen the new Jags. They're very nice, Beck. *Especially* the one that you're getting. The S-type."

Raven and Becky had no immediate plans to leave the Summerwood Apartments. They knew that they would eventually, but for now, they were going to remain there. And besides, they still enjoyed living there.

    * * *

The following week was very busy for Raven. She had read and signed her contract, and she had also received her script for, *Heartless War.*

The movie took place in 1948. Raven's character, Myrtle Jane, was a young, sassy, African-American woman who had begged to become a maid in order to feed her two children. Myrtle Jane's husband, whom she had married at age fifteen, had been killed by the Ku Klux Klan.

Raven had to work on her dialect. She transformed her impeccable-English into Ebonics. Myrtle Jane used broken-English, and she didn't know how to read, write, or count. So, what else is *new*? thought Raven. What else is new?

Myrtle Jane had a strong will though. She was also a survivor. Those were two things that Raven had in common with her character, in addition to race and gender.

In a matter of days, Raven had the script memorized, and she had Myrtle Jane's character down pat. Raven had skillfully mastered the maid's talk, walk, personality, and her feelings. Raven's performance was uncanny. She stepped into her character's shoes, and became her in *every* way. Raven made an otherwise ordinary role, extraordinary, as only she could, thought Andrew Spellman, as he stood and watched her rehearse. Myrtle Jane was no ordinary maid, because Raven Kensington, was no *ordinary* woman.

Raven recited her lines for Becky and John. They both sat, watching in awe. Raven Kensington was a natural. She was the best of the best. And as Becky sat watching and listening to her best friend, she knew that the world, was about to sit up and take notice of this *exquisitely*-beautiful and very talented young woman, who at age twenty-three, had grown even more beautiful.

"*Well*? Someone say *something*! What do you two think? Did I sound *unedumacated* enough?" Raven joked.

"And the Oscar goes to ..." said John. "That was a *stellar* performance, Raven!"

"I second that, Sis. That was acting at its very best. Off the hook! *Spectacular* performance. Spectacular! Go knock 'em dead, Sis! Or should I say, Myrtle Jane? What a name! But not even a name like that overshadows your *flawless*-performance," Becky said with assurance.

* * *

Raven arrived on the set early. Her face was pure. She wore no makeup, because Myrtle Jane didn't. But even without cosmetics, Raven was beautiful. She was a *natural*-beauty.

Andrew Spellman had also arrived early. He wanted to be there for Raven. He had seen her rehearse, but he figured she'd still be nervous. After all, this was her first movie. He had fought tooth and nail to get her this part. Andy knew that the only thing Raven needed was an opportunity. The opportunity to shine ... And *shine*, she did!

Everyone had expected to do a lot of retakes. The producers and directors thought that Raven would be nervous and mess up a lot, which would be understandable, they'd all agreed. She was new to this. And all of this, was new to her.

Raven Kensington quickly put all of their minds to rest. If anything bothered her, it certainly didn't show. Raven delivered her lines even better than she had for Becky, John, and Andrew. There were no retakes. Raven had even added some lines that had enhanced Myrtle Jane's character. The writers loved, and approved, Raven's changes to the script. Her delivery of the maid was strong, passionate, convincing, flawless, and *moving*. Raven mastered the character.

Most of the cast came out of their dressing rooms when they heard Raven speak. Everyone stood watching and listening to this incredibly-beautiful and talented woman. Raven was very pleasing to look at, and equally-pleasing, to listen to.

Lyle Krause, the executive producer of the movie, watched Raven in awe. He had never seen anyone perform so well. His eyes lit up as he watched her. Not only was Raven very beautiful, thought Lyle, she also had incredible acting depth.

No one would have ever guessed that this was Raven's first movie. She was *calm*, she was *smooth*, she was … *Raven Kensington*.

Raven received a loud round of applause from everyone, except Tessa Winters. Tessa watched Raven. She kept trying to remember *that* face. And finally, after racking her brain, she remembered! This was the "black gal" whom she'd seen at The Beverly Hills Hotel years ago. How could she forget? She hated her then, and she hated her now. Why was everyone clapping for *her*? God! She's *only* a maid. *I'm* the star!

No one was eager to go on after Raven. Not even Tessa Winters.

Raven Kensington was perfection on-screen.

Andy rushed over to Raven. He gave her a big hug. "Pretty lady, you were awesome! Everyone loved you too." Andy was elated. His instincts about the sultry-beauty had been right on point. He had given Raven Kensington the ball, and she had delivered, like no other. I knew it! Andy thought to himself. I knew it!

Andy gave Raven a ride home. During the entire ride home, Andy marveled and talked endlessly about her performance. "Lyle Krause doesn't give compliments easily, but he couldn't stop raving about you. Keep it up! See you in the morning, pretty lady!"

The next morning, Raven arrived on the set early again. Andrew saw the way that Tessa Winters looked at her. It was obvious that she hated Raven. Raven knew it too. She read people very well.

"Don't let Tessa get to you, Raven. She may be a bigot, but she's also jealous," said Andy. He'd heard Tessa make a number of racist comments before. This was not Andy's first time working with Tessa Winters. "She's very jealous of you. That is so very obvious. If she knew that she was making herself so obvious, she'd really be sick. You have to have tough-as-nails skin in today's world, and the entertainment world is not any different. With your looks and the way that you carry yourself, you'll always be the envy of many, especially females. But don't let any of it get to you, pretty lady."

Raven had been the target of hate looks for most of her young life. She wasn't surprised by it. She had decided years ago, as long as she knew that she hadn't intentionally hurt anyone's feelings, or hurt them in any way, if they chose to not like her, even if many of them didn't even know her, that was *their* problem, not hers. And Tessa Winters was no exception.

* * *

Raven continued to give flawless-performances for the entire three weeks. Becky and John would come watch Raven perform, whenever their schedules would permit. Raven Kensington had made a name for herself on the set.

The cast and crew loved Raven's beauty, as well as her immense-talent. They also loved the way that she carried herself, her beautiful, trademark smile, her professional work ethic, and her sense of humor. Many of them hated that her part wasn't longer. It had ended too soon. They had all enjoyed working with Raven. And they hoped to work with this young lady again.

Lyle Krause kept Raven Kensington's name, and face, etched in his mind. She's good, he thought to himself, *damn* good.

* * *

On Raven's last day on the set, Becky picked her up.

"Where are we going, Beck?" Raven asked. "You look like you're hiding something. Are you and John getting married?"

Becky shook her head no and laughed. "We're going to the BMW dealership."

"I'd like to go home first. I'll probably go tomorrow." Raven kept looking at her six-figure paycheck. She was definitely going to make a copy of it. I might even frame the copy, thought Raven, smiling. She had never had so much money in her life.

Becky drove to the dealership anyway.

"Beck! Not today. Tomorrow, *please.*"

"But your car is ready! You don't want your car?" Becky asked.

"What are you talking about? I haven't *bought* a car yet. I've only *looked.*"

The salesman came out immediately when he saw Becky get out of her Jag. He greeted them with a big smile. "Hello, ladies. It's almost ready! It's being shined up, as I speak."

"Guys, what are you'll talking about? Someone tell me *something*," said Raven.

Becky reached in her purse and handed Raven a note. It was from Andrew Spellman. It read: Thanks for a job well-done, pretty lady! Enjoy your new BMW! It's on me! See ya when I return … -Andy

"Sis, Andy bought this car for you! He wanted to surprise you with it. I told him that I would do the honors. Andy had to leave L.A. due to a family emergency. The paperwork's already been taken care of. You're the owner. No car payments. And it's a convertible! He really likes you, Sis! Correction, he really *loves* you!"

Raven stood in the parking lot, speechless. She couldn't stop smiling. *Unbelievable*, she thought. Unbelievable! Hollywood certainly had its perks.

Becky was thrilled for her best friend. If anyone deserved all of the great things that were happening to her, Raven did.

Andrew Spellman knew the six-figure paycheck was more than enough for Raven to buy a number of BMWs, but he wanted to buy the car for Raven anyway. She had earned it.

When the manager drove the shiny red BMW around for Raven, Becky locked her Jag and got in the BMW, where Raven was anxiously waiting to take off. They went on a long drive. They knew L.A. very well now. After Raven drove for several hours, she turned the Bimmer over to her best friend.

Raven now knew, how BMW's slogan was created. It drove like an ultimate driving machine. The car hugged the road. The suspension was world-class. Raven smiled. The car was *awesome*. It was a *driver's* car. Raven had always loved BMWs. Bimmers had sporty good looks, combined with prestigious luxury, and uncanny-performance.

Raven and Becky phoned their families. The Kensingtons and Simms were very happy for them. Mae and Sonya reminded Raven and Becky to always be very careful.

Raven told her mother how much she had received for playing Myrtle Jane.

"Call me next time! For *three hundred and fifty thousand dollars*, I'd play a maid with a *quickness*," said Mae Kensington. "After all, the only thing better than being a maid, is being a *well-paid* one."

Raven laughed in answer.

Raven and Becky *loved* their new luxury cars. It was very nice not having to catch the bus. Having a car was also a great convenience. They could now go wherever, *whenever*. And having a car was also safer.

    * * *

Heartless War had finally wrapped. Everyone was excited about the movie. It had received rave reviews.

There was an invitation-only, movie premiere party scheduled the following Friday. Raven was invited. She wasn't going to go at first, but Becky and Andrew convinced her to attend. It still bothered her, playing such a stereotypical role.

    * * *

The morning of the premiere party, Raven and Becky went shopping. Raven needed something to wear, something nice and fancy. She knew that everyone would be dressed in fancy attire. This was more than just a premiere party, it was, as Andy told Raven, "a fancy-smancy one."

Raven and Becky went to Viene's on Rodeo Drive. It was well-known for its class, style, and impeccable customer service. Andrew Spellman recommended the store. He also offered to pay for Raven's attire, but she politely declined. Andy had already been more than generous buying her a new luxury car. And besides, she had money. Raven wasn't a millionaire, but she wasn't a pauper either.

* * *

When Raven and Becky arrived at Viene's, a nicely-dressed man in a black and white suit, identified himself as "valet." He then took Raven's car keys, handed her a claim card, then parked her car.

The ladies were greeted immediately upon entering the store, and offered a glass of champagne.

"You know, Beck," Raven whispered, "they figure, you come in, they get you drunk, and you'll buy *anything*."

Becky laughed in answer.

Raven declined the champagne offer. Becky accepted. Raven was driving, but she wasn't a drinker, anyway. She'd drink champagne and wine occasionally, and it took her all day, literally, to finish one glass.

A lady named, Vera Fuqua, assisted them.

Raven, Becky, and Vera walked the store, searching for *the* perfect gown for Raven. As they continued to walk the store, Raven spotted it. It was a gorgeous, black, Valentino gown. The gown also enhanced Raven's sparkling, dark eyes.

"This is it! *This* is the one," said Raven excitedly.

Raven was a size eleven, but because European gowns came in even-sizes, Vera removed a size-ten and a size-twelve gown from the racks for Raven to try on.

"Try them on, young lady. Let's see how it looks. If it looks as good as I think it will on you, they'd all better watch out!" said Vera.

Raven went to the dressing room to try the gowns on. She tried the size-twelve gown on first. It was too big. Please, let the ten fit, Raven thought to herself. *Please.* She really loved the gown. She tried the size-ten gown on. And it fit! Raven studied her reflection in the mirror. Her eyes danced with approval and excitement. She loved the way the gown looked on her. She also loved the way it felt. It hugged her body in all the *right* places, yet, it still left "things" to the imagination. Raven had a very nice, curvaceous body, but she always dressed, and carried herself, like a lady.

Raven left the dressing room to show Becky and Vera, who were eagerly waiting. She walked out of the dressing room, slowly. Raven didn't have to ask them what they thought. It was written on their faces.

"You look gorgeous, Sis! The gown enhances your eyes too."

"Splendid, young lady. Lovely, elegant. You'll be a smash hit!"

"Thanks." Along with the evening gown, Raven also purchased matching shoes and a purse. "Hmmm ... I have the gown, the shoes, the purse ... Something else is missing. Jewelry! Not too much though." Raven told Becky. "Just a nice pair of diamond earrings, a diamond bracelet, and a nice diamond necklace. And, oh yes, a ring. What are you looking at me like that for, Beck? Diamonds are a girl's best friend. Let's go see, Harry!"

Becky laughed. "A woman with *expensive* tastes."

Raven winked at her friend. "Beck, you will usually remember quality, more so than the price."

"'Tis true, Sis, 'tis true."

Raven and Becky enjoyed shopping on the famous, Rodeo Drive.

Raven's bank account had also diminished by thousands of dollars, but she was far from broke. Raven had always managed her money very wisely, and as she'd always said, it's good to treat self sometimes. When you work hard, you deserve to buy nice things for yourself, Raven thought to herself, as she skillfully maneuvered her BMW in the busy, Beverly Hills traffic.

When they made it home, Becky went to see a movie with John, and Raven went to take a nap. She had stayed up most of the night writing. Writing was another one of her passions. Raven planned to write a movie that she and Becky would star in. She would love to star in a movie, opposite her best friend. Raven didn't know when she'd have time to actually start writing the script, but she was determined to do it. It was definitely on her future to-do list.

Raven set her alarm clock, before stretching out on her bed to catch some z's. She fell asleep as soon as her head hit the pillow. Raven was so exhausted, she slept like a baby.

* * *

The phone woke Raven hours later. It was Becky. She phoned to give Raven a wake-up call. Becky didn't know if Raven had set her alarm clock, and she didn't want her to be late for the big, movie premiere party. "I'll be there to help you get dressed," said Becky. "I'm on my way."

Raven slept for another hour.

Becky was frantic when she saw Raven still in bed. "Sis! You're going to be late! Are you feeling okay?"

"Yes, Beck, I'm fine. Relax! I plan to be late. I'm going to be *fashionably*-late. I want to be the last to arrive, and the first to leave."

"Oh, I get it, save the *best* for last." Becky smiled. "Raven Kensington, you're too much!"

* * *

Raven sat in the tub, enjoying her bath and watching the clock. After bathing, washing and conditioning her hair, and brushing her teeth, Raven went to her room to get ready for her "big night."

She checked her voice mail. Andrew Spellman had called a dozen times. He wanted to make sure that Raven was going to come to the movie premiere party. Andy even insisted on picking Raven up.

* * *

Becky called the limo company that John had recommended for Raven. The owner was a good friend of John's. The white limo would be there on time, and the driver, Frank Everett, would stay with Raven until she was ready to leave.

Becky helped her friend get ready.

Raven laughed at Becky, who kept making a big fuss over her. It brought back memories, when they were little girls playing dress up. But this time, it was for *real*, and the finished product, was breathtaking! The limo driver gasped when he saw Raven.

Raven and Becky hugged before she got in the limo. "Knock 'em dead, Sis!" said Becky. "I want a *full* report when you come home!"

* * *

Andrew Spellman paced nervously around the lavish ballroom, where the movie premiere party was being held. Raven was nowhere in sight.

The last person to arrive was Tessa Winters. She looked lovely in a green, Calvin Klein gown. She was a very attractive lady. She waved and smiled for the cameras, *loving* the attention. Tessa's arrival was calculated. She wanted to be the last person to arrive.

When Tessa entered the ballroom, she looked around to see if Raven was there. No Raven. "You know, I'm not surprised that *black gal* didn't come," she told a cameraman. "She played a *maid*, for chrissake! If I'd played such an *embarrassing* role, I wouldn't show my face either."

The cameraman walked away. He liked Raven. He, like many of the cast and crew, were hoping that Raven would come. She had worked harder than anyone. And she deserved to be there as much as anyone, if not more so. The cameraman thought of Raven's flawless-performance. She had upstaged everyone, *including* Tessa Winters, who hated to be upstaged by anyone.

* * *

Lyle Krause looked at his Rolex. He walked over to Andrew Spellman. "Andy, where's Raven? You said that she would be here. She certainly *deserves* to be here."

"She'll be here, Lyle," said Andy, with more assurance than he felt. Don't let me down, pretty lady. *Please*, don't let me down, Andy thought to himself.

* * *

The white limo pulled up to the front entrance of the Ritz-Carlton.

Photographers readily aimed their cameras. *Who* could it be? They thought everyone had arrived.

Frank got out first. He walked over to Raven's door and opened her door for her.

Raven stepped out of the limo, dressed to the nines. Flashbulbs went off like an electric storm. The cameras *loved* her. And so did the photographers and entertainment reporters. They had no idea who Raven was, they just knew that she was one of the most beautiful women that they had *ever* laid eyes on. Her looks were *staggering*. Her body was a man's dream.

"Miss, *who* are you?"

"Were you *invited* by someone?"

"Are *you* in this movie?"

"What *role* did you play?"

"Are you *married*?" That last question slipped. Brad Creet was very interested in the young woman, personally; he didn't mean to ask *that* question out loud, but he had. Brad was in awe of the stunning-beauty.

Raven flashed her dazzling, trademark smile, as she answered all of the questions that were asked of her.

Frank finally intervened. "Miss Kensington has to go. Thank you! Thank you all!" said a very experienced and skillful Frank. It was obvious that Frank had been around the Hollywood scene for a while. He was very smooth and relaxed. Frank watched Raven with quiet admiration. He smiled. She definitely knew how to work the cameras.

Photographers continued to take photo after photo of Raven. They wanted to get as many photos of *her* as possible.

Frank opened the brass, double door that led to the ballroom, where the cast and crew, their families and friends, and many of Hollywood's elite, were all mingling, and sipping on expensive champagne.

As soon as the door opened, everyone looked to see who it was. All eyes were glued to her. *All* eyes, were on Raven Kensington. It was as if time had come to a screeching-halt. A standstill. Everyone stared, some whispered, some pointed, but most of them who saw her wanted to know, *who is that lady*?

Raven entered the room dressed impeccably. The eye-popping beauty was simply stunning. She was *beyond* beautiful. Raven's makeup was flawless, enhancing all of her naturally-beautiful features. Her long black hair was twisted elegantly, in a French twist. There wasn't a hair out of place. Raven Kensington was breathtaking! And as always, she was in full control. Her all-seeing, dark eyes danced, taking in everyone, and everything. All eyes remained on this showstopper. Raven flashed her dazzling, million-dollar smile, as she moved across the room ever-so gracefully. Raven walked with perfect poise. She was poetry in motion.

Raven's beauty, elegance, and presence were unmatched. She was incomparable. There was no question who the "lady of the evening" was. Tessa Winters may have had the starring role in the movie, but it was obvious to *everyone*, who the star was, *now*. A young black woman from Tunis, Texas. *Raven Kensington*.

Everyone kept staring at Raven, studying her. *Who was she*? Where had she been? Raven had them *all* mesmerized.

But no one, was more mesmerized by Raven, than Tony Dash. He stood, never taking his eyes off her. Raven Kensington defined *everything* that he wanted in a woman. She was everything, that he thought a woman should be. And if anything, she raised the bar. She was like a rare, beautiful diamond.

Tony had dated and bedded many beautiful women, but he had never seen a woman more beautiful in looks, movements, or class. Raven was also incredibly-sexy. No woman had ever captivated him, but *this one did*. She took his breath away. Tony continued to study her. It was as if he were in a trance, she was so intriguing. Her smile, melted his heart. Her eyes were like beautiful black pearls, that shined, as bright as the diamonds she wore. Her skin was flawless. Raven Kensington was every inch a woman, in looks, and more importantly, in *actions*. He *wanted* her. Tony Dash had *never* wanted a woman, so badly.

It wasn't long before Raven was surrounded. Andy quickly, and happily, walked over to her. He'd stood watching Raven admiringly, along with everyone else. He was elated that she had come. Raven had always been a woman of her word, but when it got later and later, Andy thought that she had changed her mind. He was so happy that she hadn't. And from the looks of things, so was everyone else. Everyone except, Tessa Winters. Andy looked at Tessa when Raven arrived. He tried to conceal his laughter. Tessa looked like she had swallowed a canary, several of them, in fact.

Andy knew that it didn't matter what time Raven would have arrived, she would have stolen the show anyway. How could she not? Very few had the kind of beauty, elegance, and presence that she possessed. Raven Kensington was the kind of woman who made other women feel insecure, no matter who they were.

Andy greeted Raven with a hug and kiss. He offered her a glass of champagne, which to his surprise, she accepted. Raven didn't intend to stay long. She had accomplished what she had come for, in a matter of minutes.

Funny, Andy thought, the person who played the maid, ends up being the maid of honor, literally. It was no surprise to Andy, Raven drew people like a magnet. Many people seek the spotlight, Raven Kensington lived, in the spotlight.

Raven was introduced to "everyone," who Andy thought was anyone, in the world of show business. Most of the men were just happy to look at her. The women continued to watch Raven. Many of them wanted to be her, if only for one night. And even the jealous ones had to admit, Raven Kensington, was in a class all by herself. Everyone who saw her knew it. Others simply paled by comparison.

Reva Barnett, a Hollywood legend, studied Raven. She was very impressed with the young beauty. Raven exuded glamour and elegance. Reva had seen a private screening of, *Heartless War*. She loved it. Raven's performance was unforgettable. She's going to set screens and hearts on fire, for years to come, thought Reva, as she continued to study Raven.

After mingling for a couple of hours, Raven excused herself, then went to the ladies' room. She didn't need to freshen up, she simply wanted a break from the crowd.

Tessa Winters quickly followed suit.

Raven stood, looking in the mirror, as she checked her makeup, which looked like it had just been applied.

"Well, well, well, if it isn't, *Miss Maid*. Hi, *gal*. I need my floors and windows scrubbed. Would you be up for the job? I know that *your* kind cleans so well," said Tessa.

Raven ignored her.

Tessa went on. "You walk in *this* party, thinking you're the *cat's meow*, the *dog's bark*. Your kind is *dirt*. Blacks aren't worth anything! You'll are *dumb*. History *proves* that. And even today, you'll are *still* dumb. You'll are *far* beneath us. Maybe you're confused. I've watched you. You think you're so beautiful, it's *sickening*. Hollywood is *white*, like everything else in this world. It will *never* be diverse. There aren't many of you on the big screen, or on TV. I can count your kind on *one* hand." Tessa smirked. "Beware, *gal*! I'm like a tiger."

"With *no* teeth." Raven addressed Tessa for the first time.

"You listen here, I worked my *ass* off to get where I am now!"

Raven smiled. "So that explains where it went." Tessa was livid and speechless, as Raven went on. "I think I'm the cat's meow? No, Tessa, those are *your* thoughts. That's what *you* think. You think I'm all that, and then some. There's a difference between thinking and knowing. I *know* who I am. I *know* what I am. And I certainly know what I'm not. I'm very proud of who I am. You use the word *black*, as if it's shameful to be black. It's an *honor*, to be black, Tessa. I am just as proud to be black, as you probably are to be white. Whatever race anyone is, they should be proud of it, and they don't have any reason to be ashamed. *All* races are beautiful, and when put together, we're like a rainbow. My philosophy has always been to be proud of who you are, that *includes* whatever race, look, shape, or size that God made you. And *dumb*? *History*? Let's *talk* history, Tessa. Agricultural chemist, *George Washington Carver*, is in the World Book Encyclopedia. Mr. Carver made *many* incredible contributions to this country, and to the world. He created *hundreds of inventions* with the peanut, alone. His crop-rotation method *revolutionized* southern agriculture. Mr. Carver's science of crop-rotation, saved the farming resources of the south. This *brilliant* man transformed the south from a one-crop land of cotton, into *multi*-crop farmlands. During Mr. Carver's era, America's economy was very dependent on agriculture, which made his inventions immensely-*significant*. President Franklin D. Roosevelt honored him with a *national* monument, dedicated to his *brilliant* accomplishments. *Madam C.J. Walker* was the *first* African-American female millionaire. *Self-*made." Raven smiled. "I happen to know a few things about you, Tessa. I know that your mother had open-heart surgery last year."

Tessa shot Raven an angry look. She also wondered why Raven had even brought that up.

Raven continued. "Don't get lost, Tessa, stay with me, please. Anyway, I'm happy to know that she's doing fine. I brought that up to let you know, that a *black* man, *Dr. Daniel Hale Williams*, was the *first* person to perform open-heart surgery, *successfully*. Dr. Williams was the *first* surgeon to open the chest cavity, without the patient dying from infection. His procedures set standards for *future* internal surgeries. Dr. Williams was also the founder of Provident Hospital, the *first* interracial hospital in the United States. You can also thank *my* kind for the blood transfusion that saved *your* life when you had your car accident. *Dr. Charles Richard Drew* was the medical researcher who discovered the way to store blood for long terms, making blood banks possible. Dr. Drew's discovery *revolutionized* the medical profession. He was the *first* director of the American Red Cross blood bank. He also organized the world's *first* blood bank drive. Tessa, I assume that you stop at traffic lights. Well, *every* time that you look at a traffic light, *every* time that you stop at one, you can thank us, thank *my* kind, for that too. *Garrett A. Morgan*, a *black* man, *invented* the *traffic signal*. And that *same* man invented the *gas mask*, the item that saved your daughter's life last year when your mansion caught on fire."

Tessa gave Raven a deer-in-headlights look.

Raven Kensington still wasn't finished. "Let's see, I *assume* that you use *refrigerators, golf tees, lawn mowers, pencil sharpeners ...* " Raven smiled. "Must I go on? *All* of these things, were *invented*, by *my kind*. Many eons ago, many ingenious blacks were inventors, who still persevered despite facing the *worst* possible circumstances, such as racism. Now *that's genius!* So obviously, we couldn't have been dumb at all, to create and invent such *incredible* things, that have made *everyone's* life *a lot safer*, *easier*, and more *profitable*. Including, *racist* people like you. And *my kind*, also helped build this country. I'd think of *another* description if I were you. Something like, *superbly*-intelligent. I could go on and on about many other *major* inventions and very *significant* contributions that African-Americans are responsible for, but you see, Tessa, I would probably never leave, and you're not worth that kind of time. You mentioned earlier that you could count the number of black actors on one hand, well, there aren't *enough* hands, to count the inventions and contributions that African-Americans have made to *this* country, and to the world. And regarding your statement of my thinking that I am *so* beautiful, the mirror *never* lies. But more importantly, I am very beautiful on the *inside*."

   * * *

If looks could kill, Raven would have been dead. Tessa shot her a hated look that had topped all of her previous daggers.

Raven went on. "And, yes, Hollywood's had their run. A very long one, but it's time for change. And it's *long*, long overdue. Tessa, whenever you count *my kind*, on your hand again, make sure that you include *me* in that count. It's obvious that you're a very *insecure* and *miserable* woman, who thinks that putting me down will somehow raise you up, make you look better. But the thing is, Tessa, you're not putting me down. Words *can't* put me down. It will take a lot more than words to do that, it will take *me*. Only I can do that. The things that you do and say, say more about you, than they do about anyone. To make a long story short, knowing who I am, makes it *easy* to deal with people like you. People like you, just reminds me, that I am who, and what, they would like to be. It reminds me that I'm doing something right, and doing it very well. And, oh yes, it also reminds me of what I don't want to become, what I *never* want to be. It's usually not the losers that many hate and envy, it's the *winners*." Raven flashed her trademark smile. "*Thanks*, for the compliment." Raven Kensington had read, written, and erased Tessa Winters, who was now fuming. "Try to have a better evening."

What a *smart* bitch! Very smart bitch.

As Raven went to leave, Tessa cut her off. She hated the smug look on Raven's face. The truth had cut Tessa deep like a knife. Tessa wanted Raven to feel the massive pain that she was feeling. Hate and jealousy were eating her up inside. Tessa raised her hand to slap Raven, but Raven grabbed her arm and held it.

"Let go of my arm! Oh, no, look what you've done! You've broken my nail!" Tessa scowled.

Raven looked Tessa straight in the eye. Her eyes were like black ice. "If you *ever*, raise your hand to *me* again ... If you *ever*, *touch* me ... I will *break* more than your nail. Now, get out of *my* way."

Tessa knew that Raven meant business. She quickly stepped aside, as Raven left the ladies' room.

* * *

After Raven left, Tessa Winters plopped down on a leather chair. She couldn't stop crying. Raven's handprints were very visibly-imprinted on her arm, and Raven's words, were imprinted on her mind. Tessa now realized, there was nothing that she could do, or say, to stop Raven Kensington. *Nothing*. Everything that she had said and done, so far, had failed. *Miserably*.

Tessa hated Raven with a passion, because as Raven had so wisely and accurately pointed out, she was *everything* that Tessa Winters wanted to be, but wasn't. Tessa was unable to stop crying. Never in her life, did Tessa *ever* think, that she would be jealous of a …

* * *

Frank was waiting for Raven in the hallway. He had no idea what had just taken place in the ladies' room. "Are you okay? You were in there for a long time. I was about to knock on the door, but I figured you were in there chatting with other beautiful women."

Raven laughed. "I was *chatting* all right, with the Wicked Witch of the West."

Frank looked puzzled.

"As you can see, Frank, I'm fine." Raven smiled.

No kidding, Frank thought to himself. You are *very* fine.

Raven looked at her watch. "Gosh, it's late! It's time for me to leave."

Frank laughed. "Okay, *Cinderella*, I'll tell valet to bring the limo around."

Raven told Andy that she was leaving.

Andy couldn't stop smiling, as he bid Raven farewell, and thanked her for coming. He was elated that she had come. And from the looks of things, Andrew Spellman wasn't the only person elated that Raven Kensington had graced them with her presence.

* * *

Tony Dash walked around everywhere looking for Raven. Finally, he went to ask the valet attendant if "the lady" had left.

"The *lady*, sir?" the valet attendant asked.

Tony nodded, as he described Raven to a T.

The valet attendant smiled and nodded. "Yes, Mr. Dash. Miss Kensington has already left. She left about fifteen minutes ago, sir."

"*Kensington*? What is her *first* name?" Tony wanted to know.

"Raven, sir. Her first name is *Raven*. Is there a problem, sir?" the valet attendant asked.

"No. There's not a problem. Thanks. Please bring my car around. I think I'll call it a night too."

Tony's date, Mindy Rice, had long since left. She'd called him every name but a child of God, as she spilled champagne on his Armani suit. "You can pick your chin up. You're *drooling*," she'd told him. Mindy saw the way that Tony was staring at Raven. "You look like you've never seen a beautiful woman before!"

He *hadn't*, Tony started to tell her. Not like Raven Kensington, anyway. Tony Dash was *smitten*. He couldn't stop thinking about *her*. Raven was the *highlight* of his evening. He didn't care about the champagne-spill on his Armani suit, nor did he care about Mindy leaving, although Tony didn't mean to be so obviously rude, but he couldn't help it. Raven Kensington had made him lose his mind, in a *good* way. Tony had never felt what he was feeling before. Never! This woman had such a powerful effect on him, and he didn't even know her. *Who was she*? Tony wanted to know everything about Raven. *Everything* about the rare, very beautiful, breathtaking lady, with those gorgeous, magnetic eyes, and that dazzling, million-dollar smile.

Raven was etched in his mind. *That* face, *that* body ... the way that she moved, the classy, ladylike way that she carried herself. And somehow, when he'd first laid eyes on her, Tony Dash *knew*, that Raven Kensington, was also *etched*, in his heart.

* * *

"Tell me *everything*!" said an excited Becky, the moment Raven walked in. "Everything!"

Raven yawned, pretending to be tired. "I'm sorry, Beck, I'm wiped out. I'm going to bed now. *Tomorrow.*"

"Oh, no! *Inquiring* minds want to know."

Raven smiled at Becky. "I was just kidding, Beck. Well, I'd say that things went well. *Very* well," said a beaming Raven. "I did what I set out to do. Many of Hollywood's elite were there too. Andrew's going to call me tomorrow. He was excited. He acted as if there was something he wasn't telling me, or at least not yet. But I think that whatever it is, I'll know soon." Raven gave Becky every detail, small and large. She told her who was there, what they did, what they wore, and what her reaction was to the entertainment reporters, and photographers.

Becky became angry when Raven told her about the *showdown* in the ladies' room. "That witch! The nerve of her! She's one very sick, ignorant, and jealous woman," said an outraged Becky.

"I know. I've known that Tessa Winters hates me, for a while now. But it doesn't matter to me. The world doesn't revolve around her, at least my world doesn't anyway. She doesn't know me. But she knew enough not to try to hit me again, that's for sure. I started to ignore her, but it was in me to tell her *everything* that I told her. And it was very effective too. Sometimes you have to speak. There is a time to speak, and there is a time to be silent. And regarding her trying to slap me, I let her know in no uncertain terms, that if she ever tried such a *foolish* move again, I would break more than her nail, and I meant that. And if she's not sure, she can always try it again. I don't usually warn people twice," said Raven. "Tessa desperately needed to be schooled."

Becky laughed. "She couldn't have picked a *better* teacher. Tough talk, met *tough* cookie."

Raven and Becky talked for hours. After talking about Raven's big night, they talked about Becky and John's romance, which was becoming more serious each day.

"I love him, Sis. But I'm not ready to get married," said Becky honestly.

Raven listened to her friend intently. "Well, you're right, Beck. If you're not ready to get married, then *don't*. Marriage is a very big step. It's not anything to be taken lightly." Raven yawned. "I'm sleepy, Beck, we *both* need to catch some z's."

"Good night, *Cinderella*."

"Good night, Beck."

* * *

The next morning, Raven jumped up quickly when she heard Becky screaming. She ran to see what was wrong. "Beck! What's wrong? Is everything all right?"

Becky was smiling broadly, and holding the *Los Angeles Times*.

"You scared me to death!"

"Raven! You're in the paper! You are on the *front* page! Look! Look, Sis! Look!" Becky showed the newspaper to Raven.

Raven *finally* found her voice. "*Oh... my... gosh*! I *am*! That's... *me*!" Raven couldn't believe it. "*Wow*."

There was a photo of Raven getting out of the limousine when she'd arrived at the movie premiere party. The headline read: "Hollywood's *Most* Beautiful, Best-Kept Secret!"

Becky read some of the article aloud. "We can't compare her to anyone, past or present, this young, sultry, eye-popping beauty is in a class all by herself. She's a *mega*-bombshell! I've seen the movie, *Heartless War*, and her performance was flawless. Where has *she* been hiding? She's one of the most *beautiful* women that I've *ever* seen. Her presence is uncanny. Raven Kensington is a siren!" Becky looked at Raven smiling. Both women were beside themselves with joy. "If *this* doesn't boost your career, Sis, *nothing* will!"

Raven couldn't stop smiling. She was ecstatic. And shocked. She hadn't expected to be front-page news.

* * *

Tony Dash slept very little after coming home from the premiere party. His thoughts were on the "woman of his dreams." He couldn't stop thinking about the woman who had raised his temperature. Literally. She's *so* beautiful. But it was much more to Raven than her immense-beauty, Raven Kensington was unlike any woman he'd ever seen. Tony regretted that he was with Mindy for most of the evening, he so desperately wanted to meet Raven. Talk to *her*.

"Who are you, Miss Kensington?" Tony said aloud. "*Please,* God, don't let her be taken. Don't let her be married. Please!"

Tony's thoughts were interrupted by a knock on his bedroom door.

"Mack, is that you?"

"Yes, Mr. Dash."

"Come in."

Mack Simon had been Tony Dash's butler for eight years. Mack enjoyed working for Tony. Not only did Tony pay his employees well, he also treated them well. He was a great boss to work for.

"Good morning, Mr. Dash. Here's your coffee. Just the way you like it. And, here's the morning paper." Mack smiled.

Tony had a small staff that worked extremely well. They delivered big. They'd all been working for him for a number of years. And because of the size of his estate, many people thought that he had an enormous staff. They were always surprised when they found out that his staff was small.

Tony liked all of his employees, but Mack was his favorite. There were very few things that Mack couldn't do. And whatever Mack did, he did extremely well.

When Mack left, Tony took a sip of the fresh coffee. As he opened the paper, he almost spilled the hot coffee on himself. "It's *her*. It's ..." Tony was ecstatic. He stared at Raven's photo for a long time, before finally reading the article. Tony hoped to find out something about her from the paper. And he did! He breathed a huge sigh of relief. *She*, wasn't married. Raven Kensington was not married! Tony was elated, there was hope. He cut her picture out of the paper and framed it. When he woke up every morning, Raven's beautiful face was the first thing that Tony Dash wanted to see. His emotions were running high. He had to get to her. He figured he'd start at Spago. According to the paper, that's where she used to work. Tony was very determined to find Raven. He smiled; there's no better time like the present, thought Tony, as he went to shave, shower, and brush his teeth.

* * *

When Tony arrived at Spago, he placed an order, even though he wasn't hungry. Food was the last thing on Tony's mind. He was just hungry for information, about *her*. He studied the waitress. Would she tell me anything? Tony wondered. He knew because of obvious reasons, that no employee should give out information about a current, or former, employee. He had very few options. A desperate Tony decided to throw caution to the winds.

"Here you are, sir," said the waitress, as she placed Tony's food and iced-tea in front of him. "May I get you anything else?"

Tony figured he'd go for it. He might as well. "Yes, actually, you can. My name is Cliff Caters. I work for a talent agency. I was told that a *Miss Kensington* works here, or *used* to, rather." Tony described Raven. "From what I hear, she has *exceptional*-talent."

Sandra Pommer knew exactly who Tony was talking about. She hoped the two close friends made it big. And from what she'd heard, they were both well on their way. Sandra was very happy for Raven and Becky.

"*Used to* is right. I'm sure you're talking about Raven. Raven Kensington. And from what I hear, she doesn't have to either. Work here, I mean. She's doing pretty well now financially. She's already landed her first movie role!" said an excited Sandra.

"I'd like to speak with her about an opportunity. Do you have *any* idea how I would be able to contact her?" Tony asked.

"No. I didn't know her that well. Raven was friendly, but private, *very* private. Unfortunately, the person who does know her very well, her best friend, Becky, would be able to help you, but she's gone too."

"Is that so?"

Sandra smiled. "Yes. They're both about to make it big! I'm so happy for them!" Sandra tried to keep her voice down.

"*Please*. Is there *anything* that you can think of that could help me find, *Raven Kensington*?" Tony pleaded; he sounded desperate, and he was.

Sandra may not have been the sharpest knife in the drawer, but she was no dummy either. This man was interested in Raven for *personal* reasons. His interest wasn't professional. Sandra was certain of it. He sounded more like he was *love-struck*. Sandra pondered, as she looked the immensely-handsome gentleman over. He seemed harmless.

"*Okay*. I know that Raven was off every Sunday."

Tony looked at Sandra as if she had lost her mind. "Off on Sundays? *And*? Is that *supposed* to mean *anything*?"

"It *means* that ... I'll need a *nice* tip, if, you want *my* tip."

"I'll leave you a tip, but *only* if the information's worthwhile."

"Raven goes to church *every* Sunday." Sandra held her hand out for the crisp, one hundred dollar bill that she saw in Tony Dash's hand. "Give me the money, and I'll tell you what church she goes to. If you are as interested in her as you seem to be, you'll go there if you *really* want to talk to her."

Tony smiled. "*What* church? *Which* church does *she* attend? I'll give you the money. I'm a man of my word."

"City of Angels Church of Christ. On Oaklawn Drive."

Tony paid for the meal that he hadn't even touched, then he placed the one hundred dollar bill in Sandra's hand. He looked up at her smiling. "*Thanks! Thanks a million!*"

* * *

Chapter 4

Raven's phone rang. It was Saul Chambers, a movie producer whom she had met at the movie premiere party. Saul was one of the most powerful men in Hollywood. He told Raven that he wanted to meet with her, to discuss an upcoming movie role. "It's *big*, Miss Kensington!" Saul told her. "Very big!"

Becky sat watching Raven and waiting for her to hang up the phone. She felt it was the call that Raven had been waiting for, hoping for. Another acting role. "*Well*? Don't keep me in suspense! Who was that?" Becky asked.

"A movie producer. Saul Chambers was at the party last night. He said that Andy gave him my number. Saul also said that Andy's going to meet me at his office on Wilshire Boulevard, in a couple of hours. He sounded excited. Perhaps it's another movie role." Raven told Becky.

"Sis, you don't look or sound excited." Becky looked at Raven in disbelief. She didn't know why, but Raven didn't look the least bit excited. "Am I missing something here? Most people would be jumping up and down. They'd be very excited. Why aren't you? Is there something you're not telling me?"

"There was something in his eyes that I didn't like. That's it, in a nutshell. I can't explain it, but I don't have a good feeling. I don't know. Maybe it's nothing. I'm going. Don't worry about that."

"Sis, I'm not worried about *that*, I'm worried about *you*. You're my *first*, and *only* concern. Andy's going to be there. Do you want me to go with you?" Becky offered.

"No, Beck. Thanks!"

"Take your cell, Sis. Call me if you need me," said Becky.

"I will."

Raven's phone rang again, but she didn't answer it; she didn't have time to talk. She had to get ready or she would be late. Raven never liked being late for meetings or appointments. Whoever it is, thought Raven, they can leave a message on my voice mail.

It was a very excited Andrew Spellman calling.

* * *

Saul Chambers sat in his lavish office staring out the window. His thoughts were on Raven Kensington. She was one, *sultry*-beauty. Saul remembered *everything* about Raven, especially her full breasts and round buttocks. He got aroused just thinking about her. Raven Kensington had a body that just wouldn't quit. Saul smiled.

He'd had sex with too many females to count, all wanting to be stars, and doing whatever they had to do to become one. Saul figured Raven wasn't any different. She may *act* like a lady, but behind closed doors, the *real* her will come out. Saul looked at his watch. Raven was due to arrive in less than an hour. He was very excited and very hungry. Saul wasn't hungry for food though, he was hungry, for Raven. He felt that Raven would be the best sex he'd ever had, or certainly close to it. He couldn't wait to touch her breasts, kiss those lovely lips, not to mention ... She has curves for days! Saul smiled again.

His thoughts were interrupted by a knock at his door. She's early, Saul thought. But it wasn't Raven, it was his two bodyguards. Lester and Rich had worked for Saul for over ten years. They knew what their boss did. Many times, he would also let them in on the action. The bodyguards hoped that they could have a piece of Raven too.

* * *

"Are we *in*?" Lester asked Saul. He looked at his boss grinning from ear to ear. Lester wanted this one, *badly*. Like Saul, he had also seen Raven last night. And, what a *woman*! The big, burly Lester couldn't wait. They were going to have a sexual feast. All three of them.

Saul grinned. "Sure! Why not? You both are in, big guys. How does a train sound?"

Rich looked ecstatic. "Choo-choo! I have already sent the secretary home. It will only be the three of us, and our fresh meat. I have always preferred dark meat. It tastes so much better than white meat. Looks better too. She's dark and so very lovely!"

All three men laughed, as they nodded their heads in agreement.

* * *

Raven arrived twenty minutes later, dressed in business attire. And as always, she was early. Raven knocked on Saul's office door. She was escorted in by Saul's bodyguard. There was another big guy sitting on the sofa. Raven reluctantly went in anyway. She looked around for Andrew.

"Hello, Miss Kensington. It's a *pleasure* seeing you again!" said Saul, as he kissed Raven's hand. "These are my two bodyguards, Lester and Rich."

"Nice to meet you, Miss Kensington." Lester spoke first.

"You're a *very* beautiful woman," said Rich. Raven Kensington was a beautiful sight to behold. Rich just stood, staring at her.

"Thank you," said Raven.

"Okay, guys, leave us alone for a while, please. I'd like to talk with Miss Kensington in *private*."

Lester and Rich left their boss's office, but they didn't go far. They stood outside the door.

"Would you like something to drink? Have you had lunch yet?" Saul asked Raven.

"I'm fine, thank you." Raven replied, as she kept an eagle's eye on Saul. "You said Andrew Spellman would also be here. Where is he?"

Saul had lied to her. Andy wasn't coming, nor did he know anything about this.

"He called a little before you arrived. He's running late. *Traffic.* Don't worry your pretty little head. He'll be here." Saul tried to take Raven's mind off Andy. He asked her what her dreams were.

They talked for an hour. Saul was getting impatient. He felt that he had pretended long enough. Saul sat, eyeing Raven. He knew that his bodyguards were outside the door. Saul also knew that no one else was on his floor. The well-built walls and floors were also soundproof. It's time. I'm not going to wait all day, Saul thought to himself. He promised his wife that he would take her shopping at Saks later that afternoon.

"Saul, when you called me, you said that you wanted to discuss a possible role." Raven felt something was very wrong. Andy was never late, and he certainly wouldn't be *this* late.

"Oh, yes. I was just making small-talk. And wanting to get to know you better. I hadn't seen you before last night. But, regarding the role, how *badly* do you want to be a star?" Saul cut right to the chase.

Raven looked at Saul. She knew that she had made a *big* mistake coming here, especially, alone.

"What do you mean, how *badly* do I want to be a star?" Please, not *that* again, Raven thought to herself. She was trying to stall Saul with the question, while her mind was contemplating. She knew that she was in trouble. *Big* trouble. Raven also sensed that Lester and Rich were close by.

"Raven, you strike me as a very smart girl, I don't think that I have to tell you what I mean by that."

"I'm a *woman*, Saul. And yes, by all means, tell me. Tell me *exactly* what you mean," said Raven.

Saul looked at the young beauty, annoyed. His patience had worn thin. The others were always quick and easy, except for the last girl they'd all had sex with. Lindsey Procter tried to fight back. She didn't want to have sex with any of them. Saul, Lester, and Rich had raped and beaten her, very badly. Lindsey was currently in the hospital, fighting for her life. We may have to rape and beat this one too, thought Saul. She asks far too many questions, and she's not easy like I thought she would be.

Saul spoke candidly. "*Favors*. I'm a very *sexual* guy." He was tired of playing games with Raven. Let's get on with it, thought Saul. He was so hungry for her. "You have very *lovely* legs, Miss Kensington. What time do they open?" Saul smiled wickedly.

Raven found his sense of humor, sickening. "I'm leaving. I'm *not* having sex with you." Raven told Saul.

Saul caught her off guard. He slapped Raven so hard, she could taste the blood in her mouth.

Raven was angry, but she was determined not to be frightened. She knew that fear would only make things worse. She also knew that she was in danger. *Grave* danger.

When Saul went to slap her again, Raven moved quickly, causing him to miss her. Saul wouldn't give up. He raised his hand to hit her again, but this time, Raven broke his arm, then she kicked him with all of her might, right between his legs.

Saul fell to the floor, in excruciating pain and sheer agony. It took a while for him to find his voice. "You slut! You black whore! Lest-er! Rich!" Saul squealed.

His bodyguards came in right away.

"This tramp just broke my arm and she kicked me between my legs! Forget sex! Boys, *beat* the hell out of her!" Saul ordered them. He had never been in so much pain in his life.

"There's no *hell* in me," said Raven. "All of the hell's in the three of you." *God, help me*, Raven prayed silently. *Please*, give me the strength. Please get me out of this. I know that I shouldn't have come, but it's too late to think about that now. God ... *help* me.

"Aren't we the comedienne?" said Rich, walking towards Raven. "Beautiful and funny, what a combination. I like that! Stand back, Les, you can have her when I'm done."

"I'll go slip into something more comfortable. Like my *birthday* suit," said Lester. "Be back in a sec." Lester went to the adjoining room to remove his clothes.

It happened so quickly, Saul nor Rich, saw it coming. Before any of them knew it, Rich was on the floor.

Saul was very frightened. He thought Rich was dead because he wasn't moving, nor was he saying anything. His eyes were also closed. Rich wasn't dead, Raven put him to sleep.

Raven tried to leave through the same door that she came in, but it was locked from the outside. She had no choice. She had to go through Lester.

"Lest-er! Get in here! Now!" Saul yelled. "Lest-er!"

Two down, one to go, Raven thought.

"Lest-er! Get your ass in here! Lest-er!" Saul yelled again. "Now!"

Lester ran back into the room in a matter of seconds, naked. "Is it my turn, boss?"

"*Yes*, it is." Raven answered.

"Oh … shit!" said Lester, when he saw Rich lying still on the floor. "Holy fuckin' cow!"

The expression on Lester's face made Raven want to laugh. "You might want to cover *that* up." Raven told Lester.

Lester stared at Rich's still-body. "She's *killed* him! Oh, God! Rich was like a brother to me!" Lester was shaking visibly, as he looked at Raven. "Damn! What are *you*, some kind of *wonder-bitch*?" Lester had never been frightened by a woman before, but he knew that he wanted *no part*, of this one.

"Stop talking and get her!" yelled Saul, who was still lying on the floor with his hands between his legs. Raven had kicked him a good one. "What are you standing there for?" Saul roared at Lester.

"Because I wanna remain standing, that's why! She's kickin' ass and takin' names. I ain't touchin' her, boss! No freakin' way!" said Lester, shaking his head nonstop. "No freakin' way!"

"You, punk!" Saul yelled. "You girlish, sissy punk!"

* * *

"Boss, how can you call me a punk and she kicked your ass? You're lying on the floor, unable to get up, and *I'm* a punk? And look at Rich! Rich is a two hundred and fifty pound man, and he's on the floor, dead as a *freakin'* doorknob! He might as well have been a rag doll, the way she handled him. And *you*. Naw! No way! No freakin' way! I ain't touchin' her! I don't care what you call me. I'd rather be a smart punk than a dumb and dead one *any* day." Lester couldn't remember Raven's name, nor did he want to.

Saul turned his eyes on Raven. "No matter how cliché this may sound, you are *finished*! You hear me? You will *never* work in this town again! Never!"

Raven watched Lester and Saul very carefully, as she quickly left the room. She ran down the hall as fast as she could. When she made it to the lobby, no one was in sight.

Raven knew that the best thing to do was get out of there. And she did.

On the drive home, tears streamed down her face. "Thank You, God. *Thank You*, for sparing my life. And thank you, Daddy, for insisting that Angie and I take martial arts."

Raven had never been so happy that she was a black belt, than she had been that day. However, she knew that being a black belt didn't have anything to do with being foolish. She knew that she had been very foolish. She had learned a very valuable lesson. Raven had put her life in danger.

Always follow your instincts. And always follow your first mind. Raven knew that if she would have done that, she would not have put her life at risk. She never would have come. Never again, thought Raven, as the tears kept falling. *Never* again.

* * *

When Becky saw Raven's face, she knew something awful had happened. "*Sis*, what's wrong? *What happened*? Did he hurt you?"

Raven told Becky what happened.

Becky immediately dialed 911. "Oh … Sis … I should have gone with you." Becky cried, as she hugged Raven.

"Don't blame yourself, Beck, it wasn't *your* fault. I shouldn't have gone. I should have followed my instincts. They were *so* strong too. I shouldn't have gone anywhere, without contacting Andrew first, to verify."

Becky nodded in agreement.

Two officers from the L.A.P.D. arrived within minutes. One officer completed a police report, while the other officer immediately dispatched police to Saul Chambers's office.

The officers stayed with Raven and Becky for a while, after the report was completed. They could see how visibly-shaken Raven was.

"Thanks for everything, officers. I'd like to be left alone now," said Raven. "Beck's here with me."

"Okay, Miss Kensington. As long as you are all right. You don't need to see a doctor?" the officer with the chestnut-brown hair asked.

"That's not necessary. Thank you," said Raven. "I'm not hurt. At least not *physically* anyway."

"Here's a copy of the police report, Miss Kensington. We'll need you to come down to the station to identify the three *animals* who tried to rape and beat you. Someone from the station will contact you ASAP."

Raven and Becky thanked both officers again.

After the officers left, the two women sat on the sofa in silence.

Becky was very happy that her friend had escaped alive. She cringed thinking about what she would have done if anything would have happened to Raven. It was a loss she couldn't even fathom.

Raven's phone was ringing off the hook. She didn't know who was calling, and after what had just happened to her, she wasn't in the mood to talk to anyone.

"Gosh, who's calling like that? Back-to-back. Would you like me to answer it?" Becky asked Raven.

Raven shook her head no. "I'm going to my room now. *Thanks* for everything, Beck. What would I do without *you*?"

* * *

"What would we do without *each other*? I'm here for you, Sis. I'm not going *anywhere*," said Becky.

Becky called John to cancel their date. When John asked why, Becky told him that she had caught a virus that had been going around. After all that had happened, Becky wanted to stay with Raven. "It's contagious. I don't want you to get sick too," Becky told John, when he insisted on coming over anyway. "You just started your new job. It wouldn't look good missing days already."

John reluctantly agreed. "Yeah, you're right, Becky."

Jonathan Sparks was now Vice President of Trakton Systems, Inc., a Fortune 500 company. John was very excited about his new position, the six-figure salary, and all of the great benefits and perks that came with his position. He could easily take care of himself and Becky now.

Raven and Becky were very happy for John. He had worked hard for years, and he was *finally* reaping the rewards, as they were.

As Becky and John talked, Raven's phone continued to ring, nonstop. Whoever it is, thought Becky, they're very insistent on speaking with Raven.

It was Andrew Spellman. "Raven, where are *you*, pretty lady? Please call me! It's *very* important. Got great news! You're not going to believe this." Andy left message after message on Raven's voice mail. After hours of trying to reach her, he finally stopped calling. "She and Becky are probably out somewhere. She'll call me when she gets the messages," Andy said to himself. "All *hundred* of them." He smiled a broad smile. Raven Kensington was going to be ecstatic! And *rich*!

Raven gave the police officers Becky's phone number, so Raven knew that it wasn't them calling. Becky also had Call Waiting, and Call Waiting ID, and no one had called while she and John talked on the phone.

John did most of the talking. Becky's mind was on her best friend. She was ecstatic that Raven was okay. It scared her every time she thought about what could have happened to Raven. Becky breathed a huge sigh of relief.

"Sweetheart, you're very quiet," said John. "I'll let you go get some rest."

"I'll call you later."

"Okay. Get well soon. I love you, Becky."

"I love you too, John."

Minutes after Becky hung up from talking with John, her phone rang. "Hello."

"Raven Kensington, please."

"May I ask who's calling?" Becky asked, even though she knew from the Caller ID that it was the police.

"Sergeant Miller, with the L.A.P.D."

"Please hold," said Becky, as she took Raven the phone. "It's Sergeant Miller," Becky whispered to Raven.

"Hello, Raven Kensington speaking."

Raven sat on the sofa shocked when she was informed of the news. Saul, Lester, and Rich, had been murdered, shot to death, at Saul's office. They would have called sooner, the officer told Raven, but they wanted to identify all three "animals," and they wanted to get as many facts as possible, before phoning Raven.

"I didn't kill them," said Raven, although she wanted to. This was becoming more and more like a nightmare by the minute.

The officer quickly put Raven's mind to rest. "We know that, Miss Kensington. Valeria Procter has been taken into custody. She was still there when police arrived at Saul's office, and so was the murder weapon. Their blood was all over her. She admitted to killing them."

Sergeant Miller told Raven that Valeria Procter shot all three men in the head, and she had also shot Saul between the legs. He was the one who had raped her fifteen-year-old daughter, Lindsey, repeatedly. The other two, Lester and Rich, beat the young girl to within an inch of her life. Lindsey Procter had died that day. And that's when her mother decided to take the law into her own hands.

   * * *

A police report was completed when Lindsey was first hospitalized, but Saul was so clever, there wasn't any evidence when the police arrived at his office, hours later. The three men weren't even in sight. Supposedly, they weren't even in town. They all had alibis too. Saul paid a pretty penny to the general manager of the Fairwinds Hotel in San Francisco, to lie for them. The manager of the hotel gave police fraudulent-receipts, showing that all three men were at the hotel during the time of Lindsey's incident.

Raven thanked the officer for the information, while also thanking God. She breathed a huge sigh of relief. Raven knew that she would have been the main suspect. She shared the news with Becky.

"My heart goes out to the mother," said Becky. "Those *animals* got exactly what they *deserved*. I don't feel *any* remorse for them at all. The world will definitely be a *much* better place without those *bastards*. I can only imagine how many females those animals used and abused! To tell you the truth, I could have killed them myself. If something would've happened to you, Sis, I would have killed them," Becky said honestly. "I'm *so happy* that you're okay. I'm so happy that you made it out of there alive! I have also learned a very valuable lesson from this. *Neither* of us, will *ever* go anywhere alone like that again. *Ever!*"

Raven nodded her head in agreement, as the two friends hugged.

"Have you checked your messages, Sis?" Becky asked. "Your phone's been ringing like *crazy*. It's been ringing all morning, non-stop. *Someone* wants to talk to you very badly."

"No, I haven't checked my voice mail yet. Right now, I just want to talk with my *best* friend in the whole wide world, and continue to beam about my making front-page news. Just *think*, what a *difference* a day makes! Just last night, I was at this fancy-smancy movie premiere party. Just this morning, we were celebrating my being front-page news. And just hours ago, I was in an office, fighting for my life. Fighting off three punks who wanted to have sex with me, and who tried to beat me into oblivion when I refused to have sex with them. This sounds like the making of a very *bad* Hollywood movie!"

Becky laughed. "Let's go back to the *good* now. *You* making headlines!"

Raven smiled. "Yes! A sister from a small Texas town *outshines* the big-city folk!" Raven changed her voice. After all that she had gone through that day, Raven was trying to cheer herself up. Having a great sense of humor always helped in life. She often used it to cheer others up, and she had always used it whenever she needed, or wanted, to cheer herself up too. And, as always, it helped. It was working. Laughter really is the best medicine, Raven thought.

Becky laughed. "Sis, you are *crazy*! I have *only* been telling you that for practically *twenty* years now. C'mon, Sis. Let's go to the beach!"

                    * * *

The sound of the water was very soothing. It was just the medicine that Raven needed. She would never forget what she'd been through. It was truly a lesson learned. Even the wise do foolish things sometimes, but Raven promised herself that she wouldn't make it a habit. Raven knew it was one habit that she could not afford.

Raven and Becky stayed at the beach for hours. Afterwards, Becky drove along the coasts. The views were breathtaking. The water and mountains were beautiful.

Raven's cell phone rang. She looked on her Caller ID before answering, as she always did. "It's Andrew. It must be important. He *never* calls my cell. Hello."

"*You're on TV! Where are you?*"

Becky looked over at Raven. She could hear every word that Andy said. So could half of the people in L.A. He was *screaming*.

"*I'm* on TV? *How*? *Why*? *What* channel?" Raven had tons of questions. She couldn't believe it. *Oh, no*, Raven thought, I hope it's not for what happened with Saul. But she quickly decided it wasn't that. Raven didn't think Andy would be excited about that. That was not anything to be excited about. "Beck! Slow down!"

Becky had put the Jag in speed-motion. She was trying to make it home to see Raven on TV.

"I don't want to see myself so badly on TV that you and I end up wrapped around a pole."

Becky laughed. "Okay, Sis. I'll slow down a bit."

"You're on *Inside Edition* and *Entertainment Tonight*," said a very excited Andrew. "Tell Becky she doesn't have to speed, both programs come on again at midnight. I'm also recording them. So, either way, you'll see yourself, *Miss Star*! What did I tell *you*? I *told* you! *Everything* that I said is coming true. Don't forget that *I'm* your agent. I represent the very beautiful, the *immensely*-talented, Raven Kensington. I'll just sit back and wait for my phone to ring. And *trust me*, pretty lady, it's going to ring. You *deserve* everything that's happening to you now. I *mean* that, Raven. Talk to you soon, pretty lady!"

Andy hadn't told Raven yet, but he and Lyle Krause had another project for her. It was big too, but Andy was making sure that everything was a done deal first. He didn't want to get Raven's hopes up. Lyle had assured him that the deal was as good as done, but, as good as done, wasn't good enough for Andrew Spellman, nor would it be for Raven. Lyle told Andy that he would call him in a few days to confirm.

   * * *

Raven and Becky didn't make it home in time to see either program, but they eagerly waited for the midnight hour, when both shows aired again.

Entertainment Tonight came on first. And there *she* was! They sat speechless, as they watched Raven on TV, getting out of the limo, smiling that dazzling, trademark smile, and answering the reporters' questions like a pro. Raven looked like a million bucks. Raven Kensington looked like the megastar, that many knew, she was well on her way to becoming.

Tears filled Raven's eyes. She began to cry.

Becky was happy beyond words. She felt nothing but sheer happiness for her best friend. She *knew* this would happen. And as she had always told Raven, it was just a matter of time. And it looked like Raven Kensington's time, was close at hand.

"*Sis?*" Becky didn't say anything else. She didn't have to. Becky knew the tears were from past and present struggles.

Raven cried for all the years of being looked over, instead of being looked at. Looked over, because she didn't fit the description of Hollywood and society's ideal of beauty. She wasn't what "they" were used to seeing. Her kind of beauty and size were rarely celebrated on-screen. And unless someone had been under a rock, everyone knew what Hollywood and society's ideal-beauties were. In a nutshell, white and *stick*-thin. But, like the fighter that she was, Raven Kensington kept fighting. Raven fought, not only for herself, but *for all those* who were wanting the same thing she wanted. And for all those who would come after her. And although things were looking up for Raven, she vowed to continue to fight, for a Hollywood, for *all*.

Raven knew as she'd always known, that talent and beauty weren't enough to make it in Hollywood, because she had both. Raven also knew that she wasn't the only one with beauty and talent shunned by Tinseltown. Even white females who weren't thin, or thin enough, were also overlooked. But in their case, it was because of their size. If they chose to lose weight, they would meet Hollywood's criteria, then. But for nonwhites, that was impossible. None of it mattered to Raven, because the *only* criteria Raven Kensington ever considered, was her own. And she had always met that criteria.

Raven continued to sit and think about all of her struggles in Hollywood, as tears kept falling. She thought of all the times when she'd tried out for parts, putting her heart into each audition, performing flawlessly, only to have the part given to a female, a white one, a thin one, who had little, or no talent.

* * *

Raven knew that making it in Hollywood was difficult for anyone. But it was, as she'd so wisely stated in sixth grade, years ago, much harder for blacks, other minorities, and females who weren't toothpicks. Even now, in the 21st century. Even after Halle's Oscar in 2002.

And as far as the males, Raven saw what she already knew, that for them, potbellies and not-so-handsome faces were okay. It was acceptable. Certainly more acceptable. How unfair, Raven thought. How ridiculously unfair. But many things in life were unfair.

Raven thought of Becky. Even though she was white, it hadn't been a cakewalk for her best friend either. Becky was a very talented actress. She would usually lose roles to many less talented, rail-thin, white females. And to the ones who agreed to bed the decision-makers.

Becky was a tall and slender size eight. She was far from fat. Becky was also at a healthy weight. So was Raven. But they were still not thin enough, according to Hollywood. As far as Raven was concerned, Hollywood's ideal-weight, was not having *any*.

"They need to put up signs that read: only toothpicks need apply." Raven told Becky one day, after leaving yet another audition.

One phrase that Raven grew sick and tired of hearing was, "This part wasn't written for a black female." Raven figured that whites made movies for whites. TV and movies largely supported her conclusion.

"The proof is in the pudding." Raven told one writer before leaving. "How about writing for *people, human beings*? How do you write for races?" Raven wanted to know.

The writer just gave Raven a blank stare.

Raven also knew that African-Americans paid their money to see movies. She felt that if she and other blacks paid to see movies in theaters, they should also be able to see people who looked like them, on-screen.

"Who do these bigots think they are?" Raven asked Becky one day. "This isn't the white man's world, it's *God's* world. And we are *all* His creations! All races are movie-goers and turn movies into box-office hits, not just whites. It's okay to take our money, but it's not okay if we'd like to be on-screen, instead of sitting in the seats, eating popcorn, and watching from the sidelines. It reminds me of the time when blacks had to sit at the back of the bus. It was okay for us to keep the white man in business by paying our money to *ride* the bus, but it wasn't okay for blacks to *drive* the bus. In other words, we could be passengers, *backseat*-passengers at that, but *not* drivers. Despite the fact that we were driving their business in a *big* way. That was then, this is *now*, and no one, is going to keep me from being a driver. *No one!*"

The world is diverse, and as far as Raven Kensington was concerned, TV, movies, and magazines, should be a reflection of the *real*-world. And if white writers only wrote scripts for whites, and cast their own race, as they had done for many years now, and still often did, they were just as racist as the white owners and managers in the *working*-world, who hired only-white employees, or mostly-white employees.

Raven felt certain that discrimination would always exist, but she was determined to do whatever she could do to make things better. Not only for herself, but for all those who would come after her. Raven continued to think about all of her past struggles in Hollywood. And the tears continued to stream down her face.

Raven looked at Becky, as she smiled through her tears. Things were looking up for the young women from Tunis, Texas.

* * *

Becky phoned the Kensingtons and Simms to tell them about Raven being on TV and in the newspaper.

They already knew.

Everyone in Tunis was calling the Kensington household. Everyone was overwhelmingly-happy for Raven.

Tanya Riley gasped. She was ecstatic when she saw Raven on *Inside Edition*. "I knew it!" she told her husband. "I knew it! She is more beautiful than ever. Honey, that's the one! I told you about her years ago, Larry." Mrs. Riley beamed. She was very happy for Raven. But she wasn't at all surprised. Tanya Riley's thoughts immediately went back to the twelve-year-old girl who had stood before the sixth grade class, and told all of them what would happen. Tanya shook her head. "I *knew* it! I, *knew* it!"

Mitch Peters, Raven and Becky's former boss at McDonald's, also recorded Raven. Many people had. It wasn't every day that one could say they knew celebrities, *especially*, personally.

Angie phoned Raven at one-thirty in the morning. She couldn't conceal her excitement. "We recorded it, Raven! I can't wait to show my boyfriend! Every guy will be trying to date *me* now."

Raven laughed at her sister. "You haven't changed, girl. Not one bit."

Angie proceeded to scream.

"You're going to wake up the whole neighborhood, Ang!"

"They're already woke. Everyone can't stop talking about *you. My* big sister. The lovely, the very beautiful, *Tunis-born* star, Ra-aa-ven Ken-sing-ton!"

Raven laughed. Angie was a character. She missed her little sister a lot. "You stay out of trouble, Ang. And *listen* to Mom and Dad too."

"I'm good," said Angie. "You know me."

"I sure do, that's why I said what I said. I know you too well, little one. Too well. Hollywood hasn't given me Alzheimer's. I *mean* it, Ang, be good. Stay out of trouble. Keep your grades up. Love you!"

"I love you too, *star*! Give my love to the other star too."

"Will do, Ang."

* * *

The following Sunday, Raven arrived at the City of Angels Church of Christ, as she had for years now, since moving to L.A.

Many of the church members congratulated her. They saw Raven in the newspaper, and on TV.

Raven thanked them, as she walked into church, eager as always, to hear the word of God.

Tony Dash walked in minutes later. He wanted to arrive early, but traffic had killed that plan. Tony sat at the back of the church. His eyes wandered. Where is *she*? He didn't see Raven. Tony began to wonder if the waitress at Spago had lied to him, or if Raven just hadn't come to church that Sunday. His eyes rested on a woman wearing a lavendar, wide-brimmed hat. He kept his eye on the woman. It could be *her*, Tony thought to himself. He couldn't see the woman's face. Tony sat, staring at the woman's back, hoping that she would turn her head enough so that he could see her face.

She never did.

When offering time came around, the mystery woman was revealed. It was her! Tony's heart raced. "*Thank You, God*," he whispered to himself. "*Thank You*." Tony was not what one would call a religious man by any means, but those were the first words that came out of his mouth. Tony knew that he was thanking God because He made *her*.

He watched Raven with the same awe and admiration as he had at the movie premiere party. "Poetry in motion. *My, my, my* ..." Tony was so enthralled by Raven, that he didn't hear the usher.

"Will this side *please* stand?" the usher asked again.

Tony quickly rose to his feet, a little embarrassed. He knew the usher saw him watching Raven. And *all* of the women, were watching *him*.

When church was over, Raven greeted many of the members, including the pastor. She had never become friends with anyone at the church, especially any of the ladies. It wasn't because she thought that she was better than anyone else, it was because of what many of them did. Gossip, gossip. And *more* gossip. They seemed a lot more interested in talking about people, instead of talking about God.

Raven thought it humorous, how supposedly-Christian folks would be in church praying and shouting one minute, then rolling their eyes and talking about others, the next minute. Raven had never been into gossip, even as a child. She was always the kind of person, that if she had anything to say about anyone, she would say it *to* them. Talk to them, not, about them, which is how it should be done.

Raven knew that gossip was something that many people loved to do. To each their own, Raven thought. It's their prerogative to do what they do. And it's my prerogative to do what I do.

Tony was greeted by men and women alike. Many of the women agreed that he looked familiar, but they couldn't remember where they had seen him before. The men knew exactly who *he* was. How could they not?

Tony kept a very close eye on Raven. He didn't let her out of his sight. When he saw her walking out to her car, he excused himself from the crowd, and walked quickly, to catch up with her.

As Raven unlocked her car door, Tony called her name. "Miss Kensington!" He hadn't come this far to turn around. The usually-suave, cool, and confident Tony Dash was very nervous. He had *never* been so nervous in his life.

Raven stopped and waited. She had seen this man watching her. She had always had the ability to see people and things, without them being aware of it. Her all-seeing, dark eyes were like a scope.

"Miss Kensington," said a very nervous Tony again.

"*Please*, call me Raven."

Wow. She's even *more* beautiful up close. Tony had never seen a more beautiful face in his life. And *that* voice ... Tony had always wondered what Raven's voice sounded like, and now, he knew. Raven's voice was like sweet music to Tony's ears. Her voice was very beautiful, eloquent, sultry, clarion ... The voice suited the staggeringly-beautiful woman to a T. Tony tried to speak, but he couldn't. Raven had him speechless, dumbfounded. Tony just stood there, staring at Raven. He was mesmerized. *She*, was the *ultimate* woman.

Raven looked at the man who stood before her, her eyes never left his. A number of questions crossed her mind. *Who* is this man? It was obvious that he knew her name. Perhaps from the paper or TV. She remembered her fifteen-plus minutes of fame.

Who was this *immensely*-handsome and *sexy hunk* of a man? He stood, Raven guessed, about five feet, nine inches tall, and was roughly, two hundred and twenty pounds, of pure *fineness*. He had broad shoulders and a very muscular, powerfully-built body. His honey-brown skin was clear and smooth. His eyes were dark, though not as dark as hers. He had thick eyebrows that made his dark eyes look even sexier. His mustache was neatly-trimmed. His short, black, wavy hair was trimmed to perfection. His hands were well-manicured.

Tony Dash was very debonair. The man standing before Raven was a very handsome, fine, well-dressed man, who obviously took very good care of himself. He also has expensive tastes, Raven thought, as she eyed his impeccably-tailored Armani suit. And although there wasn't a ring on his left hand, Raven knew that it didn't mean he wasn't married. He looked to be in his mid-to-late twenties. Raven sensed that he was a little older than that. The man who stood before her looked young, yet very mature.

"*Yes?*" Raven asked, after checking Tony out with one quick glance. It was also very obvious to Raven, that the man was very nervous.

Tony Dash took a deep breath. "I ... I saw you at the movie premiere party the *other* night. I was among those fortunate enough to see a private screening of *Heartless War*. Your acting was *superb*. I loved it!" And I love you, he wanted to say, but didn't. "I'm sorry. My name is Tony. *Tony Dash*. I'm just *nervous*. I'm not usually *this* nervous," Tony said honestly. "The reason ... that I wanted to talk to you ... I ... I want to know if we, if we could, exchange phone numbers. I ... I would like to take you out to lunch, or dinner. *If* ... that's okay with you." Tony looked at the woman who was driving him crazy, and had, since the first time he'd laid eyes on her. He was trying to read her, but he was unable to.

Vintage Raven.

Raven just looked at Tony. She knew that her silence was making him even more nervous. She liked that. Raven liked keeping people in suspense. Sometimes.

They could have stood there all day and it wouldn't have bothered Tony one bit, he loved looking at her. Raven was *quite* a vision. She was beyond beautiful. *Those* eyes ... Tony loved Raven's dark, mesmerizing eyes. They were the most beautiful eyes that he had ever seen. She had the kind of eyes that a man could stare into night and day. And *those* lips ... He yearned to kiss those very pretty lips of *hers*, but he knew that was totally out of the question.

"*Please* ..." Tony pleaded. "*Please*, Miss Kensington. I'm sorry, *Raven*."

Raven looked as if she were debating, then finally, she gave Tony her phone number.

Tony's hands were shaking as he wrote Raven's number down. "I'm not an alcoholic, I promise. I'm just nervous." Tony joked. He was a man with a sense of humor.

Raven laughed at Tony's comment. "It's quite all right. If I thought you were an alcoholic, *believe me*, I wouldn't have given you my number. I would have given you the number to AA instead."

Tony laughed hard. "I'll write my number down for you."

Raven smiled, as she shook her head no. "You can call me."

There's *that* dazzling, million-dollar smile again. Tony loved everything about Raven, so far. "*Thank you*, Raven. Thank you so very much."

Tony continued to stand there, with his eyes fixated on Raven. He was within arm's reach of her. Not only did Raven look good, she also smelled good. Very good. Tony stood there thinking that a perfume could be made from her scent.

Raven looked at her watch. "Tony Dash, it was nice meeting you. I have to go now."

Tony opened Raven's door for her. He had never done that for a woman before. "Have a great day, Raven." Tony stood watching the shiny red BMW, until he could no longer see it. "You don't know how you've made my day." Tony Dash was elated. "You just don't know!"

"Don't know *what*?" said Pastor Daly, smiling.

"Reverend! I didn't see you," said Tony, looking startled.

"You didn't hear my sermon either. I'm sure you wouldn't be able to tell me what I preached about today to save your life, now, would you?"

"Reverend!"

"Don't *reverend* me, young man. Your eyes were on Sister Kensington the entire time that you were in church, not to mention your mind. You look like you're the happiest man alive! It's easy to see that you're crazy about her. To be truthful, so are most of the men at my church, including some who are married. Anyone can see that she's a very *fine-looking* woman, but she's also very wise and classy. She is a very classy young lady. She's every inch a woman. *Don't* look at me like that, Son. Best wishes, young man. You better *not* do anything to hurt her, or you'll have me to answer to." Along with the rest of the men at the church, the pastor started to say. Pastor Daly shook his head and laughed. "Come to my church, to get the woman of your dreams' phone number. You *need* Jesus!" The pastor patted Tony on the back. "See you later, young man. Come again, but *next time*, come for the *right* reasons!" The pastor laughed, as he wagged a finger at Tony.

* * *

Three female church members were standing outside. They had watched Raven and Tony the entire time. Renee Walker, Allie Travis, and Jean Jones were all members of the City of Angels Church of Christ, and had been, for over fifteen years. They were also three of the *biggest* gossipers in the church.

"*Girl*, look a there," said Jean, pointing at Tony, "that man's *so* fine, it ought to be against the law."

Renee and Allie laughed, as they nodded their heads in agreement.

"I've never seen him before," Allie said. "I sure hope he comes again. Jean, you sho' right, he's a fine one, ain't he? And *pretty* too."

"And don't think he don't know it either, honey," said Renee. "He *knows* it. How could you be *that* pretty and fine and *not* know it?"

"Aren't we all pitiful? We all married and standing on the church grounds, acting like a bunch of *teenage* girls." Renee laughed. "*Drooling*, over that very *fine* specimen of a man."

"Girls, I done told you'll before, I love my husband, Lutha, but he does *not* satisfy me. He knew I was a sex machine when he married me. Lutha even tried Viagra and it didn't help. So honey, anyone knows, that if Viagra and Marvin Gaye *can't* help you, you know you in *big* trouble. Very *serious* trouble," said Allie, being careful to keep her voice down.

Jean and Renee laughed hard.

"Barry White didn't do no good either y'all."

"Girl, quit it," said Renee. "Allie, what are you doin' listenin' to *that* kinda music anyway, and you a saved, Holy-Ghost-filled, Christian woman?"

"We're *listening*, Allie," said Jean. "Answer. Or do you have *selective*-hearing again?"

"I *listen* to that kinda music, *because*, I want my husband to do *exactly* what those songs say do," said Allie candidly, as she quickly changed the subject. Allie's thoughts went back to Tony Dash. "You know, I should've known that *pretty* boy was after *Miss Prissy. Miss*

Prim and Proper, Miss Holier Than Thou. Girls, that Raven Kensington's holier than us, and she ain't even got the Holy Ghost like us. I've been saved for thirteen years now. What about you two sisters in the Lord?"

"Me too, girl. 'Bout the same amount of years. *Hallelujah!*" said Renee, throwing both of her hands in the air.

"Me three," finished Jean. "My life has been changed ever since. I'm glad to be a true woman of God; there are so many phonies out here. They ain't gone do *nothin'* but bust hell *ocean*-wide open."

"*Girl*, you know you right," said Allie.

"So many out there sayin' they got the Holy Ghost, when if anythang, they filled with the pure dee-devil." Jean replied.

"*Amen*, Jean," said Renee. "I'm glad I'm a Christian too. Anyway, I never did like that girl. She walks in the church, a house of God mind you, as if she *owns* the place. My bad, *Miss Thang* don't walk, honey, she *struts*."

"Girl, I hear ya. The walk kills me too, girl. I know she don't *really* walk like that. *Prancing* around like she's *Miss America*." Jean quipped.

"Naw, *Miss Universe*, girl," said Renee. "She walks like she's saying, I *know* I look good. I'm *all* that, and then some! Is it just me, or do you'll agree too? And she see the men looking at her like they never saw a woman before. They be looking at Miss Thang, just a *droolin'*! I told one of 'em, I said, put your tongue back in your mouth. The man acted like he was going to break out in a cold sweat." Renee shook her head. "I think she got *breast implants* too, you'll. Those tits ain't real!"

"Honey, you know you right!" said Allie. "You know they ain't real. And since she's been in the paper and on TV, you sho' can't tell her *nothin'* now. You couldn't talk to her *before*, and you sho' *can't* talk to her now. Her head's *so big*, I'm surprised she could actually fit it in the door to come to service today."

The three women laughed.

* * *

"And what about the *voice*? She talk *white*," said Renee.

"White as snow," said Jean. "Correction, *lily-white*. She talk *just like* those white folks. Just like 'em! She wanna be white. And if she got a best friend, I bet her best friend is white."

"And if she ain't already moved into a white neighborhood, it won't be long fo' she do," said Jean. "And she *always* smilin'. What's *that* about?"

"She's a *show-off*. Nothing but a show-off. That's all Miss Thang is," said Allie.

"She also want to show-off those straight, pretty white teeth of hers," said Renee. "She's *too* conceited for my blood. Notice what kinda car she got? Now, she could've got a nice little ol' cheap car. It didn't have to be a big-name, expensive car. She goes out and gets a *BMW*. *Fancy*, ain't we? I know none of us should be surprised though."

"And a *red* one at that." Allie added. "I'm not surprised at all that she got an eye-catching color either. She's a show-off. I wonder how many men she screwed to get that pretty little Bimmer?"

"*A lot* of 'em, girl," said Renee.

"And you know it," said Jean.

Allie laughed hard. "She's probably screwing *everything* in Hollywood. And this man who came to church today, *pretty* boy, only came to try to *get* her, *if*, you'll know what I mean. He wants to *knock* those boots, girls. Remember that song, 'Knockin' Da Boots,' by H-Town?"

"You sho' talk about sex a lot, Allie. It's obvious that you ain't gettin' *none*," said Jean, laughing.

"No, I'm *not*. However, Lutha better rev this engine soon, like he did on our honeymoon. Or *someone* else *will* be cranking *this* engine. I still got it, girls. Now, just 'cause I'm a Christian, don't mean that I *ain't* a woman. The flesh is calling me, sisters. And *loudly*, I might add. I'm going to commit adultery, and ask for forgiveness *later*. Sisters, I ain't a rabbit, but I *gots* to have it. Lutha the one that got me this way. He used to do it *so-oooo* good when we first got married. And I mean *good*. I don't know what in the world happened. That's a million-dollar question. But he best do something quick, or someone else *gone* hit. 'Cause my body's callin', I mean, yelling, *screaming*."

The ladies roared with laughter again.

"*Seriously*," said Jean honestly. "We don't know that anything that we've said about *her* is true. She is a very beautiful woman. I *gotta* give the sister her props now! She has a beautiful voice too."

"Talk to the hand," said Allie, "cause the ears *ain't listening*! I ain't even *tryin'* to hear it."

"Why would that *ultra-fine* brotha want *her*, instead of *us*?" Renee asked.

Jean looked at Renee in disbelief. "*Now, Renee, do you really* want me to answer that question? *Face it*, what man wouldn't want a *woman like that*?"

No matter what they said about Raven, they couldn't take anything away from her, Jean thought to herself. None of them were Raven. Jean had always secretly admired the young woman. In fact, she admired Raven a lot. She knew that her friends would give her a hard time if they knew what she *really* thought of Raven. She also knew that they were envious of Raven. So was she.

"I don't know about *you'll*, but I *know* I look good," said Allie. "And none of us are old. I don't know why we always calling ourselves *old*. We're only fifty-six. I look just as good as Tina Turner." Allie laughed.

Jean cleared her throat. "Allie, honey, don't even go there."

Allie laughed. "Honey-child, I done already went."

"I'm willing to bet that she's had plastic surgery too," said Renee, her thoughts going back to Raven. "*No one* has a face like *that*. Not naturally anyway. Her features are *too* perfect. That's not natural. It's not normal."

"I have to agree with you there, Renee. I'm also curious about her skin. It's *too smooth*. Girlfriend ain't got a bump, mark, *nothin'* on her face," said Allie. "Her skin is as smooth as a baby's ... uh ...

butt."

"*Oooh*, Allie!" Jean laughed.

"I said *butt*," said Allie.

"Her skin's smooth like marble," said Renee. "Usually, you will have some marks *somewhere*. Who knows what that girl's had done?"

"*Miss Weave*. You'll know that long black mane ain't hers either. *No way*. It look real, but it *ain't*," said Allie.

"Allie, I hate to change the station, but you're a devil's reject," said Jean.

"Girl, what do you mean by *devil's reject*?" Allie inquired.

Jean laughed. "Allie, you so bad and terrible, that the devil himself don't even want you. And girl, you *know* you bad, when the devil rejects you. When the devil see you coming, he runs the *other* way."

The ladies were so deep in conversation, they didn't see the pastor walk up behind them. The three ladies loved gossiping. It was their favorite pastime.

"Hello, sisters! What are you'll talking about so?" Pastor Daly asked them.

Allie smiled nervously. "The sermon, Pastor Daly." Lord, forgive me.

"You preached a *great* sermon," said Renee, avoiding the pastor's eyes.

"Sho' did, Pastor Daly." Allie replied. "'Bye, Pastor Daly. Good-bye, sisters. Lutha ready to go." And he better be *really* ready to go *tonight*.

"Well, Pastor Daly and Sister Walker," said Jean, "I best be goin' home too. My sister and her family's coming to my house for Sunday dinner. I'll see you'll Wednesday at Bible study."

"'Bye, Sister Jones. Save some of that delicious food for me." Pastor Daly told her. "You never know, Hazel and I just might stop by."

"Come on by, Pastor Daly, you'll know you'll are welcome anytime. There will be plenty of food. More than enough," said Jean.

"I'd better be goin' too," said Renee, looking at Pastor Daly, nervously. She hoped that he hadn't heard them. He might think we ain't *true* Christians. And God knows we are!

    * * *

On the drive home, Tony Dash used his cell phone to call the phone number that Raven had given him. He hoped it wasn't a phony number. When Tony heard Raven's voice on the voice mail, he was elated. "Yes! It's *her* number." Tony couldn't stop smiling. He was on cloud nine, as he turned on the radio.

"Swe-eeet la-d-dy, would you *be mine*?" Tyrese sang.

Tony laughed. How appropriate. How very appropriate. He couldn't stop thinking about Raven Kensington. She had hit him like a freight train. Tony couldn't describe the very strong feelings that he had, for a woman he didn't even know. The *incomparable* Raven Kensington.

Tony was used to dating beautiful women. He'd never had any feelings for any of them though. They weren't decent women either, they were "easy." There was nothing respectable about them. They weren't the kind of females that you would want to bring home to momma, or daddy either. Tony knew all too well what his parents would have thought, and said, about them.

Tony always used protection whenever he had sex. He was never foolish like some, to have sex and not protect themselves. Sex wasn't worth a disease of any kind, nor was it worth him risking his life, or fathering a child out of wedlock. Although being the responsible man that Tony Dash was, if he would have fathered a child, he would have been a father to that child, in *every* way.

At thirty, parties and sex, no longer peaked Tony's interest the way they once did.

Tony's mother always told him. "Son, you haven't found the *right* woman yet. But one day you will, and when you do, you'll know it. You will *know* that it's *her*. *Believe* me."

"*Raven* ..." Tony whispered. "*Raven Kensington* ..."

"*Miss Kensington*, is there something you're not telling me?" Becky asked. She knew Raven very well.

Raven smiled. "I gave a guy my phone number today."

"Wait a minute! *You* gave a guy *your* number? Sit down! I want to hear all about *this* guy. He must be *some* guy for you to have given him your number, *Miss, I Don't Want to Date At This Time.* Let's see, you've only dated, maybe three guys, since we moved here."

"I've always told you, Beck, it had to be a guy that peaked my interest. It had to be the *right* one. I don't know him, but I found him interesting. I didn't get a bad feeling about him either. He was just very nervous. But being nervous isn't a bad thing. We all get nervous sometimes."

Becky sat down, she was all ears. "Where did you meet this guy?"

"At church. He came to church today. He looks very familiar. I'm sure that I've seen *that* face before. He said that he saw me at the movie premiere party the other night."

"What's his name?"

"Tony. Tony Dash."

"Plate number?" Becky knew that Raven had that information stored in her photographic memory bank.

"Dash 1. Why?" Raven asked.

"Sis, after what just happened to you, why would you even ask me that question? I'm going to have John do a *thorough* background check on *this* Tony Dash, *if* that's even his real name. With the kind of exposure that you've received, and that you're going to continue to receive, especially when *Heartless War* hits theaters, you're going to have all kinds of people trying to get a piece of you, and wanting to get in on the action. Some good, some bad. And you know as well as I do, especially in the business that we're in, we have to be very careful."

Raven nodded. "You're right, Beck."

Becky phoned John with all of the information that Raven had provided her with. The license plate number was especially helpful.

John told Becky that he'd run a thorough background check on the mystery man. "What's his name again?" John asked.

"Tony Dash."

"Naw. It can't be him," said John, shaking his head.

"What do you mean it *can't* be him? John, what are you talking about?" Becky asked him.

"There's just this big-time, professional football player with the same name, who retired this year because of a knee injury, that's all. But, there are plenty of people with the same name. I will call you as soon as I complete the background check."

Becky felt better. She knew that John would be very thorough, and that's what she needed. Becky also hoped that Tony Dash was a nice, decent guy. Knowing Raven, she had to have seen something good in Tony to have given him her phone number. Raven had gone out very little since moving to L.A. Becky would only be happy once John called her with good news. *Please*, don't let this guy turn out to be an axe-murderer.

* * *

Raven was in bed reading, when Tony phoned her. She liked the sound of his voice. Tony sounded more relaxed. Maybe because he's on the phone, thought Raven. Their conversation was very enjoyable and interesting. So enjoyable and interesting, in fact, that they talked … *for* … *hours*.

* * *

True to his word, John phoned Becky, days later. It didn't take him long to run a background check on Tony. "Is it okay if I come over? Is Raven home?"

"Yes. We'll be waiting for you," said Becky.

"*Well?*" said Raven, when John arrived. "Shoot, Sherlock."

"Tony Dash doesn't have a criminal record of any kind. His record is spotless. He doesn't even have a speeding ticket." John began.

Becky cut in, "Okay, this guy is probably trying to get next to Sis because she's about to become rich and famous. I doubt if he's some kind of millionaire who has money to burn."

John laughed. "You're right, Becky, he's *not* a millionaire."

"See, I knew it!" said Becky. "Not that being rich is a requirement."

"Sweetheart, I'm not finished," said John. "Put it this way, he doesn't drink, but he can buy the bar! He has more connections than the electric company."

"John, I thought you said he's not a millionaire," said Becky.

"He's not, Becky. Tony Dash, is a *billionaire*!"

Becky's jaw dropped.

Raven listened. This newfound information didn't change anything, as far as she was concerned. Raven wasn't surprised that Tony had money, his clothes and a number of other things reflected that possibility. She was impressed by the man, not his money. Raven was a very independent woman who made her own money anyway.

John went on. "Tony Dash was a big-time, professional football player who retired this year. He was the *greatest* running back to ever play the game. He made hundreds of millions of dollars playing professional sports, and signing major endorsement deals. Mr. Dash has an MBA. He's a *very* successful businessman who turned his millions, into billions. He's *not* married. He lives in Pacific Palisades, and you have to have money to live there. *Big* money! Let me see … What else?" said John, reading his notes. "According to sources, he's a ladies' man. But, we can't look at that as a bad thing. Before I met you, Becky, I was kind of a ladies' man too. Very few guys aren't. And vice versa. I'm living proof, that when you find the one that you *love*, your *true* love, that makes all of the difference in the world. Well, Raven, Becky, I hope this information was helpful. And, oh yes, he's thirty years old." John smiled and shook his head. "What a *small* world! *Who* would have known? *Where* did you meet the *great* sports icon, T.D.?" John inquired. He had admired Tony Dash for years. He was amazing to watch.

"At church," said Raven.

"I'll say this too, if this guy came to church to meet you and try to talk to you, that's saying *a lot*. A whole lot. He's filthy-*rich*, he's very handsome, and he's single." John reminded Raven again. "My dad and I are *huge* fans of his. Tony Dash was *by far*, the *best* running back to *ever* play the game of football!" John shook his head in amazement. "*What* a *small* world." John couldn't believe it. "This is *unbelievable*. Unbelievable!"

"Thanks, John," said Raven.

"Yeah, thanks, sweetheart. You were *thorough*. I knew you would be," said Becky. "Well, I do feel better, Sis. But as we've said before, be very careful, no matter *who* it is."

"You too Beck. We *both* need to be careful. *Everyone* needs to be careful for that matter. It's the kind of world we all live in. Although, it's not the world, but some people in the world," said Raven.

"Sis, aren't you supposed to go out to dinner with Tony Friday night?" Becky asked.

"Pending the investigation, yes."

All three of them laughed.

"I'll go now. But I'm going to drive my own car. When I get to know him better, if it goes that far, then things will obviously be different. But until then, I'll play it safe."

"Where are you'll going?" Becky and John asked in unison.

"To Palm Biernat's on Rodeo Drive."

"*Fancy smancy!*" said Becky. She had heard about the new, upscale restaurant. "Just be careful, Sis."

"I will, Beck. You be careful too."

* * *

On Friday afternoon, Raven's phone rang.

It was Andrew Spellman. "*Brace* yourself, pretty lady. We've hit *pay* dirt! You know me, I'm going to get right to the point."

Raven could hear excitement in Andy's voice. "Shoot, point man."

"If you accept the two offers, you'll be very busy for the rest of the year, but, you'll also be *rich*! Lyle has agreed to pay you *six million dollars* for two movies. In the first movie, you'll be co-starring opposite Norman Sheers. Have you heard of him?"

When Raven heard the dollar amount, she almost dropped the phone. "Of course, Andy, who hasn't heard of Norman Sheers? He's one of the biggest stars in Hollywood!"

"He sure is. You'll play a sexy private investigator. You'll be Norman's partner, but he will end up falling *madly* in love with you, like the rest of us," said Andy. "It's similar to a James Bond flick, only *better*. The movie, *Gun Shy*, will be filmed in the Los Angeles area. Filming begins in two months."

Raven listened quietly. She was speechless.

Andy went on. "The second movie is called, *Before Midnight*. Filming will begin in mid-October for that one. This movie will be filmed in L.A., and possibly Manhattan too. Lyle hasn't decided yet. I have the contracts in my hand for you. But *you* did it, pretty lady! You're the one who delivered. You *fought hard* and *long*. You *never* took *no* for an answer. And you *believed* in yourself. And oh yes, how could I forget, although *Heartless War* hasn't hit theaters yet, there's a *heavy Oscar* buzz, regarding your performance. You certainly gave an *Oscar-winning* performance, Raven. Pretty lady, you're going to be the *biggest star* that's *ever* graced Hollywood!" There wasn't a doubt in Andrew Spellman's mind.

This time, it was Raven who screamed. "Beck! Beck!"

Raven and Becky almost collided.

"*Sis, what's* wrong?"

Raven felt breathless. "I ... just spoke with Andrew Spellman! I have *two* movies lined up for *this* year! He has the contracts for me to read and sign. And the *money* ... *Beck*, I am going to be paid, *get this, six million ... dollars*, for *two* movies. *Six million dollars!* Can you believe *that*?" said a very ecstatic Raven.

"*Yes*, I can. I've *always* told you, Sis, it was just a matter of time. I'm elated, I'm very happy for you, but I'm not at all surprised. You *still* haven't seen nothin' yet. You're going to be the *biggest* star that the world has *ever* seen. And, Sis, you can take those words to the bank, and you can also *cash* the check!"

Raven laughed at Becky's last statement. "Thanks, Beck! You've always believed in me."

"*Yes*, I have, Sis. But *more* importantly, *you*, have always *believed* in *you*. You're very sure of yourself, Raven. You have the confidence of a champion. You wave confidence like a flag. What else?" Becky pondered. "You're very beautiful, inside and out. You're one superbly-intelligent lady. You are classy, very sophisticated, elegant, strong, witty. You have a *great* sense of humor. And above all else, you have a *big* heart! You care about others. I can't say enough *great* things about you, Sis. You're very uplifting to me. And you're the *best* sister that *anyone* could *ever* have."

Tears filled Raven's eyes. "*Oh, Beck* ... You're going to make me cry! You're also the *best* sister that anyone could *ever* have. I *love* you, Rebecca Simms. And whenever I can, I will be tuned in to, *Day's Dawn*. And whenever I *can't*, I'll record it. I'll watch you *every* day. You're going to do *fabulous*, just fabulous! You know that I'm in your corner. *Always!* You can *always* depend on me, Beck."

The two longtime friends hugged. Things were finally looking up, *way* up, for both of them.

"*S.F.L.*, now, *go* answer your phone! It's ringing. *Again*."

"That's right, Beck. We are *sisters for life!*" said a teary-eyed Raven.

"*Sis*, your phone!" Becky laughed.

"I'm going! I'm going!" Raven walked quickly to her room to

answer her phone. "Hello?"

It was Tony. "Hello, Raven. How are you doing?"

"I'm doing fine, thanks. How are you, Tony?"

"I'm doing well, thank you. Is it a good time? Do you have time to talk?"

"Yes, I can talk now." Raven told him.

"Are we still on for dinner tonight?" Tony asked.

"Yes," said Raven.

You don't know how much I'm looking forward to seeing you again, Tony wanted to tell her. He was so excited. "I'll see you tonight, Miss Kensington. Until then …"

Raven heard a smile in Tony's voice. "Until then … Mr. Dash."

Tony had grown more comfortable with Raven. They'd talked on the phone every day, since Sunday. Tony loved talking with Raven. It seemed he could open up to her. Raven wasn't just a great talker, she was also an equally-great listener. Tony also loved the fact that he could hold intelligent conversations with Raven. He flashed a big smile. *Beauty, and brains.* Tony couldn't wait to see Raven again.

He picked up her photo. "Oh … *Raven* ... What are you doing to *me*? Whatever you're doing to me, *keep* doing it. I'm *loving* it."

Tony went to his home-gym to workout. Afterwards, he took a long shower, shaved, then brushed his teeth. Tony took extra preparation getting ready for *this* date, which was also something that he had never done before.

"*Wow*, Mr. Dash! You look very nice," said Mack, who saw Raven's photo in his boss's bedroom. There wasn't a doubt in Mack's mind that his boss wasn't in love. Tony had never framed any woman's picture, except his mother's. "*This* woman *must* be very special."

"She *is*, Mack. *Raven Kensington* is *very* special," said a beaming Tony.

"Well, have a great time, Mr. Dash."

"Thanks, Mack. I'm sure I will!"

* * *

Raven arrived at Palm Biernat's fifteen minutes early, dressed to the nines.

"You look very lovely this evening, ma'am," said the valet attendant, who flashed Raven a flirtatious-smile.

"Thank you," said Raven. She spotted Tony as soon as she walked into the lobby.

"*Hello*, Raven," said Tony. His eyes lit up instantly the moment he saw her. "*My*, you look gorgeous, as usual!"

"Thank you. You don't look *too bad* yourself." Raven teased.

"Well, *shall* we?" said Tony, extending his arm to Raven.

Raven smiled in answer, as she linked her arm with Tony's.

Raven and Tony walked into Palm Biernat's, arm in arm.

They were greeted immediately by the manager, who recognized Tony. "Good evening, *Mr.* Dash." The manager smiled at Raven, and greeted her too. "As *always*, you have the *best* seat in the house! Let me show you to your table."

"Thank you." Tony smiled, as he and Raven followed the manager.

As they were escorted to their table, they received many admirable stares. Raven and Tony made a very *striking* couple.

Tony couldn't stop smiling. It was truly an honor, to have a woman like Raven Kensington, on his arm.

* * *

Chapter 5

Palm Biernat's was a five-star restaurant that had impeccable service. Live music played softly in the background. The setting was very romantic. It was the *perfect* place for dinner, dancing, and romance.

Tony pulled Raven's chair out for her.

Chivalry's not dead, thought Raven. She thought Tony very charming. The fact that Tony was filthy-rich didn't matter to Raven. She knew it was the man, not the money, that she would have to like, love, fall in love with. And besides, she was also rich. *Now.*

"A penny for your thoughts," said Tony.

Raven smiled. "How about a penny for *yours*?"

"Well, right now, I'm thinking about how *elated* I am to be dining with the *most* beautiful woman in the world. And ... I'm thinking about how your million-dollar smile, lights up the entire room. I'm also thinking about ... how very much, I'd love to dance with *you*." Tony held out his hand. "Miss Kensington, may I *please* have this dance?"

Raven smiled. "Yes, Mr. Dash, you may."

Tony took Raven by the hand and led her to the dance floor. They danced to a number of slow, romantic ballads. As they danced, Tony closed his eyes. It felt so good to hold Raven in his arms. Her skin was so soft. *She,* was so soft. He could smell the sweet scent of her perfume. It was very difficult for Tony not to become aroused. They danced through four songs, before the band stopped for a break.

Why did they have to stop? Tony was disappointed. He wanted to hold Raven in his arms, forever. And as they danced, when he looked into those mesmerizing eyes of hers, that is exactly what he saw. *Forever.*

After dancing, Raven and Tony went back to their table and looked over the menu to order dinner. When they had both decided what they wanted, Tony beckoned for their waiter.

What a gorgeous woman, the waiter thought to himself, as he took their order. She's simply stunning! "Drinks?"

"Raven?" Tony asked.

"I'll have a glass of white wine," said Raven. "Thanks."

"And you, sir?"

"A glass of Cristal. Thank you."

They had a very pleasant conversation as they waited for their drinks and meals. Tony's eyes lit up every time he looked at Raven. He loved being with her.

Raven was the most extraordinary woman that Tony had ever met. He looked at the stunningly-beautiful woman that sat across from him. And as Tony continued to look into Raven's eyes, he knew, that Raven Kensington was the woman, that he had been destined for. *She*, was his wife.

Tony didn't want their date to end. No woman had ever made him as happy as Raven Kensington made him. She unlocked feelings in him that he never knew he had.

At the end of the evening, Tony walked Raven out to her car. "When may I see you again?" he asked her.

Raven smiled. "I don't know. When would you *like* to see me again?"

"Is tomorrow too soon?" Tony asked.

"No, it's not."

Tony smiled. "You told me you like parks. Maybe we can go to the park tomorrow. Is that okay with you, beautiful?"

"Sounds like fun."

"I had a wonderful time tonight, Raven. I hope you did too." It was important to Tony that Raven was happy.

"Yes, Mr. Dash, I did. *Thank you*, for a very beautiful evening."

"You made it beautiful, *beautiful*," said Tony. His eyes reached deep into Raven's. "I know it's late. I'll let you go. Drive carefully."

"Thanks, Tony, I will."

"Okay, beautiful, I'll see you tomorrow. Oh, yes, what time? I'm flexible."

"How about oneish? One o'clock," said Raven.

"And which park?"

Raven gave Tony the name and address of the park. She told him that she would meet him there.

"Good night, beautiful."

"Good night, Tony."

* * *

Tony drove home on cloud nine. When he arrived home, he called Raven. He wanted to make sure that she had made it home safely.

Tony couldn't stop thinking about their wonderful, fairy-tale evening. "Oh ... *Raven* ..." Tony smiled, as he remembered how good it felt to hold her in his arms. He also remembered how good Raven smelled. "Good night, my love," Tony whispered in the dark.

* * *

"So, how was your date?" Becky asked. She could tell by the look on Raven's face, when she came home, that it had gone no less than splendid.

"*Great*, Beck. Tony Dash appears to be a very charming man. However, aren't they all when you're dating? That's the time when they will do *whatever* it takes to impress us. But, I don't know ..." Raven's instincts told her that Tony Dash was different. "This guy seems different. He seems genuine. Nothing to worry about, like with all things, time will tell. It always does." And as always, Raven gave full details. She smiled the entire time. "Beck, I feel like I've known *this* man my *entire* life."

* * *

"Sis, it sounds like he's smitten with you. I think you like him too. But, I think that he's more taken with you. There is definitely a bond between you two. Did Dr. Simms analyze this correctly?"

Raven laughed. "Yes, Dr. Simms, you sure did."

"When will I get to meet, *Big Money*?" Becky asked.

"Maybe tomorrow. Tony and I are going to the park. I might bring him by afterwards, I don't know yet. But if things progress, you know that he *has* to meet my sisters. I told him I have two sisters, one who lives in Texas, and one who lives in L.A. And Beck, his billions aren't a factor. Money *doesn't* buy love."

"I know that, Sis, I was just kidding. I know you. There aren't too many things that I don't know about you."

"And vice versa," said Raven. "What did you and John do tonight?"

Becky told Raven earlier that day, that she and John had big plans for the evening.

"We had a great time. Actually, John's *big* plans, were attending the Lakers game, but to my surprise, I enjoyed it. And there were *a lot* of celebrities there too. As usual."

"Yes. I know Jack was there."

Becky laughed. "You know it, Sis. He sure was!"

"He has always been a huge Lakers fan. In Los Angeles, celebrity-sightings are common. And speaking of celebs, I'm talking to one now," said Raven, referring to her best friend.

"And so am I, *Miss Six Million Dollar Woman*!"

* * *

The white Bentley Azure convertible pulled up at the park forty minutes early. Tony got out of the car carrying a number of items that he'd brought, for the *surprise* picnic. He wanted to have everything ready before Raven arrived.

Tony was dressed in a light gray Sean John sweatsuit. Black, stainless-steel, Armani sunglasses rested on the top of his wavy black hair. Several joggers stared at Tony, admiring the movie-star handsome, powerfully-built man. Tony Dash was a man who commanded attention. He symbolized power, and that was something he had plenty of.

Tony found a nice, quiet, isolated area, and it was there, that he spread the blanket over the grass. Ironically, their meal was specially-prepared by a good friend of Tony's, Wolfgang Puck. There were gourmet ham and swiss-cheese sandwiches on French bread, Greek salad with shrimp and creamy garlic dressing, strawberries, chips, bottled water, a variety of soft drinks, and plenty of ice. Wolfgang had also put *extra* goodies in the box for them. Tony also purchased a dozen of red-stemmed roses. He smiled as he waited for Raven. He had everything set up, beautifully.

Shortly before one o'clock, Tony saw the red BMW pull up at the park. He waved at Raven, and she smiled and waved back.

"Hello, beautiful." Tony greeted Raven.

"Hello, Tony. *Wow*, Mr. Dash, this is a lovely surprise!"

"Close your eyes, beautiful. *Please*."

Raven closed her eyes.

"Okay, you may open them now." Tony handed Raven the roses. "These, are for you."

"*Thank you*, Tony. They're so lovely! They're beautiful."

They sat and talked, until they became hungry. Neither of them had eaten breakfast that morning.

"I'm at the right place," said Raven, looking at all of the goodies. "You don't miss a beat, Mr. Dash."

"I try not to."

Their eyes locked and held.

"I'm sorry for staring, but you're *breathtaking*, Raven. I am *blinded* by your beauty."

Raven laughed. "You'll get your sight back in a day or two."

"A beautiful woman with a great sense of humor. I'm going to hold you to that, Dr. Kensington. If I *don't* get my sight back in a day or two, I'm going to give you a call. Or better yet, a *visit*."

Being with Raven made Tony think of Christmas for some reason. Perhaps it was because being with her brought him so much joy and excitement.

"Why is Christmas your favorite holiday?" Tony asked Raven.

"Christmas is by far my favorite holiday. It has always been for a number of reasons. I love the music, the decorations ... I love seeing the excitement in children's eyes. I love the *whole* atmosphere. I love when it snows during the holidays too. Although I am in the wrong place for snow." Raven's eyes lit up as she spoke of Christmas, her favorite holiday.

"You're from *Tunis*, Texas?"

"Yes."

"I've never heard of Tunis. Where is it located?" Tony asked Raven.

"It's about twelve miles from College Station. Have you heard of Texas A&M University?"

"I sure have," said Tony. "Aggieland. College Station is also George H.W. and Barbara Bush's adopted home."

Raven nodded in answer. "Yes, it is."

"I do a lot of business in Dallas and Houston."

"Well, Tunis is about three hours from Dallas, and an hour and a half away from Houston."

"I see."

* * *

After eating lunch, Raven and Tony strolled through the park. It was a beautiful sunny day. Tony noticed an elderly couple watching them.

The couple smiled and waved.

Raven and Tony smiled and waved back.

"*Oh* ... to be *young* again," the elderly lady said to her husband.

"Being young was good," said her husband. "But I like where I'm at now. I've had many great years and I've learned a lot. Oftentimes, we want to turn back the clock. We will never be able to turn back the hands of time, so we might as well go forward. Enjoy the present. And look forward to the future. I love you. Don't ever forget that. You're *still* beautiful to me."

As Raven and Tony walked past the elderly couple, the old man told him and Raven something, that neither of them, would *ever* forget.

"Young folks, the only thing better than *falling* in love, is *staying*, in love," the old man told them.

"You know, I've never heard that before, but I like that. It's very true too. It also makes *perfect* sense," said Tony, as he pondered what the old man said. "It's great to see couples who are still in love and have that same look in their eyes after many years of marriage."

After walking for what seemed like miles, they sat near the water. Tony looked at Raven. "Raven, what are your ingredients for a happy and healthy relationship?"

"Obviously love," said Raven. "It *has* to be based on that. Several kinds of love come to mind: *unconditional* love, agape love, passionate love, and being *in* love."

Tony laughed. "You're very thorough, Miss Kensington, aren't you?"

"Yes, I am."

"You're also very intelligent. And, you're a deep thinker."

"I've always been a deep thinker."

"I'm listening, beautiful. Go on."

"Trust, understanding, communication, commitment, maturity, respect, chemistry, romance, similar morals, values, integrity, and hmmm ... *Regular* maintenance is also very essential. And being *friends*, preferably, *best* friends. Being equally-yoked is also very important. Many think that all we need is love, and that's not so. The things that I've just named are all important, at least to me, in addition, to love. Using my motto: It takes more than one ingredient, to make a good cake. Expectations should also be realistic. We're human beings. We're all imperfect. We will make mistakes. We also may get on each other's nerves sometimes. It's also important that both people in the relationship meet the needs of the other. Going back to communication, it's very important to talk *openly* and *honestly* with each other. About *anything*."

Tony nodded as he listened intently. He hung on Raven's every word. He found her intelligence amazing. He loved listening to her speak.

Raven also enjoyed talking with Tony. He was a man of great intellect. Tony also seemed genuinely interested in her thoughts and feelings, and that meant a great deal to Raven.

Since they had first met, they'd had a number of long, interesting, and enjoyable conversations. More importantly, their talks were always open and honest. They could talk about anything, and they often did.

Raven also loved how they could communicate in silence.

Tony broke the silence. "I agree with all of the things you said. I don't think anything you said was unrealistic either. The regular maintenance is one that I've never thought of, but it's true," said Tony, looking pensive. Raven always made him think. Tony liked that. He knew that he could learn a lot from her. He loved her eyes. They were full of beauty and wisdom. Raven had the wisest eyes that Tony had ever seen. "Oh wise and beautiful woman that you are, please finish. I'm enjoying this," said Tony.

Raven flashed her trademark smile as she continued. "Like with *anything*, if not maintained regularly, it can, and often will, break down. Relationships aren't any different. And it's also important to do what we're doing now."

Tony looked at Raven. "Talking?"

Raven nodded. "Yes. And getting to know each other. Dig deep *before* you leap!"

Tony laughed.

"The relationship, should *always* come *before* the marriage. And you, Mr. Dash?" Raven liked calling Tony, Mr. Dash. "What is your *ideal*-woman like?"

"Well, that's easy. Like you. *Correction*, she *is* you," said Tony.

Raven was silent.

Tony's eyes never left Raven's. "I *meant* that, Raven." And he did mean it. Tony knew from the first time that he laid eyes on her, that Raven Kensington was everything he wanted in a woman. She was everything he thought a woman should be, and more. He was smitten with her. She made him do things that he'd never done. She made him think about things that he had never thought of before. She made him feel things that he had never felt. She made him happy to be alive. Raven made him happy, to be a man. She was unlike any woman that he'd ever known. He had never met *anyone* like her.

Tony was smitten with Raven. It was more than her immense-beauty, her elegance and class, her uncanny-intelligence, her beautiful body, *that* smile, *that* voice, *those* eyes ... He, *loved* her. It was hard to explain. Could one love a person on sight? He didn't understand it. Yet, Tony *knew* in his heart, that he was in love with her. He loved Raven Kensington. And he loved her, deeply. However, he decided to keep those thoughts to himself for now. He didn't want to scare her off. Tony laughed to himself. Raven didn't seem like the kind of woman who would scare easily, if at all.

"Raven? You're quiet. I hope I didn't say anything to upset you."

"No, Tony, you didn't."

"I would like to go to church with you tomorrow. Is that okay with you?" Tony asked Raven. He would do anything to see her, and he would go *anywhere*, as long as *she* was there. Tony wanted to spend as much time with Raven as possible.

Raven smiled. "Yes, that's okay with me, Mr. Dash."

Tony asked Raven if he could come to pick her up for church.

She politely declined. Raven didn't get a bad feeling about Tony, but after what had recently happened to her, she was being *extra* careful.

It was almost dark, when the two finally decided to call it an evening. And as always, Tony hated to see it end.

* * *

"Thanks, Tony. For *everything*. I had a wonderful time."

"*Thank you*. I'll see you tomorrow, beautiful. Is it okay if I call you later?" he asked her.

"Sure, I don't mind."

"'Bye, *Raven*."

"'Bye, Tony."

* * *

Over the next several months, Raven and Tony dated and talked on the phone, regularly. They would talk on the phone for hours at a time.

Tony knew that he was in love with Raven Kensington. He wanted to ask her to marry him, but he felt that it was a little too soon. A few more months, at least, thought Tony. He had even taken Raven to meet his parents. His mother called him the same night that he'd brought Raven over to meet them. She had nothing but great things to say about the woman he loved. His father strongly-agreed.

Carol and Theodore Dash could easily see how much their son loved and cared about the beautiful young woman, whom they recognized as the new star on the rise.

Raven had been on TV and in the paper, often, since *Heartless War* hit theaters. Many people recognized her now. Raven was ecstatic when a little girl, who reminded her of Becky when she was little, asked for her autograph. "One for my brother too, please," said the little girl. "He thinks you're *real* cute!"

Raven laughed, as she gave the little girl the autographs.

Tony knew all too well what being famous was like. He'd played pro-football for twelve years, before retiring, reluctantly, because of a knee injury. He still did a lot of commercials. Tony endorsed automobiles, soft drinks, athletic wear, exercise equipment, the list was endless.

Companies loved Tony Dash because he was a superstar-athlete with great conduct on the field, as well as off the field, and he was movie-star handsome to boot. Tony also had the people's ears. They listened to him. If Tony Dash said the product was good, they would go buy it. Tony only endorsed products that he actually used.

* * *

Becky finally began taping *Day's Dawn*. She played the beautiful, rich, and ruthless seductress, Samantha Matthews.

Raven watched *Day's Dawn* every day, and whenever she couldn't watch, she would record it and watch it later. She couldn't explain the immense-joy that she got watching her best friend on TV. Raven smiled. Their dreams were no longer dreams, but *reality*.

Everyone in Tunis was ecstatic. And they too, tuned in daily to watch their hometown girl on the daytime soap.

John also watched every day. Everyone at his job knew that "John's girl," was on TV. John was very happy for Becky. He was also happy for Raven. He smiled, remembering when the two friends came to California years ago, and he carried their luggage up to their suite. The three of them had come a *very* long way. A very long way, indeed.

* * *

Sometimes Raven and Tony would watch "Becky's show," as Raven called it, together. There weren't too many things the lovebirds didn't do together. They were practically inseparable. Raven had also practiced her part, for her upcoming movie, with Tony. And like the natural that she was, she gave flawless-performances each time.

Andy told Raven that when filming began, she would be working long hours. "We'll try to give everyone weekends off."

Tony sure hoped so. If not, he would find a way to see his sweetheart. He enjoyed the months that they had spent going to the movies, going to dinner, going dancing, going to one of Raven's favorite places, the park, going driving ... Tony had even enjoyed going to church too, and his mother was very pleased about that. Raven made *everything* exciting. Tony didn't care what they did, as long as they were together. He would follow Raven to the ends of the earth.

On the weekend before Raven was scheduled to start filming her next movie, she and Tony went to the park. They watched two guys play touch-football.

Raven watched with interest. "I'll go referee," she said, jokingly.

"What do *you* know about football?" Tony challenged her.

"Enough. You get the ball and run!" said Raven.

Tony laughed. "We'll see what you know. Let's go get my football out of my car. Who was your favorite quarterback?"

"Was. *Still* is. *Joe Montana*!" Raven said without hesitation.

"Great choice! Ladies first," said Tony, handing Raven the ball.

Tony laid down the ground rules and marked a number of places with branches. He went over the rules with Raven to make sure she understood them.

"Ready?" he asked her.

"I'm as ready as I'll ever be," said a very confident Raven. "I hope you brought your A-game."

Tony laughed. "Trash-talkin', huh? I *always* bring my A-game! I'll signal with my hand. When I do, try to make a touchdown. Ready ... set ... go!"

Raven ran quickly. Tony was impressed by her speed and her moves, but he deliberately let Raven get a touchdown, and she knew it.

"No, don't go easy on me, T.D. You *let* me get that touchdown. You could've stopped me. Let's do it again."

"Okay, Raven. I won't go easy on you this time." Tony shook his head. Nothing got past Raven. *Nothing*.

They started over. Raven started running again, full speed ahead. And *this* time, Tony came after her. It was very evident that he was a pro. He was lightning-quick. Tony tackled Raven, playfully. And as he tackled her, they both fell on the ground, laughing.

Their eyes met and held. And for the first time, Tony kissed Raven. He'd wanted to kiss those beautiful lips of hers, from day one. He kissed her gently at first. It was a heart-felt kiss. Kissing Raven was everything Tony thought it would be.

Tony loved the taste of Raven's lips. He moaned as he kissed her again. The second kiss was breath-stealing, passionate, and long. It was filled with the deep emotions that they both shared.

"Oh ... *Raven* ... *God* ... how I *love you*," Tony whispered.

"I love you too, Tony," Raven whispered back. And she did love him. She'd known that for some time now. It felt as if she had known Tony Dash her entire life. There was an immensely-strong, and very special bond between them.

Tony looked at Raven. "You *love me?*" he asked, as his eyes searched hers.

"Yes, Tony, I *love you*. I don't go around telling anyone that I love them. If I say something, it's genuine. I have always been very careful with hearts and minds."

"Can we seal our love with *another* kiss?" Tony asked Raven. Her lips were so soft and sweet, and they tasted so good. He knew that if kissing her drove him this crazy, he could only imagine what making love to her would be like. "Well, may I? May I kiss those *beautiful* lips again?"

Raven nodded in answer.

Tony didn't want to stop kissing Raven, but reluctantly, he did. "Do you think that couples complete each other?" Tony asked Raven.

"No," said Raven. "I don't. I hear that a lot. If anyone completes you, then that means you're not a whole person. And *everyone*, is a whole person, not a half of a person. One, *is* a whole number. Another thing that I often hear people say is that a relationship should be fifty-fifty. I also disagree with that. Like with anything you do, you should never give half. You should always give your all, one hundred percent. So having said that, I feel that *each* person should give one hundred percent. I don't believe in doing anything, *half-heartedly*."

Tony sat and listened. He loved listening to Raven. She was very wise. His mother was also impressed by Raven's wisdom.

"Let's see, another thing that some often say is, I hope to find someone to make me happy. You *can't* find happiness in someone else. For example, if I don't love myself, how can I love anyone else? If I'm not happy with myself, as an individual, there's no way that anyone else would be able to change that. Only I would be able to change that. We can't change others, but we *can* change self. Oftentimes, we look to others for answers, that lie within us. And sometimes, the answers are right in front of us. Always enter a relationship being independent, not dependent. If I don't have anything going for myself, individually, how could I bring anything into a relationship? There are two people in a relationship, therefore, *both* people in the relationship, are *equally*-responsible, for *contributing* to, and *maintaining* that relationship, in order to keep it *healthy* and *happy*, the way that relationships *should* be. It's great to be in love. It's great to be loved. But again, as long as you're wanting a companion, not a crutch."

Tony kissed her on the lips. "You know, you're as wise as you are beautiful. Well-said!"

"Thank you, Mr. Dash. Why all the questions about love and relationships?"

"*Because*, I'm *madly* in love with you, and it's very important that you and I are on the *same* page. *That's why*, Miss Kensington."

"Well, we're *not* on the same page," said Raven, playfully.

"We are! What makes you think we're not?" asked Tony.

"Because, I'm on page *twenty*, and you're on page *ten*."

Tony laughed. "Come here you!" He held Raven in his arms as they lie on the grass. It felt so good to hold her. "I *love* you, *Raven Kensington*."

"I *love* you too, *Tony Dash*."

"Do you *really love me*?" Tony asked.

"*Yes*, Tony, I sure do."

"Will you tell me again? I *love* hearing you say it."

"*I ... LOVE ... YOU ... TONY ... DASH!*" said Raven, in-between kisses.

* * *

Filming *Gun Shy* was a great experience. Raven continued to give Oscar-winning performances. The director told the cast that the movie would probably wrap ahead of schedule, which is what everyone was hoping for, for one reason or another. Norman told his agent that he enjoyed working with the "lovely" Raven Kensington.

Even while filming her second movie, Raven and Tony saw each other regularly. It was no secret the two were very much in love. They were the best of friends too, which was a *key* ingredient in happy relationships. They got along extremely well, and they enjoyed each other's company, immensely.

* * *

Several months later, Raven and Tony were dining at Palm Biernat's, which had easily become one of their favorite places.

"Why aren't you drinking your champagne?" Tony asked Raven.

"You know me, Tony. It takes me until Christmas to finish one glass." This was Tony's third time asking her that question. Why is that? Raven wondered. "Are you hoping that I get drunk?" she asked him.

Tony laughed. "*No*, sweetheart. I'm not hoping that. Although if you did get drunk, you'd be in the *best* of hands."

Raven started drinking her champagne. As she raised the glass to her lips, tears filled her eyes. "*Tony! Oh … Tony …*"

A *beautiful* ten-carat diamond ring was at the bottom of Raven's champagne glass. Tony was beaming. He'd been wanting to do this for a *long* time now.

Raven's eyes were glued to the enormous rock.

"May I see it please, Raven? I *promise*, I'll give it back to you."

Tony walked over to where Raven was sitting. He flashed a broad smile, as he kneeled down on one knee, and proposed.

All eyes were on Raven and Tony.

"*Raven*, I *knew* when I *first* laid eyes on *you*, that you were the woman of *my* dreams. But I want you to be *much more* than that. You're a woman worth having for *several* lifetimes. I *want* you to be *my wife. Raven Kensington, WILL YOU MARRY ME?*"

Tears filled Raven's eyes. "*Yes*, Tony Dash. *Yes*! I *will marry you*!"

Tony smiled, as he slid the ring on Raven's finger.

Afterwards, the newly-engaged couple shared a passionate kiss, then they hugged.

Onlookers shouted and clapped.

Tony looked into his fiancée's eyes. "*Raven*, you have just made me the *happiest* man in the world tonight. Champagne for everyone!" said an overjoyed Tony Dash. "Champagne for everyone!"

"This is a *big* rock! I'm not going to be able to hold my hand up," said Raven, flashing that trademark smile of hers.

"I can get you a *much* smaller diamond if you'd like."

"I don't think so, Mr. Dash! *Forget* about that."

"That's what I *thought*!" said a beaming Tony. "I *love* you so much, the future *Mrs. Dash. Mrs. Dash*, I *love* the sound of that. But, not *nearly* as much as I love *you*." Tony's eyes reached deep into Raven's. "Raven, I want to spend the rest of my life with *you*. I want us to grow old *together*."

They decided on a Valentine's Day wedding, which was just five months away. Raven wasn't sure if she wanted a big wedding, or if they'd have a small, private one.

Tony told her that it was up to her. It didn't matter to him, as long as they got married. And the sooner, the *better*. Tony signaled to the band leader, and the band immediately started playing, "Ribbon in the Sky," which was one of his and Raven's favorite songs.

"I would love to dance with my future wife. May I please have this dance?" Tony asked Raven.

"You certainly may," said Raven, who kept staring at the gorgeous rock on her finger.

"I'm very *happy* that you love the ring. I was hoping you would, beautiful." Tony told her as they danced.

* * *

Everyone in the world knew that Raven Kensington and Tony Dash were getting married. They were front-page news. "Former NFL Superstar-Running Back Turned Billionaire Business Magnate to Wed Beautiful New Movie Star Siren." News of their engagement was also on every major channel.

Paparazzi took photos of Tony proposing to Raven. Publicity was something that Raven knew she had to get used to. It was obvious the bigger you became, the less privacy you would have. It was incredible how paparazzi seemed to get pictures, even in the most private of moments. They seemed to be everywhere, and sometimes they would surprise celebrities by appearing out of nowhere, with camera in hand.

Raven, like Tony, had been too caught up, enjoying their very *special* moment, to see paparazzi snapping pictures of them. The only people that had mattered to them at the time, were each other.

Tony didn't care if the entire world knew that he loved Raven Kensington, because he did. And she loved him too. That was *all* that mattered to Tony.

* * *

Mae Kensington phoned Raven early the next morning. "Is this *the future*, Mrs. Dash?"

Raven laughed in answer.

"*Missy*, you didn't have to tell me that you're getting married! After all, I'm *only* your mother."

Raven was going to call home and tell everyone, but she knew that she didn't have to now, the media had already done it for her.

"Mommie! I was going to call you this morning. Tony proposed last night. When I made it home, it was *well* after midnight. I was bubbling with excitement, but I wasn't going to wake you up at that hour. I was going to call and tell you something else too."

Raven had received her monstrous check.

"What's that, Miss Future Bride-to-Be?"

"You can *retire*, *and*, you can build your *dream* home!"

Mae Kensington was silent.

"*Mommie?*"

"I'm here, honey. *Repeat* what you just said." Mae Kensington wanted to make sure that she'd heard her oldest daughter correctly.

"I *said* that you can *retire*, *and*, you can build your *dream* home!" Raven said again. "Tell Mr. Ed, *good-bye!*"

Raven thought about her mother all the time. She was the *best* mother that anyone could ever have. Mae had worked hard for many years, to help provide financially for her three children. She was determined to give them a much better life than she had. She worked so that her children would have the *best of everything*.

Charles had always been a good husband, father, and provider, but things were still so expensive, that it took two salaries to make it. So, like many mothers in the world, Mae worked. Even though she worked, her family *always* came first. And now, Mae's days as a restaurant manager weren't just numbered, they were over! And one of the homes that she often looked at in *Elite Homes*, would soon be hers. *She*, was going to be the proud owner of one of those big, luxurious homes.

Mae Kensington was speechless. Raven had kept her word. Mae remembered when Raven was in elementary school. "Those homes are *gorgeous*, aren't they, Mommie?" a then-seven-year-old Raven said to her mother. "*One day*, I'm going to buy you one!"

Tears filled Mae's eyes, as she thought of her oldest daughter. Raven had always sent her hefty checks from her earnings, when she started making money from acting, but she had never been in a position to retire her mother and build her her dream home. But now, with her six-million-dollar movie deal, she was. Hollywood, *no one*, could ever erase what her mother had done for her, and all that she had sacrificed.

Raven had always been very grateful for her mother's unconditional love, parental guidance, and discipline, that she had given her, Trey, and Angie, since birth.

Mae finally found her voice. "Oh, baby. Thank you!"

"No, Mommie, *thank you*. What you've done for *me*, what you have given me, is *priceless*."

Tears fell from Mae's eyes. "Raven, Angie wants to talk to you. She's been standing here reaching for the phone ever since I dialed your number. She acts as if she's about to have a seizure. Here she is." Mae smiled through her tears, as she handed Angie the telephone.

Angie took the cordless phone and walked to her room. She wanted to talk to her sister in private. "Raven?"

"Hi, Ang."

"First of all, congratulations on your engagement! I'm *very* happy for you."

"Thank you."

"Well ... I'm sure you already know, I bought a car earlier this year."

"Yes."

"I ... uh ... need to borrow some money. Tunis Chevrolet is going to pick up my car, if my payments aren't caught up by next Friday. It's my last year of high school. My grades are good. I'll pay you back. *Please*, help a sister out! *Your* sister. I know you're not going to leave your baby sister hanging. Raven?"

Raven laughed. "Angie, how are you going to pay me back and you don't have *nobody's* job?"

Angie laughed hard in answer. "Raven! Please! Come on. I know you got it."

"I *what*?"

"I know you *have* it," said Angie.

"That's *correct*. Just kidding, Ang. I use slang myself *sometimes*, when I'm playing around. But the most *important* thing is *knowing* how to speak *proper*-English. And I know that you know how to, and so do I. And knowing when to speak properly is *key*, like for *example*, when you go on job interviews next week to get a job, in order to pay me back."

Angie laughed. She missed Raven a lot, she always made them laugh.

"How much are we talking, Ang?"

"Six hundred dollars."

"Did you by chance, think that you'd be able to finance a car, not pay for it, and still get to keep it?" Raven asked her sister.

Angie laughed again. "No."

"Looks that way to me," said Raven. She knew that Angie's payments were two hundred dollars a month. Therefore, she was three months behind. Raven smiled, thinking of her baby sister.

Angela Kensington, like many teenagers, loved boys, "cute" and "fine" ones, especially. She loved the latest fashion trends, and she also loved parties and music. Angie was very good with hair. She could cut, style, curl, braid, and weave with the best of them. Angie could do *any* type of hair too. Her customers were of various races, backgrounds, and from all walks of life. Angie made pretty good money doing hair on the weekends.

Raven thought, knowing Angie, she was more than likely using all of her money to buy expensive clothes, instead of paying her car payments. Like many teens, Angie was young, wild, and irresponsible, but Raven loved her little sister, dearly. She was very happy that her sister's grades were very good. And so far, Angie was also staying out of trouble.

"Okay, Ang. And no, you *don't* have to pay me back. I was just kidding. But please learn to manage your funds responsibly. You're *never* too young to learn. Are you picking up, what I'm putting down?"

"Oh yes, Raven. I understand what you're saying."

"*Good.* Have you been paying your car insurance?" Raven was curious.

"Yes. I wasn't going to risk that! I can't afford to have my license taken away."

That statement was very funny to Raven. "Okay, let me *analyze* this *very humorous* situation. Ang, you *really* have things out of order. You're willing to pay your car insurance, but risk having your car repossessed? Did it *ever* occur to you that having car insurance doesn't matter, if you don't have a car?" Raven shook her head. "Do me a big favor, Ang."

"Anything, Raven."

"*Please*, don't tell *anyone* that we're related. I don't know about you, Angela."

Angie laughed hard in answer.

"I'll help you, but remember what I said."

"Thanks a million, Sis!"

"You're quite welcome."

"How's Becky doing?"

"Beck's fine. She's sleeping."

"Tell her hi and give her my love."

"Will do."

"Thanks, again, Sis! Raven?"

"Yes, Ang?"

"Is my future brother-in-law really a *billionaire*?"

"Yes, Ang."

"Does he have *any* brothers, cousins, or young uncles?"

Raven laughed. "Get off the phone, Ang! Give my love to Daddy, Trey, Stephanie, and the kids! I love you, *crazy* girl!"

Shortly after Raven hung up from talking with Angie, their brother Trey called. He congratulated Raven on her engagement, and her success in Hollywood. He told her that he would be coming to L.A. in three days, on business.

Raven wrote down Trey's flight information. "I can't wait to see you!" Raven told Trey. They hadn't seen each other in a year, which was too long by Kensington law. "Oh, no!" said Raven, after hanging up the phone. "I have to be on the set next week." She immediately called Andrew. Raven explained the situation to him. "Andrew, my brother's coming to L.A. on Wednesday. I'd like to pick him up from LAX and spend some time with him. We haven't seen each other in a while. I would like to, if at all possible, take that day off."

"Sure, pretty lady. I don't think that will be a major problem. In fact, I'll contact Lyle. Just go ahead and plan to have that day off. That's hardly anything for anyone to have a heart attack about."

"Thanks, Andy!"

"Are you ready to knock 'em dead again on the set?" Andy asked her.

"You know it! I stay ready," said Raven.

Andrew Spellman laughed. "I know you do. Call me if you need me. And, oh yes, where are my manners? *Congratulations* on your engagement! Mr. Dash is one, *very* lucky man! You're an *extraordinary* woman, Raven. And, if Tony's as awesome as a husband as he was as a running back, you've got a *great* man. And please, pretty lady, don't quit acting because you're *filthy*."

"*Filthy?*"

"*Yes*. Filthy-*rich*. *Billionaire* future husband, along with your six-*million*-dollar movie deal. Need I say *more*?"

Raven laughed in answer. "Don't worry, Andy, I *love* acting."

Raven sat on her bed, thinking about Andrew's last comment. There's no way that I'm going to quit now. I am rich, but that was never my *sole* purpose for becoming an actress. Raven smiled. It was great not having to worry about money though.

Raven was also pleased that she was now able to make other people's dreams come true, family and strangers alike. She had already started donating money and time to some reputable and authorized charities. Raven didn't just want to make a difference in Hollywood, she also wanted to make a difference, in the world.

There was so much, so many things that Raven knew needed to be changed. She hadn't even scratched the surface. But, as she continued to think, she thanked God for the great distance that He had brought her, thus far. Raven certainly couldn't overlook any kind of progress. She had struggled, and she had progressed. She knew that she would continue to struggle. Life was full of struggles. Struggles were a part of life.

Raven smiled, she was playing the game *her* way, and *winning*! Raven felt that she was winning because she was playing the *right* way. She'd always felt that acting should be *more* about a person's talent, and less about the package.

And in Raven's opinion, music wasn't nearly as good as it used to be either, because like Hollywood, it too, was based more on looks and size, instead of *actual* talent.

Raven smiled again. So far, she had kept the promise that she'd made to herself, and to her mother. She had kept her morals and values. She had not become a prostitute, nor had she changed her size.

Raven Kensington was a fighter! And she was determined to continue to fight, not for how Hollywood was now, but for how she wanted it to be, for herself, and *for all those* ...

* * *

On Wednesday, Raven went to pick her brother up from the airport. They were both very happy to see each other. Trey gave his sister a big hug, as he kissed her on the cheek. "Hey, Sis. *Miss Hollywood*!"

Trey laughed as he and Raven were immediately surrounded by autograph seekers. He stood and watched, as his sister graciously gave autograph after autograph. Raven never wanted to take her fans for granted. They played a *large* role in her success. And she loved and appreciated them.

Afterwards, Raven and Trey went to get his luggage, then they left the airport. Raven didn't want to spend a lot of time there. She was eager to be alone with her brother, to catch up on what was happening in his life.

"Wow! *Nice* BMW, Sis. It doesn't surprise me though, you have *always* had *expensive* tastes. Very *nice* car!"

"Thanks," said Raven, as she drove to her and Becky's apartment.

* * *

"Nice pad, Raven. Very nice. Where's Becky?"

"You must have forgotten. She's at work. You know she's the *star* on the new soap, *Day's Dawn*. And speaking of *Day's Dawn*, it's on *now*," said Raven, turning on the TV.

Trey's jaw dropped. "Oh, my, God! *Look* at *Becky*! *Miss Rebecca Simms*, from *Tunis*, Texas. Look at her!" Trey was beside himself with excitement. This was the first time that he had seen *Day's Dawn*. And, like everyone else in Tunis, he was elated seeing two hometown girls doing so well. Raven and Trey watched, "Becky's show," together.

After the show was over, Trey shook his head again. He had watched the show in awe. "*Small* world."

"Yes, Trey, it sure is. Very small world," said Raven.

"Is there a park nearby?"

Raven smiled. "Yes, there is."

Trey knew how much his sister loved parks. "Why don't we get something to eat and go to the park?" Trey suggested. He needed to talk with Raven.

They went to Subway, then headed to the park. Trey looked at his sister. "You're beautiful, Sis. You've always been. You're also wise. I *need* some advice."

Raven sat and listened. She could tell that whatever it was, it was obviously of great concern to her brother. "Shoot."

"I'm thinking about getting a divorce. Things aren't the same between me and Stephanie. The fire's out. We no longer make love, we have sex. And even that doesn't happen that often. She's gained weight. We used to talk, we used to be best friends. Raven, I don't know what changed. We used to be so much in love. I work long hours, but I'm glad that I do. At least when I do come home, she's already asleep. I know how awful that sounds." Trey shook his head. "I don't know, Raven."

"How did it get from where it used to be, to where it is now?" Raven asked her brother.

"I don't know."

"Trey, c'mon now, *of course* you know." Raven could hear all that he didn't say.

Vintage Raven, thought Trey. She could take crumbs and make a cake.

"*Well*, for *one* thing, you know how important making it to the top was to me. Well, as you know, Sis, I *finally* did that. I make six-figures now. I have the big nice house in the suburbs that I've always wanted. I have the black, S500 Benz, that I've always wanted to drive."

"You have money and material things. Are *you* happy?" Raven asked. She could clearly see that he wasn't.

Trey hesitated. "No. No, Sis, I'm *not*. To be truthful, I'm *miserable*." And he looked it too.

Raven took in everything that Trey told her. She looked at her brother. His eyes were that of a very sad man. "Trey, *remember* the things that made you fall in love with Stephanie in the first place. As far as changing, we all change. Change is inevitable. But *how* you change, is what matters. We should all try to change in a positive manner. It's also important to grow, *together*. You also said something that's common, she's gained weight. You've also gained weight. I'm looking at a little gut right now. Trey, you're not exactly the chiseled man that you once were either."

Her brother laughed.

"Where is the *unconditional* love? Unconditional love means loving someone without stipulations or requirements. No fine print. Loving them for *them*, no matter how they look, how they are, etc. *Real* love isn't about Coca-Cola-shaped bodies. Looks aren't everything. And a relationship should *never* be based on looks anyway. Looks can fade away at anytime, for various reasons. Be with someone because of *love*, not looks. If a marriage is based on anything other than the things that it *should* be based on, it's doomed from the start."

"Very true, Sis."

"Attractive things, and attractive people, naturally catch the eye. We are all drawn to pretty things. But *love*, catches the heart. Learn to see with your heart, Trey. It sounds to me like you have neglected your marriage, and focused most of your time and energy, on making money. And as you can see, money's not everything. A relationship has to be built and maintained. Nothing from nothing leaves nothing. You have to put something in, in order to get something out. You are not putting anything into your marriage, and yet you expect to get something out of it? There's *no way* that you should be complaining. You should always make *Stephanie*, your *priority*. Not your business, anything, or *anyone* else. If you weren't going to be a husband to her, then in my opinion, you shouldn't have married her. You should have built your business first, and then, if you chose to get married, you should've done it then, but only if you were willing to commit to it. Marriage is a very serious commitment. You and Stephanie have been married for eight years now. You've lasted longer than many. But try to make it 'til death do you'll apart. And don't just be present, Trey, be *happy*. Don't be so quick to throw in the towel either, not until you've given it *everything* that you've got. And you haven't! Talk to Stephanie. Be open and honest with her, even about your fears. Tell her everything that you have told me, and then some. Take *full* responsibility for your actions. Even if you leave, or divorce Stephanie, you'll be sitting here again, singing the same song. Many people think that the quick fix is to change partners, when sometimes, we need to change *self*. The one and only person that you can change, Trey, is *you*. You have to deal with you. The same problems and habits that you have now, you would carry them into your next relationship, if you were to leave Stephanie. Trey, you're going to have problems with *anyone*, and there are no ifs, ands, or buts about that. The *best* relationships, have problems. We can't escape them. It's how you deal with those problems. Handle your problems, don't let them handle you. Don't give up, Trey, get up! And I don't mind giving you advice, but always go to your partner, in this case, your wife. Open up to her, talk to her, talk *with* her, tell her what you're telling me. After all, you two are the ones in the marriage. Stephanie's a *good* woman. Good women are very hard to find. In a nutshell, if you want a *better marriage*, Trey, you *need* to be a *better husband*."

Trey sat, looking pensive. "You're right, Sis. You are right."

"Anything that's worth having is worth working hard for. It's worth *fighting* for. Relationships are work, but they can also be very rewarding. There is *no* perfect mate. *Every* rose has thorns. And in your case, don't change partners, change *you*. If at all possible, love the one you're with."

Tears filled Trey's eyes. "I still love Stephanie."

"Then *build* on that love! And *fight* for her, fight for you, fight for my nieces and nephew. Fight, for your marriage. And, *boy*, get yourself and your priorities straight! It's obvious, that if money made you happy, you wouldn't be so miserable now. Money is great to have, as long as it doesn't have you. And money will never be a replacement for love. *Never*. Love, is priceless. It's also free."

"Oh, Sis, I love you! What would I do without *you*?"

Raven didn't see Tony watching them. He had decided to surprise Raven, and take her out to lunch. Tony knew that even when Raven was filming movies, she would often go home for lunch, or go to the park. He had gone to her apartment, and when he didn't see her car, he figured she would be at the park. And she was. With *another* man.

Tony sat and watched Raven and Trey. The two seemed to be having a very serious conversation. He'd even seen Raven touch the man's hands, a number of times. When Tony saw them hug, he drove off. He couldn't watch any longer.

"*Raven how* ... could you do this to *me*? *How* ... could you do *this* ... to *us*?" Tony felt as if his heart had been ripped out of him.

* * *

"Speaking of my nieces and nephew, how are they? I'm sure they're getting bigger every day," said Raven.

Trey smiled, thinking of his babies. "Yes, Sis, they're definitely getting bigger every day. Trey Junior's almost as tall as I am."

"How old is he now? *Fourteen*?" Raven asked, trying to calculate in her head.

"*Close*. Fifteen. Sabrina and Lillie are a handful! Lillie reminds me a lot of Angie."

"Save her *now!*" Raven laughed. "One Angie's *more* than enough."

Trey looked at his sister, lovingly. He had always thought highly of her. Raven was just that kind of person. "Raven, it has been a long time since I've smiled, *sincerely.* I can't thank you enough for talking sense into me. I feel so much better. It was obviously the will of God that business brought me to where you were. I knew that if *anyone* could talk sense into me, you could. I probably would have done something very foolish otherwise. I could always talk to you. You are wise, trustworthy, and you have the ability to look at the whole picture. You've always been honest with me too. You don't tell me what I want to hear, you tell me how it is. I like that. You're also a great listener. I love you, Sis."

"I love you too, Trey. Some conversations aren't phone conversations. Perhaps God brought you to L.A., for another reason, besides business. And speaking of business, *always* take care of business at home, *first*. Call me if you need me. I love you."

Brother and sister hugged again.

"Are you coming home for the holidays?" Trey asked his sister.

"I plan to. Maybe I'll bring Tony too."

"You love him a lot, don't you?"

"Yes, Trey, I sure do. I love him very much."

"He'd better be good to my sister!"

"He will. We'll be good to *each* other. And Trey, make sure that you and Stephanie do the same."

"We will. I'm sorry, Sis, but I'm going to cut this trip short. I won't be spending the night in L.A. after all. I'm going to cancel my business meetings too. I need to go home and make things *right*. Take me to the airport."

* * *

On the drive to the airport, Raven and Trey continued to talk.

"Raven? Any *other* advice?"

"Just remember, Trey, we women like to feel *special*. Treat your wife like she's the *only* woman in the world. Treat her like a *queen*. And don't just tell Stephanie that you love her, *show* her. If your actions don't show it, the words are meaningless. Open the door for her. Don't wait for Valentine's Day to buy her flowers … cards … candy. Call Stephanie from work, let her know that you're thinking of her. *Show* her that *she's* the *most* important human being in your life. Because as your wife, she *should* be. Don't take her for granted. *Always* reserve quality time for the two of you, no matter what. And, the word that I really love, *cherish* her, Trey, cherish her! You two *need* to take care of each other. And, who knows? Stephanie may even start watching football with you! You would be *surprised* what a woman will do, when she's *happy*."

Trey laughed. "*Stephanie*? Watching *football*? That'll be the day! You know, Raven, you could have easily been a psychiatrist. I *never* understood where all of your wisdom came from. I guess it comes from God. I am certainly not complaining though. Especially since you don't charge me for advice."

"Says *who*? Your bill will be in Tunis before you get there."

Trey laughed hard in answer.

When they made it to LAX, Raven pulled up curbside and got out to hug her brother. "I love you, Trey. Give my love to Stephanie and the kids. And everyone back home."

"I love you too, Sis. What would I do without you?"

This time, Raven wore a hat and dark sunglasses. She wanted to have a private moment with her brother.

The two hugged again, before parting ways.

* * *

Raven checked her voice mail. Tony still hadn't called. Raven decided to call him. "Tony, hi, baby. Call me when you get this message. I love you." She tried his cell phone. Voice mail. Again. Raven left a similar message, before going to martial arts class.

When Raven returned home hours later, she checked her voice mail again. Tony still hadn't called her back yet. That wasn't like him. *Hmmm* … Raven thought. Where are *you*, love? He's probably on the golf course. Raven knew how much Tony loved playing golf.

* * *

Tony locked his bedroom door. He sat on his bed, thinking about Raven. And although he tried very hard to fight them, the tears came anyway. And they came, in droves. Tony was devastated. He had never cried over a woman before, but he had never loved a woman before either. He *loved* Raven, with *every* fiber of his being. Tony knew that he would never love another woman the way that he loved Raven. *Never.*

Tony got drunk. He knew that he would be sick the next day, but it wouldn't come close to the sickness in his heart. *Nothing* would. All he could think about as he sat on his bed, was *why? Why, Raven? Why?*

* * *

Raven sat on her bed. Her thoughts were on Tony. He was such a *wonderful* man. God couldn't have sent her a *better* man. Tony was so kind and considerate. And it was very obvious to Raven that Tony loved her deeply, and unconditionally. He was also *in* love with her. They were in love with each other. Raven smiled, remembering the very nervous man standing in front of her, when he'd approached her at church, a year and seven months ago. They had come a long way since then. They were very compatible, especially in the ways that mattered most. Raven was looking forward to becoming ... *Mrs. Tony Dash.*

"Did Tony meet Trey?" Becky interrupted Raven's thoughts.

"No. I forgot to tell him that Trey was coming today. So much has been on my mind lately. I called Tony, but he hasn't called me back yet. But it's too late, Trey's gone now."

"*Gone?*" Becky asked. "I thought he was going to spend the night in L.A."

"Yes, he was," said Raven. "But he decided to go back earlier."

"Everything all right with Stephanie and the kids?" Becky asked.

"Hopefully they will be. He and Steph's having some problems."

"Oh. Well, I know that you gave him a *good* talking to." Becky laughed.

"Yes, I did. I think they'll be fine. I *hope* so anyway. As I told him, everyone has problems. Whether you're in a relationship or not, there will *always* be problems."

"*No kidding*. John and I have a very good relationship, but we still have problems, and disagreements," said Becky.

"Tony and I do too. That's what I told Trey. He seemed better after our talk. How was your day? Is John coming over later?"

"My day was *great*! I'm *loving* this! It's what I *love*. It's what I've dreamt of. And to answer your other question, *no*, John's not coming over later. I'm going to shower, eat dinner, and relax. What about you?"

"I don't think I'm going anywhere. I'll just talk with Tony on the phone, our usual, nightly-talk, and rest and relax too. I have to arrive on the set early in the morning, so, like you, I *need* sleep."

Raven checked her voice mail again, Tony still hadn't called. He hadn't returned her pages either. I hope everything's all right. It's not like you, Tony. Where are *you*? Are you okay? Raven wondered. She called him again. Voice mail. Night came and went, and Tony still, had not called.

    * * *

Tony woke up the next morning with the *worst* hangover imaginable. He stayed in his bathroom, vomiting, for most of the morning.

"Mr. Dash, are you all right?" Mack asked. He was concerned about him. He'd seen Tony when he came home, and his boss looked like someone who he had loved dearly, died. When Mack asked him if everything was okay, Tony shook his head no, as he went to his bedroom and closed the door behind him. It was obvious to Mack that his boss wanted to be left alone.

Tony finally stopped vomiting long enough to answer Mack. "Uh! *Oh*, Mack. I'm *sick* as a dog!"

When Mack saw the empty bottles of Jack Daniel's on the dresser, he knew that his boss had a hangover. "I will be right back,

Mr. Dash."

Mack left to get Tony some Alka-Seltzer. He also brought him a cold glass of 7-Up, and some Excedrin, for his headache. "Here you are, Mr. Dash. This should help. This, and *no more* drinking for the next five years," said Mack. "Oh yes, I forgot to tell you, your mother came by yesterday while you were out. She wants you to call her."

"Thanks, Mack. I'll give her a call later. The *only* thing I want to do now is feel *better*."

"Care to talk about it?" Mack asked. He and his boss were pretty good friends. And they had been for some time now. Mack couldn't help but wonder if Tony and the sultry-beauty on the photo had a fight. If he was right, it had to have been a very *big* one, from the looks of things.

"No, Mack, I don't want to talk about it. Thanks," said Tony. He appreciated everything Mack had brought him, but it was his heart, that hurt most. And, unfortunately, there was only one remedy for that.

After showering and brushing his teeth, Tony checked his voice mail. Raven had called a number of times. He didn't listen to her messages completely, because it was *far* too painful hearing her voice. *That* voice. He had even placed the photo face down. Looking at *her*, was even *more* painful.

How am I supposed to live my life without *you*, Raven? *How*? Tony was wise enough to know that he could live without her, but he didn't want to. Without the woman he loved, he was going to be one, very *miserable* man. He went to sleep, with Raven, on his mind, and still very much, in his heart. And Tony knew, that she would *always* be.

    * * *

When Tony awoke hours later, everything was feeling better. Everything, except his heart. And he knew that that would *never* heal. He decided to go to his home-gym to workout, which is something he did daily. Tony was in the gym for hours, when he looked up and saw his mother, walking through the door.

"I'm glad I'm not that punching bag!" Carol Dash looked at her only child. He looked awful. Something was very wrong. This was not the Tony she was used to seeing.

Tony managed a weak smile. "Hi, Mom." He kissed his mother on the cheek. "I would hug you, but as you can see, I'm all sweaty."

"What's going on, Tony? What's wrong? You've been on my mind. And from looking at you, it's very obvious that something's going on. *What* is it?"

"*Mom*, I ..." Tony couldn't lie to his mother. She wouldn't have believed him anyway. She knew him far too well. And his parents also raised him to be honest. Tony hit the punching bag hard a few more times, as he took a deep breath. "Mom, Raven and I ... are ... *no* longer." It almost killed Tony to say that.

Carol Dash looked startled. "Tony, what do you mean, you're *no longer*? *What* happened? Let's go outside on the terrace and talk. Get your mother some iced-tea first, please."

"Yes, ma'am."

Mack shooed Tony out of the kitchen. "I'll get that for you, sir. That's one of the reasons you pay me. And very well, I might add. Get out of here! I'll get it. Two iced-teas coming right up!"

True to his word, Mack brought two deliciously-cold glasses of iced-teas on the terrace.

"Thanks, Mack," said Tony and his mother, in unison.

"You'll are welcome. Please let me know if you need anything else."

"We will, Mack, thanks," said Tony.

Carol Dash looked into her son's eyes. "I'm *listening*, Tony. What happened?"

"*Another* man," said Tony. "I saw Raven in the park yesterday, with another ... man."

His mother sat and listened. It was hard to believe. She'd spent time with Raven. She didn't strike her as the *cheating* kind. But many didn't, thought Carol. "Wait a minute. You saw Raven with *another man*? Doing *what*?" his mother asked.

"*Talking*. She would also touch his hands from time to time, not to mention, I saw them hugging." Tony's voice cracked.

His mother's heart went out to him. But she was certain that Tony had misread the situation.

"*Tony*, I'm touching your hands now. That doesn't mean that I'm your lover. You and I both know that it's just an affectionate gesture of love, between a mother and son. Now, *if* you saw Raven *French* kissing the man, that would certainly be *a lot* different. Did you see that? Or anything *sexual* in nature?"

Tony didn't hesitate. "No, Mother. Nothing sexual in nature. Just a young, handsome man. They were having a deep conversation, and what I shared with you before."

Carol Dash began to put the pieces together. "Does Raven have a brother?"

"Yes. But he lives in Texas."

"Have you ever seen her brother?"

"No, I haven't."

Tony's mother looked pensive. "She's not cheating on you, Son, or playin' you, as you young folks say. I bet my life on that. Raven doesn't strike me as that type of woman. I know that people aren't always who they seem to be, but I don't think that's the case with Raven. I *really* don't."

"God knows how I wished that were true, Mother. I don't know, maybe it's God's way of paying me back for my earlier behavior."

"*Earlier* behavior?" his mother asked.

"Yes, Mother. I'd sleep with females, using them for sex. I didn't care about *any* of them. I never loved them either. And when I *finally* find a woman, who I am *knee-deep*, in love with, the tables turn. Maybe it's just payback. We all have to pay the piper," Tony said sadly.

"*Son*, those girls were just as much to blame as you were. You didn't *rape* them. And it's not surprising to me that you didn't care about them, or love them. *Most* men, when they *do* get married, they look for women like Raven Kensington. A woman who dresses *respectfully*, and leaves *things* to the imagination. A woman with morals and values, great integrity. *Anyone* can see that Raven's an *extraordinary* woman. Men don't often marry the easy, or the sleazy females, who they can have their way with. The ones who have slept with Tom, Dick, and Harry. Those kind of females are not respected either. Son, you were also targeted because they knew who *you* were, make no mistake about that. They wanted money. You wanted sex." Carol Dash pointed a playful finger at her son. "And *you*! I've always told you to wait until you got married before you had sex. But *no-oo* ... like so many of you guys, and girls, you'll just can't wait. Abstinence seems out of the question."

Tony laughed.

"Your father and I raised you well. I can't control what you do as an adult, but you were a very good boy growing up. You always behaved, always made straight-A's in school, and you always did what your father and I asked you to do. You never gave us any problems. You've turned out to be a very good man. You are a *great* man, Tony Dash. I'm very proud of you, Son."

"Thanks, Mother. I haven't slept with *anyone*, since I met Raven. She's the *only* woman I want, in bed and out of bed. Once you go Raven, you *never* go back."

His mother laughed. Carol Dash could easily see how very much her son loved Raven. He was *crazy* about her.

Tony went on. "She's *incomparable*, Mother. I've never known *anyone* like her. And I doubt if I ever will. I'd give her the world. There is nothing, that I wouldn't do for Raven. *Nothing*. Her happiness means *everything* to me. She, means everything to me. I have *never* loved so deeply in my life."

Carol could tell by her son's eyes, that he meant *every* word. She hoped and prayed that it was a male friend, or even better than that, a relative. If Tony was right, Carol Dash couldn't begin to imagine, what losing the woman he loved so deeply and dearly, would do to her son. Carol knew that losing Raven would leave a *permanent* hole in her son's heart, and a very *big* one at that.

"Mother, what did you think of Raven when you first met her?"

His mother had already told him, but Tony wanted to hear it again.

"*Jackpot.* I *knew* that you had hit the jackpot, Son. Raven's a *gold mine.* She's a very *distinguished* woman. *Rare.* She's a woman *ahead* of her time. I thought her *exquisitely*-beautiful. She's very intelligent, classy, elegant, respectful, and respectable. Raven is a woman of great integrity. And I knew, *correction*, I *know*, that she will be a *great* wife. She's the *best* daughter a mother could have."

Tony smiled.

"And by *all* means, you *better* be very good to her too. I'll tell you something else that I've *never* told you about Raven Kensington."

"What's that, Mother?" Tony was very curious.

"She's going to touch the lives of many, many people."

"She's an *actress*, Mother. And a great one at that, not to mention the *most* beautiful woman that I have *ever* laid eyes on."

Carol Dash shook her head. "*No*, Son. Raven touching lives, has *nothing* to do with Hollywood. It has *everything* to do with *her*, as a person. As a human being. Raven Kensington's going to touch many lives, before she leaves this world. *Many.*"

"Mother, what about *us*?"

Carol's heart went out to her son. She had never seen Tony look so miserable in his life. "You and Raven?"

Tony nodded.

"*Sweetheart*, I'm *not* worried about you two. You'll are going to grow old, *together.*"

"If only that were true," said a heartbroken Tony.

"*Tony Dash*! No matter how old you get, Son, you will *never* catch up with me!"

Tony laughed.

"What do you mean, if only that were true? It *is* true, Tony. Do not question your mother. I'm not just *talking.* *Everything* that I've told you, is *true*. Your paths crossed for a reason, as with *all* things. Everything, happens for a reason. *Nothing* happens by chance. Now, *stop* talking to me, and *call* Raven! I want you to talk with *her*. Not over the phone either. Tell her what you've told me. Also, let me know what happens. Sometimes, we're quick to assume. *Never* assume, always *know*, find out, *first*. You didn't handle this right, Son. You should have talked to Raven, first, instead of jumping to conclusions. It would have saved you from that *awful* hangover!" Carol had seen the empty Jack Daniel's bottles in the trash can. "And communicating with her, would have saved you from the *greatest* ache of all, in this case, *temporary*-heartache. *Always* communicate, Tony, always! Communication is very important in healthy and happy relationships. It's a *must*. *Learn* from this. Lay your cards on the table. Raven is your companion, and when you two get married, you'll be as one. I love you, Son. Don't forget to call me later."

"Mother?"

"Yes, Son."

"Where did that come from? How do you know that Raven will touch the lives of many people?"

"Just *trust* me on that one. I knew that when I first saw her. We don't always know how or why, but sometimes, God lets us know things. I love you, Son. Now, *go* make things right. I suggest you move fast, Tony, a woman like that has a line around the corner!" Carol Dash knew that a woman like Raven Kensington didn't come around often. Any man would be elated, to have her as a wife.

After his mother left, Tony immediately called Raven. He knew that she was on the set still. He left a message on her voice mail. He told her that he had to talk with her. "It's very important. I *love* you so much, Raven." Tony couldn't deny that he loved Raven, nor did he want to. Whatever happened, Tony wanted Raven to know, how very much he loved her.

* * *

When Raven came home, Tony was waiting for her. He drove them to his house, so they could talk in private.

Raven and Tony sat by the pool, sipping on the iced-tea that Mack had brought out to them. When Mack left, Tony cut right to the chase. He *had* to know, the suspense was killing him. So was his heart.

"Raven, I saw you yesterday, at the park. My emotions got the best of me. When I saw you touch the man's hands, and I saw you'll hug, I left. The first thing that I thought was ... you were cheating on me. Are you, Raven? Are you *cheating* on me?" It was as if Tony's heart stopped, as he waited for Raven's answer.

Raven quickly put two and two together. Tony didn't know that it was her brother, that he had seen her with at the park. "Tony, *look* at me. Look into my eyes." Raven's eyes reached deep into Tony's. "*No*, I'm not *cheating* on you, nor would I ever cheat on you. You are the *only* man that I want, Tony Dash. I love *you*. If I wanted to end our relationship, I would come to you and tell you. I wouldn't do a thing like *that*. That's not me. That's *not* who I am. I thought you knew me better than that. The man that you saw was my *brother*, Trey. I was touching him, out of *sisterly*-love, affection. He and his wife are having problems right now. I love *you*, Tony Dash! And *only*, *you*." Raven shook her head. "*Oh ... Tony*. Don't you *know* how much I love *you*?"

Tony breathed a *huge* sigh of relief. "Raven ... you don't know how ecstatic I am to hear that! I'm so sorry. I didn't do things the *right* way. I should have talked to you first, instead of assuming. My life was in a tailspin. Losing you was *unthinkable*. Still is. As long as I have *you*, Raven, I have *nothing*, to lose. I love you more than life itself. You know how much I love you. This is one time in my life, that I am very happy, to have been *wrong*. I *love* you, beautiful. I love you *so* much!" Tony told Raven that he loved her, repeatedly. "*Thank You, God*! *Thank You*! I'm *so sorry*, baby. I'm so sorry, beautiful."

"Your apology is accepted. I love you too."

Raven and Tony shared a long, passionate kiss.

* * *

"*Wow!*" said Tony. "*What* a kiss! Maybe we should fight more often," he joked.

Raven laughed. "If you want to call it that. It was simply a misunderstanding. Although it could have been a very costly one. *Never* assume. Come to me. Communicate, sweetheart. *Always.*"

"I promise, I will. I will *never* assume again." Tony took it as a lesson learned. Raven was right, it could have been very costly.

They sat poolside, talking for hours. Tony watched Raven with love and admiration. He loved her more than anyone, and more than anything in the world. Tony couldn't imagine life without Raven. She, was his life.

Tony drove Raven home later that evening, and kissed her good night. "I love you very much, beautiful."

* * *

Carol Dash was elated when Tony phoned her with the great news. And, like any mother, she was happy that her baby was happy. No matter how old her son got, he would always be her baby.

* * *

Raven checked her voice mail. Trey had phoned with some great news of his own. He had left the kids with the sitter, and he and Stephanie had gone away for the weekend. In her brother's words, his and his wife's weekend getaway had been romantic, great therapy, and filled with renewed promises and hopes. Raven smiled, that was *exactly* what she wanted to hear.

Raven took her bath and went to bed. And like clockwork, Tony called later that night. They talked for hours, before Tony heard sleep in Raven's voice.

"I hear sleep in that beautiful voice of yours. Good night, Sleeping Beauty. I *love* you."

"'Night, baby. I *love* you too."

Tony stayed awake most of the night thinking about Raven. Time wasn't moving fast enough for him. He couldn't wait for Valentine's Day to arrive. Raven's face was the *last* face that Tony wanted to see, when he closed his eyes at night. Tony smiled. It was also the *first* face that Tony wanted to see, when God opened his eyes every morning.

* * *

When Raven arrived on the set the next day, there were two dozen, red, long-stemmed roses waiting for her. She smiled, as she read the card that was attached. "With *all* my love, *Tony*!"

"Whew! Someone *loves* you!" said Chad Steele, a co-star in the movie. He knew that more than likely the roses were from Raven's fiancé. The media had notified the entire world of their engagement. Chad remembered the headlines when he'd first seen the announcement in the paper. He had read the entire article. Chad also noticed that the media often referred to Raven as a bombshell. He agreed with them. She was a very beautiful and sultry woman. Chad wasn't the only man who shot Raven admiring looks on the set. He, like a lot of men, would have loved to trade places with Tony Dash. Who wouldn't want a woman like Raven Kensington? "That Mr. Dash is an *extremely* lucky man!" Chad told Raven, who only smiled in answer.

* * *

Raven went to her trailer to phone Tony. "*Thanks*, baby! The roses are *beautiful*! I have to go now." Raven heard Andy calling her. "I *love* you!"

"I *love* you too, beautiful," said Tony.

After hanging up with Raven, Tony phoned Bruce-Hexton Builders, which was one of the companies that he owned. It was the same company that built the home he lived in now. Tony was very pleased with their work. They were the best in the area, and had been, for many years.

When Tony was informed that Joseph Bruce and Brice Hexton were selling their company, Tony purchased it. But not before *thoroughly* checking out the company, *including*, seeing *all* business records, *past* and *present*. When Tony knew that it would be a very solid, and immensely-profitable business investment, he wrote a check.

Tony was young, but he had already made a *big* name for himself in the business world. He was a very shrewd and successful businessman. And although Tony had an MBA, he learned a lot from working with his father, who was a very successful entrepreneur for many years.

Tony arranged to meet with Joe Junior, the previous owner's son, who now worked for him. They planned to meet the following Saturday, to sketch out the plans, to build his and Raven's *new dream home*. In *Malibu*.

* * *

Chapter 6

Tony picked Raven up the following Saturday.

"Where are we going?" Raven asked him.

"We are *going*, to Bruce-Hexton's. They're going to build our home in Malibu." Tony smiled. He saw Raven's eyes light up. He knew that she wanted to live by the water. "I figured we'd better get things started. Do you want a big home or a small one?"

"Small. *Very* small," said Raven. "*Hmmm*, probably about two rooms."

Tony laughed, he knew that she was kidding. "*C'mon*, beautiful, let's have *at least* three rooms!"

"*Hmmm* ... that's *pushing* it, sweetheart, but okay."

A half-hour later, they were standing in Joe Junior's office.

Joe Junior greeted his boss with his usual firm handshake and smile. He liked Tony. He was a good man to work for. Joe Junior thought Tony Dash a business genius. Sales had more than doubled each year under Tony Dash's ownership.

Tony paid his employees well. It was important to him that his employees, and their families, be able to live well. Tony knew that his employees worked hard to keep his business successful, therefore, they deserved a piece of the pie too.

"Hi, Joe Junior. How's it going? Joe Junior, this is ..."

"*Raven Kensington*! *Oh … my … God*! I had *no* idea ... *Oh …*
Miss Kensington! It's a *pleasure* to meet you! You're even more
beautiful in person! *Wow.* May I *please* have your autograph?" said
Joe Junior, handing Raven a pen and paper. "My son is in love with
you. May I *please* get an autograph for little Joey too?"

Raven flashed her trademark smile. "Sure."

Joe Junior finally calmed down and got down to business. He
looked at Tony, who had been totally forgotten, for a moment
anyway. "I'm sorry, boss, I didn't mean to lose it. But it's not every
day that you see a *big* celebrity face-to-face." Joe Junior took a deep
breath. He shook his head. He couldn't believe it. *The*, Raven
Kensington, was in *his* office. Standing right in front of him!

"It's okay, it's quite all right," said Tony, who knew what being
a celebrity was like. Tony also knew that even if Raven wasn't a
celebrity, she would still get a lot of attention, because she was a
stunningly-beautiful woman. "Now, are we *ready* for *business*?"

"Yes, sir, boss!" Joe Junior was still beaming.

Raven, Tony, Joe Junior, and his assistant, Malik Jones, spent
hours drawing the designs for Raven and Tony's fifty-thousand-
square foot, beachfront mansion, in Malibu. The palatial home would
sit on twenty acres. The secluded, monstrous estate, would boast
thirty-two rooms, complete with two spacious guesthouses, heated,
Olympic-size indoor and outdoor pools, three marble Jacuzzis, movie
theater, game room, wet bar, and tennis and basketball courts. The
home would also have walls of windows and French doors, with
city-to-ocean views. There would also be a huge library, wine cellar,
skating rink, built-in fish tanks, a huge, state-of-the-art gym, gallery,
golf course, and waterfalls. The home would also feature twenty-
foot-high ceilings, crown molding throughout, and marble flooring in
all ten bathrooms, hallways, utility rooms, and in the huge, gourmet
kitchen. Floor-to-ceiling, marble fireplaces, would also be in most of
the rooms, including a large, see-through fireplace, in the all-white,
marble master bath. The grand living area would have a magnificent,
winding staircase. Cream-colored, ankle-deep carpet would cover

most of the floors. The main living area would have a cascade waterfall in the center of the room, along with a skylight. A large terrace would be adjacent to the master suite. Two spacious rooms would serve as offices, for Raven and Tony. The home would also be equipped with an indoor carwash, a twenty-car-attached garage, and a state-of-the-art recording studio.

"Elevators too. In case we ever break a leg," said Raven.

The entire home was Raven-designed. Tony made it very clear that the builders were to do, whatever "his baby" wanted. The foursome went over the plans thoroughly, checking for accuracy. Finally, Raven gave her seal of approval.

Joe Junior assured Raven and Tony that they would begin building immediately.

Raven and Tony thanked Joe Junior and Malik before leaving, after a long, but successful afternoon.

When Raven and Tony left, Malik looked puzzled. "Wasn't that? *No.* It *couldn't* be. But ..."

Joe Junior nodded. "It was *her*! *Raven Kensington*! I got her autograph too, dude!" Joe Junior smiled. "Well actually, I got two, one for my son and one for *me*. I *like* her! She's also down-to-earth. She's not snooty like a lot of them are."

Malik nodded. "I agree. She's very nice, not to mention very easy on the eyes. I don't blame Mr. Dash, I would marry a woman who looked like *that* too." Malik shook his head. "*Boy*! Talking about a stunner!" Malik looked pensive. "Dude, she's like the *total* package ... She's *all* that! Beauty, brains, and *that* body. I *love* her voice too. Raven Kensington's like *whoa*! Don't you dare tell Mr. Dash that I said this, but he's one *lucky* dog!"

"Boy, is he ever!" said Joe Junior. "He's crazy in love with her too, dude. Does she have *exceptional*-tastes, or what? This is going to be the *most* lavish home that we've ever built! A *true* beauty. As gorgeous, timeless, and elegant, as the woman who will own it."

* * *

"Well, I feel better." Tony told Raven when they got in the car. "I wanted us to get the house taken care of." He kissed Raven's hand. "I love you, beautiful."

"I love you too, sweetheart."

Raven and Tony went back to Raven and Becky's apartment. Becky and John were there watching a movie.

The foursome spent the rest of the evening watching movies and talking. Tony and John talked a lot about sports, while Raven and Becky talked show business.

Later that evening, when the guys left to go get dinner platters for everyone, Raven showed Becky the floor plans of her and Tony's dream home in Malibu.

"Wow! Sis, it's going to be *breathtaking*, not to mention *humongous*. Are you and Tony sure you'll have *enough* room?"

Raven laughed in answer.

"On my way to the studio Friday, I saw a *gorgeous* home in Beverly Hills that's for sale. I don't want to build a home from the ground up yet," said Becky.

"Are you and John going to get married?"

"We've been engaged for a few years now, but I still don't want to get married yet. We'll more than likely live together first."

"Whatever floats your boat," Raven told Becky. "As I've always told you, don't get married unless you're ready to, which will be when it's right for the two people involved. It's also very important that you are right for each other."

"Like you and Tony."

Raven smiled. "Like me and Tony."

     * * *

John shook his head in amazement, as he sat across from Tony at the dinner table that evening. It had taken him a while getting used to the fact, that the guy who he had posters of in his room, was now a pretty good friend of his. And although John had seen and met a lot of celebrities, as far as he was concerned, star-athletes, especially superstar-athletes like Tony Dash, were on another level. John was a sports fanatic. And he had always been a huge, Tony Dash fan.

* * *

After dinner, Becky suggested they all go see a movie. And since she and Raven had chosen the last movie that they'd all gone to see, it was the men's turn to choose this time. Tony and John chose an action flick, which wasn't a surprise to Raven or Becky.

* * *

By year's end, Raven Kensington was Hollywood's hottest star. She was the most photographed person in Tinseltown. She had wrapped her second movie, which received rave reviews from critics and fans everywhere. Raven was on the cover of countless magazines. Her face graced the cover of *People* magazine's "100 Most Beautiful People."

Raven was also on countless talk shows. Norman would often join her, as they worked together to promote their new movie, *Gun Shy*. Norman was happy to spend time with Raven for any reason. And promoting their new movie was a good excuse to do just that.

Andrew Spellman couldn't keep up with the many offers that flooded in often, for his most sought-after client. Raven was now in a position to choose her roles. She was also in a position to command a higher salary.

Fans couldn't get enough of Raven. Parents *loved* her, they thought her the *epitome* role model. They loved everything that the young beauty stood for. And didn't, stand for. Males drooled over her. Females loved her beauty, class, and elegance. Children were also crazy about Raven. Little girls around the world chose Raven Kensington as the celebrity they most wanted to look like, and be like.

Raven's fans made it clear that *she* was the reason that they had gone to see *Gun Shy*, not Norman Sheers. The beautiful and multi-talented Raven Kensington, had arrived!

Raven beamed every time she saw all of the massive fan mail that poured in daily for her. She also received a number of threatening letters, some with racist dialogue. Raven refused to let cowards stop her. Raven was always as careful and as cautious as anyone could possibly be, but she'd decided long ago, that she was going to live in faith, not fear. Raven laughed to herself, she couldn't worry about "the haters," as her sister, Angie, called them.

Raven sat at the desk in her office. She skimmed through the *People* magazine. Raven was doubly-thrilled because Becky was also on *People's* "100 Most Beautiful" list.

Raven flashed that trademark smile of hers, as she looked at her face on the cover, staring back at her. *Finally*, it's happening ... to *me*. It's happening, to *us*, thought Raven, thinking of Becky. And as far as Raven Kensington was concerned, success couldn't be happening to two better people.

Raven's thoughts went to the upcoming holiday. The next day was Thanksgiving. She had so much to be thankful for. Her life, good health, her family, which included Becky, her friends, Andy, her career, and last but not least, the love of her life, her future husband, Tony Dash.

Raven's *favorite holiday*, as *everyone* knew, was definitely *Christmas*. The day after Thanksgiving, through New Year's, was Raven's favorite time of year.

Raven sat looking out the window at the City of Angels. Traffic was light. Raven figured it was because many people were out of town for Thanksgiving. She was going to spend Thanksgiving in Brentwood with the Dashs, and Becky was going to spend hers with John and his family, in Woodland Hills.

⸎ ⸎ ⸎

The following month, Raven, Tony, Becky, and John flew to Texas for Christmas. Raven and Becky received a warm welcome from their families, and the entire Tunis community, who were very proud of them. Everybody and their momma had a copy of the *People* magazine, as well as all of the magazines, that Raven and Becky graced. Everyone followed their careers very closely. Many still couldn't believe it, but they knew, that the two hometown girls, had made it *big*.

Angie Kensington told everyone about her celebrity sister. She loved telling anyone who had ears, about *her* sister, the movie star. She also talked proudly about Becky, her sister's best friend, who was also a big star in Hollywood.

Angie remembered when she and Raven sat in their parents' bedroom the night that Raven had graduated from high school. She knew that her older sister was going to make her dreams become reality, and that's exactly what she had done. Angie was so proud of Raven.

Mae Kensington loved the lavish, eighty-two-hundred-square-foot, gated home, that Raven had built for her. Mae could have built any size home that she wanted, but as far as she was concerned, eight thousand plus square feet, was more than enough room. For anyone.

Charles Kensington also loved the new home. He could have retired, but he decided to keep working. It was very comforting to Charles to know, that if he were ever laid off, or if he just didn't want to work anymore, he wouldn't have to worry about his family being taken care of. He, like everyone else, was very proud of Raven. Charles continued to keep her in his prayers. He knew that it wasn't the easiest life one could have, but his daughter seemed happy, so he was happy.

* * *

Before Becky left the Kensingtons that evening, she turned to Raven. "Sis, maybe we should send Susan Porter a copy of *this People* magazine. I'm sure she's *very* busy eating crow now." Becky had a good memory, and a very good point. "What was it that she'd said? *Fat chance*? Well, as you told her that day, it was a *very fat chance* that she was right. And, as usual, you proved her wrong. Apparently, she had no idea *who* she was talking to."

Raven flashed her trademark smile. "Crow's a *tough* bird to eat, isn't it, Beck?"

Becky laughed. "It sure is, Sis! It sure is."

* * *

The holidays at the Kensington household were busy and festive. Raven arrived in time to help her mother and Angie prepare Christmas dinner. Tony offered to help, but Mae Kensington shooed him playfully out of the kitchen.

"Get out of here, Tony! Charles and Trey, get him out of here! You're just trying to keep an eye on Raven. She's *not* going anywhere," his future mother-in-law teased.

Everyone laughed.

Most of Raven's family were in awe of Tony at first. This was the guy whom they had watched for years, running down the field. The *unstoppable*, "T.D." Tony had shattered every record imaginable. And because of his unmatched-talent, he was also the richest athlete. He signed the most lucrative contract in the history of professional sports, ever.

Tony, Charles, and Trey sat in the den, watching sports, and discussing who they thought would win the Super Bowl. All three men agreed that the Dallas Cowboys, who were playing better than they'd played when they were the team to beat in the '90s, would win.

"My baby's team is going to win," said Tony, who knew that Raven was a huge Dallas Cowboys fan.

"*Your* baby? Raven's *my* baby!" Charles Kensington joked.

Trey laughed. "Men, *stop* it! She's *both* of your baby. *Okay*?"

* * *

The Kensington home was beautifully-decorated. The big white Christmas tree had every ornament imaginable. And everyone had a stocking hanging over the fireplace, including Tony.

Raven's family welcomed Tony with open arms. Mae made special preparations for Christmas that year, because she knew that her future son-in-law would be coming. She also knew that Christmas was her oldest daughter's favorite holiday, and she wanted it to be special, the best one ever.

* * *

Mae stood in her elegant and spacious living room, looking at the beautiful tree. She thought about how much Raven *loved* Christmas. Her oldest daughter always made a big fuss about Christmas. Every year, Raven would put the tree up the day after Thanksgiving. And she loved watching the Christmas cartoons. Especially her favorite one, *Rudolph the Red-Nosed Reindeer*. Mae smiled, as she thought about then and now. She was very blessed. She had a healthy family who loved each other. Mae was also happy, that although her children had grown up, they were still very close. And that meant a lot to her. God and family, were *everything* to Mae Kensington.

   * * *

On Christmas Day, after exchanging gifts, everyone washed their hands, then went to the formal dining room, where Christmas dinner was awaiting them. There was turkey, ham, dressing, all kinds of vegetables, dinner rolls, yams, pies, cakes of every kind, the list was endless.

Before eating, everyone held hands and bowed their heads, as Charles Kensington blessed the food. Everyone was hungry. It didn't take anyone long to start digging in.

"Wow! Raven was right, Mrs. Kensington, you are an *awesome* cook!" Tony had never tasted food so good. His mother was a great cook, but no one came close to Mae Kensington. No one.

Mae Kensington smiled. "Thanks, Son."

The Kensingtons *loved* Tony, and he, loved them. And everyone could easily see, how deeply, he loved Raven. There wasn't a doubt in anyone's mind. Raven's family knew that Tony would take very good care of her. And that was very important to all of them.

Whenever Tony was out of earshot, Angie would ask Raven, repeatedly, if Tony had any brothers, even though Raven had already told her a thousand times that he didn't.

Angie read the *People* magazine article aloud that evening to everyone. She was very proud of Raven and Becky. Their success did something else for her. Angie realized that she could also turn her dreams into reality. Angie knew that it hadn't been easy for her sister. And although it hadn't been easy for Becky either, her race, made it easier for her. I may be young and wild, but I'm not as naive as people think I am, Angie thought to herself.

    * * *

    The next day, when Raven, Tony, and Angie decided to go to the mall, Angie was stunned to find paparazzi outside the gates of their home, taking photos. Angie loved it. She let down the car window. "Hello, everyone! I am the younger sister of the very beautiful and talented movie star, Raven Kensington. And, as you can all see, good looks run in our family! I shall be going now. I love you all!" said Angie, blowing kisses.

    Raven shook her head. "I don't know what we're going to do with you, Ang. I really don't know. Baby, what do you think we should do with her?"

    "Please, beautiful, leave me out of this. *You* decide."

    Angie sat in the backseat laughing.

    "There's nothing we can do. There's just no hope for you, Ang."

    Tony picked Becky and John up so they could go to the mall with them.

    "Let's go visit Mrs. Riley first," said Becky. "Momma says she's always asking about us."

    "Sure," said Raven. She looked at the others. "Does anyone mind if we pay our sixth grade teacher a visit?"

    "Not at all," Tony, John, and Angie spoke in unison.

    * * *

Tanya Riley was very surprised, but elated, to see Raven and Becky. She, like everyone else in Tunis, followed their careers very closely. Tanya Riley knew, years ago, that the beautiful little girl with the attention-getting eyes, and Miss America smile, was *going* to "make it." There was never a doubt in her mind.

The teacher gave Raven and Becky big hugs. "What a *pleasant* surprise! How are you two doing? I am *so* proud of both of you! I knew you ladies would make it though. I *knew* it! *Look* at the two of you. You'll are so beautiful. I've followed *everything* the two of you have done so far. *Brilliant* acting, you two, simply brilliant!"

They visited with their sixth grade teacher for about an hour.

Raven invited Mrs. Riley to her and Tony's wedding. "In fact, please give me your address, Mrs. Riley. I'll also mail you an invitation."

"I'll be there. With bells on!" Mrs. Riley looked at Tony and smiled. "You are a very *lucky* man. *Very* lucky."

"Yes, I am, Mrs. Riley. I couldn't agree with you more," said Tony.

* * *

They were shopping at Saks Fifth Avenue, when someone recognized Raven, Becky, and Tony.

"*Wait* a minute ..." said the clerk. "Didn't I go to school with you'll? *Oh, my, God*! *Raven Kensington* and *Rebecca Simms*!" The clerk looked at Tony. "I would know *that* handsome face and *fine* body anywhere! Your posters are all over my brother's room! *Tony Dash*! It *is*! Oh, my! *Everybody*!" Sun-Yoo screamed at the top of her lungs.

John looked uneasy, as they were immediately surrounded by screaming fans, wanting autographs.

Raven, Becky, and Tony started giving autographs, while Angie and John stood by and watched.

"I guess *no one* wants *my* autograph." Angie joked. "Just *act* like you don't see *this* celebrity! It's okay though."

The crowd roared with laughter.

They left the mall quickly when things started getting out of hand. There were people pushing, shoving, running, and screaming. There weren't enough security officers to maintain and control the ever-growing crowd.

"Whew!" said John, as they ran to the car and quickly drove away. "The price of being a star."

Raven and Becky were now used to being recognized wherever they went. They would disguise themselves sometimes, in order to have privacy. They were very grateful for their fans, but they were also human.

"They treated me like I was *chopped*-liver," said Angie. "And *this* Miss Kensington doesn't like that one bit!"

* * *

After spending a week in Texas, Becky and John headed back to California, where Becky had to resume filming *Day's Dawn*, and John had to return to work.

John loved his job. The money and perks were fantastic. John also loved the challenges of his new position.

Raven and Tony went to New York City to ring in the New Year.

On New Year's Eve, they dined at 21. Afterwards, they bundled up and joined thousands at Times Square to watch the ball drop. It was all so exciting, especially for Raven. It was one thing to watch it as she had for years on TV, it was another thing to actually be there, in the *heart* of it all. She and Tony had a ball!

At midnight, Tony picked Raven up, hugged and kissed her, and told her how much he loved her. "*Happy New Year*, beautiful!" he yelled, as he planted a big kiss on her lips. It was the best New Year that Tony had ever had, because he was with Raven, the love of his life. *She*, was the *best* thing, that had ever happened to him.

Raven and Tony called their families and friends to wish them all a Happy New Year. When Raven called Becky, Becky told her that she and John had dined at a new restaurant in Santa Monica. Becky also told Raven that John had popped the question. *Again*.

John thought that Becky would finally say yes, since it was a new year, but he had no such luck.

"I told him that I would *think* about it," said Becky.

Raven laughed. "John's certainly *adamant*, isn't he? And you're certainly adamant too, about *not* getting married. Well, Happy New Year, Beck! Tell John that Tony and I wish him a Happy New Year too. I *love* you!"

"I *love* you too, Sis. Happy New Year to you! And Tony!"

* * *

The next morning, Raven and Tony took his private jet back to L.A. Raven slept on the way. Tony slept very little. He was too excited to sleep. His thoughts were on their wedding the following month. They had everything ready. And Tony couldn't wait.

Raven and Becky had gotten an early start. The wedding planner, Jackie Vienet, dubbed the best in the business, was very professional and super-good at what she did. The invitation-only wedding was going to take place at the Old Bethlehem Baptist Church in Tunis. The wedding reception was going to be at the Hilton, fifteen minutes away.

Becky was going to be Raven's maid of honor. John would be her escort. Angie, Stephanie, Raven's niece, Sabrina, and eight of her cousins, were all going to be bridesmaids. Trey was going to be the best man. Raven's niece, Lillie, was going to be the flower girl. All of the main positions were filled.

Jackie was looking forward to going to Texas. She'd never been there before, but she had heard a lot about it. She was very curious about Tunis. She had only heard of the larger cities in Texas, like Houston, Dallas, and Austin. Raven and Becky told her that Tunis was a very small town. "Similar to Mayberry," they told her.

Tony had *big* plans for their honeymoon. Raven didn't know where they were going. Tony wanted to surprise her. He was taking her to *Paris*. Becky told Tony that Raven had always wanted to go there. She also assured Tony that his secret was safe with her. And true to her word, Becky hadn't breathed a word to Raven.

Tony had arranged for them to stay at the Belle Etoile Suite in the Hotel Meurice.

* * *

When they arrived in L.A., Tony took Raven home, per her request. She was very tired and still very sleepy. She'd stayed up late each night in Texas, and the late nights finally caught up with her.

Raven kissed Tony before he left. "I'll call you next year when I wake up. I now know how Rip Van Winkle felt."

Tony laughed. "Okay, beautiful, get some rest."

And rest, she did.

* * *

As Raven sat in the tub later that day, she thought of her future husband, their wedding, and their life together. She also thought of Tunis. No matter where she lived, or where she went, Tunis would always, be her home.

She and Tony had a very enjoyable time with her family. Raven was very happy to see Trey and Stephanie beaming at each other like newlyweds. She wished them well. Trey had even told her, when the two of them were alone, that Stephanie was now watching football with him sometimes.

Raven laughed. "I told you!"

Raven also thought about her sixth grade teacher. She went to visit her mainly, to *thank* her. Mrs. Riley had believed in her, *before* she actually went off to make her dreams become reality, before she'd had any success in Hollywood, and that meant a lot to Raven. She was also hoping to see Clint Stanton. She was curious to know what he was doing with his life. Raven sent him an invitation to her wedding.

As she was towel-drying her body, her phone rang. "Coming!" said Raven, as if the person who was calling her, could hear her. "Hello."

"Hi, beautiful. You sound *rested*. You certainly slept *long* enough." Tony teased. "It was very nice meeting your family. They made me feel at home."

"They're crazy about my baby," said Raven.

"I'm *crazy* about them too. Your mother can *burn*. I can still taste her food."

Raven laughed. "I told you she's the *best*. I wasn't saying that just because she's *my* mother."

The lovebirds talked for several hours, before finally hanging up. Each anxiously awaiting their wedding day. They had even invited Pastor Daly and the entire City of Angels' congregation. Pastor Daly assured them that he wouldn't miss it for the world. His wife had family in River Oaks, a Houston suburb.

The pastor laughed, as he remembered Tony coming to his church that first day just to make contact with Raven. He would never forget that. The pastor had been happy to see Tony coming to church every Sunday with Raven, since that time. The two rarely missed a Sunday.

* * *

Becky came home later that evening.

"Hey, Beck. How was your day?" Raven asked her.

"My day was *great*." Becky shook her head. "Sis, I still pinch myself sometimes. *My* dreams, *our* dreams, we're *living* them now."

"I know, Beck. And what a *feeling*!"

"Sis, I want to show you the home in Beverly Hills that John and I are going to get. You *gotta* come with me! You have to get dressed quickly though, we don't have a lot of time."

"They're meeting you there *tonight*?" Raven asked. It was already after seven o'clock.

Becky nodded. "Yes, they are. I mean, *she* is. This was the only time that I could actually go. The real estate lady will be waiting for us. She's very nice."

"And obviously very flexible. But money talks. I'll be ready in five," said Raven.

Minutes later, Raven and Becky were driving to Beverly Hills. They arrived a little before eight. The real estate lady was anxiously waiting for them.

* * *

The home was gorgeous! It was twelve thousand square feet, and it boasted fifteen spacious rooms. There was a huge swimming pool, tennis court, guesthouse, and a ten-car-attached garage.

Becky looked at Raven. "So, you *like*?"

"I like! I like! Beck, this is a *beautiful* home! *Absolutely* beautiful! Who wouldn't like it? Has John seen it?"

"No, not yet. He just told me that as long as I was satisfied, he'd be satisfied," said Becky. "I'll make sure that I bring him to see it tomorrow evening though."

Raven laughed. "*Men*."

They walked the home and property repeatedly. Becky didn't want to leave. This was the kind of home that she had often seen on *Lifestyles of the Rich and Famous*. And she was now a part of that elite group. So was her best friend, Raven.

"I'm very *happy* you like the home, Miss Simms. Please don't wait too long. This home is below market value. The owner wants to sell it quickly. I've had *a lot* of calls regarding this home."

"Consider it sold!" said Becky, writing the real estate lady a check.

Nona Walden's eyes lit up. She knew that this sale made for a very handsome commission. Nona was very happy that she'd agreed to show that night. She started to call and cancel, but she was very happy that she hadn't.

Becky's new home was within walking distance of The Beverly Hills Hotel. Who would have ever guessed that she would be a homeowner in one of the most exclusive communities in the world, thought Becky. *Who* knew?

"I told you, Beck!"

Rebecca Simms smiled. "Yes, Sis, you sure did."

Becky made arrangements to meet Nona the next morning to read and sign all of the paperwork. She was elated. And as always, Raven was also very happy for her.

* * *

The following weekend, Raven and Tony joined Becky and John, as they shopped for furniture for their new home. Afterwards, the foursome went to Malibu as Raven and Tony had been doing on a regular basis, to see how their home was coming along. It was almost complete.

"Wow!" said Becky. "You guys' home is *five-star*! Excuse me, I mean, *palace*. This is definitely you, Sis. All the way!"

Raven laughed. "I can't wait to move in. I'm so excited!"

Raven and Becky spent countless hours shopping for furniture for the Malibu mansion.

Later that day, as Raven and Becky sat at the park, Raven smiled, as she silently-thanked God for their many blessings. So many great things were happening to them, and, for them.

Raven's thoughts shifted to Tony. He loved her so very much. And she loved him very much too. God couldn't have sent her a better man to spend the rest of her life with. She was ready for marriage. If she wasn't ready, she would have followed the same advice that she had given Becky, she would have waited. Raven knew that marriage was a big step and a big commitment. It wasn't anything to be taken lightly. She was ready to take that step, and she knew in her heart that Tony was also ready. She and Tony were equally-yoked. They were so good together. Their love and chemistry were immeasurable.

"Thinking about Tony, huh, Sis?"

Raven smiled in answer.

"Now how did I *know* that?" Becky asked as she laughed. "He loves you *so* much. I know he'll be good to you. If he isn't, he will *definitely* have to answer to *me*."

"John had *better* be good to you too, Beck. I don't think he wants to answer to me," Raven told Becky.

"Sis, *no one*, wants to answer to *you*!"

Raven laughed in answer.

* * *

The weeks flew by ... *February ... finally ... arrived.* And *no one* was happier than Raven and Tony.

On February seventh, Raven, Tony, and everyone who was going to be in the wedding, flew to Texas. All last-minute preparations and practice for wedding participants took place at the church in Tunis.

Mack was flying in the following Thursday. He was one of Tony's honored guests. Mack was very happy for his boss. He had never seen Tony happier, since meeting the sultry-beauty.

* * *

The night before the wedding, the Kensingtons and Dashs threw Raven and Tony a pre-wedding party. Most of the people in the Tunis community came, along with many of Raven's childhood friends, who had moved away, and were in town for the wedding.

Angie told Raven that Clint wasn't coming. "You know how his mother is. Do you *honestly* think that she gave him his invitation? *C'mon* now, Raven," said Angie.

"You're probably right, Ang."

"Angie is right," said Becky. "I doubt if Mrs. Stanton gave Clint his invitation. I also doubt that you're going to look as beautiful as you can look with bags under your eyes. Call it a night, Sis!"

"You're right, Beck." Raven yawned, as she and Tony thanked everyone for the wonderful party.

Tony kissed his fiancée good night, as he flashed a broad smile. "Just think, this time tomorrow night, we will have been husband and wife, for exactly, *nine* hours," said Tony, as everyone laughed.

Tony said good night to everyone, as he kissed Raven again, then went to his hotel room.

* * *

Raven was too nervous to sleep. The next day, she would be getting married. Tony was the person who Raven loved more than *anyone* in the world. She smiled. She would soon be ... *Mrs. Tony Dash. In a matter ... of ... hours ...*

**The wedding day ...*

"Get up, lady! It's *your wedding* day!" Mae Kensington kissed Raven on the forehead. "This will be the *most* memorable day of your life, sweetheart."

Raven flashed her trademark smile. "I'm nervous, Mommie. But it's a *good* kind of nervous."

Her mother nodded. "I know, sweetheart. Being nervous is common. I was also nervous when I married your father. I'm sure Tony's nervous too."

Everyone started getting ready for Raven and Tony's *big* day.

The extra bathrooms, in times like these, proved to be very useful. Mae still marveled at the huge, elegant home.

Mae, Becky, Stephanie, and all of her aunts, helped Raven get ready. Angie did her hair. Becky did her makeup. Everyone wanted to help the bride-to-be in some way. They all made a fuss over Raven. She didn't have to do anything. She was waited on hand and foot.

Shortly before the limos arrived to take everyone to the church, Stephanie got a rare moment alone with Raven. "Raven, *thank you.* There was a *big* change in Trey after he returned from Los Angeles. I know you had a hand in that. I want to also thank you for being unbiased. You didn't take his side, simply because he's your brother. I love you, Raven. You're the *best* sister anyone could ever have." Tears welled up in Stephanie's eyes.

"You're welcome, Steph. I'm glad that I could help."

"The limos are here! Let's *go!*" Angie yelled excitedly.

* * *

Jackie earned every penny of her money. She took the otherwise common burdens that every bride-to-be faced off Raven, by executing everything, perfectly. She juggled everything like a circus act. Jackie Vienet was a pro.

"Miss Kensington, I'll take care of *everything.*" Jackie told Raven. "Don't worry your pretty little head." Jackie knew what getting married was like. She had been happily-married for ten and a half years. Jackie remembered it, as if it were yesterday. The couple were already nervous enough, thought Jackie. They certainly didn't need to worry about things not running smoothly. Jackie had always believed that if someone paid you to do a job, you ought to do that job very well. Tony had paid her a very pretty penny. It was very obvious to Jackie that Raven's happiness was everything to him.

Jackie gasped when she saw Raven. She was the most beautiful bride that she had ever seen. Jackie checked to make sure that Tony was in a separate room, so that he wouldn't see Raven. Raven and her father were escorted in through a side door. Jackie didn't want to take any chances on Tony seeing his bride, before it was time.

The wedding began on time, to no one's surprise. Jackie was a woman of her word. Raven and her father waited in an undisclosed room at the back of the church.

Jackie notified Raven and her father. "It's *time*, Raven. Your husband-to-be awaits!"

Raven looked at her father, who was fighting back tears. He was about to give her away. Charles knew that he couldn't be giving her to a better man than Tony. He also knew that, no matter what, she would always be his baby, she'd always be his little girl. No wedding would, or could ever, change that.

Charles Kensington looked at his beautiful daughter. "Raven, you are the *second* most beautiful bride that I have ever seen. Your mother was the first. And Angie, will be the third."

Raven and her father stood at the door waiting. When they heard the music, that was their cue. Father and daughter began walking, slowly, down the aisle.

Everyone stood, watching them.

Raven looked at the beautifully-decorated church. Nothing, was as beautiful to Raven as the bridesmaids, they all looked very beautiful.

And everyone thought Raven breathtaking. She was eye-popping! She wore a long, white, Vera Wang wedding gown, that had an endless-train, a pair of diamond earrings, and a diamond necklace that Becky bought for her as a wedding gift, from Raven's favorite jeweler, Harry Winston.

Tony's eyes lit up instantly at the sight of Raven. His eyes were glued to her. He loved her so very much. *This*, was the moment, that he had been waiting for. And *this*, was the woman, that he wanted to love, honor, and cherish, for *all* of his days. Raven was the woman, that Tony wanted to grow old with. She was the woman that he loved, needed, and wanted. And in Tony Dash's heart, he *knew* that Raven was the *only* woman for him. He was very blessed to have her. Tony knew that a woman like Raven came along *once* in a lifetime.

Raven's eyes locked with Tony's. The unspoken, immensely-strong love that they shared was easily seen and felt.

Tears streamed down Mae Kensington's face, as she watched her daughter walk down the aisle.

Everyone took their seats, when Raven stood beside Tony.

Pastor Morton wasted no time getting things started. "Dearly beloved, we are gathered here today, to join these two wonderful people, in *holy* matrimony." The pastor looked at Tony. "Do you, *Tony Dash*, take *this* woman, *Raven Kensington*, to be your lawful, wedded wife, to have and to hold, from this day forward, in sickness and in health, for richer or for poorer, for better or for worse, forsaking *all* others, keeping *only* unto her, as long as you *both* shall live?"

The answer was in Tony's eyes, before he even spoke the words. "*I do*."

Pastor Morton turned to Raven. He had her repeat the same vows.

Raven smiled through her tears, as she repeated the vows, then ended with … "*I do*."

Raven looked at Tony. He looked so handsome, and happy. They were taking their vows before God, their families, and their friends.

Raven and Tony had another thing in common, neither of them

had middle names. And Tony's real name was not Anthony, as with most "Tonys," it was Tony.

Pastor Morton asked if anyone had just cause that Raven and Tony not be married, he asked that they come forward. And as expected, no one did. "By the power vested in me, I *now* pronounce you *husband, and wife!*" Pastor Morton smiled at the handsome groom. "You may kiss your *beautiful* bride!"

Everyone cheered and clapped, as Raven and Tony shared a heartfelt-kiss. Raven couldn't stop crying.

"I *love* you *so* much, Raven *Dash*," Tony whispered to Raven. "You have made me the *happiest* man in the world."

"I *love* you too, Tony Dash."

After congratulating the bride and groom, the guests drove to the Hilton for the wedding reception.

The reception was held at the posh, L'regne Ballroom. Each guest was greeted upon entrance and escorted to one of the lavishly-decorated tables. The seating was prearranged.

The reception was professionally catered by the Hilton staff, who were instructed by Raven and Tony to wait on their guests hand and foot. They didn't want anyone to have to lift a finger for anything. The only thing Raven and Tony wanted their guests to do, was have a great time celebrating with them, on the *happiest* day of their lives.

Everyone loved the beautifully-decorated ballroom. There was great music, an open bar, and a wide variety of delicious food and drinks, for the eight-hundred-plus guests in attendance.

Guests dined on caviar, iced jumbo shrimp, oysters, honey baked ham, chicken, and all dishes in-between. They had their choices of the finest of wines, beer, hot tea and iced-tea, juices, all kinds of soft drinks, and water. Raven and Tony wanted to make sure that no one left their wedding reception hungry, or thirsty, for that matter. The newlyweds wanted everyone to eat, drink, and be merry. And that is exactly, what everyone did.

* * *

Everyone ate until they couldn't eat anymore. The food was delicious. The service, impeccable. Many decided to dance off their meals, by cutting some steps on the adjoining dance floor. The deejay played current hits, as well as oldies, like Ray Charles, the Temptations, Smokey Robinson, the Supremes, Otis Redding, Martha and the Vandellas, Stevie Wonder, the Four Tops, Marvin Gaye, and Percy Sledge.

Raven and Tony had their first dance as husband and wife. They slow-danced to "Love of My Life" by Brian McKnight. Raven also danced with her father.

Everyone had a ball! It was truly an unforgettable day. The huge wedding cake, with miniature look-a-like Raven and Tony dolls, was beautifully-decorated, and delicious.

All of the single females eagerly lined up when Raven announced that she was about to throw her bouquet. Raven stood in a chair, turned her back to those awaiting, then slowly counted to three, as she tossed her bouquet, which was caught by her best friend, Rebecca Simms.

John was thrilled that Becky had caught the bouquet. He took this as a sign that Becky would finally change her mind and marry him. He didn't want to remain Becky's fiancé, he wanted to be her husband.

Raven and Tony's *exquisite* wedding reminded John of just how very much, he wanted one of his own.

It was Tony's turn next. He tossed the garter to the bachelors, which was caught by Mack.

Everyone laughed as Mack stood speechless.

Raven laughed hard when she saw the expression on Becky's face. "It's *not* the end of the world, Beck!" Raven told her, when John went to get more wine. "Beck, is there something you're not telling me? Do you think John's *not* the right one for you?" Raven knew that Becky knew John far better than she did.

"To tell you the truth, Sis, no, I don't know if he is *the one* for me. It's confusing sometimes, because I do love him. Then again, maybe I like things the way they are. I don't know. But I do know that I'm *not* ready to get married."

Raven nodded. "Do what's *best* for you, Beck."

As time began to wind down, no one was as happy as Tony. He was ready to be alone with his beautiful bride. He had shared Raven with others all day. And as he watched her in deep conversation with her mother, he thanked God again for blessing him, with such an extraordinary woman.

It had been two years since he had first laid eyes on her. Tony remembered that day, as if it were yesterday. And he knew that it was a day that he would never forget. He still appreciated Raven's stunning-beauty, her immense-wisdom, her huge heart, her great sense of humor, her independence. Tony loved Raven more than life itself. And he loved her unconditionally, which was of utmost importance.

After hours of celebrating at their wedding reception, Raven and Tony were both ready to call it an evening. The newlyweds walked onstage and thanked everyone for coming to celebrate the most important day of their lives with them.

"Keep us in your prayers!" said Raven. "We love all of you!"

Raven and Tony joined hands, then ran towards the door, as rice was thrown on them, along with lots of well-wishes.

The elevator whisked the newlyweds to the top floor, to their honeymoon suite. They were going to spend the night at the hotel, then take Tony's private jet to Paris the next morning. Their suitcases were already packed and ready at the Hilton suite. Tony also had their passports. Everything, was planned to a T.

Tony unlocked the door. "Wait," he told Raven, as he picked her up and carried her through the door. "*Tradition.*"

The suite had a breathtaking-view of College Station.

"Would you like a glass of wine, beautiful?" Tony asked his wife, as he kissed her.

"Sure," said Raven. "Thanks."

After Tony handed Raven the glass of wine, he told her that he would be back.

"Leaving me *already*?" Raven joked.

Tony laughed. "*Not* a chance! I'm going to take a shower."

Raven nodded. She was going to take a bath after Tony came out of the bathroom.

As the water and soap cleansed his body, Tony smiled. He would *finally* get to make love to Raven. He knew that Raven was nervous. In some ways, so was he. But one thing about nature, thought Tony, it always takes its course.

Tony came out of the bathroom after a long shower, wearing only a pair of black satin briefs.

Raven eyed her husband's muscular, powerfully-built body. He looked very handsome and sexy.

Tony liked the pleasing look that he saw in Raven's eyes.

"My turn!" said Raven.

When Raven went to take her bath, Tony put his and Raven's song, "Ribbon in the Sky," on repeat. Both he and Raven loved that song.

Tony poured himself a glass of wine and sat down to wait for the woman of his dreams, who was now, *his* wife. *Finally*. Tony smiled a broad smile. Raven was no longer "the future Mrs. Dash," she was *now*, Mrs. Dash. *Mrs. Tony Dash*. And Tony was ecstatic. This was the *happiest* day of his entire life.

After her bath, Raven put on the black lingerie that Angie bought for her from Frederick's of Hollywood. She sprayed a little perfume, *here* and *there*, then she brushed her long black hair, which she left hanging loose. After taking a deep breath, Raven walked out of the bathroom.

* * *

The fireplace was burning. Tony also lit candles throughout the suite. When he heard the bathroom door open, he immediately looked in that direction. "*Whoa ... you ... look ... wow.*"

Tony's eyes were enraptured. Raven Kensington Dash was an extremely beautiful and sultry woman. Tony had always thought that, no matter what she wore. He continued to feast his eyes on her. *All*, of her. And all of the love that he felt for her, was in his eyes. Angie told Raven that her husband would be pleased. And Raven had to admit, her little sister was right. Tony was very pleased.

Tony walked over to his wife. His eyes were dreamy. "I love you, Raven. I love you *more* than anyone, or *anything*, in this world. Don't *ever* forget that," he whispered, as his lips hungrily found hers. Tony always loved kissing Raven, her lips always tasted so sweet. Kissing her, drove him crazy.

Raven could feel how much Tony wanted her.

Tony moaned. His entire body ached for Raven. When he couldn't stand it any longer, he picked his bride up and carried her to the bed. Tony placed Raven gently on her feet, as his eyes and hands undressed her slowly. "*If* this is a dream," said Tony, his voice husky, "*please, don't wake me up.*"

Raven's lingerie fell to the floor. Her lingerie was very sexy, but not as sexy as the naked body that stood before him. Tony swallowed long and hard, as if drinking *her* all in. His eyes combed his wife's voluptuous body. Raven was eye candy. Tony continued to look at her from head to toe. His was a look of love, promise, appreciation, and hunger. Tony was speechless. He had never wanted a woman so badly. Tony didn't just hunger for Raven's body, he also hungered, for her heart. Tony pulled the covers back, picked Raven up again, and gently laid her on the bed, as he climbed in beside her. He was about to remove his briefs, but Raven stopped him.

"Allow me. Let *me* do it," Raven whispered, in that beautiful, sultry voice of hers.

Tony smiled. His eyes never left Raven's. "I *love* you, *Mrs. Dash*." His eyes said it, before his words did.

Raven's eyes reached deep into her husband's. "I *love* you too, *Mr. Dash*."

Their suite was the picture of romance. The fireplace roared. Candles were everywhere. Their favorite song played softly in the background. Rose petals were sprinkled throughout their suite, in the shape of hearts. But most of all, they, were the picture of romance. They were soul mates, who loved each other more than life itself.

Tony made love to Raven like there was no tomorrow. He was starving for her. He explored Raven, with a fiery, primal passion. His lips, tongue, and hands, were like magic, as he slowly combed every inch of her. There wasn't a part of her, that he didn't caress … kiss … taste … Tony did things to Raven, that he had never done to anyone.

Raven moaned, as Tony stirred her. He was an extraordinary lover.

After what seemed like hours, Raven then, explored Tony. She was incredible, as she took him to new heights. She made him feel things that he had never felt before. Tony moaned in ecstasy, as he whispered Raven's name.

After they had explored each other, repeatedly, Tony entered Raven. *Gently.* They, were *one.* They loved each other deeply, and their passionate lovemaking reflected that.

Making love to Raven was so powerful, so addictive. It was the *ultimate.* Tony felt as if he were in a different world. And what a *wonderful* world it was! Tony couldn't get enough of Raven. It was as if he wanted to devour her. He made love to her, repeatedly, then finally, they came. *Together.* Afterwards, they lie in each other's arms, immensely-happy, and *sated* …

"*Wow. Mmmm … oh … Raven …*" Tony's voice was husky. His eyes were glazed. "You didn't think I was ever going to stop, did you, beautiful?"

Raven laughed in answer. "No, sweetheart, I didn't."

"I didn't think that I was either." Tony was on cloud nine. Making love to, and with, the woman he loved, was everything that Tony thought it would be. "Raven, you drive me *cra-azzy*, but, in a *great* way." Tony continued to caress Raven. He couldn't bring himself to stop touching her. "I *hate* to be the bearer of *bad* news, *especially* since we just got married. However, you and I have a very *open* and *honest* relationship, so I'm going to tell you."

Raven looked at her husband. "*Oh? Tell* me, Mr. Dash, tell me the bad news. I'm *listening.*"

Tony tasted his wife's lips, before he answered. "We're going to be spending *a lot* of time in bed. And you have *yourself* to blame. It's something *you* will have to live with, for the rest of *our* lives." Tony moaned. "The *only* trouble that we're going to have *in* bed, is getting *out*, of bed!"

Raven laughed hard in answer.

Tony looked at the woman that he wanted to grow old with. "Raven, you just don't know what *you* do to me. I *love* you so much, beautiful." His eyes searched hers. "Baby, did I satisfy you?"

Raven nodded. "Yes, sweetheart, you *satisfied* me. Did I satisfy *you?*"

"Oh, *yes!*" Tony quickly answered. "Making love to you is a *pleasure* that I can't possibly measure. You make me sing the Campbell's soup song, *mmm-hmmm ... go-o-o-od ...* You are like a variety of very delicious dishes, but, there is absolutely nothing, like the main course meal. You make me not want to get out of bed. *Ever!*"

His wife laughed.

Making love to Raven nearly drove Tony out of his mind. What he shared with her was a passion he had never believed could exist. Tony smiled. Making love had never felt *so* good.

"Beautiful?"

"Yes, love?"

"If there *ever* comes a time when I don't satisfy you, in or out of bed, *promise* me, that you'll tell me."

"Yes, Tony, I promise. I will tell you. And, *likewise*, will you promise to do the same?"

"Yes, beautiful, I will." As Tony looked at Raven, he knew in his heart that he would love and protect her. *Always.* "I want to grow *old* with you, *Mrs. Dash. I love you.*" Tony whispered again, before falling asleep. Tony had given Raven all of him. Including, his heart.

    * * *

"I love you too, sweetheart." Raven whispered back.

Raven stayed awake for hours. She had *never* been happier in her life. Not even the success that she had attained in Hollywood had given her *this* much joy and happiness. She thought of their *beautiful* wedding and reception. Raven thought of their families and friends, who came to celebrate this very special and unforgettable day, with them. She would never forget this day. Never! Or *this* night. Raven smiled, as she thought of their immensely-passionate lovemaking. They had made love, repeatedly. It was as if Tony couldn't get enough of her. It was obvious to Raven that her husband had an insatiable appetite for her.

Raven had waited to have sex. She had always known that her husband would be the *first* man who would make love to her, not to mention, the *only* man, to do so. Tony never pressured her when they were dating. It was as if he already knew that she wasn't going to sleep with him, until they were married. Raven was very happy that she had waited. Her *first* time had been very *special*, and *unforgettable*. It was very important that the man loved her. And she him. Loving out of bed, was first and foremost. Not her body, not her looks, but he had, to love her. *Unconditionally* too. She looked at her husband and smiled. Tony Dash had more than proved how much he loved her, a thousand times over.

"*I love you,*" Raven whispered to Tony in the dark, before finally falling asleep.

The newlyweds slept soundly, throughout the night, in each other's arms.

* * *

Tony awoke in the wee hours of the morning. He propped up on one elbow, as he watched Raven sleep. He loved the way the moonlight shone on her face. She was so beautiful. "*My* Sleeping Beauty." Tony whispered. "*Raven ... you* make *me* so *happy*."

* * *

Tony was looking forward to their honeymoon in Paris. They would be leaving in a few hours. They were going to spend three weeks there. Tony was very excited. He knew that Raven would love Paris.

Tony had recently purchased a new jet. It was fit for a king and queen, fit for royalty. It had every kind of comfort and luxury imaginable.

Jerry and Cret Barker, who were father and son, were flying them to Paris. They were both very skilled pilots. They were also skilled mechanics. The Barkers had extensive training and many years of experience, in all aspects of aviation. Tony also liked them because they were very thorough. They would always check every inch of the aircraft before take-off.

Tony had a number of mechanics and pilots who worked for him, but Jerry and Cret were the best. And as a result, they were always Tony's first choice.

Mack, whom Tony often referred to as his right-hand man, would also be accompanying them to Paris. Mack was very happy about going to one of the most beautiful places in the world. Tony certainly didn't need Mack to go with them, it was more of a perk, special incentive, for being Tony's favorite employee.

Months prior, when Tony had informed Mack and the Barkers of his honeymoon plans, he had sworn them to secrecy.

As Tony looked at his beautiful bride, who was sleeping soundly beside him, he thought of Paris. It was going to be a pretty lengthy flight, but Tony knew that everyone would be very comfortable and well taken care of. That was important to him. It was *especially* important to him that Raven be comfortable and want for nothing. And as he watched her sleep, he knew that she would never want for *anything*. Ever. He would move heaven and earth for her.

Tony couldn't resist kissing Raven. When he kissed her on the lips, like Snow White, she awoke. And as they shared a passionate kiss, Tony became aroused, and he made love to Raven again. Tony couldn't get enough of Raven. And he wasn't sure if he ever would.

She, was insatiable.

"*Oh ... Raven,*" said Tony. "You're *insatiable. Addictive.* I don't think that I'll *ever* get used to you, not to mention, get *enough* of you." Tony smiled. "But, that's *okay* with me." He *loved* making love to her. "What can I say? I *love* to love *you.* You're an *extraordinary* woman, Raven. You're unlike *any* woman I've *ever* known." Tony had sensed that about Raven when he'd first laid eyes on her. "You've certainly taken me places that I've *never* been. *In,* and *out,* of bed." He kissed the nape of her neck as he spoke. "You're so rare, *precious.*" He looked into his wife's eyes as he said this. *No one* had ever made him feel the way Raven made him feel, sexually or otherwise. He loved her with *every* fiber of his being. Tony's eyes bore into Raven's. "I *adore* you, Raven. I *never* knew what it was to need, or want, until *you.* Then came, *you.* My heart, is in *your* hands."

"I *promise* to handle it with *care,*" said Raven, as she kissed her husband's lips. "I love you very much, Tony Dash."

"And I *you.* I have an *insatiable* appetite when it comes to you, Raven." She was like an addiction, a very good one. Making love to her was incredible. "I'm *addicted* to you, baby. And like *any* addict, I will keep coming back for *more,* and *more,* and *more ...*"

Raven laughed in answer.

"You're gonna *have* to face it, *I'm* addicted to love. *Your* love, Raven. You know, beautiful, I took *many* a cold shower *waitin'* on you."

"Is that *why* you're making me pay for it now?" Raven teased.

Her husband laughed. "On a *serious* note, I admired and respected you for waiting, doing it the *right* way. And, sometimes, doing things the right way isn't always easy, but it's always the *best* way," said Tony. "*Good* things come to those who wait. And you were *definitely,* worth the wait!"

Raven knew that many couples made love a lot during their honeymoon-stage, then lovemaking would usually die down. But somehow, she didn't sense that about them. She sensed that this was the way it would always be, or at least, most of the time anyway. She didn't mind it. And she didn't think that she ever would. She loved her husband very much. And she wanted to please him, in and out of bed.

"Raven, will my *frequent* lovemaking bother you?" Tony asked.

"No, baby, I don't think that it will bother me. As long as I'm the *only* one you make love to. And *with*." Raven smiled, thinking of her husband's passionate lovemaking. Tony Dash didn't disappoint. Then again, neither did she.

"Raven, my love is *only* for you. You're the *only* woman that I love. I will *always* love you, Raven. *Always*. And you are the *only* woman that I want, in *and* out of bed. It's been that way since the first time that I laid eyes on you. I've *never* been very religious, but I've *thanked* God every day since then. I am *truly*-blessed." Tony meant every word.

"I am also *very* blessed, Mr. Dash, to have *you*." Raven knew that Tony was a very good man.

She and Tony had always made love to each other's minds, way before they had actually made love, and doing that, along with their deep, obvious love for one another, made making love *in* bed, unbelievably-satisfying. Their lovemaking was very magical, to say the least.

"It feels so good holding you in my arms. I don't ever want to let you go. I want to hold you in my arms *forever*. In *my* arms, is where *you* belong, beautiful." Tony told Raven, as the phone rang.

It was Mack, giving them a wake-up call.

Tony refused to tell Raven where they were going, no matter how many times she tried to get it out of him. "No matter how often you pout, or how beautiful you look pouting, I ain't tellin' you nada, *nothin'*, Mrs. Dash. You can keep sticking your lips out, I'll just *keep* kissing them."

Raven finally stopped asking, and she also stopped pouting. Her husband was adamant. He wasn't going to tell her.

   * * *

Raven and Mack waited inside of the airport, while Tony, Jerry, and Cret thoroughly inspected the entire aircraft. Afterwards, Tony came inside to get his wife and Mack.

Everyone boarded the jet and buckled up, as the jet took off smoothly. And, on time.

Mack stayed in the mid-quarters of the jet, where everything was at his fingertips: magazines, a big-screen TV, a variety of drinks, food, and a lavatory. The seats were ultra-comfortable. The jet was also equipped with pillows, beds, blankets, and first aid kits. Passengers could even watch movies. The jet was *first-class* all the way.

* * *

Although Tony didn't fly planes often, he knew how to fly them. He flew planes enough to keep his skills sharp. He'd paid Jerry to teach him how to fly, years ago, before he'd put Jerry and his son on his payroll. And, as with many things, Tony Dash was a quick learner. He had a photographic memory.

As the plane headed for Paris, the newlyweds, who were in the back of the plane in their *private* quarters, fell asleep holding hands.

* * *

"Hi, beautiful. Did you sleep well?"

Raven smiled and nodded.

Tony had also slept well. He felt revitalized. He looked very well-rested, as did Raven.

"I'm going to get something to drink. Would you like anything?"

"Sure, ginger ale, please."

Tony laughed. "Okay, ginger ale woman." After washing his hands, Tony came back with an ice cold glass of ginger ale for his wife, and a glass of white wine for himself.

The lovebirds gazed into each other's eyes as they sipped on their drinks.

The plane hit an air pocket, causing it to shake.

Tony purposely spilled some of his wine on the front of Raven's blouse. "*Oops*! Sorry, sweetheart, *clumsy* me. Looks like we've got a spill," said Tony, trying to keep a straight face. Tony changed his voice. "Alert! We have a spill on aisle two. Repeat, there's a spill on aisle two!"

Raven laughed.

"Don't worry, I'll *fix* that, beautiful."

"I *bet* you are sorry, Tony Dash!" Raven knew Tony all too well. Her blouse was wet. "Tell me, Mr. Dash, how is it that you *accidentally* spilled your wine on my *chest* area? *Nice* aim."

Tony laughed. "*Raven*, every man's *innocent* until proven guilty. I'll fix that. You don't have to lift a finger." Tony unbuckled their seat belts. "But, in order for me to help you, you'll have to follow *my* instructions. Okay?"

Raven nodded. "Okay."

Tony led her to the bed. "Sit here, beautiful. I'll be right back."

Tony went to get blankets and pillows.

Raven knew what Tony was up to. She saw that familiar, dreamy look in his eyes. It was the exact same look she remembered seeing, every time that he had made love to her.

"I have to *warn* you now. I sometimes have a *strange* way of doing things, but the end result will be successful. Okay?"

"Okay."

"Okay, beautiful wifey, don't be alarmed." Tony told Raven to lie down.

Raven followed her husband's instructions.

Tony began slowly unbuttoning Raven's blouse, using his mouth.

Mission accomplished.

"Oh, my! Your bra is also wet. I'll have to *remove* that too. The last thing I want you to do is catch a cold. Especially, on *our* honeymoon." Tony smiled, as he unhooked Raven's bra. "Please, sit up now," said Tony, as he extended his arm to Raven.

Raven sat before him, topless.

"*Wow*!"

"Tony!"

Her husband didn't answer her.

"*Tony Dash*!" Raven said again.

"I'm sorry, sweetheart, I was just admiring the *breathtaking-*view." Tony continued staring at Raven. She was an eyeful. "I am very *pleasingly*-distracted."

"Please bring me a T-shirt or something." Raven looked at the door. "Hurry! Tony, someone could walk in."

"Only if they're a ghost. Don't worry your pretty little head, the door is *locked*."

"I *still* want to cover myself." Raven insisted. She wanted to give her husband a hard time.

"Why, baby? We're *married*. No one else can enjoy this breathtaking-view, but your husband should be able to."

Raven looked at him and shook her head. "Tony, *get* me something."

Tony went to get another blanket. "Don't look at me like that! You said get you *something*."

"Funny, Tony. *Very* funny."

"I'll relax with you," said Tony, removing his shirt. "Now, Raven, you did say that you would *cooperate* with me, didn't you?"

"Yes, but ..."

"*Ah-ah-ah ... no buts*. You *can't* go back on your word now, Mrs. Dash. I'm cold now. I think I'll climb under the blankets with you." As soon as Tony got under the blankets, he kissed Raven. "*Mmmm ...*" his voice was husky. They kissed for a while. Tony was about to go further, but Raven stopped him. "Raven!"

Raven smiled. "Sweetheart, I have a *taste* for strawberries. Do you eat those?"

"Among *other* things." Tony returned his wife's smile.

"Very *naughty* boy, Tony Dash. Very naughty!"

"Okay, beautiful, I'll get you some strawberries."

When Tony returned with the strawberries, Raven sat up and began to eat one.

Tony watched her lips as she slowly chewed the strawberry.

Raven was driving him insane, and she knew it.

Raven took another bite, then she lip-fed the rest of the strawberry to Tony. Raven licked her lips. "*This* ... is ... very good. It's *delicious*."

"That's it, Raven! *Enough* is enough," said Tony.

"Baby, what are you talking about?" said Raven, feigning innocence.

Tony reached for her.

"No, no, *no*. We ... are ... *going* ... to ... *play* ... *my* ... game ... *now*," Raven whispered, as her eyes searched Tony's. "The game is called ... *Eye On the Sparrow*."

"Eye on the ..."

Raven ran a pretty, well-manicured finger, across her husband's lips. "*Ssshh-ssshh* ... don't talk now. I've noticed that your eyes keep wandering down to my breasts. My *eyes*, are up here, Mr. Dash."

Her husband blushed.

"Now, you'll have one minute, *sixty* seconds, to keep your eyes on *mine*. They *can't* look below, as they have been doing since you removed my bra." Raven looked at the clock. "Okay, when I count to three, the game starts. *If* you lose, I don't *think* I have to tell you what that means for you. *One* ... *two* ... *three* ..." Raven counted slowly, as her eyes locked with Tony's.

Five seconds passed. Raven pretended to look away, but she could still see Tony's eyes in the corner of her eye. He quickly looked down at her breasts.

"My, my, my, *Mr. Dash*! Looks like you have *failed*. How weak you are, my love. How very *weak*."

Tony tried to reason with his wife. "I'm only weak for you. And anyway, it's all *your* fault. I can't help it if you make me *lose* my mind. *Please*! C'mon, beautiful! *Please*!"

"A man who begs. Interesting. Please *what*? What on earth are you *begging* for, sweetheart?" Raven asked.

"What I'm *begging* for, is not on earth. She's ... on a plane, in the air. I'm looking at her, talking with her, *dying* to make love to her. *Raven!*"

His wife finally surrendered. "What are you trying to introduce me to, Mr. Dash, the Mile High Club?"

Tony laughed hard in answer.

"You know, sweetheart, if I'm not able to walk, I'm going to blame *you*."

"Don't worry. My big strong arms will carry you," Tony whispered, as his lips found Raven's.

The newlyweds were on a flight-of-love, for hours. Then finally, they came. Raven and Tony lie in each other's arms, happy and spent.

Tony looked in his wife's eyes. "You're looking quite pensive. What's on that beautiful mind of yours?"

"I'm *thinking* of what your pet name should be. How about ... hmmm ... *Rabbit*? *Tonagra*? You're like the Energizer Bunny, you keep going and going and *going* ..."

Tony was a very passionate and virile lover.

Tony laughed. "*Tonagra*?"

"Yes. I simply combined your name with the popular drug that's known for ... I don't have to say it. You already know what it's for. You're no *minute*man, Mr. Dash. Far from it. Another untrue stereotype."

Tony smiled. "I may need Viagra one day, who knows? But this is *all* natural, one hundred percent Tony Dash. No help needed. You're *more* than enough to get my engine roaring, and then some. Besides, as long as you made me wait, you're *going* to pay for it, Mrs. Dash. For the rest ... of *our* ... lives."

Raven laughed.

"If a woman like you couldn't get me roaring and blazing, there's *no way* that *anything* else could, including, Viagra. I *love* you, beautiful. Don't *ever* forget that. And speaking of the minuteman-myth, it depends on who you're with too," said Tony seriously. "But, as you now know, Mrs. Dash, your husband is *no* minuteman. And besides, you bring out the *best* in me, Raven. *All*, of me."

Tony held Raven in his arms, as he caressed her. He loved the way she felt. It felt so good to touch her, hold her, make love to her. Tony looked at his wife, who was the woman of his dreams, and he knew that he would always love and cherish Raven. *Always*. Tony also knew that he would always be devoted and committed to her. His heart, was truly, in *her* hands.

"Mr. Dash, I know from experience, that you're *no* minuteman. You're like a *tiger* in bed."

"*Grrrr-rrrrr!*" Tony growled, as Raven laughed. "In all seriousness, beautiful, I can't stop thinking about how incredibly-blessed I am to have you in my life. Raven, I will *always* love you. You'll always be my baby. Always!"

Raven kissed her husband tenderly on the lips. "I love you too, Tony, *my* Prince Charming. I too will *love* you, *always*."

The newlyweds fell asleep, in each other's arms.

* * *

Jerry's voice woke them, hours later. "Mr. and Mrs. Dash, please prepare for landing."

Raven and Tony smiled at each other, as they got dressed.

"*Where* are we?" Raven asked. "You *never* told me where we were going."

"Have patience, Mrs. Dash. *Please*, a little patience woman. You will know soon enough."

The jet landed smoothly at the Charles de Gaulle Airport. They, were in Paris!

"Okay, mon amour, I'll tell you *now*. We ... are ... in ... *Paris*."

Raven's eyes lit up. "*Oui*! *Oui*! Oh ... *Tony*! *Paris* ..." Raven had always wanted to go to Paris. From what she'd seen and read about Paris, it was a very beautiful and romantic place. Even the language was romantic. Raven was ecstatic.

The airport was about fourteen miles north of Paris. Tony told Raven that their hotel was approximately forty-five minutes away. A limo was waiting for them when they arrived. Tony had everything carefully planned. Like a true businessman.

* * *

When they arrived at the Hotel Meurice, Mack, Jerry, and Cret checked in, then said their good-byes to Raven and Tony. "We'll see you lovebirds in three weeks!" they all said in unison. They immediately left the newlyweds alone, to enjoy their honeymoon.

Raven observed the posh hotel. It was even more lavish than The Beverly Hills Hotel. Their suite was as large as most people's homes. The three-thousand-square-foot terrace had breathtaking, panoramic views of Paris. The enormous suite boasted fireplaces in the living room, bedroom, and bathroom. The suite was also equipped with chandeliers, a wet bar, hot tub, large, garden-size tub, two separate showers, and an accessible, private elevator.

Tony smiled, as his wife's eyes danced with excitement.

"*The City of Lights*!" said an overjoyed Raven.

The newlyweds wasted no time putting the hot tub to use. It was very relaxing. They sat in the hot tub for hours, listening to music, sipping on champagne, and enjoying each other.

Afterwards, Raven and Tony showered, dressed in elegant attire, then went down to the Le Cresque for dinner. The Le Cresque was one of the finest restaurants in Paris.

As they entered the restaurant, Tony noticed the men *gaping* at his staggeringly-beautiful wife. It was annoying to him sometimes, especially when men acted as if he were invisible.

Raven's eyes searched her husband's. "Tony, *you* are the *only* man who matters to me."

Tony laughed in spite of himself. "Woman, is there *anything* you don't see? I don't know what to say about you and those *gorgeous*, X-ray eyes of yours."

"Baby, don't think that women don't stare and drool over you. I'm *not* dumb. Nor am I blind. You are a *very* handsome and charming man, Tony Dash." Raven didn't say it, but Tony was also a very rich man. His money didn't matter to her, but Raven knew that to many women, it certainly would have mattered. Their relationship, their marriage, was based on their love for each other, *not* money, or material things.

"I don't care about *other* women," said Tony. He reached for his wife's hands. "*You* are the *only* woman, who I *love, need,* and *want.*"

"The feelings are *mutual,* sweetheart," said Raven. "*Always,* remember that."

Raven and Tony dined and danced. They had a very enjoyable time. Before leaving, Tony left a handsome tip for their waiter.

As the lovebirds strolled around the hotel, a number of guests recognized the star-couple, but they respected their privacy. They simply pointed and whispered excitedly.

The hotel had a tea gallery, huge fitness center, pools, an extensive health spa, a full-service spa, elegant bars, and several very exclusive restaurants. There was also a twenty-four-hour business center, which didn't matter to the newlyweds, because they were there for *pleasure,* not business. After touring the hotel, Raven and Tony went back to their suite.

* * *

The newlyweds stood out on the terrace, admiring the breathtaking-view of Paris. It was a lovely night in Paris, though windy.

Tony laughed, as the wind combed Raven's long black hair. "Beautiful, isn't it, *beautiful?*" said Tony.

Raven nodded. "Yes, Tony, v*ery* beautiful indeed."

The newlyweds stayed on the terrace for hours, before going back inside.

* * *

As they lie in bed, Tony propped up on one elbow and looked at his wife. "Raven? What *other* dreams do you have?" He wanted to make *all* of her dreams come true. He wanted to make and keep her happy. *Always.* Raven's happiness meant *everything* to Tony.

"*Hmmm* … well, let's see. I plan to open a few retail stores. The stores will be in various areas, poor and affluent."

* * *

Tony kissed the nape of Raven's neck as she talked.

"Are you trying to *distract* me?"

"No, sweetheart. You're just so *irresistible*. I'm listening, *really*, I am." And he was.

"Okay, as I was saying, before I was so *enticingly*-distracted ..."

Tony laughed.

"The stores will have name-brand clothing. The stores will cater to *everyone*. *All* sizes. *All* shapes. *All* income levels. And, regardless of the location, each store will be held to *my* high standards. Well-kept, clean, neat, organized, impeccable customer service, well-stocked, and nicely-designed on the exterior and the interior. I will hire the *best* people to get the best results. Preferably people who are smarter than I. And those people will be from all races and from all backgrounds. I'm a *firm* believer in diversity. I wouldn't hire anyone simply because of their race, but I do know that qualified people, like with all things, come in *all* colors. Diversity is also a good thing, because it can give a company more creativity and innovation. R.K. by Design will more than likely be my next project."

"*R.K. by Design*? I like that name. It's *chic*. Very ... *you*," said Tony.

"You *like*?"

Her husband nodded. "Yes, beautiful."

"*Good*. I like the name too. I'm now in a position to help others, in a *big* way. And that's always been important to me. I believe that people should also help themselves, but sometimes, we need to help them do that. Help people help themselves. R.K. by Design will be an upscale retail store. Building and opening stores will also help those needing employment. It will also make it easier for the less fortunate to be able to purchase designer clothes, at affordable prices. Again, my stores will cater to *all*: poor, rich, *all* sizes, *all* shapes, *and all* colors. When I say everyone, I do mean, *everyone*. Too many have been left out for *far* too long. When we're not being separated by race, we're being separated by sizes, or looks, or by money. By the have-*nots*, and the have-*yachts* ..."

Tony laughed, as he looked at his wife with love and admiration. "That's only one of the *many* things that I love about you, beautiful, your larger-than-life heart. That's a great idea! So, not only are you this *drop-dead gorgeous*, multi-talented movie star, you also have an entrepreneur spirit. You're a *shrewd* businesswoman, Mrs. Dash."

Raven nodded. "I'm not done yet! I have *another* idea. You're a man with *incredible* taste for fashion. I would like us to have a clothing line with both of our names combined. I like Ravetone. To me, that sounds better than Tonerave. What do you think?"

Tony smiled. "Either name. You know me, whatever my baby wants, she gets." His wife was right. Tony had great fashion sense. "Our line will include fancy evening attire, sportswear, casual dress, the whole nine yards! What else, beautiful?"

Raven flashed that trademark smile of hers. "I also want to continue to donate money, and help raise money, to help the less fortunate. I've been donating time and money to help the homeless, the hungry, people with cancer, people with disabilities, abused women and children, and schools. *Poor* schools. I also donate my time and money to many other worthy causes. I want to help people all over the world." Raven's dark eyes lit up as she spoke. "I just think that if those who were wealthy did more of that, more people would be able to benefit from it. Especially, the have-*nots*. And speaking of domestic violence, there are currently more animal shelters, than there are domestic violence shelters. That's horrible! I love pets, but they are *not* more valuable to me, than human beings."

"That is horrible, sweetheart. There's a very *special* place in your heart for the poor, and the less fortunate, isn't it?" her husband asked.

Raven nodded. "*Yes*, there is. Let's face it, those are the people who are *excluded* most of the time, besides minorities and those who aren't lollipops. People can do as they so wish, and God gave us the freedom of choice. He gave us free will. However, I have yet to understand how some rich people will donate hundreds of millions of dollars to schools that are already wealthy, and donate little or *noth-*

ing, to poor schools. The poor schools are the ones in need. They're the ones that would benefit greatly from those hefty donations."

Her husband nodded his head in agreement.

"It's just common sense to me, to put money where it *needs* to be, *first*. That may explain why the rich gets richer and the poor gets poorer."

"Could be." Her husband laughed. "*Lollipops*?"

Raven told Tony about her sixth-grade book report, and Clint Stanton.

"Okay, I *get* it. Clint was right though. So were you. You proved that Susan girl wrong. Boy was she wrong! She's eating *lots* of crow now." Tony smiled. "My baby proved her wrong. Didn't she know *never* to bet against you? I would like to see her face now. I know she knows how *immensely*-successful you are. Your *beautiful* face graced every major magazine cover this year alone, not to mention the massive media attention you receive on a regular basis. The cameras *love* you. They eat you up, Mrs. Dash. They can't get enough of you. Neither, can I! You have come a *long* way, baby. I am very *proud* of you, beautiful." Tony looked at his wife, admiringly, she was a beautiful sight to behold.

"Thank you, Tony, you are my *biggest* fan."

"I sure am, and I always will be. And that's because *no one* loves you more than I. I *love* you to pieces," said Tony, as he kissed his wife. Tony loved tasting Raven's lips. "*Mmmm* ... I *love* tasting those sweet, pretty lips of yours. They *taste* so good. Oh, yes, there's something else you *need* to know," said Tony, in-between kisses.

"What?" his wife asked.

"*If* you leave me, I'm *going* with you."

Raven laughed. "*Tony*! If I leave you and you come with me, then I wouldn't be leaving you then, would I?"

"That's my point *exactly*. Very wise woman, Mrs. Dash. Brains, and beauty." Tony looked into Raven's eyes. "I hope you don't mind being stuck with me for ... the next *hundred* years. *At least*."

    * * *

"No, sweetheart, I *don't* mind. You aren't a bad man to be stuck with." Raven kissed Tony tenderly on the lips. "In fact, you're the *best* man that I could be stuck with. Going back to Susan, it was always interesting to me how whites who supposedly *hate* blacks, go out and get tanned, and usually deep, dark tans at that. It's been said the deeper and darker the tan, the happier they are. The prettier the tan looks. Many of them have their lips enlarged too. What's *that* about? The race they claim to hate so much, they want to *look* like?" Raven shook her head. "That's never made any sense to me. Do they know what they are *really* saying? Becky and I have always found that very ironic, not to mention interesting. That would be like me saying I hate white people, and yet, I go and get my skin bleached, hair dyed bleach-blonde, and maybe throw in some blue contacts while I'm at it. I'm not talking about *all* whites either, only the bigots, racist ones."

Tony nodded. "It's true. And you're right, it's very interesting, to say the least. I never understood that either."

Raven and Tony loved talking. They would always talk honestly and openly, about anything. And they would share their innermost thoughts and feelings with each other. They didn't agree on everything, but the few things that they didn't agree on, was acceptable to both of them. They knew that it was okay to disagree. After all, no matter how much you love anyone, you are still individuals. You're not going to agree on everything.

Raven lies in Tony's arms, thinking. They were quiet now. Raven loved the way their relationship was. She knew of couples who talked to everyone except their mate, not to mention couples who very seldom talked to each other at all. Raven never wanted a relationship, or a marriage, like that. She prayed and hoped that their marriage would stay on the right track. She also prayed that she and Tony would always work hard to keep their marriage on the right track. A healthy and happy marriage was very important to her. And Raven knew that it was also very important to Tony.

* * *

She and Tony had a great relationship before they had gotten married. Raven would never have married him, if it wouldn't have been.

Raven also knew that when couples were courting, they would often put their best foot forward. But, Raven believed, that if you really got to know someone, if they were wearing a mask, in time, you would be able to see right through it. And sometimes, it didn't take long. After all, one could only pretend for so long. Raven knew people sometimes ignored the warning signs and got married anyway, even when they saw red flags. No marriage was guaranteed to last. Destiny, was truly in the hands of God. But Raven knew in her heart, that Tony Dash was the man that she was willing to take that chance with. She was certain of that. And she still was.

Tony broke the silence. "Oh, yes, I know what I've been wanting to ask you. How many movies do you have lined up for this year?"

"Four," said Raven.

"Talking about a full plate! *Four*? All in town?" Tony asked.

"I think so. There's one that I'm not sure about. I still have to read the script to see if I want to play the role. But it's nice being first choice for a change. I'm very *grateful* for that."

"Please, reserve *quality* time for me, for *us*," said Tony, looking at his wife seriously. "Four movies in a year is pretty overwhelming."

"I will *always* reserve time for us. You don't have to worry about that, sweetheart. No one, or *nothing*, is more important to me than you, including, my career. I *mean* that, Tony."

Raven continued to talk about her dreams and future plans. Her list was endless. Raven had always been a person who aimed high. She had always been a person who believed in being everything that you were capable of being. And she was determined to do just that.

"Reserve time for our golf dates too," said Tony, who was an avid-golfer.

"Will do," said Raven. Thinking of the history of golf, made her laugh.

"What's *so* funny?" Tony asked.

"I was just thinking about the history of golf. Like with Hollywood, there was a time when the only faces you saw on the golf course playing, were white. And for eons, blacks were kept off the golf course, they weren't allowed to play. What is ironic and very interesting is, the person who *revolutionized* golf, didn't have a *white* face, he looks like you and me. Two words, *Tiger Woods*. He is arguably the best golfer to ever play the game of golf, not to mention the most influential and most popular person in the history of golf, to date. Ain't that somethin'? *Who* knew? But as my mother always says, keep living, you never know what you might see. It's another fantastic example that *the best* can come in *any* package. Race, color, size, are *all* irrelevant. Intelligence, doesn't have anything to do with race. And like Mommie has always said, what's for you, you're going to get, and *no one*, can stop it from happening. Actually, sweetheart, *before* Tiger Woods, there was *Charlie Sifford*. Mr. Sifford broke the PGA Tour's Caucasian-only clause in 1961. And on November 15, 2004, he was the *first* African-American chosen for the World Golf Hall of Fame. And speaking of golf, my golf game leaves *a lot* to be desired."

Her husband laughed. "That's about the *only* thing too."

"I'm not done yet, Mr. Dash! I'm on a roll. *Oprah Winfrey*. She is another great example. She is the most famous talk show host to date. She *owns* her own talk show. The *O* magazine is *still* one of the most successful magazines out today. One of the most successful magazines, ever. Oprah's still one of the most powerful and influential people in the world. I always tell children, especially, African-American children, that your race has nothing to do with how successful you can become, or how smart you are. If that were the case, we wouldn't have a *Tony Dash*, *Raven Kensington Dash*, *Oprah*, *Tiger Woods*, *Venus* and *Serena Williams*, Colin Powell, Dr. *Bill Cosby*, Dr. *Condoleezza Rice*, or *Freddy Adu*. You *can* be the best, the smartest, without being white. The *only* thing that the color of your skin determines, is simply that, your color. Race. That's *it*. It *doesn't* define you. The sky is the limit. And it's not what's on you, it's what is *in* you. What's inside of us makes a world of difference. And although it's obvious, that *we* still don't have level playing fields, we can't let that, or anything, stop us from becoming everything that we are capable of being. Even if your mountain is rockier than someone else's, you *can* still climb it, *if* you want to. *No one* made it to the top without scrapes, bumps, blood, bruises. Everyone has mountains they must climb, and it doesn't matter what race you are either. Getting to where I am today wasn't a piece of cake, nor was it I'm sure, for you, or the Williams sisters for that matter, just to name a few of us, but we didn't let race, anything, or anyone, stop us from doing what we *wanted* to do. People look at us and say we made it, we're big-time, but what they *don't* see, is what we went through, to get to where we are today. Very few things come easy. Success rarely comes without a price. That is why I cannot emphasize enough, how very important *knowledge* is. We're certainly not the only examples of blacks who made it to the top, there are others too. And hopefully there will be more and more of us, who are powerful and influential. And more importantly than those things, hopefully, there will be many people, in general, who will touch the lives of others, people of *all* races. And being successful doesn't mean you have to be rich or famous either, success is an *individual* thing. It's not everyone's desire or dream to be in entertainment. Or to be rich and famous. Whatever floats your boat. Getting back to Venus and Serena, there aren't words to describe what they did to, and with, the game of tennis. And speaking of power and influence, hopefully, those who are powerful and influential, will use it to *help* others, use it to make a difference, in a *positive* manner. It's senseless to have anything, and not put it to use. *Good* use."

Tony nodded in agreement.

"Two of the *whitest* sports on the planet, dominated by African-Americans. Who would have thought that the *best* golf and tennis players, would one day, be African-American? Who knew, sweetheart? *Who knew?*"

The newlyweds continued to talk. Raven told Tony that she was also going to have her own clothing line, and maybe a *Raven* doll.

"If the Raven doll looks like you, she will be a *stunning*-beauty," said Tony.

Raven smiled, her husband was clearly her biggest fan. Raven also told Tony that she was going to write a movie that she and Becky would star in. "I'm also going to build a park and an activity center for the Tunis community, which will give the children in the area a nice place to go for fun and recreation. A convenience store is a possibility too." Raven told her husband. She knew there was also a big need for that in her hometown. "*Hmmm*, I think that's it for now. Oh, yes, maybe I'll even record a music CD."

"You're a great writer. You have a very beautiful voice too. You're a *phenomenal* woman, Mrs. Dash. Your heart is also immensely-beautiful." Tony laughed. "You left out everything *except*, running for President of the United States."

Raven laughed. "Yes, what was I *thinking*? I forgot about running for the highest office. I'll make history in two ways. I'll be the *first black* president. I'll also be the *first female* president, if, Barack Obama and Hillary Clinton don't beat me to it."

"*Trust* me, Raven, I certainly wouldn't bet against you. Few who knew you would," said her husband.

Raven asked Tony what his dreams and future plans were.

He told her that he was going to continue to grow their businesses. Tony loved the business world. It had always been a passion of his. He also told his wife that he was going to continue to contribute time and money to the poor communities, and various charities, as he'd done for years now. Tony gave Raven a long, serious look. "*Nothing* means more to me, than *you*, Raven. No one, or nothing, comes *remotely* close."

His wife smiled in answer. She felt the same way, and she told him so. "I feel the same way, Tony. I love you very much, baby."

   * * *

The newlyweds shared a passionate kiss.

"The other day, I read a magazine article that said, according to polls, guess what was the *most* important thing that men looked for in women?"

Tony looked at his wife with a straight face. "The kind of *shoes* that she's wearing?"

"More like the kind of *boobs* that she's wearing."

Tony laughed hard.

"Mr. Dash, we both know that your answer is incorrect. It's looks! What a surprise. Isn't that *something*? The woman can be dumb as all outdoors, as long as she's a sight for sore eyes, that's what counts with a lot of men. Again, according to *this* magazine article."

"What did the poll say about women?" Tony asked, turning the tables.

"*Money*, honey. All 'bout the benjamins. The dollar, dollar bill. And going hand in hand with that, social status. He could look like something the cat dragged in, but if he's a lawyer, doctor, businessman, professional athlete ... In a nutshell, as long as he's a *moneyed-honey*, a walking *ATM*, we'll love him! What are *your* thoughts?"

"I've always loved the sight of a beautiful woman," Tony said honestly. "Few men don't. *However*, it took *a lot* more than that with me. A woman's beauty wasn't the *only* thing that had to impress me. I'd always wanted the *entire* package to be beautiful. *Heart, mind*, etc. Not all women are beautiful on the outside, or on the inside either, for that matter," said Tony. "But, I will be the first to admit, that I've always wanted to marry a woman who was beautiful." Tony looked at the woman that he treasured, and flashed a broad smile. "God answered my prayers. And *boy* did He ever! Raven, *you* were the *first* and *only* beautiful woman, who made me feel, made me love. Made me get down on bended knee. I fell *hard*. I'm *knee*-deep in love with you, Raven. You're in a class all by yourself. You are the *ultimate* woman." Tony studied his wife. "For instance ... you have a face, that is *beyond* beautiful. You have that *dazzling, signature, million*-dollar smile. A very *well*-equipped body, *ooh-la-la* ... You have eyes that I could stare into night and day. Your eyes are *mesmerizing* and full of wisdom. Your skin is *baby*-soft, beautiful, flawless. You have long, raven-black hair, that I love playing in. You are *breathtaking*, Raven. But there is so *much* more to you, than the *exquisite*, outside-beauty, that you possess. You have a beautiful mind. *Genius*. You are a thinker, doer, innovator. You're a fighter. A *survivor*. You're very inspiring. Very *sophisticated*. And *most* importantly, you have a *huge* heart. You love and care about *people*." Tony's eyes searched Raven's. "You also *listen* to me. You care about my thoughts and feelings. I can tell you *all* of my hopes. *All* of my fears. And *all* of my dreams. I can talk *to* you. I can also talk *with* you. About *anything*. You don't know how much that means to me. How much, *you*, mean to me, Raven. And in addition to being the woman who I love *more* than life itself, you're also my *best* friend. So, to sum up my very *thorough* observation of you, Mrs. Dash, you are *exquisitely*-beautiful, *inside* and *out*. When I first saw you, words of Roberta's song came to mind ... *First time ever, I saw your face*." Tony framed Raven's face in his hands. "Raven, you give *new* meaning to the word *beautiful*. I felt as if I had been hit by a freight train. I had *never* seen a woman as beautiful as you. Still haven't. Not that it would matter if I ever did. You are the *only* woman who I *love*, *need*, and *want*. I love you *unconditionally*. I still pinch myself sometimes, it's *so* hard to believe. *Never* ... in *all* of my wildest dreams, did I *ever* think, that I would be *this* happy. *Never*. Raven, *you*, are the *best* thing that *ever* happened to *me*. The reason that I bought you a ten-carat diamond ring, is because *you are, my* ... *perfect ten*. It doesn't hurt that you like sports either. Especially, *football*."

Raven laughed, as her dark eyes grew serious. "I *love* you, Tony Dash. *My*, Prince Charming."

After the newlyweds finished talking, they watched TV. Raven popped popcorn, while Tony searched for a good movie. It was after three in the morning, when they fell asleep.

* * *

The newlyweds slept until noon. The maid smiled to herself when she saw the *Do Not Disturb* sign on Raven and Tony's door. She knew the newlyweds would phone room service when they were ready to have their suite cleaned.

Martha Price had been working as a maid for the Hotel Meurice, for over fifteen years. She enjoyed it too. She'd seen the young couple when they first came in. It was obvious to her that they were very much in love. Newlyweds, she immediately said to herself when she first saw them. They couldn't stop beaming at each other. They were *glowing*. She thought them a beautiful couple too. The woman looked very familiar to Martha. She didn't want to stare, but she was certain that she'd seen that beautiful face before. Martha also knew that they were doing well. Apparently, very well. They had the most expensive suite in the hotel. Martha was happy for them, in more ways than one. She wasn't doing too well financially, but she always thanked God for the things that she did have. And she was doubly-pleased, to see her kind, doing so very well.

* * *

"Good morning, beautiful. Or should I say good afternoon?" said Tony, kissing a still, slightly-sleepy Raven.

Raven smiled. "Good morning, baby. How are you this morning, *pretty boy*?" Raven teased.

They had stayed up most of the night making love, after watching TV.

"*Pretty boy*?" Tony laughed.

Raven nodded. "Yes. You are *pretty*. You are a *very* handsome fella, Mr. Dash." Raven's sense of humor kicked in. She started imitating a valley girl. "I came to Hollywood to become this *really* big star, dude. Some of the people in Hollywood are like, *totally-*weird. And everyone wanted to like, *sleep* with me. I was totally-*flabbergasted*, dude. I told them that I wasn't that kinda girl. I told them that I have like, morals and principles and things. I told them that there was no way that I'd sleep with them on the *first* date, they'd have to at *least* wait until the *second* date. And they were like totally-*shocked*. Like totally-shocked out of their minds, dude!"

Tony laughed at his wife. Raven had the voice down to a science. He loved her sense of humor.

The newlyweds finally got out of bed, brushed their teeth, bathed each other, then got dressed. Neither were hungry, so they called room service to have their suite cleaned. Raven and Tony were eager to explore the beautiful and romantic city of Paris. *Together.*

* * *

"Room service!"

Raven looked through the peephole before she opened the door. "Hello. How are you doing?" Raven greeted the middle-aged lady, with the slightly-graying hair.

"I'm well in the Lord, thank you for asking. And besides being the *most* beautiful woman that I have *ever* seen, how are you, young lady?" Martha stared at Raven. Her beauty was staggering. She loved Raven's voice too. Very articulate. And *beautiful*.

Raven glanced at Martha's name badge. "I'm fine, Ms. Price. Come in."

"You can call me, Martha." Very respectful too, the older lady thought to herself. And although Martha didn't know Raven, she still decided that she liked the young woman. "Well, if you *want* to call me, Ms. Price, you can."

"Ms. Price, this is my husband, Tony."

Tony greeted Martha and shook her hand.

"*Newlyweds*?" Martha asked, as she started cleaning their suite.

Raven and Tony laughed.

"Is it *that* obvious?" Raven asked.

Martha nodded. "*Yes*, it is, young lady. *Oh, my!* Aren't *you* ... *Raven Kensington*?"

The answer was in Raven's face.

* * *

"Oh, it *is* you! You know, I knew when I saw you two come in yesterday that I'd seen you before. Oh, my ... I *can't* believe this! What a *small* world! Don't worry, Ms. Kensington, I'm not going to advertise it. I can keep a secret. I know you want your privacy. Especially being on your honeymoon and all."

"Please, Ms. Price, call me Raven."

Raven and Martha chatted for a while longer, before the newlyweds left to explore Paris.

Raven and Tony wore matching sweatsuits and very comfortable shoes. They planned to do a lot of walking. They also donned hats and sunglasses.

The hotel was located in the most elegant district in Paris. There were a host of nearby art galleries, boutiques, museums, restaurants, theaters, and parks, all within walking distance.

Tony laughed when he saw the parks. He knew that they would *definitely* be visiting the parks, probably every day.

Paris was one of the most beautiful places that Raven had ever seen. The newlyweds strolled hand in hand, as they explored the *City of Lights*.

* * *

Over the next several weeks, Raven and Tony continued to explore Paris. They did lots of shopping, dined at restaurants, went dancing, watched a number of plays, enjoyed the parks, and they also visited many of the historic landmarks.

There were also days, when the newlyweds would do *nothing*, but stay inside of their hotel suite, making love, and having heart-to-heart talks. Raven and Tony were having the time of their lives! *Neither*, had *ever* been ... *happier*.

* * *

Chapter 7

Tony whisked Raven away for three days to the South of France. Before they left for the South of France, Tony surprised his wife with a gorgeous diamond bracelet that he had purchased for her at JAR's.

They rented a convertible and packed a few things for their short stay. The ten-hour drive was very enjoyable. Tony loved how the wind combed Raven's long black hair.

Tony had visited the South of France a number of times. There weren't many places he hadn't been. He had always loved the serenity of La Faviere, the little "French" town where they were going.

He felt Raven would love it too. And from the look in her eyes when they arrived, there was no question, she did love it. Her eyes lit up when she saw the water, the sailboats, the dock ... It was a place where one could get away from it all. It was very peaceful and quiet.

The newlyweds strolled hand in hand for a long time, before sitting on a dock. As their bare feet dangled over the water, Tony began humming Otis Redding's classic, which couldn't have been more appropriate. Then, as if on cue, Raven and Tony began singing, "Sittin' on the Dock of the Bay."

Tony concluded the song by whistling at the end, just as the late Otis Redding had done. He smiled as he looked into his wife's eyes. "We make *beautiful* music *together*, don't we, beautiful?" Tony meant that in more ways than one.

Raven smiled. "Yes, my love. We *sure* do."

There was a long silence, as their eyes locked and held. What they felt for each other, transcended words. They gave each other something no one else did.

Tony finally broke the silence. "You and I weren't even thought about when that song first came out, yet, we both know the lyrics."

"Oh, yes, baby, that's a *classic*! It's also one of my *favorite* songs," said Raven.

The newlyweds continued to sit on the dock of the bay. They sat quietly, admiring the beautiful scenery.

* * *

Raven and Tony returned to Paris days later, as planned. The three weeks went by far too quickly for them. Although the newlyweds were definitely going to miss Paris, they were both very excited about starting their new life, together, and moving into their palatial, Malibu dream home.

Before leaving Paris, Raven left a thousand dollars in an envelope for Martha. Somehow, she felt that Martha could use the money. And although it may not have been a lot to some, Raven knew that it would help her.

Tears filled Martha's eyes when she came in to clean the suite and found the envelope, with her name written on it, and the money inside. Martha didn't know how Raven had sensed that she needed money, but God knew, thought Martha. She smiled, now she had enough to pay her rent. She had missed three days of work, due to illness, which had in turn made her paycheck short. But, thanks to the beautiful black woman, who was apparently just as beautiful on the inside, she would be fine.

"*Thank you*, Ms. Kensington," Martha whispered, as if Raven could hear her. "Thank you!" And last but not least, she also thanked God, who made *all* things possible.

* * *

The jet took off just as smoothly as it had landed. Raven and Tony sat on the plane, talking about their *unforgettable* honeymoon and their futures.

Tony kissed his wife tenderly on the lips. "Our honeymoon's *not* going to end just because we're leaving Paris. We will continue it! Our honeymoon was very *memorable*. Wasn't it, beautiful?"

"*Unforgettable!*" said Raven smiling. "*Unforgettable!*"

It seemed they had made it back to L.A. in no time. Even the pilots and Mack hated leaving Paris. Everyone had enjoyed themselves immensely. But none more so than the newlyweds.

Becky and John had already moved in together. All of Raven's belongings had been moved to Tony's home in Pacific Palisades, before they'd left for Texas to get married. Raven and Tony spent the night there. The movers were arriving early the next morning.

The newlyweds decided to sell the Pacific Palisades home. The home was sold to a new comedy star, who made Raven and Tony an offer they just couldn't refuse.

Tony Dash owned a number of homes; there was the sprawling ranch in Wyoming, a home in the Hamptons, Aspen, an apartment in Trump Tower that overlooked Central Park, and a home in the Bellhaven community in Greenwich, Connecticut. And now, there was his and his wife's newly-built home in Malibu, to add to that list.

* * *

Raven lies in her husband's arms, unable to sleep. She was so excited about moving into their new home.

Tony was equally-excited. But nothing excited him more than spending the rest of his life with his beautiful wife, who was the woman of his dreams. It didn't matter to Tony where they were, as long as they were together. There was no greater joy, as far as Tony was concerned, than being with Raven.

* * *

The movers arrived promptly the next morning. Raven laughed. They looked like a small army. Like most people, Raven hated moving. It was nice not having to lift a finger for a change. The movers were going to pack everything, transfer their belongings to the home in Malibu, and put everything where Raven wanted it.

"My wife's in charge," Tony told the manager. "If you have *any* questions, see her."

The manager brought more than enough men to get the job done as quickly as possible. The movers were very professional, and they handled everything with care. They were also quick. It was obvious they had done this many times before. They had the job completed in record time. Raven could see why Tony always used the same moving company. They were awesome, to say the least. The very last item was brought into the Malibu home late that afternoon.

Tony thanked the manager and gave him a fat tip, which put a big smile on the manager's face. "Please share that with your workers," said Tony. He knew the entire crew had worked very hard.

     * * *

Becky and John came over later that night. They marveled as Raven and Tony gave them another tour of their lavish estate, per their request. The home *shouted* immense-wealth and style. John was thrilled that the basketball courts were now finished. He loved playing basketball.

Tony had a top-notch security system installed to cover the monstrous estate. Cameras were everywhere, including, outside the gates.

After the tour ended, the guys went to shoot hoops, while the ladies sat in the living room talking.

"Honeymoon-look, *huh*, Sis?" Becky teased.

Raven laughed in answer.

"I feel ya!" Becky was elated for Raven. She had never seen her so happy. Becky listened as her best friend gave her all of the exciting details, of her and Tony's unforgettable honeymoon in Paris.

After Becky and John left, Raven called her family and Tony's, to give them their new phone number and address. Everyone was happy to know that they had made it home safely. No one had to ask how the honeymoon went, the answer was in Raven's voice.

Raven smiled, as she thought about what Becky had said to her earlier. She was every bit as happy as she looked. Raven Kensington Dash, was very happy. She had never, been happier. And it clearly showed.

Andrew called Raven's cell phone. *"Welcome* back, pretty lady!" Andy commented on their beautiful wedding and reception. And then, like the point man that he was, he got straight to the point. Andy reminded Raven that her next film would begin shooting in three weeks. The movie would be filmed in Manhattan and Philadelphia, Andy told her.

Raven was happy that she had three more weeks before filming her next movie. She still thanked God every day to be working and to be where she was now. She had come a long way, but Raven knew that she still had not reached her peak. She was the kind of person who always strived to continue to grow, in *all* aspects of her life, including, becoming a *better* person. And no matter how successful she became, she vowed to never forget where she came from. Nor would she ever forget the *true* meaning of life. *Living.*

Tony overheard some of Raven and Andrew's conversation. He was happy for his wife. He knew what she'd gone through to get to where she was now. Tony knew that she had worked very hard, and long.

Raven smiled at her husband. "My new film will begin shooting in three weeks. It won't be here though. The director has decided to film it in Manhattan and Philly. If everything goes well, the movie should be wrapped in about three months." Raven looked at her husband. She hoped he was going to travel with her.

Tony nodded. They hadn't been married anytime at all, and they were already reading each other's minds, *and* finishing each other's sentences. Becky had even picked up on that too. *"Of course,* I'm going with my baby. There's no way that I want to spend *one* night without you, Raven." Tony meant it too. He didn't think there would ever come a time, when he would grow tired of his wife.

   * * *

Raven and Tony went outside and walked the grounds. It was a beautiful day in Malibu. Tony had a surprise for Raven. Mack knew what it was, but he had been sworn to secrecy. *Again.*

"What's *that* for?" Raven asked, pointing to what looked like a huge doghouse.

"That's where I'll be *staying* when I make you angry." Tony joked.

Raven laughed in answer.

"Shall we go *see* what it is?"

They walked over to the doghouse, but it was empty.

"Mrs. Dash? Perhaps you're looking for *this*," said Mack.

Raven turned around to see the cutest little Yorkie that she had ever seen. Tony had bought her a Yorkshire Terrier. She'd mentioned that she liked Yorkies. The Kensingtons had a Yorkie named Trixie. And Trey had a Yorkie named Skippy.

Besides showering Raven with lots of love, Tony also wanted to spoil her. And continue to spoil her, he did. It was obvious that Tony Dash was a man of his word.

"Oh, baby! *Thank you!*" said an elated Raven, giving her husband a kiss. Her eyes danced, as Mack handed her the little Yorkie, who wasn't any bigger than a shoebox. He had the cutest little baby-doll face. The little Yorkie's eyes were big and dark. He was very friendly, and he seemed very happy, as he wagged his tail back and forth.

Raven smiled. "*Hello, Pugs Dash.* Welcome to the family."

Tony and Mack laughed.

"*Pugs Dash?*" her husband asked. "How *cute.*"

Mack nodded his head in agreement.

No one could deny how cute "Pugs" was. And the men had to admit, Pugs was also a cute name for a pup.

The spacious, well-equipped doghouse would keep Pugs warm in the winter and cool in the summer. Tony knew how Raven felt about dogs being in the house, no matter how cute they were.

Mack went back inside.

Raven and Tony stayed outside and played with Pugs. Mack watched them from the living room window. They were so happy together. Mack could tell they were deeply in love. He had never seen his boss so happy. Watching Raven and Tony brought a smile to Mack's lips.

Raven and Tony stayed outside playing with Pugs for hours, before coming in the house to eat the lunch that Mack had prepared for them. Cooking was also another one of Mack Simon's specialties.

Raven and Tony washed up, then went on the terrace to eat lunch. They asked Mack to join them, but he declined.

"He's a little shy, isn't he?" Raven asked her husband.

"Yes, he is. It took him a while to actually start talking to me, on a personal level. At first, he was all business. Mack's a quiet man."

The two sat on the terrace, eating and talking. And as always, they talked about any and everything. Tony congratulated his wife again on being nominated for Best Supporting Actress in a Motion Picture, for her role as Myrtle Jane, in *Heartless War*.

Tony laughed. "*Myrtle Jane*? What a name! Especially, for such a *lovely* lady."

Andrew told Raven on the day of her wedding, that her nomination was no longer speculation, it was official.

Raven was elated, but her main hope was to *win*.

Many were rooting for Raven: Tony, of course, her family, the Dash family, Becky, and the entire Simms family, John, Andrew, the entire Tunis community, and all of her millions of fans, that she now had all over the world. Raven-mania was in full force.

In less than a week, Raven, Tony, Becky, and John, were all going to the Oscars, together. And ironically, the Oscar ceremony was on Raven's birthday, *March 9th*. What a great birthday present that would be, thought Raven, not to mention, what winning an Oscar could do to her already successful career. If Raven did win, it would be the third Oscar, won by an African-American woman, playing the role of a maid. Hattie McDaniel, the actress who played in *Gone With the Wind*, was the first.

After finishing their lunch, Raven and Tony went to visit Becky and John. Becky showed them all of the countless magazines that had the newlyweds on the front cover.

Raven glanced at one of the headlines that read: "Beautiful Movie Star Siren Weds Billionaire Business Magnate / Former Superstar NFL Running Back, in Lavish, Valentine's Day Wedding."

Some magazines gave Raven top billing, others gave top billing to Tony. Raven and Tony's wedding was in every national newspaper and magazine known to man. Their wedding had also been broadcasted on every major news channel. And although security had been tight, paparazzi still managed to get photos. As always.

Paparazzi had even flown above the Kensington home, the church, and the Hilton, in airplanes, enabling them to take photos of the bride, groom, and many of their families and friends.

Becky shook her head laughing. "Paparazzi were determined, weren't they, Sis?"

"Yes," said Raven. "That's a well-known fact in Hollywood. They always seem to find a way to get pictures of the stars, no matter what."

Tony and John went to the game room, leaving the two women alone to chat. Raven reminded Becky that she had caught the bouquet.

Becky only laughed, she still wasn't ready for marriage.

The two ladies talked for hours, before the Dashs left Becky and John's.

When Raven and Tony arrived home, they went to check on Pugs, who was sleeping soundly in his doghouse.

Raven later joined Tony in their home-gym, where they often worked out together. The Dashs' spacious, well-equipped gym, rivaled that of a world-class gym.

The newlyweds worked out for a couple of hours. Afterwards, Tony decided to go for a swim. He asked Raven to join him.

Raven shook her head. "I can't swim, honey."

"We'll have to *change* that. I'll *teach* you."

"Tomorrow, maybe? I'm ready to take a bath and relax."

Raven went to take a bath, while Tony went swimming.

When Tony came upstairs to their bedroom, he kissed his wife and went to shower. He felt good. He loved exercising and staying in shape. He also loved going swimming after working out. The water from the pool always felt good. Tony also enjoyed working out with his wife. He made a mental note to teach Raven how to swim.

* * *

Raven was in bed reading when Tony got out of the shower.

"What are you reading, beautiful?" Tony asked.

"*Twelve Inches*," said Raven.

"*New* book?"

"Yes. It's very good so far. It's hard to put down. It's what I call a *glue*-book. I bought one for Aunt Dolores for her birthday last month. She loved it. So, I decided to buy one and read it too. Everyone's been talking about what a great book it is, and so far, it seems they're right. I'm certainly enjoying it." Raven read a good portion of the book, before turning off the light. She had gotten up very early that morning, and her eyes were heavy.

Tony watched TV, until he fell asleep.

* * *

Tony woke up in the middle of the night. "Raven?" he whispered in the dark. "Sweetheart?"

His wife stirred. "*Hmmm*? Yes, baby?"

"I'm hungry."

"*Tony*! *O-kay* ... I suppose you want me to be a good wifey, and go get you something to eat. *O-kay*. You spoil me, so I *guess* I can spoil you too." Raven threw the covers back. She was about to get out of bed and go fix Tony something to eat, but he stopped her.

"Don't get out of bed, baby."

* * *

Raven looked at her husband. She saw that all too familiar, dreamy look in his eyes. She knew instantly what Tony wanted. It never failed, every time he wanted to make love to her, which was often, his eyes would get *that* look.

"I'm *not* hungry for *food*."

Raven hit him with a pillow. "Tony Dash! *Baby*, I'm *tired* and sleepy. *Another* time?"

"You're tired and sleepy?" her husband asked.

Raven nodded.

"Not a problem."

"Thanks for being understanding, sweetheart."

"*Relax*," said Tony. "I'll do *all* the work. *Self*-service, is one of my specialties."

"Tony Dash, you're *too* funny. What am I going to do with *you*?"

"*Love me ...*" said Tony, as he reached for Raven. Tony skillfully removed his wife's black satins, as his lips found hers. "Oh … *baby* … I *love you*." Tony's mouth and hands were electrifying, and like magic, as he explored every inch of his wife's body.

Raven moaned in ecstasy, as Tony made love to her, hungrily, and with a fiery passion. And as always, their lovemaking was magical. Tony's appetite for Raven was insatiable.

Hours later, they lie in each other's arms, happy, and sated.

"I *love* you, Raven."

"I *love* you too, baby. *Tonagra. Now*, may I *please* go back to sleep? Tony, *promise* me that you'll be a *good* boy."

Tony laughed. "Yes, beautiful, you may go back to sleep now. I *promise*, I'll be good. At *least* 'til morning," he added.

Raven laughed. Within minutes, she was fast asleep. And so was Tony.

* * *

The next morning when Raven awoke, Tony was out of bed. She turned on the TV to watch *CNN*.

"*Good morning, beautiful!*" Tony entered the room carrying a tray. He had made breakfast for her.

"Good morning, love. *Oh ... Tony ...*" Raven smiled. "Breakfast in bed?"

Her husband had cooked her pancakes and bacon.

"Tony, you're spoiling me so much! When the honeymoon-period ends, I'm going to have withdrawals."

"You will *never* have withdrawals, because I'm *not* going to stop. I'll always love and cherish you, beautiful. *Always*! That's not going to end after a honeymoon, or after the first few years of marriage. I'm going to do my *best* to stay in honeymoon-mode."

"Wow! I can certainly get used to this. *Thank you* so much, baby. Where is yours? Have you eaten?" Raven asked her husband.

Tony flashed a big smile. "I ate *a lot* last night."

Raven blushed. "Tony Dash! You are *such* a *bad* boy!" Raven began eating the delicious breakfast that her husband made for her. "This is great. You're a very good cook, baby."

"Thanks. I'm not as good as your mother though. I've never tasted food so good. Don't you dare tell my mother that I said that either. My mother's a great cook, but Mae Kensington can burn!"

Raven laughed. "Your secret's safe with me, sweetheart."

"I got the report this morning on *our* businesses. They're *all* doing extremely well." Tony smiled. "I *love* making money when I'm sleeping, or even *better* than that, when I'm *making love* to my beautiful wifey."

"Speaking of *making love*, Tonagra, I've told you before, I'll blame *you* if I'm unable to walk. Just *think*, not so long ago, I was a *virgin*. You have only *touched* me, a *thousand* times, since our wedding night."

Tony laughed hard. He looked at his wife, who sat topless, before him. "Beautiful woman with a sense of humor. If you don't cover *those* up, I'm going to *touch* you *again*, *before*, you finish your breakfast."

Raven laughed, as she reached for her robe.

"*Ah-ah-ah* ..." said Tony. "I was just *kidding*. I don't want you to cover up. The view is far too beautiful to hide. And like I've told you before, if there ever comes a time when you *can't* walk, I'll *carry* you. Gladly! You're in the *best* of hands, baby. What do you want to do today?"

"Absolutely nothing. I just simply want us to enjoy doing nothing. Much to do about *nothing*. That sounds like fun. Let's enjoy our time together, enjoy our beautiful home, and little P.D. Pugs looks just like Trixie, our dog in Tunis. The main difference is that Trixie's a female."

Tony nodded in agreement. "Pugs and Trixie do look just alike. They look like twins. Same color, everything." Tony laughed. "*P.D.?*"

"Pugs Dash."

"*Cute*. Doing nothing's great. No arguments here. I fed Pugs this morning. I also gave him water, so he's a *happy* camper. Aren't the Oscars this week?"

Raven nodded. She tried not to think about the *big* night. She was a little nervous. But now that her husband had brought it up, she thought about what an Oscar could do for her career. Although, there were exceptions. In some cases, actors and actresses had won Oscars, but it did very little, or nothing, for their careers. Those were exceptions though. Winning an Oscar was truly the *greatest* honor. Oscars were to actors and actresses, what Grammys were to musicians, or winning a Superbowl ring was to an NFL player, thought Raven, thinking of Tony, who had seven Superbowl rings. It was a symbol that you were the best. The very *best*.

Raven thought of her next film. They would leave for the East Coast approximately two weeks after Oscar night. She looked forward to going back to Philly. She had many great childhood memories in *The City of Brotherly Love*, which was now also referred to as, *The City that Loves You Back*.

Raven had one exception in all of her contracts, to have every weekend off. Now that she was a married woman, she wanted to spend quality time with her husband. No one, or *nothing*, including her love for acting, meant more to her than Tony. Their marriage. Raven was determined to follow the same advice that she had given Trey, she vowed to always take care of business at home, *first* and *foremost*.

* * *

Later that day, Tony drove Raven to an empty building on Rodeo Drive. "Don't you think this would be a *great* location for R.K. by Design?" Tony asked his wife.

Raven looked at him. "A *perfect* location."

The building was for sale. Tony told Raven that he'd also looked at a number of locations in South Central L.A.

Raven decided that she would start with two locations. One in South Central L.A., the other, in Beverly Hills. Raven told Tony that they would hire a good management team to run the stores. They both knew how crucial good management was. The Dashs didn't just want good employees, they wanted the best. And that, was what they were going to get. As Tony already knew, even if you're an owner, you must stay on top of things. You must know what's going on with your business, on a regular basis. They both knew that it wasn't wise to entrust everything to others, including your management staff.

Tony loved every aspect of the business world. He used the same philosophy that he had used in sports. Learn, know and master your game, work harder than anyone else, be a leader and a team player, put the best team together, and always strive to be the best. And although Tony knew there was no perfect human being, that *never* stopped Tony Dash from striving for perfection. And, just as he'd done when he played sports, when it came to business, he always played to win. Tony also knew that when it came to business, *results*, were the bottom line. And the *best people* produced the *best results*.

After leaving Rodeo Drive, Raven and Tony drove to South Central L.A. Tony showed Raven the vacant building on Crenshaw.

The newlyweds examined the building and the location. The building was in an area that had heavy foot traffic.

Raven smiled. Another great business location, another great business opportunity.

Raven and Tony spent the next several days putting together strategic business plans for the two locations, which would be R.K. by Design. They were very pleased with the results.

Tony knew that he was going to purchase the two buildings. They were both prime locations. Tony knew a great business opportunity when he saw one. And apparently, so did his wife.

"That's it. No *more* business now!" said Tony. "Let's go swimming."

Raven and Tony donned swimwear. It was time to teach his wife how to swim. Raven entered the pool slowly. She held on tightly to the bars that were alongside the pool. Raven was afraid to let go.

Tony laughed. "It's *okay*, baby. Hold on to me. I'll go slow. If I'm going too fast for you, let me know." Tony waited for Raven to gain her composure. "Okay, *first* lesson. Hold your breath, then *slowly*, put your head under water. Come up whenever you need to. It is very important that you learn to hold your breath, especially under water. That's probably the one thing that scares beginners the most, besides being afraid that they're going to drown. One of the most important keys to learning how to swim, is removing the fear of drowning factor."

Raven cautiously followed Tony's first set of instructions.

Tony stood beside her, watching her closely. "You're doing well, baby. *Relax.* Go at your *own* pace. Don't try to do anything too quickly. Take your time."

Raven practiced the routine, repeatedly, until she felt comfortable. She still refused to let go of the bars. She wasn't feeling quite that brave yet. But eventually, she felt better about holding her breath and going under water, and that she did, repeatedly, until she felt very comfortable doing it.

* * *

When Raven was completely comfortable with the first step, Tony moved to step two. He held Raven's body up, as she moved her arms forward, and used her legs, to kick her feet behind her.

"Don't forget, sweetheart, remember to hold your breath."

"Don't let me go, Tony!" Raven almost panicked.

"I'm not going to let you go. I would drown first, before I'd let *anything* happen to you, beautiful. You don't have to worry about that."

Raven and Tony stayed in the pool for hours, before calling it a wrapped, first lesson. Raven still had a lot to learn regarding swimming, but she was closer than she had been before. In fact, she was closer than she had ever been.

"You know, you did well, it being your first lesson and all." Tony told her. She had done well, and Tony wanted to encourage Raven and help build her confidence.

* * *

Tony continued to give Raven swimming lessons. They were in the pool every day, for several hours each time. And as a result, Raven got better and better.

Whenever Raven and Tony used the outdoor pool, they had one audience member, Pugs. He would bark and wag his tail excitedly. It was as if Pugs were rooting for Raven. The newlyweds laughed when they saw how excited Pugs seemed to get, whenever Raven went swimming.

"Do you think Pugs can swim?" Raven asked Tony.

"Probably. Most dogs, if not all, are naturally good swimmers. I have also determined why Pugs gets so excited when he sees you swimming."

"Why?" Raven asked.

"Because you look *soooo gooodddd* in your swimsuit. You're so beautiful and *sexxxy*. It's *hard* to teach you, sweetheart. You always distract me." Tony's eyes lit up, as they combed his wife's body.

* * *

Raven looked incredibly-gorgeous and sexy with the water dripping from her hair and body. She was truly, a sight for sore eyes.

Tony picked her up. "Time to *go*," he whispered.

* * *

The next day was Raven's birthday; it was also Oscar time. Tony gave Raven a surprise birthday party. Becky, John, Mack, Andrew, Tony's parents, and about thirty of their closest friends were in attendance. The party ended in more than enough time for everyone to get ready for the *big night*.

* * *

Raven, Tony, Becky, and John went to the Oscars together. Raven looked smashing in a white Chanel evening gown. Tony looked very handsome in a white Armani tuxedo. Becky looked very lovely too. She wore a light blue Calvin Klein evening gown that matched her eyes. And John, like Tony, wore the same color as his significant other. He too looked handsome in a light blue Ralph Lauren tux.

Raven sat quietly in the limo, as the driver whisked them off to the Kodak Theatre. The night that she'd tried hard not to dwell on, had finally come. Hollywood's *biggest* night, had arrived.

When the foursome exited the limo, they were immediately surrounded by reporters. The women from Tunis, Texas finally got to experience what walking on the red carpet was *really* like. Raven and Becky had watched the Oscars on TV for years. And now, they were a part of it. A *big* part of it.

"There *she* is!" one entertainment reporter shouted, pointing at Raven. Raven Kensington was the biggest star in Hollywood.

"*Raven Ken-sing-ton*! *Over here*! *Over here*!" Everyone was waiting for *her*. Lightbulb after lightbulb flashed in Raven's face.

"Miss Kensington! Over here, *Miss Kensington*!"

Fans waved paper and pens for Raven to sign autographs. And she did so, graciously. Raven had her hands full, signing autographs, and answering all of the endless questions from the media. But as always, she handled both, like a pro.

The twenty-five million dollar, loaned necklace, shone brightly on Raven's neck. The elegant gown was also loaned. Raven's phone rung all week long. *Everyone* wanted her to wear *something* of theirs. They knew all eyes would be on *her*. And they were all counting on Raven to work her magic and sell their products. If anyone could bring in lots of sales, they knew the sultry-beauty could. Raven attracted attention, like honey attracted bees.

"How does it feel to be nominated for an Oscar for your *first* movie?" an entertainment reporter asked.

Raven flashed that signature smile. "It feels great! I'm *elated*. It's *truly* an honor." And it was.

Fans began screaming Becky's name. Many of them watched *Day's Dawn* every day. It was currently the number one soap opera. And Rebecca Simms was the reason why. She received more fan mail than anyone else on the show. Fans *loved* her. And they made it clear that she was the main reason that they tuned in to watch every day, even though her character was one you loved to hate.

Finally, after being interviewed by what seemed like reporter after reporter, the foursome headed inside to find Andy. He and his wife had arrived early. It was Raven's second time seeing "the Mrs." Tandy Spellman was a slim, pretty brunette.

After a while, everyone was asked to take their seats.

"The show's about to begin! Everyone, please take your seats!" said Cramby Nokesman, the Oscar host.

Everyone took their seats.

Raven knew that she wasn't the only one nervous. She was certain that even the veteran actors and actresses were also nervous when they were nominated for Oscars, if only a little. Raven also knew that one could never win too many Oscars. She knew that it was every actors' and actresses' dream, to win at least one.

John yawned as the night went on. As far as he was concerned, it was all boring. "I'd rather be home watching football," he whispered to Becky, who laughed in answer.

   * * *

Then finally, the moment that they had all been waiting for, arrived. Tony squeezed Raven's hand, as Cramby called her name.

"And nominated for *Best* Supporting Actress in a Motion Picture ... Raven Kensington, for *Heartless War*!" Cramby finished calling out the other nominees' names, then paused, as he opened the envelope. "And *now*, for the *moment* that we've all been waiting for ... the *Oscar goes to* ..."

Raven got more nervous by the minute, Cramby seemed to take forever to announce the winner.

"*Ra-ven Ken-sing-ton*! For *Heartless War*!" Cramby roared.

Raven sat frozen. She was shocked and overjoyed, at the same time.

Tony kissed her. He was ecstatic. He had been silently-praying that she'd win. So was Becky, Andy, all of Raven Kensington's family, and her millions of fans.

Becky hugged Raven. "*Congratulations*, Sis! You *earned* it!"

John congratulated her too. He smiled. That was the only thing that made sitting through the boring ceremony worthwhile. John was very happy for Raven.

Raven walked onstage. Her dark eyes were filled with tears. She found her voice. "*Wow*! What a *birthday* present!" Tears fell as Raven spoke. She didn't try to fight them, nor did she want to. "*First* of all, I *thank God*, because with *Him*, *all things*, are possible, and *absolutely nothing*, is impossible! *Tony*, my *wonderful* husband, *my* soul mate, *my Prince Charming*. I *love* you *so* very much. Words can't express how much I love *you*. *Thank you*, sweetheart!"

Tony smiled.

"*Special* thanks to my parents, Charles and Mae Kensington, who *always* loved and believed in me. My brother, Trey, my sisters, Angie, Becky, Stephanie. My nephew, T.J., my nieces, Lillie and Sabrina. The *entire* Tunis community. Mrs. Tanya Riley ..." Raven looked at Andrew. "*Thank you*, Andy, *Andrew Spellman*, very much, for *believing* in *me*, when no one else in Hollywood did. And to *all* of my fans, thank you. I also want to thank everyone who cast their votes for me. I didn't want to take this role because of *obvious* reasons. But I realized, thanks to my mother, that sometimes, as actors, we have to take roles, that we may not want to, in order to open doors to *bigger* and *better* things. And for me, it did just that. I also want everyone out there to know that, no matter what your race, size, or monetary situation, you *can* do it! Work hard, *believe* in yourself, even if or when, no one else believes in you. Self-confidence is *crucial*! And so is perseverance. *Always, believe in yourself,* and *resist* the word, *can't*. I'm living proof of what *can* happen, when you keep fighting, even when someone else's barriers, are against you. *Remember*, the *only* barriers that matter, are the ones that we place on ourselves. *This* Oscar is a *collective* one. It's *for all those*, who came *before* me, who helped *pave* the way for me. *For all those*, who are fighting, and struggling in Hollywood now. And *for all those*, who will come *after* me. F.A.T., *for all those ... Thank* you! Thank you *all*!"

Raven Kensington received a standing ovation.

"Congratulations, Ms. Kensington! And *Happy Birthday!*" said Cramby. "I didn't know that *March 9th* was your birthday. I am sure the audience agrees with me, what a birthday present! I must add this, you couldn't have worn a more appropriate color, Ms. Kensington. You are an *angel*, to so many!" Cramby knew that Raven donated a lot of her money, and time, to help others. Especially, the less fortunate. He admired her immensely. As far as Cramby was concerned, Raven Kensington was an angel, living on earth.

The audience continued to cheer and clap.

"*Congratulations*, beautiful! You *deserved* it! I *love* you," said Tony, as he gave his wife another hug and kiss.

Tessa Winters sat in the audience, with a grim look on her face. She was nominated for Best Actress in a Motion Picture, but she didn't win.

After the show concluded, the foursome, along with Andy and his wife, made their rounds at the Vanity Fair party at Morton's, and the Governors Ball. Everyone had an enjoyable time. It was well after midnight, before they decided to call it an evening.

Andrew and his wife congratulated Raven again, before leaving. Andy was ecstatic for Raven, and as far as he was concerned, she deserved everything great that was finally happening to her. *Everything.*

Tandy Spellman looked at her husband. "I *like* Raven. She's a very beautiful and distinguished woman." Tandy had seen Raven many times, on TV and in magazines.

"She is, isn't she?" said Andy. "You know, when I *first* saw her, I *knew* there was something very special about her. I watched her for a number of days, before I spoke with her. You should've seen her boss and the other employees at Spago. They were going to have my head, if I would have stepped out of line with Raven. It was very obvious that they all cared a lot about her."

"She used to work at Spago?" Tandy asked.

Her husband nodded. "Yes, she did."

"I didn't know that. What's the story on the blonde? Are they as close as they seem?"

"*Yes.* Raven and Becky are *very* close. They've been best friends for about twenty years, I think. They both came out here from Texas to make it big in Hollywood. Both of them are *big* now. They're both doing well. *Very* well. I don't know if you've seen that new soap opera, *Day's Dawn,* but Becky's the *main* star on there. And you know how well Raven's doing. Fans everywhere love her. Raven-mania! She's driving everyone crazy. Raven Kensington's a big star now, and her star is only going to get bigger and *bigger.*"

Tandy nodded. "Her husband's *crazy* about her! Is he *smitten* or what? I wish you'd look at me the way he looks at her. He *adores* her."

It was very easy to see, how much Tony loved Raven.

"*Tandy,* what are *you* talking about? Sweetheart, you know how much I love you. And besides, they are *newlyweds.*"

"I know that Andy, we went to their wedding, remember? I don't think that it's a passing thing with him though. Maybe I'm wrong. But I think he'll *keep* that look. I haven't seen *all* women, including, *newly*-married ones, receive *that* look from their husbands. It is very *obvious* that they are very much in love. They are a very *striking* couple too."

Andy nodded. "Tony's a great guy. I wish them both well. And yes, he's very lucky to have Raven as a wife, but you know what?" Andy reached for his wife's hand. "I'm also a very *lucky* man."

Tandy Spellman smiled. She and Andrew had been married for twenty-five years. And they were still very happy. Tandy felt very lucky to have Andy too. He was a great husband, he was also her closest friend.

"It's nice to see a different kind of look and size in Hollywood. It's so very *refreshing*! For so long, *too* long, we've seen the same ol', same ol'. The white female, toothpicks, half-naked, or *completely* naked."

Andy laughed.

"Many had *little* or *no* talent, but mainly because of their race, they were given parts. Not to mention, God only knows, what they probably did behind closed doors to get those parts. To get parts, I'm sure their legs *parted* too."

Andrew laughed again. He was used to his wife's bluntness. Tandy Spellman was never one to mince words.

"Raven *contradicts* all of those things, and in *my* opinion, she's *far* more beautiful than those *dimwits*. Ms. Kensington also has a much better body. She has the boobs too, which I assume are real."

Her husband laughed again.

"She's very curvaceous. She's got it goin' on! And no, I'm *not* gay, I'm simply making a point. Not that she's the first black woman in Hollywood to ever be successful, but in my opinion, she's the first to show Hollywood, and the world, that you can be sexy, *without* being a toothpick." Tandy shook her head. "I have never thought that being skinny was sexy. Being skinny isn't sexy to me at all. Bones, straight up and down. What's sexy about *that* look? And the ones who look anorexic, they're *supposed* to be sexy? C'mon now. Please! Obviously, many of us are *blind* as bats."

Andy laughed.

"I'm small. But my size-four frame *has* curves. I'm not straight up and down. I've got boobs too. And I certainly *don't* look anorexic."

Andy nodded in agreement. His wife had a nice body.

"Ms. Kensington sends an *immensely*-strong and *positive* message that is so very badly needed in the world. *Long*, long overdue. She also has *a lot* of class!" Tandy shook her head again. "I wonder how her husband feels about *all* the men drooling over her. Raven walks in a room, and all eyes are on her. They stay on her too. I guess it would be difficult not to watch a woman like that. She's like a *magnet*. A person like that you can't help but be drawn to. She's a very *extraordinary* woman. And is she beautiful or *what*? She's a *bad* sister!"

"Raven is a very beautiful woman." Andy agreed.

"I like her *a lot*."

Andy looked at his wife. As far as he was concerned, his wife didn't *like* Raven Kensington, she *loved* her. Tandy Spellman talked about Raven all the way home. It was obvious to Andy that his wife admired Raven, immensely.

Tandy continued singing Raven's praises. "She's a woman who does things *her* way and wins. I can tell that about her, simply by what she's done, and how she's done it. Raven Kensington is wanted by men and women. Men want her. Women want to be her."

Andy nodded his head in agreement.

"Who would've thought that one day, we would live to see a black movie star, size eleven, in predominantly-white Hollywood, who is considered by many, as one of the most beautiful women in the world? The train was already in motion with more and more blacks becoming more successful in Hollywood over the years, although they still have a ways to go. However, Raven Kensington has not only carried the baton with race, but with size, also. And that is *definitely* very rare. She has made larger females be proud of their shapes and sizes, and that is *priceless*, because it may even save lives." Tandy shook her head. "Andy, you don't know how many times I've heard on the news, and read about females who have died, because they had starved themselves to death, trying to emulate super-thin females, who are constantly praised in the media. Raven is incredible! We need more people in the world like her. Finally, someone who is *truly*, the one to watch." Tandy beamed. "Watch out now! There's a new sheriff in town. Raven Kensington's *changing* the rules, and the judges!"

Andy laughed. "Not *only* are fans crazy about Raven, so is my wife."

"I told you, honey, I *like* her. *A lot*. She's also immensely-talented. Everyone *deserves* the right to be given the same opportunity as everyone else. We still have a *long* way to go on that too. But *thank God* for Raven Kensington! Thank God for *her*."

Tandy *finally* changed the subject. She and Andrew talked about their upcoming vacation. They were leaving to go skiing in Aspen the next day. They were going to spend four nights there. After leaving Aspen, they were going to head to Dallas to spend a week with Andy's brother and his family, in *tony* Turtle Creek.

"Are you coming with me to New York in a few weeks?" Andy asked his wife.

Tandy shook her head no. "I can't, honey. After we come back from Dallas, it's back to work for me."

Tandy Spellman was a legal analyst for *MSNBC*. And although she didn't have to work, she loved what she did, so she worked anyway.

* * *

Raven placed her Oscar on the fireplace mantel in her bedroom, so that she would see it when she awoke the next morning. She was *ecstatic*. *She*, had *won* an *Oscar*! That was clearly another dream that had become a reality for Raven Kensington. A *big* dream.

Raven knew the history of the Academy Awards. She knew that

very few blacks, no matter how talented, won Oscars. Raven also hoped that there would come a time, when an African-American winning an Oscar, wasn't a big deal. But unfortunately, that time had not arrived yet.

     * * *

The Kensingtons called to congratulate Raven on her win. They had stayed up to watch, hoping they'd be celebrating with her. Raven's mother told her that her father had even watched the Oscars, which was a first. But then again, he never had a *personal* reason to watch the show before now. Neither of them had.

Raven and Tony offered to fly her parents to L.A., so they could attend the Oscars, but they declined the offer.

Mack had also congratulated Raven. He had stayed up waiting for them. He was very happy for "Mrs. Dash," as he now called her. "Congratulations, Mrs. Dash!" he'd told her, when she and Tony came home.

     * * *

"A penny for your thoughts," said Tony.

"I'm thinking about the *big* win. *My*, big win. It's very special for so many reasons. I just hope that it won't be the last one. I also hope that other *deserving* African-Americans will win more Oscars as well. Regardless of your race, win based on *talent*, when you've truly earned it. That's the way that it *should* be."

Tony nodded in agreement. "I'm very happy for you, sweetheart. That *won't* be your last Oscar either. And I too hope that other blacks will win more Oscars. I know exactly what you mean. We're not saying *give* them away, we're simply saying, give credit where credit is due. Give it to the *best* performing actor or actress. Not the best *white* performing actor or actress." Tony went on, "If we look at history, the Academy is saying that blacks don't give the best performances in movies. And like you, I'm not saying what I'm saying, because I'm black either, but no one can tell me that more blacks didn't deserve to win more Oscars, since the Academy Awards began, way back when. I also know like with anything, that the *best*, or *most* talented, comes in *all* sizes, shapes, and colors ... not just one."

Raven nodded in the dark, as she laughed. "We haven't even been married long, and you're already starting to *sound* like me."

Tony laughed. "Thanks! That's *definitely* a compliment."

"But you're right, sweetheart. Vote for the *best* man, regardless of the package that they're in. Race shouldn't even be a consideration, but as with so many things, even in *these* times, it's *still* a factor. And in many ways, unfortunately, I think it will *always* be."

"You have *never* let race stop you."

"No, Tony, I haven't. And I *never* will," said Raven. "Besides God Himself, only I, can *stop* me. Bigotry, nor ignorance, won't *ever* stop me."

"That's *my* girl!" Tony loved his wife's determination.

* * *

The next morning, Raven picked up her Oscar and held it close to her. She smiled as she touched it.

Tony stood in the doorway, watching Raven. "It still hasn't quite set in yet, has it?" He knew that winning an Oscar was every actors' and actresses' dream. Tony likened winning an Oscar to a professional football athlete, winning a Super Bowl ring. It symbolized that you were the best. And that is *exactly*, what Raven Kensington was. And no one was happier for her than Tony.

* * *

The Dashs spent their last two weeks getting plenty of *R* and *R*, before leaving for New York.

Tony instructed Joe Junior to begin remodeling both R.K. by Design locations. His and Raven's goal was to have the stores open for the holidays. They had already received a flood of resumes. Tony was going to review them while they were in New York. He knew that with his wife's very busy schedule, he would be taking care of most of the hiring, and everything else in-between. And like the awesome businessman that Tony Dash was, the train was already in motion.

Tony shook his head thinking of his wife's schedule. Raven had a very busy schedule that year. She had four movies, back-to-back, that she had signed on to do. No matter how busy Raven was, Tony knew that she was elated to be living her dreams. Tony also loved the fact that Raven's work, centered around their marriage, it wasn't the *other* way around. Tony hoped that it would stay that way.

*Chapter 8**

Raven and Tony flew to New York. They stayed at their Trump Tower apartment.

And as always, Raven had studied and practiced her part to *perfection*. She was ready to give her signature, flawless-performance.

Andrew had always loved that about Raven. She had the same outstanding work ethic that she'd had, since filming *Heartless War*. She hadn't slacked off a bit since becoming a huge star. She worked harder than ever, and she *still* worked harder than anyone. And whenever it was time for her to perform, she did so with the same flawlessness and passion, each and every time. Her *unmatched*-performances had become as trademarked as her staggering-beauty and her dazzling, million-dollar smile.

While Raven was on the set, Tony ran their businesses and made business deals from the office in their apartment. He would also visit his wife on the set, especially when it was time for her to perform. Tony loved watching her. Her talent was incomparable. And as he'd always told people, it was an unbiased opinion. Many agreed with him. The fans certainly did. Raven was an immensely-gifted actress. She could portray *anyone*, or *anything*. No matter who she was playing, Raven always raised the bar with her flawless-performances.

Many of the producers, writers, and directors, who at one time, didn't give Raven Kensington a *second* look, rang Andrew Spellman's phone off the hook. They wanted Raven to star in their movies. *Now.* They even told Andy that Raven could name her price and tell them what kind of role she wanted to play. They knew all too well, like so many, that Raven now carried movies alone. Not only would Raven's movies debut at number one, they retained that position, for months.

Raven Kensington starring in a movie, meant box-office hit, megabucks. And everyone wanted a piece of the action, they wanted a piece of the "green." Raven was the biggest money-making star in Hollywood.

Andrew politely turned all of them down. "She's *too big* for you," he told them. He meant that in more ways than one. After all, that is exactly what they had told her, once upon a time. "You'll aren't in her league. You *never* were."

As Andy had told his wife, he knew when he first saw Raven, that she had *it.* Some only saw Raven's race, and the fact that she wasn't petite. They admitted that she was gorgeous with an eye-popping figure, but they'd told Raven often, that the world and Hollywood, wasn't ready for *"her kind."* Many of them had even said that the world would never be ready.

Andy smiled as he watched Raven. Now "her kind," *she*, was the *most* sought-after actress in Hollywood. "Her kind," had just won an Oscar, playing the role of a maid. And "her kind," was recently voted the sexiest woman alive. Shows how much they knew, thought Andy, still smiling. But *he* knew. Andrew Spellman had always been very certain that Raven Kensington would be a huge star. The biggest ever! He had gone home after speaking with Raven at Spago and told his wife, "I'd bet the house on it." And because of Raven, he and his wife had their dream home. Raven Kensington was, by far, Andy's biggest client.

* * *

Andy watched Tony watching Raven. He laughed to himself, thinking about what Tandy had said. "Oh, yes! You're right, Tandy. Tony's definitely smitten with his wife. Very smitten." Who could blame him? Raven Kensington was an *extraordinary* woman.

When Raven came home after a long day on the set, Tony would run her bath water for her. He loved pampering her. Raven meant the world to him. Tony also knew how hard she worked. Even though no one would ever guess that, by looking at her. Raven was the most energetic woman that Tony had ever known. She was like the Energizer Bunny. She always looked rested too. And gorgeous. There was never a hair out of place. Tony didn't know how she did it. *All* of it. Be the *best* wife ever, be the *best* actress, a *great* philanthropist, the list went on. And Raven juggled *all* of it, like a circus act.

Raven and Tony went to Central Park often, which was certainly not surprising to Tony. They had even managed to go to a number of plays too, at some of the nearby theaters. They dined at Per Se, one of Raven's favorite restaurants, almost every night.

* * *

The following week, cast and crew went to Philadelphia. Raven enjoyed going back to her old stomping ground. Although Raven was born in Texas, and she had lived there for most of her life, she had also lived in Philly, for a number of years.

Raven and Tony toured downtown, known as Center City, ate the very famous cheesesteaks, and went to a 76ers game.

Raven also took Tony to 22nd Street and Indiana Avenue, where she used to live. It seemed the best thing Tony liked about Philly, were the delicious cheesesteaks. He wouldn't stop raving about how great they tasted.

"They are delicious, aren't they?" said Raven. "There are many restaurants in different cities and states, who use the name, Philly Cheesesteak, but when you have had the *real* thing, you *know* the difference. There's often a big difference too."

* * *

Raven and Becky talked on the phone every day. She and John were doing great, Becky told Raven. She also told Raven that *Day's Dawn* was keeping her very busy. Like Raven, Becky never took her success for granted either. She worked just as hard as she had always worked, and she was always gracious to her fans.

Raven also talked regularly to her family. Her mother told her that they'd finally seen Clint Stanton. "He asked about you and Becky. He gave me his number. He says he knows that you'll are very busy, but whenever possible, he said to please give him a buzz," said Mae.

"Okay, Mommie." Raven replied, as she wrote down Clint's phone number. "I'll also let Becky know."

* * *

After almost three months, Raven's time on the East Coast, had come to an end. Raven and Tony were thrilled to be going back to Malibu. They'd flown home every other weekend since arriving in New York.

The producers and directors threw a party the night before everyone left to head back to California. It was more of a "thank you" party. The cast and crew had done very well.

* * *

Once back in L.A., Raven had a short breather, before she would begin filming her next movie. In the coming months, she would also have to promote her new movie, which she always enjoyed doing. Her passion for acting hadn't died at all. She enjoyed every bit of it too, with a few exceptions. Raven Kensington was very *grateful*, and *ecstatic*, to be living her dreams.

Tony looked at his wife smiling. "I was just *thinking*. It was two years ago, when I *first* laid eyes on you. That night changed my *entire* life. *You*, changed my entire life. Every day I pinch myself."

"You've brought so much love and joy into my life too, Mr. Dash. Don't *ever* doubt that," said Raven. "You're *my* king. You are *my*, Prince Charming!"

* * *

Raven and Tony sat out on the terrace for hours, looking out at the ocean and listening to the water, which was always very soothing. They had just returned from their usual jog on the beach. Raven was happy they had chosen Malibu as their main residence. It was such a beautiful place.

Raven smiled. "I'm so glad to be *home*! I'm going to sleep late, watch movies, go swimming, and practice martial arts."

As they sat out on the terrace, they saw a number of couples strolling on the beach, hand in hand. Tony told Raven that he'd purchased ten, newly-built homes near the Summerwood Apartments. He hadn't decided yet, but he told her that they would probably rent them out. "What do you think, beautiful? Does that sound like a good idea?"

"Sounds like a *great* idea," said Raven, as she got up to take a bath.

"*Bath* time?" Tony asked.

"Yes."

Raven sat soaking in the tub. The hot, bubbly-water felt good.

It wasn't long before Tony joined her. "Room for *two*?" Tony asked, as he removed his clothes.

"Yes, sweetheart." Raven smiled, as her eyes combed her husband's powerfully-built body.

Tony's eyes feasted on Raven. She looked so sultry and beautiful, as the water and soapsuds dripped from her hair and body.

Tony smiled. "How about a little, *quid ... pro ... quo*?"

"*Quid ... pro... quo*?" Raven asked.

"Yes. I'll wash *your* back, *if*, you wash mine."

Raven laughed. "*Hmmm*, sounds *quite* tempting, but I don't know. I'll have to *think* about it." Raven teased, as Tony held her in his arms, which was home to her.

"I need to read you your rights *first*, Mrs. Dash."

"My *rights*?" Raven asked her husband.

"*Yes*. You have the *right*, to *remain* immensely-*beautiful* and super-*sultry*. *Anything* that you say *can* and *will* be used against you, in a court of *love*."

"My lips are *sealed*," Raven whispered.

"With a *kiss*," said Tony, as his lips found hers.

* * *

The next morning, the Dashs went to see how the R.K. by Design stores were coming along. And true to his word, as Joe Junior had told Tony when he'd talked with him in New York, which was daily, things were going extremely well.

Tony reminded the crew to make sure the stores were stylish and elegant. "Like *my* wife," he told them.

Everything was going according to plan. Raven was elated. The stores would be ready by mid-November. *Just in time ... for the holidays*.

* * *

Raven filmed movie after movie. She was happy that her last film was in L.A. She liked going home in the evenings.

At year's end, Raven had fulfilled all of her contracts, and she was looking forward to a much-needed vacation. She was also looking forward to her *favorite holiday. Christmas*.

Becky and Andrew were right, Raven's star only got bigger and bigger. Raven Kensington, was now, the *biggest* star in the world. She was also a very powerful and influential woman.

That same year, Raven won a People's Choice Award and a SAG Award. She was at the *pinnacle* of success. Her face continued to grace the cover of countless magazines, on a regular basis. Raven Kensington's face on a magazine cover sent sales soaring through the roof. Everything she touched turned to gold. She was a money-making machine, and *everyone*, wanted a piece of her.

* * *

On one of Raven's very rare off days, the phone rang, as she sat reading a book. "Andrew. How are you? Before you ask, no. No more movies, until *after* the holidays." Raven joked. "I *need* time with my family."

Andy laughed. "Whoa! *Slow* down! Hear me out, pretty lady. I am calling regarding an *upcoming* movie, but it's *next* year. And they want *you*, badly. They want to get their bid in first. It's no secret that you're the *most* sought-after star in Hollywood, *excuse me*, you're the *biggest* star in the world." Andy told Raven what the movie was about and what role she would play, if she signed on to do the film.

Raven sat and listened. The movie seemed very exciting and interesting. It would also be filmed in L.A., which was a plus for Raven. She enjoyed being home.

"*So*? What do you think, pretty lady?" Andy asked her. He also told her what they would pay her.

Raven didn't seemed fazed. The amount that Andy quoted her was far less than what she knew an actress of her caliber and clout should make. It was also far less than what white actresses were being paid. Even those who bombed at the box-office, time and time again.

"In *that* case, I'm *not* going to even consider it." Raven told Andy. "I work just as hard, if not *harder*, than *anyone* in Hollywood. My movies have made hundreds of millions of dollars, because my fans always go see my movies, and that's what they *think* is a good offer? What is Rick Dauche making per film?" Raven knew that Rick was the highest paid actor in Hollywood, she also knew that he hadn't made a hit movie in years. Raven already knew how much Rick made per flick.

"Forty."

"How *unfair*! I want *fifty* million. I also want *thirty-five percent* of *all* ticket sales. Fifty million would make me the highest paid *person* in Hollywood. *Period*. And *that's* what I want. It's another thing that's long, long overdue."

Andy sat and listened. Raven's movies were the highest-grossing movies in the world, she was certainly right about that. And her star-power was uncanny.

"Andy, let's *face* it, how long have we watched racism in Hollywood? Even where paychecks are concerned. You have black actresses, for example, not making *nearly* as much as white actresses, even if they're *more* talented. And in some cases, they can be a lot more talented, and still make a lot less. And that's ridiculous and *sickening*! I didn't just come to Hollywood to be successful, I came to do things that have *never* been done before. I came to open doors for others, who *like* me, weren't being judged by our talent, but instead, we are often *discriminated* against and *shunned*, because of our race. I'm not telling anyone to pay me more because I'm *black*, I'm telling them to pay me the *most*, because I'm the *best*! *You* know it, I know it, *they* know it, and *all* of my fans that pay to see me, know it. The script sounds great, but I will only do it for that amount. Get back to me later. I have a book to finish. Have a good day, Andrew. Please say hello to Tandy for me."

Andy hung up the phone, thinking that Raven had lost her mind. It's not that he disagreed with what she said, because he didn't. But he could only imagine what the producers' reactions would be, when he told them what it would take to get *her*.

"What's wrong with you?" Tandy asked her husband.

Andy told her what Raven's conditions were.

Tandy laughed. "I don't blame her. You go, girl!" She agreed with Raven, totally. "How *many* times, and for how many *very* long years, do you have a *white* actress making *twenty million plus* per movie, for example, and a *black* actress, who was sometimes a lot better, *barely* making *one million*? Andy, there's *a lot* wrong with that picture. And instead of *saying* what is wrong, someone *needs* to act. Someone needs to *do* something about things like this, instead of going along with it. *Raven Kensington*, is *our* woman."

Andy laughed. "She's already done *a lot* of things, that *no one* thought they would *ever* live to see."

Tandy smiled. "And apparently, she's *not* finished yet."

"She had a lot of *valid* points. As usual," said Andy.

Tandy thought so too. "Very *intelligent, razor*-sharp, isn't she? I've told you a million times, sweetheart, I *like* Ms. Kensington. She's right though. Enough is enough! It's very horrible and sad, that after all of these *many* years, things like *this* are still going on. The *real*-world, and the *entertainment* industry, *prove* that racism is very much alive and well. It's really sad, here we are, years into the new millennium, and we're *still* seeing a lot of discrimination. *Often*. It's sickening!" Tandy laughed. "There is one thing that Hollywood, and the world, hadn't prepared for. They didn't know *Raven Kensington* was coming."

Andy laughed. His wife was right. Raven was *definitely* a force to be reckoned with.

* * *

At noon the following day, Andy received a call from Matt Rickeow. He was the executive producer of the upcoming movie. "*Well*? What did *Ms. Kensington* say?"

Andy told Matt.

Andrew Spellman was very surprised by what Matt said next. "Is that *why* you didn't call me first thing this morning as you said you would? Shame on you! We want *her*, Andy, and if that's what it will take to get her, then let's go! Hell, we pay actresses who don't even have half of her talent crazy millions, and they don't even deserve it. *She does*! We have the money. And with *Raven Kensington* in the movie, we'll make that back in one day, not to mention the fact that we'll make it back many times over. She's *hot*! She's not a gamble, she's a *guaranteed* jackpot at the box-office. Raven equals, blockbusters! *Everything* that she touches turns to gold, hundreds of millions. Her last movie almost made a *billion* dollars! Ms. Kensington's as smart as she is beautiful. She's very sharp! It would be a very *foolish* business decision not to hire her for this movie. It was *tailor*-made for Ms. Kensington. And we would *not* make the megabucks without *her*. Give Ms. Kensington the script. Also, tell her that she can make changes to the script, if she'd like. I've heard she's also an *awesome* writer." Matt laughed. "Beautiful woman of *many* talents."

Andy was stunned. "Oh, *before* I forget. When will filming begin on this movie?" He remembered Raven telling him that she wanted a break.

"End of March. So, tell gorgeous that she has three and a half months to do *whatever*. She'll also have a *huge* check to add to her already super-rich bank account." Matt also confirmed that the movie would be filmed in L.A.

    * * *

Raven and Tony were decorating their Christmas tree, when Andy phoned Raven with the news. It was the day after Thanksgiving. They had spent Thanksgiving with Tony's family again that year. They planned to spend Christmas with the Kensingtons, as usual.

"*Bad* time?" Andy asked Raven. "I can call back. We have time on our side," said Andy, referring to the upcoming movie.

"Thanks, Andy. If you don't mind, I'll call you back," said Raven, holding a string of lights on each arm.

After hanging up with Andy, Raven went back to decorating the big white tree that she and Tony had bought earlier that day. This was their first Christmas together as husband and wife.

Christmas music played softly in the background, as Raven and Tony happily-decorated their tree. Tony watched his wife's eyes light up as she placed the ornaments on the tree. He could easily tell that this was indeed, her *favorite* time of year.

"*Uh-oh!*" said Tony, holding a mistletoe over Raven's head. "You know what *this* means, beautiful!"

Raven laughed, as Tony took her in his arms and kissed her.

Mack smiled as he brought hot chocolate for the lovebirds. He thought it very sweet to see two people so much in love. Raven and Tony fit together like a hand in a glove.

    * * *

"You know, sweetheart, it's funny how you *keep* finding *all* of these mistletoes." Raven told her husband.

"Here's *another* one. Pucker up, beautiful!"

Raven shook her head, and laughed in answer.

Raven and Tony took a break from decorating, to enjoy the hot chocolate that Mack had brought them. They had been decorating for most of the day, with Becky's and John's help. The tree and stockings were the very last things that they had left to do. Along with shopping for presents.

They were going to Beverly Hills the next day to help Becky and John decorate their home. Becky loved Christmas too, but no one loved it more than Raven.

* * *

Every Friday, whenever Raven was in town, she and Becky spent most of the day together. It was their day. "Ladies day out," as Tony called it. And even though they had significant others and were no longer living together, they were still as close as they had always been.

After going shopping and having "brunch," as they termed it now, they went to the Will Rogers Memorial Park in Beverly Hills. It had been years since they had gone there.

"Wow!" said Becky. "It was *what*, almost seven years ago?"

Raven nodded.

"You and I were sitting at *this* very park, after moving to L.A."

It was hard to believe that it had been that long, but it had. Time certainly flew.

"Look at us *now*, Sis. I *always* told you that you would be *huge*, and *look* at you! I hate to say I told you so. *Everyone* knows who the *great*, Raven Kensington is. Even the Arab prince! He walked over to our table and asked for *your* autograph. *Unbelievable*! Sis, you know … you might be *this* beautiful and glamorous, *larger-than-life superstar*, the *Academy Award*-winning, *Raven Kensington*, to everyone else, but to *me*, you're *just* my sister."

Raven laughed. "*Well, Beck*, you know … you might be *this* …

beautiful and glamorous, larger-than-life soap opera star, the *Emmy Award*-winning, *Rebecca Simms*, to *everyone* else, but to *me*, you're *just* my sister, who I happen to love *very* much."

The two women laughed.

"Sis, I *must* say, married life *definitely* agrees with you. It agrees with Tony too. I have *never* seen a man happier. He *loves* you to pieces. I saw the recent *Fortune* magazine with your and Tony's pictures on the cover. One of the world's *most* powerful couples. You've come a *long* way, Sis."

"Yes, Beck. A *mighty* long way. Don't leave *yourself* out. You have *only* graced every other magazine cover this year *alone*. Not to mention *all* of the big-money endorsement deals that have come your way, Miss Simms. I also recall telling you while sitting at *this* very park, years ago, that you would one day *own* a home in the ever-*so* posh, B. Hills."

They were now superstars. And as far as Raven was concerned, no two people deserved it more. They had both worked extremely *hard* to get to where they were now.

"I know you, Sis, you're *never* satisfied, are you?" Becky knew Raven very well, after all, they had been best friends for many years.

"C'mon, you know the *best* never rests!" Raven flashed her trademark smile. "You do know me very well, Beck, as you *should*. You're right. I'm not one to get comfy, in *any* avenue of my life, including, relationships. It's not just getting to the top, it's maintaining, and *continuing* to work hard, once you get there. No one stays on top forever, but I will ride the wave for as long as it will have me!"

Becky laughed in answer.

"I will enjoy it while it lasts, however long that may be. *Hopefully*, you won't get comfy or cozy either. You are a *remarkably*-talented actress, Beck. I'm *very* proud of you!"

"And I you. Speaking of relationships, Tony *really* makes you very happy, doesn't he?" Becky asked Raven.

"Yes, Beck. He sure does. Tony's a *wonderful* man. I *love* him *very* much. We love each other deeply and dearly. We make each other very happy. I am very happy in love, *and*, in life."

"I can tell. I'm very happy for you, Sis. Oftentimes we hear about the *horrible* relationships, and we lose sight of the fact that *all* relationships aren't horrible or bad. Some are *wonderful*, like *yours* and Tony's."

Raven nodded in answer. "That's very true. The *bad* always seems to *overshadow* the good. How are you and John doing?"

Becky didn't answer.

"*Beck*, is there *trouble* in paradise? *Shoot*. As I've always said, problems are easier when they're shared with friends, and in *our* case, *sisters*. Is he treating you right? He had *better* be!"

"We're doing pretty well. John also treats me well." Becky sighed. "It's just that I'm still *not* ready to marry him. And he obviously wants to marry me. He only pops the question, every *other* day. Sometimes it gets on my nerves. We'd be doing great, if he *stopped* asking me to marry him!"

Raven laughed. "In all seriousness, Beck, you don't think that John's the right man for you?"

Becky hesitated again, as she shrugged her shoulders in answer.

"As I've said before, you know him better than *anyone*. I don't really know him. I just know what I see, and how he *seems* to love you, when I see you two together. But that doesn't make me know him. I will also tell you what I have *always* told you, and that's, if you're *not* ready, for whatever reason, or reasons, then *don't* marry him. It doesn't matter how often he asks you. Is everything *else* in your life going well? Are *you* happy, Beck?" Raven wanted to know. "You know that you can talk to me about *anything*. It doesn't matter what it is."

"I know that, Sis."

"I know that I can do the same with you too." Raven loved her friend very much, and Becky's happiness was very important to her.

Becky looked at the woman sitting across from her with love and admiration. Raven was beautiful and wise. Always had been. Raven had gotten Becky through some rough times over the years.

Raven's wisdom was a godsend. It had guided Becky too many times to count. Becky had always been very grateful to have a sister, a best friend, like Raven Kensington.

"Sis, don't *worry* about me. I'm happy. I'm *living* my dreams."

"Beck, I *know* that you're living your dreams, but are *you* happy in *life*?" Raven wanted to know.

"Yes, Mother, I am. I am *happy*. *Hap-py*! *Hap-py*! *Hap-py*!" Becky sang.

"*Good*. I am happy that you're happy because I want *you* to be *happy* because that makes *me happy*," said Raven.

Becky laughed hard. "*Vintage* Raven. Beauty, brains, wit, and great sense of humor. I *love* you, Sis! What would I do *without* you?"

Raven smiled at Becky. "Beck, as I've *always* told you, what would *we* do without *each* other? Hopefully, we'll *never* have to find out. I will always be here for you, Beck. *Always*. And even if I'm not in town, call me if you need me. You *know* that I would be on the *next plane*, *bus*, *train*, *boat*, *bike* ... with a *quickness*."

Becky laughed in answer.

"I love you very much, Rebecca Simms. Don't *ever* forget that."

"I also love you very much, Raven Kensington Dash. Don't you *ever* forget that either."

The two longtime friends hugged, before parting ways.

Chapter 9

Raven Kensington's fan base continued to grow. She had millions of fans all over the world. Layla Halter, a seven-year-old girl who lived in Compton, was one of Raven's biggest fans. Layla thought the sun rose and set on Raven. She looked up to her. She wanted to look like her, she wanted to be like her, in every way. Raven Kensington, was her hero.

Layla sat at her desk talking with her teacher. She was often the only child in the class because her mother usually couldn't afford to pay for her to go on field trips with the other students.

Most of the children in Compton were poor, but some had fathers at home who helped financially. So, although still poor, they were a little better off than Layla, whose father had left Carmen Halter, Layla's mother, when he found out that she was pregnant.

"Mrs. Satchell, what do you *think*? Do you think she'll write me back?" Layla asked the teacher.

"*Whom*, sweetheart?"

"*Miss Kensington*. Raven Kensington. She's the *big* movie star. Everyone knows her!"

"Oh, yes! I've seen every one of her movies. She's an *awesome* actress."

"She's *very* pretty too, isn't she?" Layla asked.

The teacher nodded. "Yes, she sure is. She's *gorgeous*."

Layla asked the teacher again if she thought the star would answer her letter.

"I don't know. I certainly hope so. If she knew how sweet you were, I know she would," said the teacher, trying to cheer the little girl up.

Layla began writing a letter to her favorite star in the whole wide world, Raven Kensington. As she started the letter, she began to cry. Tears fell on the letter, smearing some of the words.

The teacher heard Layla sniffling. "Layla! *Oh ... sweetheart ...*" Mrs. Satchell was momentarily at a loss for words. She got up from her desk and gave Layla a hug. "Now, *why* are you crying, pretty girl?" the teacher asked.

"*Because.* Daniel Martz said he doesn't know why I'm always talking about Raven Kensington. He said that she doesn't care about a poor, old, ugly girl like me, who lives in Compton. Daniel said why would she care? She's so pretty and she has lots of money."

"Sweetheart, don't *worry* about what Daniel says. He's a bully. He's always saying things to hurt you or anyone who will be a victim for him. You're a *pretty* girl, Layla. You're also very *smart.* And as far as Compton, Daniel lives here too. Please, I know it's hard, but do your very best to *ignore* Daniel."

Layla continued to write the letter. But she couldn't stop crying. It was more than Daniel's words that hurt her. She cried for her mother, who worked two jobs and still didn't seem to get very far. She cried for herself, who very seldom got to go on field trips with the other children, because her mother couldn't afford to send her.

Layla folded the letter, placed it in the envelope that the teacher had given her, then sealed it. She wrote her home address on the envelope. She wanted Raven Kensington to write her back.

"Mrs. Satchell? Will you put a stamp on this and mail it for me, *please*?"

"Sure, sweetheart, I certainly will."

The teacher had long since gotten the address to Raven Kensington's office, which was located in Beverly Hills. She knew how much Layla looked up to the star. Layla had asked her every other day to get Raven's address. And Mrs. Satchell finally got it.

Later that day, as the teacher stamped Layla's letter and placed it in the mailbox, she thought of the little girl. She hoped and prayed the star would respond. Mrs. Satchell knew that Layla would be crushed otherwise.

* * *

The following week was very busy for the Dashs. Raven and Tony interviewed potential candidates for the R.K. by Design stores. Raven reminded her husband again, that because of her busy schedule, he would need to oversee the stores, whenever she couldn't.

After months of working, tirelessly, the staff was hired and trained for both locations. And *everyone* knew about R.K. by Design. Tony Dash was a marketing *genius*. Customers were eagerly awaiting R.K. by Design's Grand Opening.

The interior and exterior of each store was very unique, elegant, and chic. And just as Raven wanted, her stores catered to *all* sizes and income levels.

Raven made headlines that same week, as the media broadcasted the *record*, fifty million dollars that she was receiving for her next movie, along with thirty-five percent of all ticket sales that Raven would also receive.

Her father laughed when he heard about it. He couldn't resist calling Raven on her cell phone. "Wow, sweetheart! I'm in the *wrong* business!" Charles Kensington joked. Her father shook his head. As far as he was concerned, with the exception of his daughter, Tony, and Becky, they were all crazy in Hollywood. "If those folks are *crazy* enough to pay you *that* kind of money, you would be crazy *not* to take it! Those folks are out of their minds. You show up on a set, get waited on hand and foot, the hired-hand pats makeup on your nose, you recite lines, smile, look pretty for the cameras, and you're paid *many* fortunes? I am *definitely* in the wrong business!"

Raven laughed in answer. She knew that her father had never been a fan of Tinseltown, and her success hadn't changed that either.

"Give my son my love," said Charles, referring to Tony. "Give my love to Becky too. You three better be *careful* out there. Those folks are *outta* their minds!"

* * *

"Let's go home!" said Tony, after Raven hung up from talking with her father. They'd both had a very long and grueling day.

"*One* more stop. I want to go by my office. I won't be long." Raven wanted to pick up a package that Andy had left for her earlier that day.

When they arrived at Raven's office, her desk was overflowing with fan mail.

Tony looked at all of the fan mail piled up on his wife's desk. "Wow! Are you well-loved or *what*? May I?"

"Sure, read and open *whatever* you'd like. *Knock* yourself out." Raven told her husband.

Raven would read as many letters as she could, but it was impossible for her to read every letter. She didn't have that kind of time. But she was always very grateful for her fans. Raven knew that she wouldn't be where she was today, without her fans' love and support, along with her hard work and perseverance. Most of her fan mail was positive, but she still received negative mail too.

"Look! Here's a box," said Tony, opening it.

It was a pair of men's briefs. A note was also inside of the box. It was a handwritten marriage proposal.

Tony laughed and shook his head. "Men's *underwear*? Raven, I don't know about *some* of your fans. There is also a note from this *same* man, asking for your hand in marriage. Too *late* for that, partner!" Tony shook his head again in disbelief. "What a way to propose to a woman! He doesn't even *know* you either. This man has *absolutely* no taste. And as far as I'm concerned, he's missing *a lot* of screws. He's *definitely* not playing with a full deck. The *only* thing he needs to *propose* to do, is seek professional help. And *fast*."

Raven laughed.

* * *

"What's *this*, beautiful? It looks like a child's handwriting."

"Let me see." Raven always had a special place in her heart for children. She was curious about the letter. "It *is* a child's handwriting. It's from Layla. Layla Halter."

"Ready to go?" Tony asked.

"Sure," said Raven, picking up Andy's package. "Let's go."

Tony noticed that Raven was still holding the letter. "Are you taking that letter with you too?"

Raven nodded. For some reason, she wanted to read this letter.

Mary, Raven's assistant, had arrived just as the Dashs were leaving. "Hello, boss lady. Hello, Mr. Dash. Please excuse your desk, I'm organizing *everything*. You have so much mail, Ms. Kensington, but you know me, I'll have everything organized in no time."

Raven nodded. "I know, Mary. Thanks."

* * *

When they arrived home, Raven placed the letter, along with Andy's box, on her nightstand. She then went to take a bath.

And as usual, Tony joined her. "Long day, huh, beautiful?"

"Oh, yes, but successful. I'm so excited!" Raven gave her husband a long, passionate kiss.

"What a *kiss*! What did I do to deserve *that*?"

"I *love* you. I don't need a reason to kiss my baby. But, I do want to thank you for making my dreams come true. R.K. by Design is *everything* that I wanted it to be, and *more*. *Thank you* so much, baby!"

"You're quite *welcome*, my love. You've made *my* dreams come true. You mean the *world* to me, Raven. I want to keep my baby happy. That's very important to me. You are numero *uno* in my life."

The lovebirds sat in the tub relaxing and sipping on white wine.

* * *

Later that night, when Tony went to check his e-mail, Raven opened Layla's letter. She noticed some of the words were smeared. She sensed correctly, that it was a result of the little girl's tears. When Raven finished reading the letter, she had tears of her own.

Layla seemed like a very sweet little girl. Raven felt there was something more going on in Layla's life. Layla asked Raven to write her back.

After reading the letter, Raven placed the letter back in the envelope, and set it back on her nightstand. Raven lies in bed, thinking about little Layla. She'd told Raven that she was her hero. "You're a great role model too," the little girl had written in her letter. "We need more stars like you. Even my *grandmother* likes you!"

Raven smiled through her tears.

* * *

The next morning, Tony went Christmas shopping. He went alone, because he hadn't bought his wife a present yet, and he wanted it to be a surprise. He still didn't know what he was going to buy Raven, but he knew that she'd be happy with whatever he bought her. That was just the kind of woman Raven was. She was always grateful and appreciative for things that many people took for granted.

* * *

Raven decided to drive to Compton. It was a Saturday; she hoped Layla was home. The black X5 pulled up on Rosa Parks Drive an hour later. Raven wore a baseball hat and dark shades. She eyed the home. It was in very poor condition. She checked the address on the envelope, then strolled up the walkway.

When Raven knocked on the door, she saw the curtain move.

"*Yes?*" said an elderly lady, as she looked through the peephole.

"Hello, is Layla home?"

The elderly lady stood at the door, eyeing Raven, suspiciously. "Who are *you?*"

* * *

"Raven, ma'am. I'm Raven Kensington." Raven showed the lady her driver's license.

It was a while before the door opened. Tina Halter couldn't believe it. *The*, Raven Kensington, was actually standing at her door! When Tina invited her in, Raven removed her sunglasses.

"Wow! This is *quite* a surprise," said Tina Halter. "Are you *really the*, Raven Kensington, the *superstar*?"

Raven smiled and nodded. "Yes, ma'am, I am."

"You look just like you do in the movies. You're *very* beautiful!"

"Thank you."

"Layla! You have a visitor! I'm Layla's grandmother. My name is Tina Halter." Tina was shocked, and excited. *This*, was unbelievable! *Who* was going to believe that the *biggest* star in Hollywood was at *her* house?

Raven shook Tina's hand. "It's a *pleasure* to meet you, Ms. Halter."

"*Please*, sit down," said Tina.

As Raven waited for Layla to come to the living room, she noticed a number of things. The house was in badly need of repairs, there was little heat, and there wasn't a tree in sight. It was a cold day in Compton too.

Layla stood in the living room, stunned. *No! This couldn't* be. *No way*! The lady in the living room looked just *like* ... No. No way! *Impossible*.

Layla's grandmother finally broke the silence. She already knew what her granddaughter was thinking. "*Layla*, where are *your* manners? Say *hello* to ... Ms. *Kensington*."

"*Hi*," Layla's voice was a whisper. The little girl was shocked. Raven could barely hear Layla, her voice was so low.

Raven got up and walked towards the little girl. "Hi, Layla. I'm Raven Kensington. I read your letter. It was *beautiful. Thank you* for such a sweet letter." Raven flashed her trademark smile.

Layla finally found her voice as she screamed. "Oh ... my ... gosh! It *is* you! It's *really* you! *Grandma*! It's ... *it's* ... Miss Kensington! It's *the, Raven Kensington*!" Layla was overjoyed.

Tina Halter laughed. She knew how her granddaughter felt. It wasn't every day that the biggest movie star in Hollywood showed up at your door. She was still stunned herself.

"Yes, sweetheart, I know. *Hard* to believe, isn't it? It took a while before it actually set in with me too. I couldn't believe it either when she knocked on the door." Tina Halter smiled. She knew how much this meant to her granddaughter. Pictures of Raven Kensington were all over Layla's bedroom wall. Layla idolized Raven.

"I apologize for how chilly it is in here. The stove doesn't always work so well. There's an electric heater in Layla's room. It's *important* that the little one stays warm," the elderly lady told Raven.

"What's wrong with the heater?" Raven asked politely. She saw the vents, which indicated that the home did have central heat, or at least it was designed to have it.

Tina told Raven that the landlord hadn't gotten around to fixing the heater yet.

Some landlord! Raven thought to herself. It made her angry that the landlord would even charge rent for the home. It was in such poor condition, and on top of that, *no* heat. "If it's okay with you, Ms. Halter, I could have my husband take a look at it," said Raven.

Tina Halter hesitated, then nodded. It was too cold in the house to have foolish pride, thought Tina.

Raven called Tony.

Tony told her that he would be right over. "What's the address again?" Tony asked.

Raven repeated the address to her husband.

"Okay, see you in a little bit. Love you, beautiful." Tony didn't just love his wife's outer-beauty, he also loved her *inner*-beauty. Raven had the biggest heart that he had ever known anyone to have.

"I love you too." Raven told Tony.

* * *

When Tony arrived, he immediately went to look at the heating system. He'd worked on heating and cooling systems with his grandfather when he was in his teens, so he knew something about them.

"It needs a new heating duct and new filters. The old ones are badly-clogged." Tony wrote down the brand and part numbers. "I'll be back."

"Want to come to *my* room?" Layla asked Raven. She was so excited. It was still very hard to believe.

"Sure," said Raven, as she followed Layla.

"*See*, I have *all* of your pictures on my wall! You look *exactly* the same too," said the little girl, smiling broadly. Layla sat on her bed.

Raven sat in a chair. "How is school?"

The little girl's eyes grew very sad.

"*Sweetheart*, what's wrong?"

Layla told Raven that "Daniel" teased her a lot. She explained how he called her all kinds of names, and how he always teased her, about being poor. "He even talks about Momma," said Layla, sadly.

"*Layla*, first of all, kids can, and often will be, very cruel. You mentioned that Daniel calls you dumb, ugly, and poor. Are you dumb and ugly?"

"No, I'm *not* dumb. I'm very *smart*," said the little girl. "I'm the *smartest* kid in my class."

"That's great, Layla. It's good to be smart. You're *not* ugly either. Do you *think* you're ugly?" Raven asked.

Layla shrugged her shoulders in answer.

"Sweetheart, you are a *very* pretty girl. I am *not* just saying that either. You have a mirror, it will tell you the *same* thing that I've just told you."

The little girl smiled. She couldn't believe it, *this* beautiful superstar, whom she adored, thought that she was very pretty.

"Layla, my point is, if you *know* that something *isn't* true, then don't worry about it. I know that it can surely be easier said than done sometimes. But the key is, even if it *does* bother you, *act* as if it doesn't. You have to be believable and consistent though. Contrary to some people's beliefs, words *can* hurt. But I'm a firm believer that the truth will set you free. So again, especially if it's *not* true, that should make it a lot easier to ignore."

Layla smiled and nodded. "Miss Kensington? There's a girl in my class who says that she's *prettier* than me because she's light-skinned. I don't think she is though. Do you think that because someone has lighter skin, that they're prettier, or better looking, than someone who's darker, or dark-skinned?"

Raven shook her head no. "*Absolutely* not. A person's *features*, make them better looking than another person, *not* how *light*, or *dark*, their skin is. Having *light* skin does not mean pretty, or good-looking. It simply means that your skin is light, that's *it*. And vice-versa. If that were the case, *all* light-skinned blacks, Asians, Caucasians, and others, who have light or fair skin, would *all* be good-looking, and they would all look better than others who have dark skin, or darker skin. I've been called pretty and beautiful all of my life, and my skin is dark. I also know that I am better looking than some who are lighter than I. *Again*, a person's *features*, make them good-looking, or better looking, than another. If the little girl in your class *does* look better than you, it's because she has *better* looking features, *not* because she's light-skinned." Raven went on, "And for the record, as I've said before, you are a very pretty girl, with a pretty name."

Layla smiled. What her "hero" said made a lot of sense. Layla watched Raven Kensington in awe. She was the most beautiful woman that she had ever seen. And it was obvious to Layla that her hero was also very wise. "Miss Kensington, you look *way* better than Megan!"

Megan was the little girl who Layla was talking about.

"Miss Kensington, have you ever been called names?"

"*Of course!*" said Raven. "I don't think there's a person alive or dead, that has *never* been called names. Sweetheart, remember, it's *not* what people call you, it's what you *answer* to. As I told you before, ignoring it, not responding to it, is *crucial*, especially, where bullies like Daniel are concerned. I have to do that a lot too, because I'm a celebrity. The tabloids will often print things that aren't true, simply to sell papers, and I, like many stars who are in the spotlight, have to either ignore it and not let it get to us, or become upset about it and let it drive us crazy. I always try to do the first. I also know that because of the profession that I've chosen, there are many things that I will have to deal with, some good, some not so good, but it comes with the territory. Dealing with good and bad is also a part of life. If Daniel sees that it doesn't bother you, he will probably leave you alone, and pick on someone else, that he knows, will become upset by his cruel comments. He probably doesn't even know your mother, does he?" Raven asked.

"No. But he's seen her. She limps a little. She was born with polio. And he says cruel things about the way she walks. That *hurts*, Miss Kensington. It hurts a lot!"

"I know, sweetheart, but follow my guidelines. And as long as *you* love your mother and think highly of her, as you *should*, don't worry about what *anyone* says about her, or what *anyone* thinks about her. What *you* think, is the *only* thing that matters. It's ridiculous to even talk about anyone whom you don't know, but people do it all the time. Some people can and often will be very cruel. And sometimes, if they're miserable, they will try to make you miserable too. Misery *loves* company. Layla, remember, act as if it doesn't bother you, even if it does. And be consistent. He's more than likely picking on you, because he sees how much it bothers you, how much it hurts you. Try what I've said, and see what happens."

Layla smiled again. She was on a roll. "What about being *poor*? That's true. I am that."

Raven heard Tony's voice in the living room. He was back.

"Nine times out of ten, Daniel's poor too. Being poor doesn't have to be a *permanent* thing. If you don't want to be poor, you can *change* that one day. *Remember*, what's to be, is up to *you*. It's *all*, up to you!"

Layla beamed. "*Really*?"

"*Really*!" the superstar told the little girl.

"Daniel's a big bully."

"Yes, Layla, that's exactly what he is. But you don't have to let him *bully* you. Most bullies pick on kids whom they can have their way with. Is he *hitting* you?" Raven wanted to know.

"No. He doesn't hit me."

"I'm happy that he's not hitting you, however, if he *ever* does, tell your teacher, and your mother, immediately."

"I will, Miss Kensington. But he still makes me cry though."

"Sweetheart, don't give him power over you. Don't let him control you, Layla. *You*, need to control you. Have control over yourself. Don't be *his* victim. Don't allow him to make you feel bad or cry. Show him that he's not going to control you *anymore*, by standing up to him. When I say stand up, in your case, I simply mean ignoring him. Again, it's very important that you be consistent and stick to your guns. I think you'll see a change if you do the things that I've discussed with you."

"Miss Kensington, you said that misery loves company. Do you think Daniel's a happy person?" Layla asked.

"No, sweetheart, I don't. I think that he's very unhappy. I think that he's miserable. Many bullies are."

"Maybe he picks on me because I stand out. I always try hard to fit in," said Layla. "You know, be like the other kids. Not stand out."

"Layla, some of us weren't born to fit in, some of us were *meant*, to stand out."

Layla smiled. "You're so smart. You're so pretty too. I *love* your skin. You don't have any bumps. Your skin's so smooth. Like a baby's."

Raven laughed. "Thank you."

"I want to grow up to be *just like you*!"

Raven looked at Layla. "Don't do *me*, Layla. Do *you*! *Always* be yourself. And always be a person that *you* can be proud of. I'm flattered, but *always* do you, *be you*. And be the *best* person that you can be. There's only *one* Layla Halter. And from where I'm sitting, she's a wonderful person! And *if* she stays on the *right* track, she'll become a *remarkable* woman."

Layla couldn't stop smiling. She told Raven that she wanted to be a doctor when she grew up. She also told her that her mother worked hard. "She loves me and Grandma a lot. We love her a lot too. I don't have any aunts or uncles. My mother's an only child. Do you have any aunts, Miss Kensington?"

"Yes, ma'am, I sure do."

"Do you have a *favorite* aunt?" Layla asked Raven.

"Yes. I love all of my aunts, but Aunt Ruth's my *favorite* aunt. We have a very strong bond. Very strong connection. We even have the *same* blood type." The superstar laughed.

"When is her birthday?"

"October sixteenth."

"Will you tell me about the birds and the bees?" the little girl asked, she was on a roll.

Raven smiled. "Sure! Birds sing. Bees sting."

Layla laughed hard. "But, Miss Kensington, you said that we could talk about *anything*!"

"*Correction*. I *meant*, *almost*, anything."

Layla nodded. "Fair enough."

Tony came to the door and told Raven that he was done.

"Okay," said Raven. "I'll be ready in a few minutes." Raven looked at Layla. "I want you to do something for me and for yourself."

"*Anything*, Miss Kensington."

"Always, listen to, and *obey*, your mother and grandmother. Show them and tell them how much you love them, *daily*. Life is *short*, and we must *never* take the ones we love for granted, nor should we ever take being alive for granted. *Never* settle for less, *always*, be the *best*. Always learn, study, and do very well in school, because *knowledge* is *power*. Knowledge, will take you very far in life. Layla, *always* believe in a very *important* and *powerful* person, who can do *anything*."

"Very important and powerful person? *Who* is that?"

"*You!*"

Layla smiled, as Raven hugged her.

"Will you *remember* what I've told you?"

Layla flashed a big smile. "I'll *always* remember, Miss Kensington. *Always*! *Thank you* so very much!" The little girl's eyes lit up. "This is the *best* Christmas present *ever*! I know that you told me to be proud to be me, but you're *still my hero*, Miss Kensington. You will *always* be!"

Raven autographed all of Layla's pictures.

"Miss Kensington? May I *please* have *another* hug before you go?"

Tears sprung to Raven's dark eyes. "That can certainly be arranged." Raven gave the little girl another big hug.

Afterwards, Raven and Tony said their good-byes, then left.

Layla and her grandmother stood at the door smiling and waving. Their house was warming up fast. Tina Halter smiled. She thanked the Dashs for all that they had done. Tina couldn't thank Raven enough, for taking time out of her very busy schedule to visit Layla. Tina knew how much that meant to her granddaughter. And she knew that Layla would never forget this day. Neither, would she.

    * * *

Raven was very happy that she'd come. But she still wasn't finished yet. It was three weeks before Christmas. Raven decided on the drive home, that she was going to give one of the homes that Tony had purchased, to the Halters.

    * * *

The next day, Raven got busy. She had the home completely furnished. Raven filled the kitchen with food and cookware. She even took care of all the utilities. The Halters wouldn't have to do anything, except show up.

    * * *

Joe Junior told Raven and Tony that his secretary would notify the Halters and assist them with anything that they needed.

Tony was pleased with his wife's decision. He also believed in helping the less fortunate.

Raven had always had a heart for helping others. She knew that one didn't have to be rich or famous to help someone. Raven knew that just because you couldn't help everyone, it wasn't an excuse not to help someone. And in spite of her and her husband's very busy schedules, they still found time to make someone else's life better. The feeling that Raven got from helping others was priceless! It enriched her life, immensely. Raven Kensington didn't just live to help herself, she also lived, to help others. And help others she did!

Judith Raskin, Joe Junior's secretary, phoned the Halters, after being notified by Raven.

Tina Halter answered the phone.

When Judith told her about the extremely generous gift from Raven and Tony, there was complete silence at the other end of the phone. The elderly lady was speechless.

Carmen had a rare day off. She sat watching her mother. Who was on the phone? What had they said to leave her mother speechless? Carmen also saw a look of shock on her mother's face. Was it *good* news, or *bad* news? Carmen wondered. Probably bad. When it rained it poured.

"Will you, please, *repeat* what you just said?" Tina Halter finally found her voice again. "*Oh … my …*"

Judith informed her about everything, including the Dashs providing transportation and movers for them.

"Thank you!" said an overjoyed Tina Halter. "Please, give me your number." Tina wrote down Judith's number. "I'll call you back. I … this … is … I'm sure you understand."

Judith assured her that she did. Judith knew that it would be very shocking news to most people.

"Momma? *Who* was that?"

Tina looked at her daughter, wanting to scream. "Carmen? Remember when Layla and I told you that the superstar she's so crazy about, actually came by to visit her? She, well, her husband, even fixed the central heating."

Carmen nodded. "I know, that was very kind of them."

"Well, honey, you're *not* going to believe this. I still can't believe it yet myself. She ... *Raven* ... has given us, a *house*! A three bedroom, two bath, *brick* home, with a private garage. Brand *new*! It's in a very nice area too. The lady that just called, Judith, she gave me the shocking news."

Carmen sat down on the sofa, unable to speak. This, was unbelievable. Simply, *unbelievable*.

Layla came out of the bedroom that she shared with her mother.

Her grandmother asked her to go back into the bedroom. "I have to talk with your mother in private, sweetheart."

"Yes, ma'am," said the little girl, remembering what Raven had told her. Layla smiled. She remembered her and Raven's conversation word-for-word. She knew that she would never forget that conversation either. Nor would she ever forget her hero, Raven Kensington. *Never.*

"Momma, I *can't*," Carmen spoke after a long silence. "I can't accept that. God *knows* this house isn't fit for an animal, let alone three human beings. But, I don't know. I just *can't*. I want the *best* for my baby. And for *you* too, Momma. You *know* that. But I ... There never seems to be light at the end of the tunnel. I've worked two jobs for years, and *still* ..." Tears filled Carmen's eyes. She worked at two nearby fast-food restaurants that paid her minimum wage.

The Halters did what they could do to make ends meet. But it was never enough. Carmen had always wanted to be a nurse. Her dreams had ended when she became pregnant with Layla. She thought the man loved her. She also thought that Hal Purdue was going to marry her. But as soon as Hal found out that Carmen was pregnant, he cut off all ties with her.

Tina looked at her daughter in disbelief. "What do you mean, you *can't* accept the house? Would you prefer we continue to live like *this*? In *this*? It's a different story, Carmen, if or when you don't have a choice, but when you *do*, there's definitely *not* an excuse. We *now* have a choice. Not just for a very nice home, but also to live in a nice area, which is so much better for Layla too. She *deserves* it. We *all* do. She'll even go to a *much* better school."

"Momma ..."

"Carmen, please, hear me out. Let me finish." Tina pointed a finger, playfully, at her daughter. "I'm *your* mother, you're *not* mine."

That made Carmen laugh. She loved her mother and daughter so very much. They were a very close family. Carmen looked at her mother with a look of love and admiration. If it hadn't been for her mother, Carmen didn't know how she would have made it this far. She stepped in and helped her immensely, when Layla was born, and her mother still helped her a whole lot.

"I'm listening, Momma."

"God's will will *always* be done," said Tina Halter. "It was the will of *God* that this happened. *Think* about it, honey. Raven Kensington is a *huge* movie star. She gets fan mail from millions of people *everywhere*. It's impossible for her to read *all* of the mail that she receives. But God made *sure* that *our* Layla's letter, reached Raven's *hands*, and *apparently*, her heart too. That letter didn't reach Ms. Kensington's hands by *accident*, Carmen. *Nothing* happens by accident. *Everything* happens for a reason. *Everything*! And God certainly doesn't make mistakes. He's *not* like us. Layla asked Raven to *write* her back. She didn't ask her to come by, although that would *certainly* be *anyone's* dream to meet her hero. I don't like using the word idol. Raven came by instead. It was *meant* for her to come. God sent Raven Kensington, to *help* us. We never know whom the good Lord's going to use. But, it's *very* important that we *accept* our blessings, not *reject* them. It's also important that we *erase* pride. Pride has caused *many* people to fall. As it states in the Bible, pride cometh before a fall. Don't fall, honey. Carmen, don't sit questioning God either. *Accept* this huge blessing. *No one*, or *nothing*, is too big for God! And He can use *anyone*, for whatever purpose He wants to. After all, He *is* God. He can do *anything*. *Anything*! So, if you choose not to go, Layla and I will visit you. We *are* going! I'm *accepting* the good Lord's blessing."

"No, ma'am, you'll are *not*," said Carmen.

"What do you mean, we're *not*?" her mother asked.

"Because, Momma … I'm *coming* too!" Carmen sat listening to her mother. Tina Halter was right. Everything that she said made a lot of sense. Mothers are wise, thought Carmen. Or, at least my mother is.

Mother and daughter screamed.

"I'm too *old* to jump," said Tina. "But I *can* dance around!"

When Layla heard all of the screaming, she ran out of her bedroom. "Momma? Grandma, are you'll *okay*?"

Carmen hugged her daughter and shared the astonishing news with her.

All three of them were now dancing around. They were ecstatic. And still shocked. Not only had God *heard* their prayers, *He* had also, *answered* them!

"Once we stop screaming, I'll call Judith back," said Tina, laughing.

"*Call* her now, Momma! We can resume screaming after you've hung up."

Tina called Judith.

When Judith informed her that they could move in immediately, Tina told her that they were ready. She didn't want to spend another day there. The only things that they had to take were their clothing, their shoes, and a few personal items, such as photos and family heirlooms.

Judith told Tina that she'd send a driver over with a moving van.

Tina thanked her, and she also told her to say an *extra special* thanks to Raven and Tony.

The Halters gathered all of their belongings and eagerly waited for the driver to pick them up to take them to their new home. On the *other*, side of town.

* * *

The Halters weren't prepared for their new home on St. Paul Street. The twenty-three-hundred-square-foot home was gorgeous! The expressions on their faces told the story. They were elated by what they saw. This was a far cry from their old home. The carpet was plush, the walls were white, there was a big fireplace in the living room, with three stockings hanging on the mantel, with each of their names on them. There was also a big Christmas tree, beautifully-decorated, with presents underneath. The home was also completely furnished. There was a TV in the living room, and one in all three bedrooms, with DVD players. The kitchen was spacious, with white-on-white appliances. The ladies shook their heads in awe. Unbelievable! But the woman who had made this possible was far more unbelievable than this beautiful home. Tina and Carmen Halter shook their heads in amazement. This was truly a dream! A dream, that neither of them thought they would ever see, in their lifetimes.

After walking through the beautiful home repeatedly, Carmen sat on the sofa in the living room, with tears streaming down her face. It was still so shocking. She couldn't believe their good fortune. How could they ever repay Raven for *this*? *How*?

"*Thank you*," Carmen whispered repeatedly. "Thank you, so *very* much." Carmen looked up. "And *most* of all, *thank You*!"

Tina, Carmen, and Layla knelt down on bended knee and prayed. Tina led them in prayer. They all thanked God for the home. The Halters were also thankful for Raven and Tony.

"The *garage*! We haven't seen the garage yet!" said a very excited Layla, after they had finished praying.

Carmen laughed. Layla was right. They had forgotten all about the garage.

"*Look*! Someone left their car here!"

Tina Halter stood back looking at the car. She shook her head. *Raven*. She had also bought them a car! A black Toyota Camry was parked in the garage. There was a big red bow on it. Tina and Carmen cried again. They were speechless.

Layla read the card that she'd found on the fireplace in the living room. It was from Raven. "*BEST WISHES NOW AND ALWAYS*! *MERRY CHRISTMAS*! *-T&R"*

"She's as beautiful on the inside as she is on the outside. Merry Christmas, Raven! And Tony! Thank you *both*, so very much!" Tina Halter said aloud. "And *thank You*," Tina said again, as she looked upwards.

    * * *

The Halters sent a big thank you card to the Dashs. They knew that they would never be able to repay them financially. But as they'd written on the card, they would *always* be forever *grateful*. They also promised Raven and Tony that they would take *excellent* care of the home, and car.

Tina was especially grateful for the car for a number of reasons. It was much safer for Carmen, who often worked at night. Tina Halter thought of her daughter's limp. Because they had a car now, Carmen would no longer have to walk to the bus stop, so things would be much easier on her. Carmen wouldn't have to walk far at all. She would only have to walk, to the attached garage.

The elderly woman smiled, she couldn't stop crying. As far as she was concerned, Raven Kensington, was an *angel*. A stunningly-beautiful angel.

Carmen looked in the help wanted ads for better-paying jobs. She also requested information from nursing programs. Raven gave her newfound hope, in more ways than one.

The Halters settled into their beautiful new home. They also test drove their new car, went to nearby malls, and familiarized themselves with their new neighborhood, which they all loved.

Layla wrote a letter to her favorite teacher, Mrs. Satchell. She gave the teacher her new address. Layla knew that she would be going to a different school now. She was going to miss Mrs. Satchell a lot. The teacher had always been so nice to her. She didn't tell the teacher what Raven had done for the Halter family. Layla wasn't sure if Raven would like that. She wasn't sure if her mother or grandmother would want her to tell anyone either. So, she played it safe. The thought of not seeing Daniel again made Layla smile. But as Raven had told her, *Daniels*, can exist anywhere. Her hero had given her *great* armor. The armor of *knowledge*. And Layla was more than prepared to use it!

The Halters *loved* their beautiful new home and car. What the Dashs had done for them still hadn't quite set in yet. It was still so *unbelievable*. This was going to be their *best* Christmas, *ever*!

* * *

Raven mailed Christmas cards to all of her and Tony's family and friends. She was thrilled that she had several months off before filming another movie. It couldn't have come at a better time either. The holidays were always very special to her. Raven wanted to spend it as she always had, with family and friends, not filming a movie. And she was very grateful and happy to be able to do just that. Raven sat by the fireplace, watching the lights on the Christmas tree. She thought of the Halters, and smiled. *Giving*, was what Christmas was all about.

"Are you packed and ready to go, beautiful?" Tony asked Raven.

"Packed? Sweetheart, where are we going?"

"Well, I thought you might want to have a *white* Christmas. We've spent a number of weeks here at home in Malibu, so I thought that maybe you'd like to fly to the Hamptons for a *snowy* Christmas. Have the best of both worlds, so to speak. We could leave New York a few days before Christmas and fly to Texas, to spend some time with your family, then return to California from there."

Raven smiled. "Spoken like a *true* businessman. You have everything planned to a T. Sure, that's a great idea! I'll go pack now. When are we leaving?"

"As soon as you get packed."

The Dashs gave Mack his Christmas gift before leaving that afternoon. They also said good-bye to Pugs. They took their private jet to New York. Most of the time when they traveled, they used it.

Hours later, Raven and Tony were landing at John F. Kennedy International Airport. The snow began falling rapidly again, as it had earlier in New York that day. They were glad that they'd landed before the weather got too bad.

Raven loved the weather. This, was *Christmas* weather. Snow made it feel, and look, a lot more like Christmas. It was a symbol of Raven's favorite time of year.

They took a limo out to their home in the Hamptons. Raven sat in the limo, enjoying the ride. She watched all of the people crowding the sidewalks, walking swiftly. "New York-style walking," Raven had always called it. She smiled. Raven was very happy that Tony had thought of coming to New York.

      * * *

The big iron gates opened, as the white limo drove slowly through, making its way to the front entrance. The home had quiet, country-like surroundings. It was a great place to relax and unwind. It was also a far cry from the hustle and bustle of New York and L.A.

Raven and Tony were greeted at the door by Rex Measley, the butler. Rex was one of the main reasons their home in the Hamptons was meticulously-kept throughout the year. Rex had a number of assistants who worked for him, to help manage the enormous estate. Together, they all did a fine job. Tony was always pleased, as he was this time too.

There was a roaring fire in the huge fireplace in the formal living room. Two stockings hung on the fireplace mantel, with Raven's and Tony's names on them. Rex had also decorated a tree, especially for them. He wanted to make the Dashs' Christmas in the Hamptons joyous, and *Christmasy*.

Rex took Raven's and Tony's luggage upstairs to the master suite. When Rex returned, he made hot chocolate for Raven and Tony.

Tony invited Rex to sit down with them, and he gladly accepted. This was Rex's first time meeting, "the Mrs." Raven was every bit as gorgeous as he had heard she was. Rex knew that Raven was a big movie star, but he rarely watched movies or TV. He was an avid-reader.

Rex took an instant liking to Raven. She was exquisitely-beautiful and very sophisticated, with a great sense of humor to boot. Rex also liked the fact that Raven was down-to-earth. Rex could easily see why his boss fell madly in love with her. He saw the way Tony looked at his wife. He's definitely crazy about her. Very, Rex observed. He could tell that Raven loved Tony a lot too. The twosome also had a very strong, unspeakable bond, Rex thought, as he watched them.

Raven, Tony, and Rex talked for several hours, before Rex retired to the guest quarters for the evening.

After Rex left, Raven and Tony sat by the fireplace, roasting hot dogs and marshmallows, as the Temptations sang softly in the background.

Raven's dark eyes danced. "I'm so *glad* we came. *All* of this is so beautiful. *Everything.* I *love* you, sweetheart."

Raven never wanted to take her husband, or marriage, for granted. And so far, she hadn't. And neither had Tony. Raven always hoped and prayed that she would never take her many blessings for granted.

"I *love* you too, baby. I'm glad you're happy. I'm happiest when I'm with *you.* And I'm happy when my baby's happy! No one or nothing, makes me feel the way you make me feel, Raven. *Nothing* comes *remotely* close." Tony looked deep into his wife's eyes as he spoke. He loved looking into those gorgeous eyes of hers. And like Mae Kensington, Tony also referred to his wife's eyes as "X-ray" eyes. Raven didn't just look *at* people, she looked *into* them.

It was well after midnight before they turned in.

* * *

Raven lies in Tony's arms, after they'd made love, looking out at the snow, which was still falling heavily. She fell asleep after the Temptations sang one of her favorite songs, "Silent Night."

* * *

Raven and Tony slept in the next morning. It was noon when they both awoke, feeling refreshed and well-rested.

Tony kissed his wife. "Good morning, *beautiful*."

"Good morning, *handsome*. I keep saying this, but I *love* the snow. It's white, it's pretty, and it's *Christmas* weather! Let it snow! Let it snow! Let it snow!" Raven sang.

They stayed in bed for hours, watching some old TV shows. They watched *Wonder Woman*, *Kung-Fu*, *Happy Days*, *Little House on the Prairie*, *Matlock*, *Columbo*, *Good Times*, *The Waltons*, and one of Raven and Becky's favorite shows, *The Golden Girls*.

Finally, the lovebirds got out of bed, performed their hygienic duties, got dressed, then went downstairs for breakfast, even though it was well into the afternoon.

Per their request, Rex cooked them Cream of Wheat, bacon, and toast. Rex also sat a pitcher of orange juice, milk, and water on the table for Raven and Tony, along with a bowl of fresh strawberries.

After eating breakfast, Raven suggested they dress warmly and go outdoors. She wanted to go for a long walk. She also wanted to ride the snowmobiles.

Raven and Tony bundled up and went for a long walk on the grounds. As they were walking, Raven bent down, made a snowball, then threw it at her husband. The snowball fight was on! The lovebirds began laughing and playing in the snow.

Rex came outside to see what all of the screaming was about. He quickly went back inside, when Raven hurled a fast one at him.

Tony laughed. "Great throw! You have a *good* arm, beautiful."

Raven smiled. "Thanks."

Raven and Tony played in the snow, until they were exhausted, then they rode the snowmobiles, which were also a lot of fun. It was Raven's first time riding a snowmobile, but she had a ball!

Raven and Tony came inside hours later, still laughing hard, after playing like kids in the snow. They immediately went to warm themselves by the fireplace.

Rex made hot chocolate, to help warm them.

Shortly after they'd come in from outside, Becky phoned. She and John were still in California. She wasn't going to Tunis for Christmas. She and John were going to Colorado.

Raven told her about all of the fun that she and Tony were having.

Becky laughed, when Raven told her about the snowball fight that she and Tony had earlier.

The two women talked for a good while, before hanging up.

"How are Becky and John doing?" Tony asked Raven, after she hung up the phone.

"They are fine, sweetheart. They're not going to Tunis for Christmas this year. They're going to spend Christmas with John's cousin, Joyce. I think she lives in Denver," said Raven.

The two got comfy and cozy on the sofa.

Raven lies in her favorite place, in her husband's arms, as they watched movies, which they both loved to do.

Tony played in Raven's hair.

"Sweetheart, you *love* playing with my hair, don't you?" Raven asked Tony.

Tony laughed. "Not as much as I love playing with *other* things of yours."

Raven hit him playfully. "*Bad* boy, Tony Dash! Very bad and *naughty* boy!"

* * *

Raven and Tony spent their remaining days in the Hamptons as they had on their honeymoon, romancing, dining at ritzy restaurants, and having their always enjoyable heart-to-heart talks. They also built snowmen in the snow. And both enjoyed the "Christmasy" spirit that everyone seemed to be in. Everywhere they went, they heard Christmas music, saw beautiful decorations, and saw excited looks on children's faces. They also saw countless shopping bags, filled with Christmas gifts.

They left for the Kensingtons, four days before Christmas. Raven wanted to get home in time to help her mother and sister cook, as she had done for as long as she could remember. She also wanted to do some last-minute shopping.

Raven and Tony spent nine, very enjoyable days in Tunis, before heading back home to Malibu, to ring in the New Year.

Raven's eyes beamed on the plane ride home to L.A. This was the *best* Christmas that she'd ever had. She was happy to see her brother and his wife still going strong. They looked very happy. Raven hoped and prayed they would stay that way.

　　* * *

Pugs barked excitedly when he saw Raven and Tony. He had obviously missed them. A lot.

Mack greeted them with his usual warm smile. That was something the entire staff, including Rex, all had in common, thought Raven, they all had warm smiles.

Raven asked Mack if he'd gone to visit one of her R.K. by Design stores.

Mack told her he had.

Raven sensed that something was wrong. "How was it? Was *everything* okay?" Raven asked Mack.

Mack decided to tell her. "Mrs. Dash, I wasn't treated very well at all, by the manager of the store."

"Why not?" Raven asked him. "Mack, *what* happened?"

"Well ... when I arrived, the store had just opened, so there weren't many customers in the store. Anyway, I walked in, the manager just looked at me. He didn't greet me, he didn't ask me if he could help me find anything. The one thing he *did* do, was *follow* me. Mrs. Dash, everywhere that I went, he followed me. I left without buying anything. But, the store is very elegant! It's a *lovely* store. You probably already know by now, but both stores had record sales."

Raven and Tony knew about the stores' sales numbers. Tony always retrieved the sales figures every day from his laptop. The sales had exceeded expectations by a milestone. The Dashs were very pleased about that. They were going to do everything that they could do to keep the sales high, by providing impeccable customer service and quality products, consistently. And by taking care of their people, which was a company's most important asset. Tony knew that if you took care of your people, employees *and* customers, everything else would fall into place. And although they were elated about the sales figures, they weren't happy about Mack's complaint.

"I'm *so* sorry, Mack. Describe the manager to me. Do you remember his name?"

Mack described the manager. He also told Raven the man's name.

Mack had gone to the Beverly Hills store. The manager was a middle-aged Caucasian man with gray hair. His name was Byron Shanks. Joe Junior, and one of Tony's longtime assistants, had interviewed Byron. They were both impressed with him, and all of his references had checked out fine. Based on Joe Junior's word, Tony gave him the okay to hire Byron.

When Raven checked the voice mail at her office later that day, there were a number of complaints from various customers, regarding that same store.

The customers had identified their race. They were all African-American and Hispanic customers, who had shopped at the Beverly Hills location. Their complaints mirrored Mack's. Oh no, thought Raven, not this again. When will it *end*? Raven called Becky. She had a plan.

"Hello," said Becky.

"Hey, Beck. You up for an *acting* job?"

"For you? *Anything*, Sis! What's up?"

Raven told her everything. Becky was angry too. They decided to visit the store the next morning. Raven wanted to confirm these reports, and if valid, she was going to terminate this guy, right away.

Raven had provided extensive training to all of her employees. That training included, how to treat *all* customers and employees, what discrimination was, and what would happen if *any* employee discriminated against *anyone*. The policies and procedures were very clear. And along with discrimination, coming to work intoxicated, stealing, violence, drug use, and harassment of *any* kind, were all immediate grounds for termination. No second chances, no exceptions.

Raven Kensington had always been a firm believer in training. All employees who worked for her had read and signed the policy and procedure forms. Raven made sure that employees hadn't just signed the forms, she made sure that they understood every word. As far as she was concerned, good employers, provided their employees with proper training to learn their jobs, which in turn enabled employees to do their jobs. Very well.

All employees knew they would be held accountable for their actions too. Raven believed in setting all of her employees up for success, not failure. And showing appreciation, training, and being fair and supportive, were just a few things that she felt employers should do for their employees.

Raven held herself up to the same high standards and expectations that she demanded of her employees. She was a true believer in leading by example. As far as Raven Kensington was concerned, leading by example, was the *only* thing that influenced others.

Raven went over the plan with Tony, Becky, and John. They all had roles in her plan. Raven checked the schedule to make sure that Byron would be working the following day.

He was.

* * *

The next morning, Raven and Tony dressed to the nines and drove to their store in Beverly Hills. They purposely wore sunglasses. They didn't want to take any chances on Byron recognizing them, although they had never met Byron in person.

The valet attendant parked their car, as they walked inside of the store.

Raven spotted Byron immediately. He gave them an unwelcome look. No greeting. *Nothing*.

Raven and Tony walked the entire store.

Byron followed them. Whenever they would stop, Byron would also stop.

The door chime sounded, indicating that someone had entered the store. The customers who had entered were white.

Byron immediately walked over to them. He welcomed them to the store, and offered them a glass of champagne.

The customers declined the offer.

"Perhaps you would like a soft drink? We have a variety of them," said Byron, smiling at the couple.

"No, thank you," said Becky, speaking for herself and John.

Byron then asked Becky and John if he could help them find anything. He treated them like royalty. Becky and John wore ripped, white T-shirts, and torn, faded jeans. Their hair was uncombed. They both looked destitute.

"We'll wait." Becky pointed at Raven and Tony. "*That* couple was here *before* us. We'll just look around while you help them. I'll look at your evening gowns."

Byron smiled. "We've just received a new shipment of evening gowns from a hot new designer from Paris. Follow me, ma'am. I'll show you. We have the *largest* selection of designer clothes and shoes in the area. We're the *best* upscale store in Beverly Hills! Actually, we're the *best* in the Los Angeles area, bar none."

Raven walked over to Byron. She looked at his name badge. "Byron? My husband and I would like your assistance, please."

* * *

Byron eyed the beautiful and expensively-dressed woman that stood before him. He wondered where she might have shoplifted the black mink coat, diamond earrings, and dark designer shades that she wore. Byron thought, *if*, the mink and diamonds are even real. His eyes combed the black handbag that Raven carried. *Chanel*. It was the same handbag that his wife wanted, but couldn't afford. Maybe they broke into a nearby Beverly Hills mansion. Byron didn't want to keep Becky and John waiting any longer.

"I am with *another* customer!" Byron snapped. For a moment there, the woman reminded him of Raven Kensington. Byron quickly shook off that thought. He had read in one of the tabloid papers that she and her husband were in New York. It's not *her*. Byron laughed to himself, *they* all look alike.

Raven interrupted Byron's thoughts. "You're with *another* customer? My husband and I were here *first*."

Tony had already called the assistant manager, who was on his way. This was definitely Byron Shanks' last day at R.K. by Design.

Byron continued to ignore Raven and Tony. He quickly turned his attention back to Becky and John. He was certain to make a sale from the white customers. Black customers were simply a big waste of his time. They need to stick to Wal-Mart, or one of those other *dollar*-stores, something *they* can afford. *Beverly Hills*, R.K. by Design, was *way* out of their league. Byron laughed to himself again, as he continued to ignore Raven.

"I'm *so* sorry about that." Byron told Becky and John, referring to Raven interrupting him. "But, as I *was* saying ..."

"*Excuse* me," said Raven. She'd had enough of this man.

"Please, help them *first*. They were here first." Becky reminded Byron. *Again*. "We're in no hurry. But even if we were, they were here before us. And it's only *right*, first come, first served."

Byron turned to Raven with an angry look on his face. "I have had enough of *you*! Look, leave *my* store." He pointed to the sign hanging on the wall and read it to Raven. "We reserve the right to *refuse* service to *anyone*. I'm *now* going to exercise *that* right." Byron had a smirk on his face. "I'm sorry. Let me *explain* to you what that means."

It was very hard for Tony, Becky, and John to conceal their laughter. They knew this man had no idea what, not to mention *whom*, he was up against. But Byron Shanks was soon about to find out.

The stocker had come from the back of the store. Sharon had finished stocking. It was a requirement that all employees be cross-trained, and it came in handy for times like these. Tony asked Sharon to take care of the customers until the assistant manager and more employees arrived. He told her that they were on their way.

Raven removed her shades. Her dark eyes were like black ice, as she looked straight into Byron's gray ones. "*My, my, my,* now that's *no* way to talk to the person who *signs* your paychecks. *Is it*? I'd like to speak with you in the manager's office."

Byron's jaw dropped. His face was deathly-pale. He now recognized *her*. He, like many people, knew that the superstar was the owner of R.K. by Design.

Byron followed Raven into the office, slowly.

Tony, Becky, and John also followed.

Everyone sat down, as they listened to the woman, running the show.

"Byron, have you ever heard of the saying, *never* bite the hand that feeds you?" Raven asked. "Even *if*, the hands are *black*. Which in this case, they *are*."

Byron apologized repeatedly. "I'm *very* sorry, Ms. Kensington. I had no idea that it was *you*. I'm *so* sorry, Ms. Kensington. I'm …"

Raven raised her hand for Byron to be silent. "Should it matter *who* it is? Racism, is very *sickening*. Tell me something, Byron, since when can *anyone* look at a person's race, or what they are wearing, and determine the following: what they *can* or *cannot* afford, that they are *thieves* or up to no good, or that for whatever reason, they are *inferior* to whites, or *any* other race?"

Byron was silent.

Raven went on. "My husband and I came to this store, *our* store, mind you, dressed to the nines. And by the way, the mink and diamonds are *real*."

Becky laughed.

"If most people looked at my husband and me, judging from our appearance, one would assume that we had money. And in our case, that assumption would be correct. Becky and John came into the store looking homeless and destitute, and they were treated like *royalty*." The beauty shook her head. "You looked at their *race*, and *assumed*, that because they were *white*, they *had money*. It didn't matter to you how *poorly* they were dressed. *They*, were white. And by all means, feel free to correct me if I'm wrong about anything that I say, at *any* given time, as I speak. On the *flip* side of the coin, since when does being *white*, mean that you have *money*, or that you're better than *all* other races, and should therefore be treated better, or be treated the *best*? You sit here in silence now. *However*, I'll answer the questions that I've posed to you, in *two* words. *It doesn't*." Raven smiled. "When my husband and I first walked into *our* store, you looked at us as if we'd taken a wrong turn, as if we had walked into the *wrong* store. You looked at us, as if we didn't belong in Beverly Hills, period. What a shame! For the record, I will go wherever I *want* to go, and only God Himself can *stop* me. And regarding the sign that you mentioned to me earlier, that I hung in *my* stores, I reserve the *right*, and I *absolutely refuse*, to keep *bigots* like you in my stores. Byron, you obviously left that off your resume, with good reason, I'm sure. Most people don't *openly* admit that they're racist. And, no, I can't change the minds and hearts of every bigot in this world, but I can and will control discrimination in *my* stores. I don't worry about what I can't change or control, but I will do something about what I *can* change and control. Does *that* make sense?"

Byron nodded. "Yes, ma'am."

"Also, for the record, if *anyone* wanted to simply window-shop, or come to my stores to look around and not buy anything at all, they *can* do that too. Many people, of *all* races, go to stores and simply *look*, without buying *anything*. There's nothing wrong with doing that, nor is that against the law. Or at least, the last time that I checked, it *wasn't*. But, what *you* have *done*, discriminating against my husband and me, and *our* customers, is definitely, against *my* law." Raven looked at her husband. "Tony, please write Byron his *last* check."

Byron spoke quickly. "*Please*, Ms. Kensington. My wife and I have a baby on the way. *Please*, I *need* my job."

Raven looked at him. "Byron, in *all* seriousness, if you *needed* your job, you would have *done*, your job. This is your *last* day at *my* store."

Tony handed Byron his last check. "This meeting is *over*. You are hearby *dismissed*."

Becky and John left the office with Raven, as she walked the store.

Tony stayed and watched Byron, as he cleaned out the office that used to be his.

* * *

Becky and John commented on how beautiful and lavish the store was. They both loved the exterior and interior designs. The store was also meticulously-clean, neat, and well-stocked.

Becky smiled. "Sis, this is *definitely* your store. It's *you* all over."

Raven laughed in answer.

R.K. by Design was now packed with customers. Raven was pleased to see all of the customers happily-shopping in her store. She was determined to keep her customers, and her employees, very happy and satisfied.

John's thoughts were on Byron. "The *nerve* of him!"

Raven nodded her head in agreement. "I know. It happens all the time. It's *disgusting*. I'm just happy that I was in a position to remove someone like that from my store. Discrimination won't be tolerated in any business that I own, or support. However, even if blacks aren't in my position, the worst thing that we, or *anyone* who is being discriminated against can do, is absolutely *nothing*."

"You're right about that, Sis."

"Raven, the store is *beautiful*. Look at all of the celebs here!" said John.

"As long as it's understood by *all* employees, that *everyone*, is to be treated like celebs. Regardless of race, size, famous or not, and despite how they may or may not be dressed. *Any* human being that walks through *that* door, is to be treated like *royalty*. Tony and I are going to have a memo printed and distributed, reminding *all* of our employees, again, of that very thing. If anyone *refuses* to follow that, along with any other policy and procedure that's severe, they too, will be terminated."

After Tony escorted Byron out of the store, the foursome went to Spago for lunch.

Rob's face lit up instantly, at the sight of Raven and Becky. He gave both ladies big hugs. "Hello, *big* stars! Wow! Speaking of making it *big*! Both of you are having *tremendous* success. I am thrilled for you. Unbelievable!" Rob beamed at his two former employees.

Raven and Becky introduced Rob to their significant others.

All of the employees came and hugged their two former co-workers.

Sandra laughed when she saw Tony.

"Am I *missing* something?" Raven asked, looking at Tony and Sandra.

"Yes, Raven, you are. You see, *this* man came here years ago, asking about *you*. Trying to get me to give him your phone number. At first he told me that he was a *talent* scout." Everyone laughed, as Sandra went on, "It took me a little while, before I finally figured correctly, that he was interested in you *personally*, not professionally. I told him where you went to church. And as they say, the rest ... is history. It looks like the king, *captured* his queen."

* * *

Raven looked at her husband. "Tony Dash!"

Tony shrugged. "I'm a good actor, but it's a *perfect* example of what happens when you let your *feelings* get in the way."

Everyone laughed again.

Before they left, Rob asked Raven and Becky to send him autographed pictures of the two of them, so that he could place their photos on his Wall of Fame. "It's great seeing you two beauties again. Take care!" said Rob.

"It's great seeing you too, Rob. We'll get those autographed photos to you." Raven and Becky told their former boss.

* * *

It was New Year's Eve. Raven and Tony decided to join Becky and John at their home later that evening to ring in the New Year. It would just be the four of them. No one wanted to go out. They had all been invited to a slew of parties in Tinseltown, but they had politely declined.

* * *

When Raven and Tony made it home, Tony watched football, while his wife slept.

Hours later, a well-rested Raven woke up.

"Hello, *Sleeping* Beauty! Becky called when you were asleep. She wants to know if you'll do a guest appearance on *Day's Dawn*. She said that she'll talk with you tonight about it."

Raven smiled. For Becky, she would do it. There were very few things that she wouldn't do for her sister.

* * *

Later that evening, the Dashs headed to Beverly Hills. When they arrived, Becky and John gave them party hats and horns. The living room was beautifully-decorated, in true New Year's fashion.

Tony joined John in the kitchen, as he checked on their dinner.

Raven and Becky sat in the spacious living room, chatting.

* * *

"Did Tony tell you about *Day's Dawn*?" Becky asked Raven.

"Yes, he sure did," said Raven.

"*Well*? What do you say? I know that you're very busy, Sis."

"I'm *never* too busy for you, Beck. For *you*, I'll do it!" Raven looked at Becky with a worried expression. "*Beck*? *Everything* okay?"

Becky looked as if she had lost a few pounds. Nothing major, but Raven inquired anyway. She wanted to make sure that Becky was okay.

Becky laughed. "Of course, Sis. Everything's *fine*. I've just been working out a lot. That's all. Believe me, I *do* eat." Becky avoided Raven's eyes. She hated lying to her best friend.

The producers on the show were pressuring Becky constantly to lose weight. "You're starting to look *fat* on camera," they'd told her. They also told her, that if she didn't lose weight, her job would be in jeopardy.

Becky was eating one small meal a day. And she would only drink water and Diet Coke. If she got hungry, she would munch on non-fattening weight-loss bars. She also worked out, relentlessly, every day.

Raven washed her hands, and fixed plates for everyone. "Beck, this one's for you. You're *going* to eat!"

Becky assured her that she would. And, she did. She ate everything on her plate.

Raven had purposely fixed Becky a hefty plate of food. "The few pounds that you have lost, you will gain them back after eating all of the food on the plate that I fixed for you." Raven told her friend.

Becky laughed hard in answer.

The foursome had a very enjoyable evening. They ate a delicious lasagna dinner and drank white wine. Well, everyone except Raven. She wanted to be sober driving her and Tony home. And besides, everyone knew that she wasn't a drinker anyway.

"Well, actually, I will have something to drink after all." Raven joked. "I'll have a glass of vodka and ginger ale. Hold the vodka," said Raven, as everyone laughed.

When midnight came, the foursome wished each other Happy New Year, as they sung, "Auld Lang Syne."

Raven helped Becky clean up before she and Tony left.

The Dashs thanked Becky and John for a very enjoyable evening.

"You'll are quite welcome. Happy New Year, Sis! Happy New Year, Tony!" said a very cheerful and slightly-tipsy Becky. "I would walk you two out to your car, but I have to go to the ladies' room."

Raven and Becky hugged and said their good-byes at the door.

As Raven and Tony were heading back home to Malibu, Becky was in the bathroom, making herself vomit.

* * *

When the Dashs arrived home, they called their families to wish them a Happy New Year. It had already been a new year in Texas, two hours prior.

"Happy New Year, my love!" Tony told Raven again, as he kissed her.

"Happy New Year to you too, sweetheart!" said Raven.

* * *

The next day, Becky called and asked Raven if "next week" would be too soon for her to tape her guest appearance on *Day's Dawn*.

"Next week will be *perfect*." Raven told her.

Becky brought Raven her script. Raven was going to play a hip-swinging seductress, who had bedded Becky's character, Samantha's, fiancé.

"Whoa!" Raven laughed. "That's hot! A hip-swinging seductress named, Lola Lavante. *Interesting*."

"As long as the guys keep their hands to themselves," said Tony. "No one beds my wife, but *me*."

Raven and Becky laughed.

The producers were elated that Raven had agreed to do a guest appearance on *Day's Dawn*. She was the biggest star in the world, and they were going to use Raven's immense star-power to their advantage. Raven Kensington meant huge ratings, and that is exactly what they were after.

Raven taped the show, which was aired weeks later. Not only did Raven Kensington's guest appearance on *Day's Dawn* make headlines, the show received its highest ratings, ever. The producers were so thrilled with the soaring ratings, they tried to get Becky to convince Raven to make a lot more appearances on the show. They wanted her character to be recurring.

Raven politely declined. "I only did it the one time for you, Beck."

Raven knew that if she wasn't the superstar she now was, and if she were wanting the opportunity to have a role on the show, *any* role on the show, she wouldn't have been given a second look. But she was glad that she had done it, for Becky. And it was the only reason she had done it too. Working with Becky was the thrill of a lifetime. Raven still had her dream of writing a movie that the two of them would star in.

Raven's and Becky's chemistry on-screen was awesome. Both ladies played their roles, flawlessly. No one could deny that these were two tremendously-gifted actresses. They weren't just beautiful.

Everyone in Tunis watched and recorded the show. Raven and Becky also recorded the episode.

The cameramen gave Raven and Becky tapes of the two of them goofing around in-between takes. The two women had a ball. When it was time for the *real* thing, they stepped up to the plate, and became all business.

"He's one *lucky* bastard," said Lario Dearst, one of the producers of the show, referring to Tony. "One very lucky bastard!" Lario couldn't take his eyes off Raven. She looked just as good standing still, as she did moving. Lario continued to watch the incredibly-beautiful woman, with the rounded hips and full breasts. Raven simply drove him nuts. And *that* voice. That ever-*so sultry* voice of hers.

Lario's partner laughed at him when he told the errand boy to bring him a big glass of ice cold water. Raven Kensington made him very hot. Lario thought her very sizzling, in more ways than one.

Tony looked at Lario, as if reading his mind. He smiled at him. Tony wasn't dumb. He knew what the guy was thinking, and he knew what he had. Tony never took his wife for granted. He loved and cherished Raven, he placed her on a pedestal. *She*, was his queen. His beautiful, lovely queen.

The Dashs left hand in hand, after saying their thank yous and good-byes to cast and crew.

Becky waited for John to pick her up. She was beaming. She loved working with her best friend. It was an experience of a lifetime! And one that Raven Kensington, nor Rebecca Simms, would *ever* forget.

* * *

Raven and Tony went swimming. Raven was now a good swimmer. She still wasn't as good as Tony, but she was good. And each time that she went swimming, she got better and better. Raven was confident enough to race her husband to the other side of the pool now. She enjoyed their pool-races.

"You won!" said Tony.

Raven shook her head and pointed a finger at her very handsome husband. "*No*, Mr. Dash, you *let* me win. I've told you before, don't go easy on me, T.D. How many times am I *gonna* tell ya that?"

Tony laughed. "Yes, ma'am. But don't knock a man for trying!"

Pugs watched them as they swam, barking and wagging his tail, as usual.

Tony swam over to his wife and began kissing her, passionately.

Pugs stopped barking. The dog stood and watched.

As Tony continued kissing Raven, Pugs turned his head from side-to-side, as he watched them.

"Tony. *Sweetheart* ... I *don't* think we should be doing this in front of the dog."

Tony laughed. "*Kissing*?"

"*Making out.*"

"Raven! Pugs is a *dog*, he's *not* a child!" Tony kept kissing his wife.

Raven looked at the dog, who kept staring at them. "*Stop. Not* here, sweetheart. Pugs is making me uncomfortable. Did you notice that he stopped barking and wagging his tail when you started kissing me? We *need* to lead by example. Not in front of the dog, Tony."

Tony looked at Pugs, who was still staring at them and turning his head from side-to-side as they kissed. "Pugs, *look* what you've done! You're going to get a time-out for that!" said Tony, waving a playful finger at their dog, who began to whimper.

Raven couldn't believe the dog's reaction. "He didn't mean it, *Pugsy*." Raven told the dog. "Daddy was just kidding."

Pugs started barking again and wagging his tail.

"*Daddy?*" Tony shook his head. He couldn't believe his eyes, or his ears. "Let's go inside. I can't believe this! You act as if Pugs is a child, and Pugs acts as if he understands what we're doing. Or what I was *trying* to do, rather." Tony shook his head. "Unbelievable!"

"We must lead by example. *Never* make out in front of children," said Raven.

"*Woman*, what are you talking about? Let's change the subject. Are you sure you haven't been *drinking*, even just a *little* bit?" Tony teased his wife.

Raven laughed. "I sure have, sweetheart. I've been drinking, *a lotta* bit!"

"*No more* ginger ale for you, beautiful," said Tony. "No more!"

Chapter 10

Over the next several months, Raven and Becky didn't see each other as often as they would have liked to, but they still talked on the phone every day. Raven was busy preparing for her next film, *The Lorraine Shears Story*, and Becky was busy on the set of her soap opera.

Raven's new movie was an autobiography, based on the life of a very popular singer who was a big star in Paris, in the early eighties. The directors wanted the movie to be as close to reality as possible, so they moved the location to Paris. Cast and crew would be there for eight months. This was by far the longest shoot Raven had ever done, but she loved the script, so she signed on to do the film. Raven was also very happy about the location. She loved Paris. And so did Tony.

The Dashs stayed at the same hotel that they had stayed at on their honeymoon. Raven inquired about Martha, the maid whom they had met when she and Tony were in Paris before.

The manager told her that Martha had moved to San Francisco.

As always, Raven worked long hours every day on the set of her movie. And as always, Tony would pamper her in the evenings. Raven was very grateful for that. Tony had spoiled her beyond the beyond. He would often cook for her, and run her bath water.

The months flew by. The entire cast and crew clicked. The movie was the most heartfelt-movie that Raven had ever done. Her heart went out to Lorraine Shears, the woman who she was portraying in the movie. She went through so much physical, emotional, and verbal abuse, it was unbelievable that the woman was still alive. It was very easy for Raven to cry when the script called for her character to do so. It was enough to make anyone cry.

* * *

Becky needed to talk to someone. There was no one better to talk to than her best friend, her sister. Becky knew that she could talk to Raven about anything. She decided to call her in Paris. Raven and Becky talked on the phone every day, and they had talked earlier that day, but Becky told Raven that she was doing great. She hated lying to her, but she just couldn't bring herself to tell her. Becky felt that she had already betrayed her best friend enough.

Raven answered the phone. "Hello. *Hello?*"

There was silence on the other end.

"*Hello*? Hello."

Becky hung up.

"Who was it?" Tony asked.

Raven shrugged her shoulders. "I don't know. They didn't say anything."

Becky couldn't stop crying. "I'm sorry, Sis. I'm ... *so* sorry!"

* * *

The next day, Tony picked Raven up from the set, as he usually did. It was Raven's last day on the set. Things had gone well. They had been in Paris for eight months and Raven had enjoyed every minute of it. She and Tony loved it there. They decided to spend two weeks in St. Tropez, before heading back home to Malibu.

"*Breaking* news story! This just in, *Rebecca Simms*, the star of the hit soap opera, *Day's Dawn*, was just rushed to Cedars-Sinai Medical Center in Beverly Hills. She's said to be in *very* critical condition. Miss Simms plays Samantha Matthews on the hit soap ..."

"Oh … no!" said Raven. She immediately dialed information and called the hospital to confirm what they'd heard.

No one would tell Raven anything.

Raven called John's cell phone.

No answer.

Tony called Mack.

Mack confirmed it. He told Tony that he had just heard about Becky. "I was about to phone you and Mrs. Dash."

Raven and Tony quickly drove to the hotel, where they packed, headed to the airport, then jetted back to L.A.

Raven kept trying to call John. Where is *he*? And *what happened* to Beck? *Why* was she in the hospital?

So many questions ran through Raven's mind, as she cried. Raven left her cell phone on, hoping that John would call her. When her phone rang an hour later, Raven quickly answered it. It wasn't John, it was one of the show's producers. Ted told Raven that Becky was in E.R. at Cedars-Sinai, as the reporter on the radio had announced earlier. When Raven asked Ted what happened, he lied to her and told her that he didn't know.

It was difficult trying to be calm in the midst of a storm, but Raven tried hard, to do just that. She called the Simms, who had already heard. They were waiting for Becky's father and brother to come home so that they could all fly to L.A. together.

Raven also called her family.

"We're on our way, sweetheart. All of us are going to fly to Los Angeles, together." Mae Kensington told her daughter.

Raven and Tony were the first to arrive at the hospital. The producers had left, they hadn't stayed long. Becky's floor was heavily guarded by police.

Becky's housekeeper told police to let Raven and Tony through. "Miss Simms is in *there*," said Lucy, pointing to Room 154. Lucy's eyes were very sad. Raven didn't like what she was feeling.

Raven and Tony quickly walked to Becky's hospital room, but they weren't prepared for what they saw. Tubes and monitors were everywhere. Becky looked almost lifeless, lying in the hospital bed. Her face was very thin and pale. She was a shell of her former self. Her face and body were skin and bones. Her big blue eyes looked huge, as they fell on Raven's.

Raven sat down beside Becky's bed. Tears spilled down her face. She couldn't control them, nor did she want to.

Tony sat in the chair beside Raven, speechless.

Becky was starving herself. Whenever she would eat anything, she would make herself vomit. It had been nearly a year since Raven and Becky had last seen each other.

"*Oh ... Beck ...*" It was hard for Raven to speak. There was a huge lump in her throat.

Becky looked into her best friend's dark eyes. "May I please have *your* autograph?" she managed a weak smile.

"*Anytime,*" said Raven, trying to return the smile through her tears.

"Sis, I told you that we'd *make* it. Look at *you*, *always* so very beautiful. You looked like a movie star, *before* you became one. I had *always* told you that you would be a *huge* star. I was *right*. Wasn't I?"

Raven nodded. Hollywood and stardom were the last things that Raven wanted to talk about, but she was willing to, if that's what Becky wanted.

"Remember when we first came to L.A.? I drove by the Summerwood Apartments just the other day." Becky's eyes had a far away look in them that scared Raven. "We've had so much fun *together*, Sis. So many ... *many* ... great and wonderful times ... *to-geth-er*. You were the sister, that I ... ne- *ne-ver* had. I know you're mad at me. I was *weak. Foolish.*"

Raven shook her head. "Beck, there's *nothing* that you could do, that would *ever* change the fact that I *love* you. *Nothing.*"

"I knew that you would be a superstar. Your star will only get *bigger*, Sis. I just *wish* ... that ... I ... could be there with ... *you*. I had always hoped, that I would be there. That we'd be there, *to-geth-*

er. And for ... a ... while ... we *were*."

"Beck, *please* ... *don't* talk like that. You *will* be there with *me*."

"Sis, I ... will be watching *you*. And as *always*, I'll be *root* ... *ing* for you. *My* ... *sis-ter*." Becky smiled slightly. "Remember when we worked at McDonald's?"

Raven nodded.

"Mitch had a *huge* crush on you. Didn't think I knew that, did *you*?"

Raven smiled through her tears.

"I've *al-ways loved* and *admired* you, Sis. You're so ... beautiful and *strong*. You've al-ways strived to do things the *right* way. You were *al-ways* the strong one." Becky's eyes searched Raven's. "You didn't care if you had to stand a-lone. Al-though, you knew that I was *always* in your *corn* ... *er. Al-ways*. I've al-ways had the *greatest* love and *ut-most* respect for you, Sis. It was hard *not* to. You're the best. *S.F.L.*"

"*Sisters, for life*."

"I'm so sorry, Sis."

"Beck, *why*? Why didn't you *talk* to me?" Raven had to ask. "Why didn't you come to me? You *know* that you could talk to me about anything. *Anything*, Beck."

"I know, Sis. It started out *small*. I thought that I could *control* things. The producers thought ... I looked *fat* on-screen. I shouldn't have listened. I was afraid, Sis. I was *afraid* I'd lose my job. I ... was afraid of *losing everything* that I had worked so very *hard* and *long* for. In the midst of it *all*, I *panicked. We* had worked so long and hard to be-come *successful*, Sis. I didn't ... want to take the chance of going *back* ... to square one. It's too late now, but I know *now* that they ... *didn't* care a-bout me. John want-ed to tell you, but I told him *not* to."

Raven was *livid*. She wanted to kill the producers, and John. *Especially* John, who'd always said that he loved Becky. Raven wondered if John had ever loved her. His actions certainly hadn't proven that.

"Sis, the *great-est* act-ing experience that I had, was when ... you and I worked *to-geth-er* ... on *Day's Dawn. Re-mem-ber* that?"

Raven nodded.

"That was an *incredible* experience. I *love* you very much, Sis. Al-ways ... *al-ways* ... *re-mem-ber that*. Clint. He was right. There was so much truth to what he said, all those years ago. It's foolish, how we as humans, can know right from wrong, and choose wrong. One *must* be very ... strong to survive in this world. The pres-sures, the stress, life in general, it can *all* get to you, you can *con-form* to it, *if* you're not strong. The saying, *only the strong sur-vives*, is very *true*. It's very true, Sis. Tell my family, Mother, Dad-dy, my brother ... Tell *all* of them, that I *love* them very much. And tell ... them that ... I ... am *ver-y* sorry. I ... didn't mean to cause any ... one pain and heart-ache. I'm so *sorry*, Sis." And as if reading her best friend's mind, Becky continued. "May-be, may ... be John didn't love me after all. *Who* knows? May-be that's why I was re ... luctant to mar-ry him. I don't know. I did love him though." For the first time, Becky looked at Tony. "*Tony*, take ... *very* good care, of *my* sis, *my* sis-ter. Take ... very good care of *her*. She is an *in-cred-i-ble* wom-an. *Ra-ven* ... is *ir-re-place* ... *able*. Don't *ever*, take her for grant-ed. A per-son ... like *her*, doesn't come a-round of-ten. I'm *not* just ... say-ing that, because she's *my* ... sis-ter. I'm say-ing it, because ... it's *true*."

Tony nodded. "I know. I will always take *excellent* care of Raven, and I will never take her for granted. You don't have to worry about that, Becky. That's a *promise*."

"I'm ... very *tired* now. I need rest. I *love* you very much, Sis. Don't *ever* for, *for-get* ... that. *Thank you* ... for be-ing a friend, *my best* friend, *my sis-ter* ..."

"I *love* you too, Beck. I love you *very* much. And *thank you*."

Raven didn't leave. She and Tony sat in the room, watching Becky. Raven held Becky's hand, praying, and willing her to live.

Tony put his arms around his wife to comfort her. The tears wouldn't stop falling.

As Becky rested, Raven sat beside her hospital bed thinking about how much Becky meant to her. They were like sisters. They had always been, like sisters. And they *were* sisters, in *every* way that mattered. They weren't related by blood, but they were related by love, and there was no greater relation than that.

Lucy came in periodically to see how Becky was doing. She had been working for Becky for months. Lucy loved working for the young pretty blonde. Becky always treated her so nicely. It was very difficult seeing her boss in critical condition. Lucy saw how thin Becky was when she'd interviewed her for the job, but most of the women in Hollywood were rail-thin. So as a result, Lucy didn't think anything of it. It seemed normal, especially in Tinseltown. And now, she felt guilty. Lucy cried as she sat in the waiting room, thinking about Becky. If only she had known. *If only ...*

* * *

Less than an hour passed, when Raven and Tony heard the sound they both dreaded. They looked at the electronic monitor and saw the flatline. Rebecca Simms, was dead.

"*Beck! No!*" Raven cried. "*Beck! Please! Beck! Oh, no! No! No! Please ...* God! *No! Please ...*"

The E.R. medical team ran in and tried to revive Becky, although it was very clear that Becky was dead, but stranger things had happened before. They did everything they could do, but to no avail.

Raven, Tony, and Lucy were in the waiting room, praying, for a miracle.

The doctor came out to the waiting room to tell them what they had all feared most, Becky, was dead. They had done everything that they could do, he told them. The doctor also told Raven that an autopsy would be performed.

Raven ran back into Becky's room. "*Oh, Beck! Beck! Please, Beck ... come back! Come back! Please! Beck! Beck! Beck! Please ... God ...*" Raven screamed, as she collapsed in her husband's arms.

Raven had to be sedated. She was a basket case.

* * *

After the nurse gave Raven a shot, she sat down in Becky's room, dazed, staring at what was left of the woman, who had been a sister to her, for twenty-two years. It was very shocking. It was so hard to believe. Becky, was gone. She was so young, so beautiful. Raven, was *devastated*. She had never been so devastated in her life.

All kinds of things went through Raven's mind. If *only* she could have seen this coming. *Where* was John? *Why* hadn't he gotten help for her? *Why* did this have to happen to Becky of *all* people? *Why*? *Why*? *Why*?

* * *

Hours later, Raven and Tony heard the voices of Mae Kensington and Becky's parents, followed by screams in the E.R. waiting room. Apparently, they had been informed of the tragic news. The Simms and Kensingtons ran into the room, sobbing.

Becky's mother cried the loudest. Sonya Simms was clearly heartbroken. Her husband, Dax, and their son, Jeb, could do little to comfort her, or each other. Everyone was grief-stricken. It was extremely difficult for all of them to believe, that *their* Becky, was dead.

Raven's parents hugged her. They had known Becky for years. She was like a daughter to them. Angie sat beside Raven. She knew that this was a very difficult time for her sister too. Raven and Becky were like sisters. They were very close, and had been for many years.

Police did a great job keeping the media at bay.

Sonya Simms shot Raven an angry look. "*Raven*? *What* happened? Why didn't *you* tell us that Becky was *sick*? *Why*?"

"Mrs. Simms," said Tony, "Raven didn't *know* that Becky was sick." His wife was already going through enough trying to even begin to deal with Becky's death. There was no way that Tony was going to allow Becky's mother, or anyone else for that matter, to make things worse for Raven. What happened to Becky was not his wife's fault. And Tony was angry with Sonya Simms for implying that it was. At the very least, thought Tony, she should have gotten the facts, first. His heart went out to Becky's mother, but pointing fingers, especially at the wrong person, was certainly not right.

"It's *okay*, Tony," said Raven. Her voice was hoarse and her eyes were red. "Mrs. Simms, Tony's *right*, I didn't *know* that Beck was sick. The *last* time that I actually saw Beck ..." Raven's voice broke. "We hadn't seen each other much before I left for Paris. I noticed that she had lost a few pounds. She said that it was due to her exercising. And I *believed* her, because Beck had *never* lied to me. She assured me that she *did* eat. And whenever we were together, she *would* eat. I had *no* idea that Beck was sick. There is *no way* that I would've kept something like that from *you*, or *anyone* who loved her. I would have also gotten professional help for Beck. I would have done *whatever* I had to do, to get help for *her*. I would have done *everything* in my power, to help her get well. *Everything. Anything. Whatever* was needed. If, I had *known*. I *loved* Beck as if she were *my* own sister. And you should *know* that. You've known me for a long time, Mrs. Simms. Hollywood, fame, *nothing* or *no one*, could *ever* change the strong friendship and love that Beck and I shared for over two decades. I would like to talk with John. They lived together, so obviously he *knew* that she was sick. Beck also told me he knew. I don't know. I'm *just* ..." Raven's voice broke.

"It's *okay*, sweetheart," said Mae Kensington. "It wasn't *your* fault. *Erase* that from your mind."

Mae looked at Becky's mother, and like Tony, she didn't like what Sonya Simms was implying either. But she understood what might have been going through Sonya's mind. She might have thought the very same thing, if she were in her shoes. This was obviously very shocking and devastating for her, as it would be for any mother, Mae knew.

"I'm *sorry*, Raven. I ... I'm *very* sorry," said Sonya Simms. "It's just so *shocking* to me. And it's even more difficult *not* having answers. I'm so sorry, Raven. I shouldn't have blamed you. I should have gotten all of the facts, first. I know you loved my daughter very much. And God knows she also loved you a lot too. Raven, I'm so sorry, sweetheart. I ... I didn't mean to ... I am just so hurt, angry, confused. *Devastated.* She … was *my* … lit-tle girl … I didn't mean … to blame *you*, Raven. *Please*, accept my apology," said Sonya, in-between sobs.

She and Raven hugged.

Sonya found her voice again. "You know, I always thought that my children would bury me, not the *other* way around. You haven't seen or heard from John?"

Raven shook her head. "No, ma'am. I tried calling John when I first heard the news, there was no answer. I don't know where he is. I've asked Lucy too. She has the same numbers that I have. She doesn't know where he is either."

Like Raven, the Simms and Kensingtons wanted to *kill* John, and the producers of *Day's Dawn*.

* * *

The ambulance pulled up quickly to the front entrance of Trakton Systems, Inc. The police were already there. They had immediately blocked off the crime scene. They took pictures of everything. Afterwards, the police officers put on gloves and began gathering and examining evidence. An autopsy would be done to confirm how he died, and to determine time of death. Although, all of the police officers agreed, that from the looks of things, and from all of the evidence, it was clearly a suicide.

All of the employees had left for the day. The cleaning lady found him. Jonathan Sparks, was dead. He shot himself twice in the head. His blood and brains were splattered everywhere. A gun was on the desk, along with a letter, addressed to, "Raven Kensington."

One of the police officers looked at the envelope. "*Raven Kensington*? *The*, Raven Kensington? He couldn't be talking about the superstar. Could he?"

The others shook their heads no.

"I doubt it," one of them answered.

"Possibly. Who knows?" another officer answered. "It's a *small* world. You *never* know."

"If he is talking about the superstar, had she and *this* guy had an affair, and he took his life when things went sour?"

The other officers shrugged. They didn't know, but it was certainly possible, things like that happened all the time.

"Isn't Raven Kensington *married*?" another officer asked.

"Yes, Adrian, but that's hardly *stopped* the majority of the world from having affairs."

Adrian nodded, as he continued gathering and examining the evidence, and trying to put the pieces together. He shook his head sadly, no matter how beautiful, rich, and famous Raven Kensington was, she or no one, was worth killing yourself over.

* * *

After staying at the hospital for hours, Tony took his wife home.

The Kensingtons stayed at the hospital with the Simms to help comfort them. They knew that Tony would be there for Raven.

Mrs. Simms had finally given permission to have her daughter's body removed from the hospital room, so that an autopsy could be performed.

* * *

Later that evening, Trey drove everyone over to Raven and Tony's, where they all were going to stay until they went back to Texas.

It was three days before Thanksgiving. This would undoubtedly be the most difficult and saddest holiday season, ever.

Everyone was very somber at the Dashs. Mrs. Simms had refused to be given a shot at the hospital. She cried all night long. Charles and Mae stayed up with the Simms for most of the night.

Raven was heavily sedated. She slept all night. When she awoke the next morning and reality hit again, she began crying uncontrollably, for the great friend, and sister, whom she had lost. Her heart was very heavy. Raven's heart went out to the Simms family, especially the mother, who was extremely devastated. Raven knew there were very few losses like that of a mother, losing her child.

According to autopsy reports, Becky died because her body was badly undernourished. Dr. Winton didn't tell the family, but he was very surprised that Becky had lived as long as she had.

The Simms had their daughter's body flown back to Tunis, where Becky's wake, funeral service, and burial, would take place. Becky's death was very difficult for all who had loved her. It was a very tough pill to swallow.

* * *

After a week in California, everyone flew back to Texas to try to prepare for, what would clearly be, the most difficult time of their lives.

It made the Simms family even more hurt and angry, seeing their daughter's face plastered all over tabloid magazines.

"Have those *bastards* no shame?" said Jeb. "They are heartless!"

The Simms hated Hollywood like never before. They hated everything about it. Everything that it stood for. Sonya blamed John, and Hollywood, for her daughter's death.

* * *

Before leaving California, they had all found out about John's suicide. John's letter was made public by an "unidentified" source. In the letter, John expressed his love for Becky. He told of how he wanted Becky to get help, but Becky denied being sick. *She also told me not to tell anyone, especially you.* John wrote in his letter. *Raven, Becky knew that you would not have listened to her. She knew that you would've done whatever you could do to help her, including getting her professional and medical help. I was afraid of losing her, so I kept my mouth shut. We argued and fought a lot about her continuing weight loss, that spiraled down so rapidly. I'm leaving this letter to you, Raven, because I don't know Becky's family that well. But, please, tell them that I'm very sorry. I shouldn't have listened to Becky. I shouldn't have stood by and watched her die, watch her kill herself, but I did. Again, I was so afraid of losing her. Please, Raven, don't ever think for once, that I didn't love Becky. I loved her very much! I sat in my office, unable to come to the hospital. There was no way that I could face Becky's family, or you. No way! When I heard that Becky had died, I knew then, that I would take my own life, because I didn't deserve to live. I feel that I was just as responsible for Becky's death as she was, and Hollywood. Again, tell her family that I am very sorry. And Raven, I apologize to you too. I know how much you loved Becky, and I also know how much she loved you. I hope that one day, you and the Simms family, will find it in your hearts, to forgive me ... -John*

You *didn't* want to *lose* her? You lost her anyway. We all lost her. Raven was very angry at John. Her thoughts were just the opposite. There's no way that he could have loved Becky to do what he'd done. That's a kind of love that I would never want, Raven thought. When you love someone, you seek *their* highest good. You do what is best for that person, not what they want you to do. If John would have done that, perhaps Becky would still be alive. All of this was so heavy. Despite Raven's anger at John, she said a prayer for the Sparks family. She could only imagine what they were going through. Regardless of what John had or hadn't done, he was still their son. And Raven was sure that John's death was just as devastating for them, as Becky's death was for the Simms family.

* * *

Becky's funeral took place on a Saturday afternoon. It was a private ceremony for family and friends, only. Sonya Simms didn't want to see anyone from Hollywood, except Raven and Tony, at her daughter's funeral. She had security in place everywhere.

The two producers who had pressured Becky to lose weight showed up at the gate. They were immediately told to leave, but not before Raven addressed them.

Raven slapped both of the producers, viciously, across their faces. Raven's eyes were like black ice as she looked at them in disgust. She was livid. "Get off this property! The *nerve* of the two of you to show *your* faces here. *You'll are the reason* ..." Raven's voice broke, "that we are here, *today*."

* * *

The producers' faces stung like never before. Raven slapped them so hard, it felt as if their teeth had been knocked loose.

Raven looked at the security officers. "Get these *scumbags* out of here!"

Security escorted the producers off the premises, immediately.

* * *

It was the *hardest* day of Raven Kensington's life, as she sat and mourned for the woman, who had been her closest friend and sister, for over twenty years.

Tony held his wife close. His heart went out to the Simms family. Tony's heart also went out to Raven. It pained him greatly, to see everyone so devatated. Raven's eyes were filled with immense-grief and sorrow, and Tony knew that her heart was too.

Sonya Simms insisted that Raven and Tony sit on the front row with them. "It's what Becky would have wanted," said the grief-stricken mother.

Thousands came to pay their respects to the blonde beauty with the heart of gold. Mrs. Simms allowed many of Becky's classmates to attend her funeral. Clint Stanton was there. Tears fell from his eyes.

This was what he'd spoken about way back in sixth grade. It wasn't humor, it was *reality*. It hit Clint even harder, because he knew Becky, personally. And like many, he loved her a lot. Very few would ever forget, Rebecca Simms.

The Simms family received millions of letters and cards from their daughter's millions of fans around the world. Many of them wanted to attend her funeral. And like Raven, and the Simms family, they were very angry at the producers for pressuring Becky to lose weight.

"Miss Simms wasn't even *close* to being fat!" one angry fan had written to the producers. "I will *never* watch your show again! You, Hollywood, *killed* Rebecca Simms!"

Raven, Tony, and the Kensington family, spent the entire day with the Simms. Andrew and his wife also spent most of the day with the Simms. Andy didn't know Becky real well, but he attended her funeral to be there for Raven. He knew how close the two women were. Andy remembered when he'd first saw them at Spago, years ago. He could only imagine what everyone who loved Becky was going through.

* * *

Late that night, Raven and Tony said their good-byes. They flew off to their sprawling ranch in Wyoming. Raven had to get away from it all. She told Andy that she was going to take a leave. Raven told him she didn't know how long she'd be gone, but she needed time away, time off, to mourn. Raven promised Andy that she would contact him again, but she couldn't tell him when.

* * *

Raven sat in the jet, looking out the window. Tears streamed down her face, as she thought of her beautiful, blonde friend. Her *sister*. She couldn't get Becky off her mind. She knew that she would never forget her. Raven had never been so devastated in her life.

Tony kissed Raven on the forehead and asked her if she needed anything. He also asked her if she needed to talk.

Raven shook her head no.

* * *

Raven and Tony arrived in Wyoming at three in the morning, just the two of them. This time, there would be no servants or maids. It would only be the two of them. And that was the way Raven wanted it.

Tony was a godsend. He always respected Raven's wishes. He gave her space and time alone, and he was always there when she needed him. Tony was Raven's much-needed source of strength, her rock, during this immensely-difficult time in her life.

Raven wanted to come to Wyoming because it was very relaxing and quiet. She also loved the scenery, the air, the altitude. It was what she needed. No glitz, no glamour, just peace and serenity. She needed time to mourn, time to heal, and time to think, without all of the reporters, and without all of the cameras flashing in her face.

Raven prayed often. She would lie in Tony's arms at night, crying, as she thought of Becky. They hadn't made love in a while. Sometimes Raven felt bad, because she felt as if she were neglecting her husband. But Tony had been very understanding. Raven didn't have much of an appetite either, but Tony would always make her eat. He refused to take "no" for an answer.

They would often go on long walks, in silence, most of the time. Raven had been very quiet since they'd arrived in Wyoming. Her heart was very heavy. Becky occupied Raven's heart and mind every minute of the day.

* * *

Months passed, before Raven could actually sleep the way she used to, before Becky's death. She felt okay sometimes, and other times, she would break down.

One night as they lie in bed, Tony reached for Raven. He wanted to make love to her, as he had for some time now. He understood what losing Becky meant to his wife, and he had been understanding and patient, but he needed Raven too.

Raven became angry. "Tony! *Please!*" Raven got out of bed, and went to sleep on the sofa. She lies on the sofa, crying. Oh, God! What am I doing? Raven felt terrible. She knew that she wasn't angry with Tony. Raven was angry with Becky, the producers, John, and Hollywood, but not her husband. Tony didn't have anything to do with Becky's death. Becky quickly occupied her mind again. *Beck, why? Why?* How could you do this to your family, me, and *everyone* who *loved* you? *How* could you? Raven lies there, crying on the sofa for hours, before her thoughts shifted again to her husband. Raven knew that she had to make things right. She got up and walked back to their bedroom.

"Tony? *Sweetheart?*" Raven climbed into bed. "*Baby?*"

"I'm here, beautiful." Tony answered.

"I'm so sorry, baby. I didn't mean to ... I don't mean to take this out on *you*. It's *not* your fault. I'm so *sorry*. I don't mean to neglect you either. I *love* you so much. Please, don't *ever* doubt that. Sweetheart, you can make love to me, if you want to." Raven whispered to her husband, reading his mind.

Raven and Tony knew each other better than anyone. They often read each other's minds. And they had long since begun finishing each other's sentences.

"Are you *sure*, baby? I've been wanting to make love to you for a while now, but I know what a difficult time you've been having, dealing with Becky's death," said Tony.

Raven touched Tony's lips. "*Sssh* ... it's okay, baby. It's *okay* ..."

Tony unbuttoned, and removed, his wife's pajama top. He then peeled off her panties. Time came to a standstill, as Tony began to work his magic. And that night, no one or nothing, was on Raven's mind. Tony kept Raven very busy, for the *rest ... of the night ...*

Tony woke up the next morning with a broad smile on his face. He kissed Raven tenderly. "Good morning, beautiful. *Thank you*, for last night. I *needed* that. I hope you don't think that I'm selfish." Tony held Raven in his arms, as he caressed her.

"Sometimes it's *good* to be selfish." Raven laughed. It felt good to laugh. She hadn't laughed in a long time. "No, baby, you're *not* selfish. You're an *incredible* man, and you are a *terrific* husband. The *best*. Your needs don't stop when there are tragedies. Life goes on. I know that it's been very difficult for you not making love for as long as it's been. *Tonagra*."

Tony laughed.

"Again, I'm so *sorry* for how I acted last night. You've been so supportive through *all* of this. You've been a *godsend*. I *love* you very much, Tony Dash. Don't *ever* forget that." Becky's death was another reminder of just how very precious and short life was.

"And I *love* you, the *beyond* beautiful, the ever-so lovely, *Raven Dash*. And I *always* will." Tony laughed again.

"What's *so* funny?" Raven asked.

"You had me taking *many* a cold shower. *Again!*"

Both of them laughed.

Tony feasted his eyes on his beautiful wife. "And you will be *punished* for that too. I hate to punish you, but that's how it is sometimes. Just remember, it will hurt me, *more* than, it will hurt *you*."

"Yeah, right," said Raven. "I'm *sure* it … *won't*."

* * *

Raven was still quiet most of the time. She had some good moments, but very few. She enjoyed the daily walks that she and Tony took. The mountains, the entire scenery, were gorgeous.

Raven began opening up to Tony about what she was feeling. He listened to her. And he never passed judgment. Raven felt better talking to someone. Especially someone whom she loved and trusted. And there was no one who she loved and trusted, more than Tony.

Their relationship was very honest, open, deep. Raven and Tony talked openly about their innermost thoughts and feelings. They were best friends.

Raven and Tony had been in Wyoming for six months now. Raven was doing better, but she wasn't completely healed. She knew that in time, things would get better. She also knew that with God's help, she would be able to *manage* Becky's death, even if it would never be cured. Raven knew that some things were to be managed, not cured. Raven seriously doubted if she would ever heal from Becky's death.

She and Tony began riding their mountain bikes daily. They also started horseback riding. It was so nice being able to get away from it all. Their time in Wyoming was priceless.

Tony called Mack daily to see how he and Pugs were doing, as he always did when he and Raven were away. Tony laughed when Mack told him that paparazzi were staked out in Paris hoping to get pictures of Raven. Raven's publicist had purposely leaked out false information, so that the Dashs could have complete privacy, and so far, it was working, like a charm.

Raven had begun to call the Simms more, and she talked to her mother once a week now. Everyone was "managing." Angie told Raven that her movie was still number one at the box-office, but that wasn't any consolation for Raven. She would have traded fame and fortune in a heartbeat, for Becky's life, to have her alive again. And well. She missed Becky so much, and Raven knew that she would always miss her. Terribly. They were all leaning on God, and each other, to help with their immense-grief.

That night, as Raven lies in her husband's arms, she told Tony what some of her future plans were. "You know, sweetheart, I would *love* nothing more than to one day come back to this place and spend lots of time here, just *us*. It's so peaceful, serene, and refreshing. I *love* it here. It's a *great* place to get away from it all."

"We can come here as often as you want to, baby. You know that," said Tony. "Is this where you'd like to spend most of your time at, once you retire?"

"I don't like the word *retire*. Let's just say that when my career winds down, I'd love for us to spend a lot of time here. I would also love for us to do lots of traveling. I've always loved to travel."

"Sweetheart, you ain't said nothin' but a word!" said Tony. "I'd love that too. It's very nice here. And quiet. A far cry from all of the hustle and bustle of big cities, not to mention Hollywood-mania."

    * * *

After two years in Wyoming, Raven was ready to go back to work, but there was something that she had to do first. She was more determined than ever, to help other females who were suffering from an eating disorder or an identity crisis.

With Sonya Simms' blessing, Raven started *the Rebecca Simms Foundation*. Unfortunately, she couldn't save Becky, but hopefully, she would be able to help and save others.

Raven hung a huge portrait of Becky on the wall of the foundation center. Raven chose the photo. It was her favorite picture of her dear friend. Becky looked beautiful, happy, and healthy. It was the way Raven wanted to remember the woman who was like a sister to her. And it was also the way that she wanted everyone else to remember Becky. Raven had the following words inscribed beneath Becky's portrait: *In loving memory of my sister, Rebecca "Beck" Simms. You will always have a very special place in my heart. S.F.L. I will always love you! Rest In Peace - Sis*

    * * *

Andrew Spellman was very happy that Raven was ready to go back to work. He had a flood of scripts waiting for her to review. Andy also told Raven that her last film was the highest-grossing movie in history. Andy smiled every time he thought of the naysayers. They're eating a lot of crow now. A whole lotta crow!

Raven chose to do two films that year. One was a comedy, she needed to laugh, the other, a horror flick. She chose the horror flick because it was a type of film that she hadn't done before. The comedy, *A Funny Kind of Lady*, would begin shooting in two months. That was good for Raven, because it allowed her time to spend at the numerous charities that she supported. It also gave Raven time to speak out to the youth.

* * *

Raven was asked to speak at a school in South Central Los Angeles. She gladly accepted. She always loved speaking to children, tomorrow's future.

Doug Hopkins, the principal of the school, knew that few could motivate like the great Raven Kensington. Her power and influence were unmatched. The principal also knew that because of Raven's star-power, the students were a lot more likely to listen to her. Doug had always had a lot of respect and admiration for the superstar. He had never seen a role model of Raven Kensington's caliber. And like millions of males around the world, he too, had a huge crush on the breathtaking-beauty. What a woman, thought Doug, as he sat at his desk thinking about Raven. What a woman! Doug laughed as he remembered his and his secretary's conversation.

"Mr. Hopkins, if we can't get Ms. Kensington to come to our school, what other celebrity would you like me to contact? I'll make a list of your choices."

"Ready to write the list?" Doug had asked his secretary.

Carolyn had nodded.

"Raven Kensington."

"Okay. Got her. *Next?*" the secretary had asked.

"Raven Kensington."

"Mr. Hopkins, I have *her* down," said Carolyn. "Who *are* the *others?*"

"Raven Kensington."

Carolyn looked puzzled, and very annoyed at her boss.

"Carolyn, *relax. Ms. Kensington* is the *only* celeb I want on the list. If we can't get her now, we will wait as long as we have to. I don't want any other celebrity coming to talk to our kids. I *want* Raven Kensington!" The principal was adamant.

"You and everyone else." Carolyn had told her boss. She knew that everyone wanted the superstar, in one form or another. She also knew that her boss had a huge crush on Raven. What man didn't? But Carolyn had to admit, Raven wasn't just a woman who possessed enormous beauty, she was very intelligent and classy, and she agreed with her boss, she was the best role model out there. And never before, thought Carolyn, had children and the world needed, a Raven Kensington. She was very refreshing, a breath of fresh air. Parents were also crazy about her. Raven Kensington was a universal, megastar, who appealed to all. She also helped a lot of people. Carolyn admired her for that, most of all.

* * *

When the principal notified the students that Raven Kensington was going to be a guest speaker at their school, the students and staff were ecstatic. They couldn't wait for "next Monday" to arrive. Parents were strongly-encouraged to attend.

* * *

Doug gave Raven a grand tour of the school, then he escorted her to the auditorium.

When it was time for the Q&A session to begin, hands shot up immediately.

* * *

Raven smiled and greeted the audience, who was overjoyed that *the* Raven Kensington had come to their school. The mostly-black audience was also thrilled beyond words, to see someone who looked like them, so exquisitely-beautiful, and enormously-successful. The woman on the stage before them was the biggest movie star in the world. And that alone, sent a message, that if Raven could do it, so could they.

As Raven spoke, the students hung on her every word. Many of them thought her very beautiful, with an equally-beautiful voice.

Raven addressed the first hand that she saw. She smiled at the young girl. "Yes, ma'am?" said Raven. "What's *your* question, young lady?"

The young girl smiled nervously. "Miss Kensington, first of all, I want to express my condolences to you regarding your best friend, Rebecca Simms. I'm *so* sorry. I've lost a number of people who I loved very much. I know what you obviously went through, and what you're still probably going through." Sterlina Stetson was a big fan of Raven's. She had many of Raven's pictures on her bedroom wall, and she had seen every one of her movies. Sterlina looked up to the star. Raven Kensington was her idol.

"Thank you," said Raven. "And you're right, it's *still* very difficult. Great friends are hard to find. They are even harder, to lose."

"Miss Kensington, in your opinion, who bears the *most* responsibility for children? Raising and teaching them in particular. And do you think that stars have a certain responsibility to children to watch what they say and do?"

"I'm a *firm* believer that the *first teachers*, are the *parents* of that child, and the *first classroom*, *is* the *home*. In answer to your second question, *yes*, I think that celebrities should watch what they say and do, because they obviously influence children, as does the media. However, the two people in the world who *influence* children the *most*, are *still*, their *parents*. It is *not* the responsibility of celebrities, the government, TV, movies, music, etc., to *parent*, or to raise, a child. It is the parents' responsibility, to be parents to their children, and that should not be an option. It's a *necessity*. And while we may like this to be a perfect world, while we may hope and wish that stars watch their words and actions, that's not an excuse to blame them for your child's behavior or upbringing. *Parents*, are responsible, for raising their children. Children will emulate their parents, more than anyone. As a parent, *you*, need to be your child's influence, not *anyone* else, including, celebrities, and that is exactly, the way that it should be. Parents, if you want A+ children, then you need to be A+ parents."

Raven was interrupted by a thunderous applause.

"All parents, are teachers. As with anything, you can be a good teacher, or you can be a poor teacher. I am also a firm believer that *good* parents, make for good children. With children, a lot more is caught, than taught. The saying of, 'do as I say, not as I do,' doesn't work, nor will it ever work. Because it is *not*, what parents say to their children, it is what they *show* them. Leading by example, is the *only* way to lead. Parents are leaders, whether they want to be or not. Parents lead, children follow. And *whatever* example parents lead with, it is that example, *that* road, that their children will follow. The apple doesn't fall too far from the tree. Before I move on, did I make myself *clear*?"

"Yes, ma'am. You were very clear, Miss Kensington," said Sterlina.

"Good. Yes, sir?"

"Miss Kensington, do you think affirmative action needs to end?"

"No, I don't. As long as there is racism, we *need* affirmative action. Yes?"

"Miss Kensington, I just want to say that you're very beautiful and confident, not to mention very smart. I want to become an actress, but I don't think that I'm the media's *ideal*-beauty. I'm not the prettiest person."

"Thank you for the compliments, young lady. I didn't meet the criteria of the media's ideal-beauty either, however, I met *my* criteria. There is something that I want the world to know, something that I want *all* females to know. Like *many* things, beauty comes in *all* sizes, shapes, and colors, not *just* one. I have *never* had the desire to be thin. I love my curves, I love my shape, I love my size. My face. I love the package, the *entire* package, that God put me in. Self-esteem and knowledge, are very important. *Never* let anyone tell you that you aren't beautiful, or what you *need* to do to become beautiful. Don't chase someone else's ideal of beauty. What *you* think of yourself, is what matters. It is the *only* ideal that you should consider. We are *all* individuals for a reason. And God made all of us, how He wanted us to be."

There was a loud round of applause from the massive audience.

Many of the females in the audience smiled. The superstar's words of wisdom were very inspiring to them.

"Yes?" said Raven, after the clapping died.

"Miss Kensington, I'm overweight. I am exercising and cutting down on what I eat to lose weight. I've lost ten pounds so far."

"That's great, young lady! As I've said before, being *healthy* is important, but it's also important to have a healthy mind. And don't try to duplicate what the media shows we should all look like. Be *you*. And be sure to lose weight in a *healthy* manner. Consult your doctor."

"My doctor's helping me," said the girl, smiling.

Raven returned the smile. "That's good, young lady. Keep up the great work! Yes?"

"Miss Kensington, did your best friend die of an eating disorder?"

"Beck died because she starved herself trying to lose weight. Her body was badly undernourished. Her producers told her that she looked fat on camera. Beck feared losing her job, so she started doing what she thought would be simple and fast, but things quickly spun out of control."

"I've seen her. I used to watch *Day's Dawn* all the time. Miss

Simms wasn't even close to being fat. She was slender. And very pretty too."

"You're right, young man. Beck was tall and slender, but by Hollywood's standards, she still wasn't thin enough. And yes, Beck was beautiful, on the inside too. Yes?"

"Why didn't Becky talk to you? Weren't the two of you best friends?"

"Yes, Beck and I were very close. We were like sisters, but oftentimes when someone has an eating disorder, they are usually very secretive. And unfortunately, I hadn't seen Beck in just shy of a year, and whenever we would talk on the phone, which was daily, she sounded like herself. I had no idea. Things may have been different had I been in town, and saw a lot more of her. I don't know. Yes?"

"You're right in more ways than one, Miss Kensington. Come to think of it, most of the female reporters are also thin."

Raven nodded. "They sure are. Society, the media, again. Same message, be thin to look good. Requirement for any media job, literally. Yes?"

"It's obvious that the media has a very strong influence on people."

"You're right, young lady. The media has a very strong influence on people. But simply acknowledging that a problem exists is a very small step. Actions to solve the problem, are of utmost importance. Yes?"

"There's not only size discrimination. There is also the never-seeming-to-go-away, race discrimination, in Hollywood."

"You're right, young man. That's very apparent in Hollywood, *and* the world in general. Yes?"

"Jose is right, Miss Kensington, it's not just thin females who we see on the screen. The majority that are seen aren't just thin, they're white."

"Right again. Discrimination, is very *disgraceful*. My enormous success in Hollywood totally contradicted what many producers, writers, and directors, told me time and time again, when I would try out for parts, when Beck and I first came to L.A. years ago. But, I *knew* better. I *believed* in myself. I worked hard and long. I *never* gave up. I never compromised myself, or my values and morals. I proved them wrong. I *refused* to accept things the way that they had always been. And I refused, to do things their way. I didn't lose any weight either. I kept my size-eleven frame. And there was absolutely nothing, that I could, or wanted to do, about my race. I am very proud to be black. I am what, and how, God wanted me to be. I wouldn't have been happy playing their game. I won playing my own game. Because as far as I was concerned, *my* way, was the best way for me. And I wanted to be the best. And I'm a firm believer, that in order to be the best, you have to do things your way, not someone else's way. I did what many naysayers said I'd never do. I made them see, what they thought they would never see. I went through, it wasn't easy by any means, but I didn't expect it to be easy either. Many things in life aren't easy. But we must never give up. And we certainly shouldn't let hard work stop us. I said all of that to say this, don't let others tell you what you *aren't* capable of doing. Don't ever let anyone, no matter *who* it is, place limitations on you. You can do *anything* that you put your mind to. Anything! If I would've listened to a lot of people, I wouldn't be who I am today, nor would I be living my dreams. It is only when you are living your dreams, that they become reality. What is to be is your call, and your call, only. You know what you're capable of doing better than anyone. So always believe in yourself, even if no one else does. Education is very important too. Knowledge is power. I can't stress that enough. Yes?"

"Miss Kensington, I hear many politicians speaking out against the negative influences of hip-hop music, yet, I *don't* hear many at all, politicians or even many celebrities, speaking out against the deadly message, and the very negative influence, that the media continues to send, regarding females, dying to be thin."

"Great point! You're right about that, young lady. Countless of females have died, and are *still* dying, to be thin. The last time that I checked, the number of people dying from hip-hop was *far* less in number. Far less! Politicians, celebs, *all* of us, need to speak out against *this* very *deadly* message, as well. Just as musicians and record companies, are told to take responsibility for their actions, the *media*, also *needs* to take responsibility for the *very deadly* message, that they have been sending for *ages*, that's doing more than influencing, their message, is costing lives. *Many* lives. I have been speaking out against this for years. I am more determined now, more than ever before. It is very personal now. It hit home. I lost my *sister*, who I loved, *dearly*. Yes?"

"Miss Kensington, why do you think females are dying to be thin?"

"Many times, especially with youth, whatever's considered the *in*, or *hip* thing, that's what is emulated. The message that's often sent by the media, is that you have to be *thin*, in order to be *beautiful*. And many of us want to be beautiful. Therefore, many females do whatever it takes to mirror what the media considers beautiful. Oftentimes, if we see it, we want to be it. Even if, unfortunately, we may die in the process. *Anything*, that is *popularized*, is usually duplicated by millions. However, I will still stand firm and strong in saying, that good and strong parents will overcome *many* things, including, what's popular. Especially, if what is popular is wrong, and even more so, if it's deadly."

Sterlina listened to Raven intently. She was so intelligent. What the superstar said made a lot of sense. She loved the way Raven broke things down so that anyone could understand what she was saying.

The principal sat in the audience with a big smile on his face. *This*, was the reason, he wanted Raven Kensington to come. The superstar certainly didn't disappoint.

A young man raised his hand. "Miss Kensington? What is your opinion about the *n*-word? Do you think that blacks should call each other that?"

"This topic is discussed often. No, I don't think that blacks should call each other that," said Raven, without hesitation. "If it's not okay for whites to call us that, why should it be okay for blacks to call each other that? The *n*-word is *not* in *my* vocabulary, nor is it acceptable to me, no matter what race uses it. The race of the person who is saying the word, shouldn't matter. The bottom line is that, *no* human being, should call *anyone* that. That word has such *awful* history to it. What that word meant to our ancestors, especially, is enough for me not to call *anyone* that, black, white, or otherwise. And I certainly don't think that we as African-Americans should be calling each other that. Our ancestors are probably turning over in their graves, knowing that some of us are now calling each other that. I've heard many blacks say that it means homeboy, buddy, friend. Some have even said that the *n*-word is used to empower. When I posed that question to a young man last week, he told me that it was like taking the word from the white man, and using his word, and that was very empowering to him. Well, *hear ye*, hear ye. You *can't* take anything from anyone who has never owned it. That word, or no other word, is *owned*, by anyone. Just because it was used by a lot of bigots, and it's still used by some, that doesn't mean that they own that word, or *any* other word, for that matter. Imitating ignorance, or wrong doing of *any* kind, does *not* empower anyone. And out of all of the great and wonderful words that can empower, namely God, why would such a hideous word be chosen, or even considered? No excuse! Let's not use race as an excuse. I only use race, when it's appropriate. I have *never* used it as an excuse. Again, if it's appalling for whites to call us that, it should also be appalling, and inexcusable, for us to call each other that. Out of respect for myself, and out of respect for my ancestors, I don't call anyone that, nor would I *ever* answer to that word. We are all familiar with the KKK."

The audience nodded their heads.

"Well, I wouldn't place a white hood over my head, for the same reason that I wouldn't use the *n*-word. If I donned KKK gear, should it make it any *less* dreadful because I'm black? Because a black face is underneath the white hood? Would it remove what that hood *represents*? What it has *always* represented? What it *will* always represent? How would using the *n*-word, and wearing KKK gear empower me? What's empowering, acceptable, or funny about that? If it's not acceptable if whites do it, why should it make a difference if, or when, blacks do it, or any race for that matter? I will reiterate. Again, there is absolutely *nothing* empowering, about hatred, discrimination, bigotry, ignorance, or *any* kind of wrong doing. It's like condemning something, and then turning around and imitating that which you are condemning. That's *ludicrous*!" Raven noticed that many of the young men were looking around at each other. The superstar could tell that her words had hit a home run. And that is exactly, what Raven wanted them to do. "Yes?"

"My name is Luctricia, Miss Kensington. You're highly-intelligent. You know *everything*!" said Luctricia Brown, who wanted to be an actress.

Raven shook her head in disagreement. "*No*, Luctricia, I know *a lot*, but no one, knows *everything*. *Learning*, is a *lifelong*-experience. Yes?"

"Miss Kensington, you mentioned our ancestors. What do they have to do with us *now*? It's a new day and time. Our ancestors are *long* gone."

"They are long gone. But their *actions*, *contributions*, and *sacrifices*, *aren't*, nor will they *ever* be. Young man, because of *our* ancestors, we are *able* to walk through *many* doors, that were once *closed* to us. It is very important that we know *how* those doors got open. You and I are not a *new* kind of Negro. What our ancestors did, *all* of the *many* sacrifices that they made, and the regular, horrific terrors that they went through, has *everything* to do with those who came after them, meaning *us*. Not to mention the countless number of lives that were lost. They paved the way for us in countless ways. They rode on *extremely* bumpy roads, so that our roads would be smooth. So please, don't *ever* say, or think, that there is not a connection between us, and them. There will always, be a connection. We are connected to those who came before us, we are connected to those who are here now, and we will be connected to those who will come after us. You don't have to live during the same generation as someone else, to be connected to them. My great-grandfathers are both dead, but it doesn't make us any less related. We are still connected. We're still related. Being black, automatically makes us related and connected, by race and experiences. Rosa Parks stood up, so that we could sit down. Mrs. Parks stood up, by remaining seated. She didn't just do that for the blacks who were living during that time, she, like many blacks, took stands and went through, for the blacks that would also come after them. And likewise, I didn't fight so hard to change Hollywood for myself, only. I fought hard, and I am still fighting very hard, for those blacks, and those non-Caucasians, who are going to come after me, when I'm gone. I've opened doors for others, that may have otherwise remained closed. I stand on the shoulders of *all* of the black actresses and actors who came before me, that helped pave the way for me. It's like a cycle. The things that we do, *our* actions, will be *remembered*, long after we're gone. And the past will always have a connection to the future. *Always*. We must know where we have been, to know where we are going. Yes?"

"Miss Kensington? Do you think that race will *always* be an issue in this world?"

"Yes. It's not colors that separate us though. We, separate us. A color is only a thing. It has no actions. People do. It's not the color, or race, of a man, it's the actions, of that man. I thank God that race relations are better than they used to be, but racism is still very much alive and well, and more than likely, it will always exist. Little children of all races will gladly play together, but they will not always stay together, and that's usually a contributing factor from a child's parents, siblings, or others, who have influence in that child's life. Some parents teach their children to only play with, and associate with children, and or people, who look like them. Some parents will also tell their children that they are better than other colors or races. As I've said so *many* times, teaching, starts at home, not at school, not *anywhere* else. Children will usually do what they see their parents do, even if they may not always understand, or agree with it. Beck and I played together *happily* as little girls. And it wasn't that she or I didn't see that we were *different* colors, it was just that it didn't *matter* to us, or our parents. If it would have mattered, more than likely, things would've been different. My sister and I were at a Wal-Mart once, and a little white boy, who looked to be no more than three years old, pointed at us and said, 'those are very pretty nigger girls.' The woman who was with him, who I just assumed was his mother, simply looked at my sister and me, and walked on. It was obvious to me, from whom the teaching was coming. That little boy was barely out of diapers, and he's already being taught to hate. It's certainly not coming from him. Race will always matter to some; therefore, it will always matter in one way or another. Which is very unfortunate. However, to some of us, thank God, race *doesn't* matter. I see people not as colors, but as *people*. Human beings. And *individual* human beings at that. Yes?"

"The size thing? What about those of us who want to be rail-thin?"

"That is certainly your choice. I just hope that you don't risk your life being *too* thin. If you're thin and healthy, and that is how you want to be, that's great. To each their own. But for all those, who like me, prefer curves and who are just as proud of our bodies and the way we look, we shouldn't be discriminated against, because of it. And it is important to send a message that we are beautiful too. There's nothing wrong with being thin and healthy. But there's *a lot* wrong with dangerous, negative messages, and discrimination of *any* kind. And I have a *huge* problem with loss of life. I also know that *any* female, regardless of her race, would be looked over, not only in Hollywood, but even in the real-world sometimes, if they're not the *ideal*-size. I will keep hammering on race and size discrimination, as long as they exist. We would only have to look at the media, and the world in general, to see that *both* are very much alive and well. And have been for *many* years. Yes?"

"Miss Kensington? I admire you so much."

Raven smiled at the young lady. "Thank you."

"You didn't let *anything* stop you. You're unbelievable! You did things *your* way, and won. And won big too. You are now the biggest star in the world!"

"Yes, I did things my way. And won. But every time I win, it is a *collective* win, *for all those*." Raven smiled. "Yes?"

"Miss Kensington? What are your thoughts on connections? And do you believe in luck?"

"Connections are always helpful; however, it is very important to know, that someone may get you through the door, but simply getting through the door, is *not* enough. *You*, have to deliver. There is no getting around that. As far as luck, I don't believe in luck. Everything happens for a reason. I don't think that *anything* happens by chance, or by wishing upon a star. Yes?"

"You have given lots of time and money to help others. I like that. I like seeing successful people help make other people's lives better. I love seeing people give back. Was helping others a dream of yours too?"

Raven nodded. "Yes. It still is. Although everyone can help someone, despite their financial status. Help comes in so many different ways. You don't need money, to give someone a kind word, teach someone how to read, or volunteer at a hospital, to put a smile on the face of the sick, or lonely. Sometimes, what we see as small, can have the greatest impact. So you see, everyone can help brighten someone else's day, *without* the use of money. Don't ever let the fact that you can't help everyone, stop you from helping *someone*. And another thing that I'm going to do, now that I've made it to the top, is *leave* the ladder. I'm not going to pick up the ladder behind me, as some do. I want as *many* people as possible, to climb up to the top. If any of you *ever* make it to the top, *don't* pick up the ladder behind you. Leave it for others to climb up too. Always, send the elevator back down."

The audience gave the superstar another loud round of applause.

"Yes?"

"Miss Kensington? What do you think about the term, sex sells? And do you think that pretty people sell?"

"I think both statements are overplayed. It's obvious that sex does sell; however, it is also *obvious*, that when it comes to movies, it's not enough. And history proves this too. The highest-grossing movie in history wasn't *sex* or *beauty*-based. This proves that people prefer beautiful movies, over beautiful people, and sex. I love seeing producers who are more interested in making *beautiful* movies, instead of being more concerned, with casting beautiful people. Music is another example. A person can look like Daffy Duck, but if he or she puts out a song that stirs the heart and soul, a song that *moves* people, they will quack all the way to the top of the charts."

Everyone in the audience laughed.

"It's *true*. We see it all the time, solo artists and bands going multi-platinum, and they're not always the best-looking people either."

The audience nodded in agreement.

"Yes?"

"You're *extremely* successful. Your movies are always big, huge money-makers, blockbusters. You've shattered many box-office records too. How much longer do you think you'll continue acting, Miss Kensington?"

"I honestly don't know. Eventually I'll call it quits, but I can't tell anyone when that will be. Yes?"

"Miss Kensington, my name is Declan. As a writer, is it enough just to have a *good* story?"

"No, Declan, it isn't. You have to be a good *storyteller* too. *How* you tell a story, is very important. Details, are very important. Yes?"

"Miss Kensington, how does it feel to be so famous and important?"

　　　* * *

"First of all, *everyone*, is important. It's nice to be famous and important, but it's much *more* important, to be nice. Yes?"

"That's a good way to put it," said the young man, smiling. "I'll have to remember that."

"Yes?"

"You're considered by many to be the best actress in Hollywood. The best *ever* actually. Have you stopped working as hard? You're obviously on top now."

"No, I still practice and work *very* hard. Even the best can get better," said Raven. "Yes?"

"What is your opinion on interracial relationships?"

Raven laughed. "Love is color *blind*, as so many other things *should* be. I think that society, the world, needs to focus more on what human beings have in *common*, and focus *less*, on what's different about us. Human beings have *many* things in common. Beck was my sister. Race, does *not* matter to me, the *person* does. Again, I see *people*, *not* colors. And people need to be seen as human beings, *individual*, human beings, and not as colors. I can't emphasize that enough."

"Miss Kensington? I was once told by a white man, that we as blacks owe them, and this country, in general, a lot. He said we're indebted to them. Do you agree with that?"

"Absolutely *not*," said Raven, passionately. "Blacks went to wars, and fought and died, for *this* country, when this country *wouldn't* fight for *us*. We, and obviously when I say we, I mean blacks, helped build this country. That's *nonsense*. If we owe *anyone*, it would be God, and our ancestors, who suffered immensely, in order to make things *better* for us. And we owe it to ourselves to do something great and positive, with all of the opportunities that we *now* have, that once upon a time, did not exist for us. Yes?"

"Miss Kensington, do you think that blacks are dumber than whites?"

Raven laughed. "Depends on whom you ask."

The audience roared with laughter.

When the laughter died, Raven continued. "No, that's *not* true. *Intelligence*, has no color. I will use *myself* as an example. I was never as smart as *any* of my classmates." Raven paused. "I was *smarter*!"

The audience clapped wildly.

"*Anyone* can be mediocre, *anyone* can be average. *Always* strive to be the *best*. Always strive to be *better* than *anyone*, better than *all* the rest! *Never* work just as hard as anyone else, *always* work *harder*. And *never* strive to be just as smart as anyone else, be *smarter*. Education is *crucial*. As I have said before, *knowledge*, is *power*. And keep in mind that many incredible inventions that are used today were *invented* by blacks, who at the time, had *little* or *no* education or training. There's *nothing dumb* about that, young man, that's *genius*. How smart you are, has everything to do with *you*, not your skin color, hair color, etc. The *only* thing that color tells, is simply that, what color, and or race, you are. It does *not* determine *anything* else. *You* do. Yes?"

"What are your thoughts on African-American inventor, *Granville T. Woods*?"

"Granville T. Woods was one of the *greatest* inventors of our time. He was a very prolific inventor. A great electrician, and an inventive *genius*. He *revolutionized* the mode of street car transit, communications, and science. Like many inventors, his inventions, were, and are, a big part of the lives of millions of people. Millions ride subways and street cars powered by Mr. Woods' motors, and supplied by electricity by his transfer devices. He also improved air brakes. He held over thirty-five patents. Many of them were inventions for electric railways, but most were focused on distribution and electrical control. Mr. Woods' most remarkable invention, was the Synchronous Multiplex Railway Telegraph, also known as the Induction Telegraph. This invention allowed trains to communicate with stations, as well as other trains, so they knew where moving trains were, at all times. Mr. Woods' invention prevented countless accidents and collisions, which saved lives. Granville T. Woods' telegraph, allowed dispatchers to note at a glance, the location of moving trains. Before this invention, trains didn't have any assistance in locating the location of any moving train. Accidents were frequent."

"Wasn't Mr. Woods sued by other inventors?"

"You've done your homework, young man. Yes, he was sued by other inventors. Including one very famous inventor, Thomas Edison." Raven flashed her trademark smile. "He also won. Mr. Woods *successfully* defended lawsuits against his patents. And as they say, if you can't beat them, join them. Thomas Edison offered to buy Mr. Woods' company. He also offered him a partnership in one of his numerous companies. Mr. Woods wanted to remain independent, so he declined Mr. Edison's offers. American Bell Telephone Company, General Electric, and Westinghouse Air Brake Company, bought many of Granville T. Woods' ideas."

"Mr. Woods sold his inventions?"

"Some of them."

"Miss Kensington, I had no idea who Granville T. Woods was. Wow! His inventions are very impressive. Awesome!"

"They certainly are, young man. Especially from a man who was forced to leave school at the age of ten. Knowledge is very powerful, and important. So is history. African-American history isn't black history. Nor is it simply for blacks to celebrate and appreciate. It's for *all*, to celebrate and to appreciate. Because it is *American* history. Inventions by African-Americans, benefit *mankind*, not just *their* kind, meaning, African-Americans. There are many great inventors in all races, however, African-American inventors don't often receive their due. They are *much* more amazing to me, because many of them did a lot, with so little. Many of them suffered greatly, because of the color of their skin. Granville T. Woods didn't have the opportunities that Thomas Edison and Alexander Graham Bell did, yet, look what he accomplished, in spite of. If many of our ancestors accomplished a lot, with very little, what more should *we* be able to accomplish with the opportunities that we *now* have?"

Raven was interrupted with thunderous applause.

"In schools across the country, students of *all* races, learn about the inventions of Alexander Graham Bell and Thomas Edison. You don't usually hear *anything* about Mr. Woods, or *Dr. Charles Richard Drew. Great* inventors, who happened to be, African-American."

Raven brought the audience to their feet.

"Black history *isn't* one month out of the year. Black history, is every day. African-Americans are a *huge* part of *American* history. There is *much* more to our history, than slavery. Students, children, should learn about the great black inventors as well. Whether it's a school in Beverly Hills, or South Central L.A. History, is history. The *most* photographed wedding dress in American history was designed by an *African-American*. When Jacqueline Bouvier married John F. Kennedy, her wedding dress, was designed by *high-society fashion designer, Anne Cole Lowe*. Ms. Lowe also designed clothing for the Du Ponts, Rockefellers, and the Vanderbilts. Some of Ms. Lowe's gowns are in the Black Fashion Museum in Washington, D.C., the Costume Institute of the Metropolitan Museum in New York, and the Smithsonian Institution, in Washington, D.C."

"Wow, Miss Kensington. I'm very impressed!"

The superstar smiled. "It's very impressive indeed. Yes?"

"What are your thoughts about people who made it to the top and they didn't care who they stepped on, or what they had to do to get there, even if it meant hurting others?"

"No one can do anything the wrong way, and expect something right or good to come out of it. Always do things the *right* way. There is plenty of room at the top. And there is more than enough money to go around. For those who get to the top by doing wrong, they will usually have to meet the same people that they stepped on, when they fall. When you don't do things the right way, it will backfire on you. You reap what you sow. We *all* do. Yes?"

"There are so many things that I would like to do. But some people have told me that I'm trying to be something that I'm not. They've told me to do one thing, instead of trying to do a number of different things. Please advise. I would like your opinion on this, Miss Kensington."

"Again, *never* put limitations on yourself. You are the *only* person who knows what your capabilities are. I don't think that you can be anyone or anything that you're not, but it's important that you be *everything* that you're capable of being. Do what makes *you* happy. Go for it! Be *all* that *you* are."

The young lady smiled.

"Yes?"

"What about being poor, Miss Kensington? Would I still have what it takes to make my dreams come true?"

"Money is not a determining factor in making dreams come true. It's *you*, and what is *in* you, that determines that. Many people who are very successful today were once poor. It's important to be self-confident. No one can have confidence for you. Yes?"

"What are your thoughts on self-love, Miss Kensington?"

"We *must* love ourselves before we can love others, so obviously, self-love is *extremely* important. Many things start with self. The better that we are to ourselves, the better that we can be to others. Yes?"

"Miss Kensington? How do you manage such a successful career and happy marriage? You and your husband always look so happy together."

Raven was loving this. She continued to choose her words carefully. She loved speaking, especially to children, who were tomorrow's leaders.

"*Priorities* for one. *No one*, or *nothing*, is more important to me than my husband. I always make time for us, for our marriage. And I *always* will. Unlike many families and relationships today, my career revolves around my family, *not* the other way around. Tony and I work hard to maintain a happy and healthy relationship. And it makes it so much easier when you love each other the way that we do. Acting, is my livelihood. *Tony*, is my life. Yes?"

"Are you'll really *that* happy?"

Raven laughed. "Yes, young man, we are really *that* happy. Yes?"

"Miss Kensington? What are your thoughts on statistics? So oftentimes we'll hear or read about them. Does that play a part in being successful, or dreams coming true?"

Raven shook her head no. "No, *not* at all. Don't worry about, or even *think* about statistics, naysayers, *anything*, or *anyone*. *Again*, it's *all* up to *you*! And that is one thing we should all be happy about. Because if it were up to a lot of people, I certainly wouldn't be where I am today, but it wasn't their call, it was *mine*. It was all up to *me*. It doesn't matter if statistics show that one in every ten million will make it out of the ghetto, for example, don't worry about that. Just *remember*, if it *can* be done, *you* can do it!"

The crowd gave Raven a loud round of applause.

"Yes?"

"Miss Kensington, I know some white celebrities and politicians who go to country clubs that do not allow black members. Many of them have said that they are not racist. What are your thoughts on that?"

"Well, I find something *very* wrong with that picture. If I support *any* establishment that doesn't allow *other* races to attend, that's the *same* thing as *supporting* discrimination. If a person is *against* something, they would *not* support it. Actions speak louder than words. It's not what we say, it's what we *show*. Yes?"

"Miss Kensington, my name is Linda Richardson. I've heard a few actors say that blacks haven't won many Oscars over the years, because the mostly-white panel who votes, can't relate to our experiences. Do you think that's true?"

"I disagree with that, Linda. Oscars should be given to the individuals who give the *best* acting performances. Best talent and skill. Black experiences? How about *human* experiences? Race, the kind of movie, *nothing* else, except the acting performance, should be considered. But, as we've all known for decades, that's not the way that it is. I also feel that anyone who considers race, shouldn't be on the panel voting, period. I also seriously doubt if anyone on the panel will admit to ever considering race. But they don't have to. What they show, what they have shown for all of these *many* years, speaks volumes. The fact that so few Oscars have been awarded to blacks obviously proves that something is wrong. There's no way that anyone can tell me that black actors and actresses shouldn't have been awarded more Oscars, over all of these many years. There's a lot wrong with that picture, and it's the same picture that we see far too often, and in *too* many places. I don't believe in handouts, but I do believe in equality. I believe in everyone getting what they justly deserve. I have seen awesome and flawless-performances by black actors and actresses for many years, and I, like many of you, have also seen them passed over, or nominated, only. As the saying goes, may the best *man* win, regardless of race or hair color."

The audience laughed.

"But, the best man doesn't always win. So, to reiterate what I've said, saying that the panel who picks Oscar winners can't relate to *black* experiences, is ridiculous to me. That is irrelevant. The *only* thing, that the panel should relate to, is simply one thing, and that is, *acting* performance. *Period.* The end. It was truly an unforgettable moment on March 24, 2002, when two African-Americans became a part of history. Halle Berry was the first woman of color to win an Oscar for Best Leading Actress in a Motion Picture since the Academy Awards began in 1928. And Denzel Washington had finally been awarded his due, which had been *long* overdue. He received an Oscar for Best Leading Actor in a Motion Picture. It had been *thirty-nine* years since a black actor won that award."

"Who was the *first* black actor to win an Oscar for Best Leading Actor in a Motion Picture?" a young man asked.

"Sidney Poitier, who also won the Honorary Lifetime Achievement Award that same night," said Raven. "Yes?"

"Do you like Samuel L. Jackson?"

"Yes! Mr. Jackson is a topnotch actor. He's *awesome*. Yes?"

"Miss Kensington? Since Hollywood discriminates, why are you there? Why are you an actress? Why did you put yourself through all that?" Linda asked.

"I came to Tinseltown for a variety of reasons. The first reason is simply because I *wanted* to become an actress. That was *my* dream. Someone else's actions were *not* going to stop me from doing what I wanted to do, or from being what I wanted to become. I hope that you don't let anything or anyone stop you either. My *other* dream has also come true. My dream of becoming a *driver* in Hollywood, and being able to turn the bus around. I am turning the bus around, and driving it in the *right* direction, a *new* direction. And on my bus, *all* races, colors, sizes, and shapes, are welcome. I am continuously striving to make Hollywood a place where there will be a level playing field for *all*. A place where people of color, and people who aren't white, will not be looked *over*, but looked *at*. And likewise, people who aren't rail-thin, will *not* be overlooked either. My hope is to see a Hollywood for all, one day. No, it won't happen overnight, few things do, but I am elated that the train is in motion! And as far as I'm concerned, living my dreams don't matter, if I don't make a difference. A *positive* difference. And no one can make a difference, or change, by being absent."

Raven told the students that she wanted to see a lot more blacks behind the cameras too. She also told them that she wanted to see black writers being hired to write movies and shows that weren't race-based. Raven explained. "The writer doesn't have to be the same race as the cast." She acknowledged that in a number of areas, progress had been made, but there was still a ways to go.

Raven Kensington was a very powerful force behind the scenes too. She now had the power to greenlight films. Her goal was to continue to bring other minorities in also. Raven had already gotten nominations for more minorities to become members of the Academy Awards panel, as she herself had been nominated, and was now a member of the panel.

"Miss Kensington, that happens often. Black writers and black producers, being hired to write and produce black films *only*. That's awful. Same with directing."

Raven nodded her head in agreement. "It is awful. I'm also a writer. I've been writing since I was a little girl. Writing comes naturally to me. As a writer, I write about various subjects and people, not just African-American experiences or African-Americans. It's always been very easy for me to write about *human* experiences, and life in general, which are things that we can *all* easily relate to. Many in the media need to stop making excuses. Stop trying to cover up discrimination. Again, we need to look at each other as *people*, not as colors. I have never allowed myself to be placed in a box. You don't have to be the same race as the actors in a film, to be the writer, director, producer, etc., of that film. That's ridiculous, and as I said earlier, it's just another excuse for Hollywood to discriminate."

The students continued to hang on the superstar's every word. Raven Kensington's words had given them all hope. As other African-Americans, who had come before Raven, had done for her.

Dirk Morehead raised his hand. He told Raven of the time when he and his mother were on an airplane, and another boy, who was white, told him to stay away from him. The white boy told him that he was black and poor. He also told Dirk that he and his mother would be sitting in *first-class*, because they had a lot of money. "We'll be seated in front, away from you poor, black people." Dirk remembered the boy telling him.

"Is that so?" Raven asked.

"Yes, ma'am."

"*Regardless* of how much money *anyone* has, regardless of their race, or what their last name is, or isn't, *always* remember, Dirk, *no one*, is *better* than *anyone else*. Just because a person *lives* better than you, that *doesn't* make them, better than you."

The superstar received a thunderous applause.

Dirk smiled and nodded in answer.

"That's something that I want *all* of you to remember. Because it's *true*. And don't *ever* let *anyone* tell you differently. You are just as important, and just as good, as *anyone*." The superstar smiled. "I know some wonderful and classy people, who fly coach, and I know some *trash*, who fly *first-class*. There are things that not even money can buy. *Class*, is one of them. Dirk, although you and your mother were sitting in coach and the other little boy and his mother were sitting in first-class, if that plane would have gone down, *all* of you, *everyone*, would have gone down, *together*."

The principal, teachers, and parents sat in awe, listening to the megastar. They had no idea, how immensely-wise Raven Kensington was. Until now. They all sat and marveled at the young woman's wisdom. Raven was much-needed therapy and motivation, for *all* of them.

Raven continued. "That plane can also represent the world that we *all* live in, because it's *one* place, and we're *all* here. *Together*. We're *not* in separate worlds. We are all under this *one* roof, the *same* roof. Therefore, we need to *learn* to live together. We need to *come* together. I've *never* seen a war that was won, without *all* of the men and women being on *one* accord. And fighting, *together*. In order to win, everyone needs to come together. The plane will fly a lot better, if we would *all* do that. Many great things are accomplished through unity. If we don't stick together, we'll fall apart. Differences should be celebrated and appreciated, *not* discriminated. We are all different, because everyone, even those of the same race, are still individual, human beings. That's something else that we all have in common, we are *all* different. *Unity*, is far more important, than uniformity."

Dirk was very impressed with the superstar. He had never heard those words before. No one had ever put it quite that way. No one had ever said things the way that *she* said them. Raven made him think. He knew that he would always remember the "plane" theory, especially. Dirk loved it! He could not wait to go home to tell his mother. He raised his hand again to thank Raven. Dirk also told Raven that he would work hard, and study hard, to become the best black person that he could become.

"Dirk, work hard to become the best *person*, that you can become, *not* the best *black* person, that you can become. We're not crayons, we are *people*, above all else. Don't strive to be a color, strive to be a *good* person, a *great* individual. And I personally, simply want to be treated as an individual."

Dirk smiled and nodded. "Okay, Miss Kensington."

"Yes?"

"African-Americans are more stereotyped than any other race. What are your thoughts on that, Miss Kensington?"

"I think that we are too. Everyone *can't* be painted with the *same* brush. It is wrong to *assume*. Again, *every* human being is an *individual*. Stereotypes hide as much as it reveals. If I were to go out and harm someone, *my* actions represent me, and me alone. I don't represent the entire race of black people, or *any* other human being. The *only* person that I represent, is Raven Kensington. And speaking of stereotypes, I didn't see any young white males, being stereotyped, when Timothy McVeigh was convicted of murder and conspiracy in the Oklahoma City Bombing. Nor do I see, all or most, white men, who are in upper-management of large corporations, being stereotyped, because of the Enron scandal. Many pedophiles and serial killers, are white males, of various ages, yet, all white males are not stereotyped because of the actions of some. I could go on and on with examples, but I think I've made my point."

Raven thought of the book report that she had written when she was twelve. It was very appalling, that after all of these years later, many of the same things, were still going on. And, still going strong.

"Miss Kensington? If my dream doesn't come true after a certain time, does that mean that it won't *ever* come true?"

"No. Life doesn't always go as planned, and the good thing about dreams is that they don't come with deadlines, or expiration dates. Yes?"

"Miss Kensington, what are your thoughts regarding, *The Cosby Show*? Do you think that the show was *unrealistic*?"

"*The Cosby Show* was very *important* for a *variety* of reasons. I, for one, *applaud* Mr. Cosby, for sticking to his guns and not going the *usual* route. He made a *new* path. It wasn't the typical black show, that America, the world, was used to seeing. That may be why some have labeled it *unrealistic*, including some blacks. *The Cosby Show* was *not* unrealistic. There *are* well-to-do African-Americans. There *are* loving families, with *both* parents in the home, who have great morals and values, who *are* black. So to say that the show was unreal is ridiculous to me. Not real, means that something is make-believe, it doesn't exist. And there are strong black families who *do* exist and who mirror, *The Cosby Show*. I grew up in a home that was very similar to the show. Just because something hasn't been seen on TV, it doesn't mean that it does not exist. Take for instance, going *back* to the ever-present thin is the way to be. We all know the types of females who are *constantly* shown in the media; however, we also know that other sizes, shapes, and colors, *do* exist. So, again, just because something isn't seen, or seen that often, it doesn't mean that it's nonexistent. It's not surprising to me that the networks initially turned down, Bill Cosby's idea for, *The Cosby Show*. It's another wonderful example of how important it is to stick to your guns, stick to what *you* believe in. Mr. Cosby did just that, and as we all know, the rest, is *history*! *The Cosby Show* is one of the *most* successful TV shows to date. I think the show was very positive and inspiring. It was also a *universal* show. And it was great to see people, of *all* races, watching the show, and loving a show, with an all-black starring cast. We are all just that, *people*. The Huxtables were a family who happened to be black, but many of the issues that were on the show were topics that *every* family in the world could relate to, because we are all human beings, who have *many* things in common. Again, keep these things in mind and apply them to your own life. *Stick* to your guns! Like me, Bill Cosby did it his way, and won big. The saying where there is a will, there is a way, is certainly true. Don't let naysayers, bigots, don't let *anyone*, stop you, from being what you want to be. Don't let anyone, stop you, from doing what you want to do. Or, *how* you want to do it. And by all means, that includes, being turned down, being told no. Many people who are successful today, and some are very successful, were turned down *many* times over. Me included. But we kept hammering. So again, don't let being told *no*, stop you. Keep hammering, until the nail goes through. Yes?"

"Miss Kensington? I've noticed that you emphasize doing it your way. Why is that important?"

"Doing it my way is important because if I do something someone else's way, or the way that they envision it, that's not *my* dream, it's theirs. And as a result, I wouldn't be happy, nor would I be fulfilled, because I would be making their dream come true, not my own."

The student nodded.

"Yes?"

"What are your thoughts regarding priests who sexually abuse children?"

"It's horrible! Awful, sickening. It's even more awful how it's being handled, or I should say, *not* being handled. In 1985, the church first learned of priests molesting children, yet it wasn't until June of 2002, in Dallas, that a Bishops' Conference was finally held to discuss this very serious matter. Victims and their families got to speak too." Raven shook her head. "Almost two decades later?! There's a lot wrong with that picture. Yes?"

"Miss Kensington? What do you think should happen to priests who molest children?"

"They should be prosecuted to the full extent of the law, just as *anyone* else would be. No exceptions! Zero tolerance. Sexual abuse is a crime. And a very horrible one at that. A crime is a crime. It doesn't matter who breaks the law. Priests shouldn't be allowed to walk away with little or no punishment whatsoever, as many of them have been able to do. And bishops who transfer priests who sexually abuse children to other churches should also be prosecuted."

The audience clapped. It was obvious that many in the audience agreed with Raven.

"Miss Kensington, what are your thoughts on the U.S. Constitution?"

"I'm not a fan of it, or the men, who are known to many, as the *founding*-fathers. This country, the United States of America, was *supposedly* founded on the promise of freedom, equality, and justice, for *all*. America, did *not* keep its promise. If it would have, there would *never* have been slavery, discrimination, or Jim Crow. At one time, it was very acceptable, and lawful, to kill, brutalize, and openly-discriminate against blacks. *We* weren't free. Another horrible thing about the Constitution, is that when it was written, it was very *clear* that they *didn't* mean people who looked like *me*, or many of you in the audience. There is a provision in the Constitution that designated slaves, our ancestors, as three-fifths of a man. However, regardless of what *anyone* says, or shows, *all men*, *are* created *equal*. And *no* human being, is three-fifths of a man. Nor has *any* human being, ever, been three-fifths of a man. That, is a *fact*."

The superstar received a standing ovation.

"Yes?"

"I know that you've stressed how very important knowledge and education is. But education is often very expensive."

"*Ignorance*, is much *more* costly, than knowledge. Yes?"

"Miss Kensington, do whites rank at the top in academics?"

"No, young man. Asian Americans currently rank at the top in academics. Yes?"

"Miss Kensington, what are your thoughts on teenagers becoming parents?" a fifteen-year-old girl in the audience asked.

"I think that at such a young age, boys and girls shouldn't be focused on *creating* a life, they should be focused on, *living* life. Yes?"

"My Aunt Gloria told me that *how* you live your life is very important."

Raven nodded. "That's right. How we live, says *a lot* about who we are. Yes?"

"My name is Glenzola. My best friend's name is Kay. She's shy, so I'll ask the question."

"Okay, Glenzola."

The young girl smiled at the superstar. "You never wanted to follow in anyone's footsteps, Miss Kensington?"

"No, young lady. I *never* wanted to wear *anyone's* shoes either, that's why I brought *my* own pair. Yes?"

"What are your thoughts on politics? And what factors do you use when determining who you're going to vote for in elections?"

"Categories and labels, i.e.: Democrat, Republican, Independent, Liberal, Conservative, etc., are all irrelevant to me. When I cast my vote for *anyone*, it is based on that individual, their vision, their morals, and their values. I vote for people, not parties. I study the individual. I listen to what they are saying. *Facts*, are very important to me. I also consider the individual's past and present deeds, both professionally, and personally. I am also well aware of the fact, that many politicians say what they think voters would like to hear. What they think will appeal to voters, in order to get their vote. After factoring all of those things in, last but not least, I pray for guidance."

"Do you think that John Kerry served his country honorably?"

"Yes! *Anyone*, who served in Vietnam, anyone who served in *any* war, period, is a hero, medals, or no medals. Length of service is irrelevant too."

The audience gave Raven a thunderous applause.

"Ms. Kensington, what are your thoughts on negative campaigning?"

"I don't like negative campaigning. I think that candidates need to discuss important issues that affect people's lives. In a nutshell, I think that candidates should focus on issues, not insults."

"Ms. Kensington, weren't the Clintons' portraits that currently hang in the White House, painted by an African-American?"

Raven smiled and nodded. "Yes, they were. *Simmie Knox* is also a *self-taught artist*, who was born to a family of sharecroppers. Mr. Knox is the first African-American who has painted an official portrait of a President and First Lady. Yes?"

"Should we love ourselves, unconditionally?"

"Yes. Not only should we love others, unconditionally, we need to love *self* unconditionally too. Yes?"

"If I don't like the rules, especially if they're wrong, or if they don't work for me, what's your advice, Miss Kensington?"

The superstar smiled. "*Rewrite* them. Yes?"

"Miss Kensington, do you like the song, 'I Hope You Dance'?"

"I *love* that song. It's a very *inspiring* song. I also love the way Ms. Womack sings it."

The principal stood up and told the students that Raven had time for a few more questions. He knew that she was a very busy woman, and he was elated that she had come to their school.

"Ms. Kensington, do you know anything about African-American Arctic explorer, Matthew Henson? And did Robert Peary discover the North Pole?"

"I know a great deal about *Matthew Alexander Henson*. And to answer your second question, Robert Peary did *not* discover the North Pole, alone. He may have been the only white man to reach the North Pole on April 6, 1909, but he wasn't the *only* man, to reach the North Pole that day. Matthew Henson, a *highly*-skilled Arctic explorer, and four Eskimos, were with Robert Peary. Mr. Peary was an *exceptional* explorer and civil engineer. He was also the leader of the expedition. Matthew Henson's contributions were crucial, immense, and cannot be overlooked. Without Mr. Henson, Mr. Peary may not have even made it to the North Pole. Matthew Henson was invaluable. He was *indispensable*. Mr. Peary chose Mr. Henson over his white assistants. Matthew Henson was chosen, because he was the *best*. Mr. Henson was a *brilliant Arctic* explorer and seaman. He was a *proven* leader. He had great technical skills. Matthew Henson was a carpenter. He built the sleds that were needed to get to the

North Pole. He was also a mechanic. He made stoves. Matthew Henson was the *only* American, who could speak Inuit, Eskimo language, *fluently*. He was also an expert dog driver. Mr. Henson handled sleds *exceptionally*-well too. Mr. Henson was *highly*-respected by the Eskimos. Matthew Henson reached the North Pole, *first*. He also planted the American flag there. Discovering the North Pole was a great accomplishment, because prior to their discovery, the only thing that most people knew about the North Pole, is that it was a very *cold* place. It was also a place that was considered to be very unattainable during that time. Others tried to reach the North Pole, but never made it. Some even died in the process. Initially, Robert Peary was the *only* individual to receive recognition for discovering the North Pole. Mr. Peary received numerous international honors for his achievement. When Mr. Peary died, he was buried at the famed, Arlington National Cemetery. Matthew Henson's recognition came years later. In 1913, Mr. Henson was personally recommended by President Taft, to the United States Customs in New York City, because of Mr. Henson's exploits in the Arctic. In 1944, the United States Congress, honored Matthew Henson with a *joint* medal for the Peary expedition to the North Pole. Mr. Henson was honored by President Truman in 1950, and *finally* admitted to the Explorer's Club. When Matthew Henson passed away on *March 9*, 1955, he was buried in New York City's Woodlawn Cemetery. This would all change, thanks to Dr. S. Allen Counter, an African-American Harvard University professor and professional explorer. In 1986, Dr. Counter petitioned President Reagan for permission to transfer the remains of Matthew Henson and his wife, Lucy Ross, to the Arlington National Cemetery. In 1987, President Reagan granted Dr. Counter's request. On April 6, 1988, seventy-nine years after the North Pole was discovered, Matthew and Lucy Ross Henson, were reburied in the Arlington National Cemetery, beside Robert and Josephine Peary. *Co*-discoverer of the North Pole is inscribed on Mr. Henson's headstone. *More* honors followed. A postage stamp was made in Mr. Henson's honor. In 1996, the United States Navy honored him with the *USNS Henson*. In 2000, *Matthew Henson* was *awarded* the *Hubbard Medal*, which is the National Geographic Society's *highest* honor. Mr. Henson's niece accepted the award at the Matthew Henson Earth Conservation Center in Washington, D.C. The Hubbard Medal is awarded for distinction in research, discovery, and exploration. Matthew Henson received the long overdue, *national* recognition, in death, that he *never* received, in life."

The audience clapped wildly.

"*One* more question for Ms. Kensington," said the principal.

"Miss Kensington, was Jesus white with long hair?"

"Most of the photos of Jesus that we have seen for many years, is that of a Caucasian man, with long or fairly-long hair. Young man, in all honesty, I don't know what Jesus' physical appearance was, when He walked this earth. However, based on where He was from, the part of the country that He lived in, I believe that Jesus was dark-skinned. And I don't mean tanned either. In answer to your second question, I seriously doubt if Jesus had long hair, because in the Bible, it states that Jesus said that it was *disgraceful* for a man to have long hair. So having said that, I can't imagine Jesus saying that, and wearing His hair long. Because if *anyone* practiced what he preached, it was Him. Regardless of what Jesus' physical appearance was, He's still the Son of God. And however He looked when He walked this earth, didn't make Him any less the Son of God, or any more or less powerful. Race, or anyone's physical appearance, didn't matter to Jesus, therefore, it certainly shouldn't matter to *anyone*. We are *all*, God's creations."

Raven was interrupted by thunderous applause.

"Students, my time is up. *Always* remember, there is *no* star, that is out of reach! I have enjoyed this so very much. May God *bless* all of you!" Raven flashed her dazzling, trademark smile. Time was up.

* * *

The entire audience stood on their feet and gave the superstar a standing ovation. Everyone was very pleased that she had come. They wished that she could stay longer. They had all enjoyed her immensely. It was truly an honor to have Raven Kensington at their school.

The school had a special surprise for the superstar.

When Raven left the stage, she was escorted to the front row, where she sat by the principal.

Within minutes, the school choir came onstage, and serenaded Raven with, "Wind Beneath My Wings."

Tears filled Raven's dark eyes, as she sat and listened to the beautiful voices that sounded like angels.

Raven stood and clapped when the choir finished. "Thank you all! That was very beautiful! And *deeply*-touching!" said the tearful superstar. "Thank you!"

The students, staff, and parents were elated that Raven Kensington had graced them with her presence. It was truly an unforgettable day, for all of them.

* * *

Everyone thanked the superstar for her time. They also thanked her for the very generous donation that she had given to their school. It was more than enough to get the school remodeled, purchase books, furniture, new computers, printers, and other educational materials, that the school so badly needed. The students were also given an autographed picture of the superstar.

The principal couldn't thank Raven enough. Doug gave her a thank you card, and a huge bouquet of flowers. Doug smiled, as he stood and watched her leave. Raven Kensington, was a class act. The *classiest*.

Cameras flashed nonstop, as Raven got in her limo and headed back home, to Malibu.

* * *

When Raven made it home, she checked her voice mail. Tony had left a message for her. He was still at the office. Mack had left a note for Raven. He had gone out to buy groceries for dinner.

Raven fell asleep on the sofa. She felt Tony's lips on hers, hours later. "*Tony ...*" Raven whispered, without opening her eyes.

"Sleeping Beauty. Hi, love. How did you *know* it was *me*?" Tony asked as he laughed.

"I would know *those* lips anywhere," said Raven, her eyes were still closed.

"I heard a lot of your speech on the radio coming home. *Excellent*, sweetheart!"

"Thanks, baby."

Tony had a slew of business meetings that day. He was going to reschedule, but Raven asked him not to. The radio stations had replayed the speech, so he was able to hear it.

"I'm sure the children gained a lot from it. You're speaking to the kids at Beverly Hills High on Wednesday, right?"

Raven nodded. "Yes, sweetheart."

"They asked some tough questions and you gave them honest and very positive answers. You would be a *great* motivational speaker. Oh, you *incredibly*-beautiful woman, of *many* talents. My queen! I am *your* number one fan."

Raven smiled as she gave her husband a kiss. "I know that you're my biggest fan, handsome. I'm also *your* biggest fan."

Raven wasn't sure what others thought of her responses, but she didn't care. She had spoken from her heart. And she'd also spoken the truth, and that was more important to her than the opinion of others.

Raven thought of Becky. She no longer watched *Day's Dawn*, and she was very pleased that the ratings were at an all-time low. Fans continued to express anger and sorrow, because of the immense-pressure that Becky had been placed under. And many of them, true to their word, stopped watching the show. Raven had also heard that there were auditions for Becky's replacement. But no one could ever replace Becky. On-screen, or off-screen. *No one*. It still saddened Raven, and tugged at her heart, that she would never see Becky again, or hear her voice.

Every time that Raven would see a young blonde woman with blue eyes, she would instantly think of Becky. Life was so precious and short. Raven sat thinking. Becky was so young. Twenty-seven years old. She'd had her whole life ahead of her. She was the best friend, and sister, that anyone could ever have. Raven knew that she would always miss her. And Becky would always have a place in her heart. A very *special* place.

"Everything *okay*?" Tony asked.

Raven nodded. "Yes, sweetheart."

His wife didn't have to say why tears filled her eyes. Tony knew that she was thinking of Becky. The two of them had been practically inseparable for over twenty years. Raven was very grateful that she had known such a wonderful person. And as she had told the students earlier that day, it's important that *everyone*, including the media, take responsibility for the very *negative* and *dangerous* message that they are sending, repeatedly, to females. And have been sending, for *many* years.

Why aren't a lot more politicians and celebrities raising their voices about *this*? Raven thought to herself. Her heart ached immensely, every time that she would think of Becky, which was often.

Raven continued to sit and think. She knew that there was still a great deal that needed to be done, in *all* avenues of life, regarding equality and racism. Raven was going to continue to fight discrimination, bigotry, and inequality. She knew, just like the great ones before her, that she and others, had to continue to raise their voices, and fight, for the right to be treated equally, no matter how long it took. Raven Kensington was a tireless-warrior, who was determined to keep fighting, not only for herself, but *for all those* ...

Chapter 11

Filming had finally begun on Raven's new movie, *A Funny Kind of Lady*. It was filmed in L.A., so Raven got to go home every evening. The script was well-written, and that was one of the main reasons that Raven took the part. She enjoyed every minute of it too. It felt great to laugh, and to be able to make others laugh, also. Life was difficult enough. Having a sense of humor was always a good thing for anyone to have. And Raven Kensington had always had a terrific sense of humor.

A Funny Kind of Lady wrapped in six months. Raven was sorry to see it end. She had so much fun on the set. It was also the most professional and talented cast that she'd ever worked with. Everyone came prepared. They also reported on the set on time every day. Raven loved that. So did the producers and directors.

On Raven's last day of filming, as she backed her BMW out of the parking lot to head home, a truck was slowly backing up towards her car. It was obvious to Raven that the driver didn't see her car. Raven sat frozen. Usually, she would blow the horn, in cases like these, to alert the other driver, but for some reason, she didn't. She couldn't move. The truck hit her car.

The driver immediately got out of her truck. The frantic lady apologized to Raven. "I'm very sorry. I … Oh … *my* ... Aren't *you*? Oh, *my* God! It *is you*! *Raven Kensington*!"

Raven nodded.

"I'm so very sorry. I'm a *huge* fan of yours! I've *always* wanted to meet you, but not under *these* circumstances, of course! Are you *okay*, Miss Kensington? I should've asked you that first. I'm so *sorry*. I …" The lady kept staring at Raven. She was starstruck. "You really are *that* beautiful." The lady shook her head. "*Please*, please forgive me. It's not every day that I see one of the *biggest* stars in the world. Especially one who is so very *beautiful*."

"It's quite all right," said Raven. "Are *you* okay?"

The lady nodded.

Besides a few scratches, both vehicles were fine, therefore, no information was exchanged between the two women.

"Miss Kensington? May I *please* have your autograph?"

"Sure," said Raven. After giving the lady her autograph, Raven drove home. She told her husband what happened.

"Are *you* all right?" Tony asked.

"Yes, I'm fine, sweetheart."

"I want you to see a chiropractor, just to make sure everything's all right. Sometimes, even minor accidents can cause problems. Doctor's *orders*," said Tony.

Raven smiled at her husband. "Okay, Dr. Dash."

Tony called and made an appointment for Raven, who went to see the chiropractor the next morning.

Her husband wanted to go with her, but she told him that she would be fine. "I'll call you if I need you." Raven told Tony, who had a slew of business meetings that week.

* * *

Dr. Spills gave Raven a thorough check-up. He also took X-rays of her back and chest. "Miss Kensington? I'm sorry, *Mrs. Dash*, I will call you with the results of your X-rays. You'll hear from me this afternoon, or definitely by tomorrow morning. Speaking of your last name, I know many people still refer to you as Raven Kensington, don't they?"

"Yes, doctor. I do too, usually. Tony and I agreed that I would continue using my maiden name. Publicly anyway. My fans know me by my maiden name. But, as long as I know who I am, that's what's important," said Raven.

Dr. Spills laughed. "Take care, Mrs. Dash. I'll call you."

Raven went shopping afterwards. She went to get Mack a birthday present. When she arrived home, she checked her voice mail.

Dr. Spills had phoned. He told Raven to call him as soon as she received his message.

Raven called the doctor back immediately, she heard concern in his voice. "Dr. Spills, please."

"May I tell him who's calling?"

"Raven Kensington Dash."

Dr. Spills came to the phone right away. "Mrs. Dash? Thanks for calling back. I'd like you to come in so that I can discuss your X-rays with you."

"Is *everything* all right?" Raven asked.

"I'd like to go over your X-rays with you in *person*, Mrs. Dash."

"Okay, Dr. Spills, I'm on my way."

* * *

Less than an hour later, Raven was sitting in Dr. Spills' office, viewing her X-rays.

"This is a picture of your chest." Dr. Spills explained, as he pointed. "*This* is the area of concern. You see *here*, on the left side of your chest?"

Raven nodded.

"You could have pneumonia. I would like for you to see your primary care physician right away."

"It could be pneumonia, or what *else* could it be?" Raven asked.

Dr. Spills didn't want to speculate. He knew that it could also be a benign, or malignant, tumor. He didn't tell Raven that, because he didn't want to alarm her.

"Mrs. Dash, I don't want to speculate or guess. I want you to see your doctor as soon as possible," said Dr. Spills.

* * *

Raven drove to Tony's office afterwards. She repeated what the doctor told her.

Tony sat at his desk, listening to Raven. "You have called Dr. Watson to make an appointment, haven't you?" he asked his wife.

"Yes. I go see him in the morning."

"*We*, will go see him in the morning. Everything's going to be okay, sweetheart. Don't worry, beautiful," said Tony.

Raven and Tony both hoped that it was pneumonia. But the next morning, they found out that it wasn't. Dr. Watson performed a CT scan on Raven's chest. He also received two other medical opinions, before phoning Raven.

Dr. Watson told Raven to come to his office, right away.

Raven and Tony drove to the doctor's office immediately. When they arrived, Dr. Watson escorted the couple into his office and closed the door. This was clearly the one thing about his profession that he hated, breaking bad news to his patients. He looked at the woman who sat before him. Her eyes were beautiful and very wise. She was so incredibly-beautiful, and young. Twenty-nine years old. She had so much going for her.

"Mrs. Dash. You have *cancer*."

Tears filled Tony's eyes. He held his wife close. He didn't want to let her go. He'd heard so many horror stories about this horrible, life-threatening disease.

Raven looked at her doctor, she had so many questions. "Okay, doctor. I have cancer. What *kind*?"

"I have scheduled a needle biopsy for you. This will tell us the kind of cancer that we're dealing with. The biopsy won't be painful. Tissue will be removed from the malignant area in your chest. Once we've determined the kind of cancer that you have, we will then know the best way to treat it. It's very important that we begin treatment immediately."

Tony found his voice. "Dr. Watson? This Dr. Taupe, is he the *best*?" Tony wanted to know. Raven's health was everything to him, *she*, was everything to him.

"Yes, Mr. Dash. He is the *best* in the business. Dr. Taupe's the very best. Please, try not to worry. I know that it's easier said than done, but we will do *everything* that we can to help your wife *beat* this thing." Dr. Watson assured Tony. The doctor's heart went out to Raven, and to her husband, who cried openly.

Dr. Watson looked at Raven, who didn't seemed fazed. She had taken the news far better than he'd expected. This was usually the time when most patients would break down, but Raven hadn't broken down, at least not yet anyway. It hasn't quite set in yet, the doctor thought to himself.

The biopsy was scheduled the next day. Because of the size of the tumor, Dr. Watson needed to move quickly. Dr. Watson wasn't an oncologist, but he could easily see that the tumor in Raven's chest was huge. The tumor was also near her heart and lungs, so it was crucial, that they move very quickly.

* * *

The biopsy confirmed the type of cancer that Raven had. Dr. Watson referred her to the best oncologist that he knew. Dr. Taupe was an oncologist with an excellent reputation, his reputation preceded him. If anyone could help Raven, Jeremy Taupe could.

* * *

By week's end, Raven and Tony sat before Dr. Taupe. The doctor introduced himself to the couple, then he told them what they were anxiously waiting to hear.

"Mrs. Dash, you have *non-Hodgkin lymphoma*. It's also known as non-Hodgkin's lymphoma and NHL. It's a cancer that attacks the lymph nodes, which is an important component of the body's immune system. I'm always upfront and honest with my patients. The tumor in your chest is large." The doctor paused, as he took a deep breath. "It's also in the last stage." Dr. Taupe gave full details.

Since day one, Tony, who was devastated, wished that he could trade places with Raven. Why couldn't it have happened to me? he thought. Why *her*? He would have traded places with Raven in an instant. Tony held Raven's hand, as they both sat and listened.

"We *must* move on this thing, *quickly*. The fact that it's near your heart, is another reason. It's also near your lungs. My treatment plan for you is six months of *aggressive* chemotherapy, and six weeks, of *aggressive* radiation treatment. Chemo is currently the best treatment for cancer. The side effects aren't great though. One of the common side effects that women don't like about chemo, is hair loss." The doctor looked at Raven's long black hair. "You're going to lose *all* of your hair, Mrs. Dash. But keep in mind, hair is *cosmetic*. Hair *does* grow back. Your life doesn't. The *most* important thing is getting this thing into remission. Other side effects are loss of energy. You're going to feel very fatigued, weak, tired. Your appetite will also be affected. That's why many people with cancer often lose weight. You will feel very sick. Nauseous. Mrs. Dash, again, the side effects aren't great, but keep in mind, they're for a very *good* cause. In many cases, chemo is effective. Do either of you have any questions?" Dr. Taupe asked.

"When will we begin treatment?" Tony asked.

"Today is Thursday. How about Monday?"

Raven and Tony nodded.

The doctor explained to them how the chemo and radiation treatments would be done. He also told them about the regular check-ups that Raven would have before, during, and after each treatment.

Dr. Taupe was very thorough and informative. Both Raven and Tony liked him. Before the Dashs left, the doctor gave them plenty of pamphlets, with very detailed information, about non-Hodgkin lymphoma.

"*Please* feel free to call me with *any* questions," the doctor told them. "Hang in there, Mrs. Dash. You do the same, Mr. Dash."

Raven and Tony thanked Dr. Taupe, as they left his office, hand in hand.

They called their families when they got home to tell them the news. They hadn't called them before now.

* * *

The entire Kensington family took the news very hard. Everyone wept openly. Tony cried again, when Trey's daughter asked him if "Aunt Raven" was going to die.

After making their phone calls, Tony held his wife in his arms. As they lie in bed, Tony clung to Raven like never before. "It's going to be *okay*, beautiful," he told her. He was scared to death. For the first time in a long time, he prayed. Tony knew that he would have traded places with his wife in a heartbeat, if he could. Tears fell, as Tony held Raven in his arms. "You're *going* to be *all right*, beautiful. *Everything's*, going to be all right," said Tony. He said those words, as much for himself, as he did for his wife. He couldn't imagine living without Raven. *She*, was his life. She was *everything* to him. Raven, was the *beginning*, and the *end*, of Tony's world. She was the blood that flowed through his veins. *Please, God. Please ...* Tony prayed silently. He didn't finish, but he knew that he didn't have to. Tony knew that God already knew, what he was *begging*, Him to do.

* * *

Raven began her chemo treatments the following Monday, with her husband by her side. The doctor had been right, she didn't feel the greatest afterwards. But Raven's attitude was positive, and her strength was unbelievable. Raven's spirit remained intact. Tony didn't understand it. Neither did the doctors and nurses, or some members of her family, for that matter.

Raven knew what everyone's thoughts were. She knew that they all wondered why she wasn't a basket case. Little did they know, it wasn't Raven's attitude that kept her upbeat and positive. It was Raven Kensington's *faith*, in God. She knew that all things were in His hands, not the doctor's, not the medicine, but His hands, alone. God gave her life, and Raven knew that only He, could take her life. He was so much bigger than cancer, or any other disease. Raven had faith, not fear. And she had the faith of Job.

* * *

Raven continued taking her chemo treatments over the months. And, as the doctor had told her and Tony, she lost all of her hair. She was completely bald now. She wore a wig whenever she would go out in public. At home, she would sometimes go bald, and sometimes she would cover her head. Tony was with Raven every step of the way.

Tony's parents, Andrew and Tandy, visited and called Raven frequently. Andy told Raven that she was in his and Tandy's prayers.

The Kensingtons phoned night and day.

Raven received regular calls from the Simms family too. Raven was family to them.

An overwhelming number of cards and well-wishes poured in daily, from Raven's millions of fans. The Halters sent her get well cards, and Layla wrote her another sweet letter. On the cards, the Halters wrote, that they would never forget what Raven had done for them. We LOVE YOU, RAVEN! YOU'RE OUR ANGEL! MAY GOD BLESS YOU NOW AND ALWAYS! HE'S ABLE!

The President and First Lady also phoned Raven. Everyone was praying for Raven, and rooting for her, to get well.

* * *

Raven and Tony were invited to an appreciation award dinner, that was being held in Raven's honor, because of her philanthropy.

Tony told Raven that they could cancel, if she didn't feel up to going.

"No, I'm fine, sweetheart. We'll go," his wife told him.

Raven wore her stunning, R.K. by Design evening gown that she designed. Raven's clothing line was immensely-successful. The Council of Fashion Designers of America named her the top Womenswear Designer of the Year, for her R.K. by Design Collection.

After applying her makeup, Raven stood in front of the mirror, looking at her bald head.

Tony stood behind her. "Hey, *beautiful*." He kissed her. "You look *gorgeous* as always!" Tony went to the front door and opened it. "I really *love* that gown too. Wow. Move over Versace and Donna

Karan! There is someone new, and extraordinarily-better, the beautiful, the multi-talented, *Raven Kensington Dash*!" Tony looked at his wife admiringly. She was *still*, and would always be, beautiful to him. Tony studied his wife. Raven was as beautiful as ever. Her looks had not diminished in any way. Tony went to escort his wife out the door.

"*Tony*! I *don't* have my wig on!"

"Raven, I *know* you don't, nor do you *have* to have a wig on. I am just as *proud* to have you on *my* arm, as I've *always* been. You are *still* the *most* beautiful woman that I've ever seen. Now let's *go*!"

"I'm *not* the only beautiful woman in the world, sweetheart."

"No, but you're the *only* beautiful woman that I love. And that's the *only* thing that matters. *You're* the woman that I will *always* love. And *cherish*. And, *you* are *still* the *most* beautiful woman that I've *ever* laid eyes on. I *mean* that. Now, *stop* fussing and let's *go*!"

Raven looked at her husband. She had *never* loved him *more*, than at *that* moment. "I *love* you, *Tony* Dash." She kissed him tenderly on the lips. "I'm going to put on my wig, then we can leave."

"*Women*." Tony teased. "*Hurry*, woman, hurry!"

"My, my! Aren't we *impatient* this evening." Raven told her husband. "I'm coming, love. I'm *coming*!"

* * *

Raven and Tony walked into the Regent, hand in hand. And as always, they received lots of admirable stares. They were a very handsome couple. All eyes were on Raven, especially. And this time, it wasn't for her exquisite-beauty. Everyone was looking to see if Raven had changed in any way, since being diagnosed with cancer.

It was amazing to them to see, that she looked exactly the same as she'd always looked, despite the cancer that everyone knew she had. Many shook their heads in amazement. This woman was simply incredible. She was like no other. Who but *she*, could *still* look like a million bucks, despite how sick she was? Who, but Raven Kensington?

Many of Hollywood's elite were there, including Andrew and his wife. And to Raven's surprise, Tessa Winters was also in attendance.

"*That* woman is *so* amazing," said Tandy, as she eyed Raven. "*Unbelievably*-amazing! Honey? Are you *sure* she has cancer?"

Andy laughed. He knew what his wife meant. Looking at Raven, no one would have believed that she did. It was very hard to believe. She hadn't changed in appearance, or attitude. Her energy appeared to be the same too.

"Yes, she *does*. She is *unbelievable*." Andy agreed. He watched Raven, admiringly. There was no one like her. *No one*. Andy smiled. Raven Kensington, was *quite* a woman!

Tessa Winters stared at her favorite person in the whole wide world. Tessa's career had crashed and burned. She did mostly B-movies now. And porn.

"I don't *think* she has cancer," said Tessa to her assistant, who had accompanied her. "She probably said that to get attention. That's *sick*, isn't it? To be *that* desperate for attention!" Tessa scoffed.

Her assistant laughed. "Tessa! The woman has *more* attention than she wants, I'm sure. No one gets *more* attention than she does. No one. She's the *biggest* star in Hollywood, in the world, actually. She's also the biggest star that has *ever* graced Hollywood. And she is one of the *most* beautiful women that I have ever seen. Her beauty is *staggering*. Boy, have times *changed*! I'm not prejudiced in *any* way, but I *never* thought that I'd live to see the day, that a woman of color, would be as big as she. Raven Kensington knocked down *a lot* of barriers. She's also one of the *most* powerful and influential people in the world." He looked at Tony, who was standing beside his wife. "They are an *enormously*-powerful couple. They're a very *striking* couple too." Tessa's assistant added.

"Don't sing *her* praises to me. I *hate* her. Now *back* to what I was saying, how do you explain the way *she* looks? She certainly doesn't look sick. Explain that to me, Brady." Tessa demanded.

"I *can't*. Only God knows. I don't." Brady shook his head at his boss. It was sad to see so much hate and envy in her eyes, especially for a woman, that Brady doubted, Tessa even really knew.

Everyone had a great time at the party, including Tessa, who had only come to see how Raven looked these days. And she wasn't pleased with what she saw. Tessa was hoping for just the opposite. She was hoping to hear of Raven's death. I'll keep my fingers crossed. Now *that*, would be the *greatest* news that I have ever heard. Tessa smiled, wickedly.

      * * *

At the end of the evening, the Dashs thanked everyone again, before leaving to go home. Everyone was elated to see Raven obviously doing, and looking, so exceptionally-well. She hadn't changed a bit, they'd all agreed.

      * * *

Later that night, Tony made passionate love to Raven. His lovemaking hadn't waned a bit, and that night wasn't any different. When Raven was diagnosed with cancer, Tony would always ask her if he could make love to her, he had always put her first. Since Raven had come into his life, nothing was more important to Tony, than her health and happiness. *Nothing*. It had always been that way.

After they'd made love, Tony looked at Raven with glazed eyes. "*Insatiable* ... my love. I *love* loving you! *In*, and *out*, of bed." He kissed the nape of Raven's neck, as he caressed her.

When they had danced at the Regent, Raven saw that dreamy look in her husband's eyes, and she knew what was coming later.

"Your *appetite* hasn't slowed a bit, has it?" Raven teased. "You're a *hungry* man, Tony Dash. Don't worry, I won't call you a madman."

"No, it hasn't. And, it *won't*. I *told* you from the start, you drive me *crazy*. You're *insatiable*, you're simply *irresistible*. And *correction*, I'm *not* just *a* hungry man, I'm *your* hungry man. I'm *only* hungry for *you*, Raven." He loved making love to her, and with her. Tony was always hungry for Raven. "I'm crazy for *my* fox. And

I'm *mad* all right. I am *madly*, in love, with my *beautiful* wife." And he was. Tony loved Raven more than life itself. His eyes combed his wife's curvaceous body. "You have *all* of these *delicious* goodies, that *only* I ... can *love* ... *taste* ... and *enjoy*. But, as I've said *many* times before, there is *nothing*, like the *main* course meal."

Raven laughed. "What are you going to do when Mommie and Daddy arrive tomorrow?"

Raven's parents were flying to California to visit.

"*Mommie* and *Daddy?* That's *cute*. You *mean*, what are *they* going to do? Just kidding! Don't you *dare* tell your parents that I said that. You *know* how much I *love* your parents. This is a *big* house, baby. They will be very comfortable on the *other* side of the house. *Way, way*, on the other side! *Far* away from *our* bedroom. *Isolation*, can be good sometimes. Either that, or we'll issue them a pair of earmuffs. Correction, *soundproof*-earplugs."

Raven laughed. She had always felt uncomfortable making love when her parents were in the same house. She laughed again, remembering when she and Tony made love for the first time, at her parents' house. They had turned on the radio while they made love, so that her parents wouldn't hear them.

"What's the matter, love?" Raven asked her husband. She sensed that something else was on Tony's mind, besides what they had been joking about.

"What is *this?*" Tony asked. "Woman with a *sixth* sense. We're lying here in the dark, and you *know* that something is on my mind. I don't know about *you* woman!"

"I'm *waiting*," said Raven. "*Tell* me."

Tony kissed her. He decided to 'fess up. He shook his head, nothing got past Raven. *Nothing*. "I don't *like* the way *they* look at you," said Tony.

Raven turned on the lamp. "*They?*"

"*Men*, Raven. The cast and crew, *all* of your tons of male fans. *Men, males* ... Some look at you like you're a piece of *meat*, as if they are *undressing* you with their eyes. Others look at you, like they are smitten. They gawk. *Drool.* I *hate* that! Granted, if some men were in my shoes, they would probably take it as a compliment, and I guess in some ways, it is, but sometimes I want to break their necks. I'm your husband. My look is a look of love, admiration, and desire, which is perfectly natural and normal. And yes, you drove me *crazy* when I first laid eyes on you, and you're *still* driving me crazy, in and out of bed. I'm bananas! But you're *not* a piece of meat. You're the woman who I'm in love with. You're the woman who I *love* with *every* fiber of *my* being. And yes, I'm *smitten.* And I will always be smitten. They would trade places with me in the blink of an eye. I know what I have. I know how very blessed I am to have an *extraordinary* woman like you, Raven. Trust me." Tony looked deep into Raven's eyes. His fingers slowly traced her lips. "*Luscious.* So very luscious. You are the woman of my dreams, Raven. You're *everything* to me, beautiful." Everything in her husband's eyes told Raven that he meant every word.

"*Tony ... baby ...*" Raven's eyes reached deep into her husband's. "You have *no* reason to worry. You are the *only* man that I *love.* You are the *only* man that I *want.* Are you saying that you *don't* trust me?"

"I trust *you*, Raven. It's the *hounds* that I don't trust. You're the *fox*, and they're the *hounds.*"

Raven laughed.

"I'm *serious*, sweetheart. That's what they remind me of."

Raven's dark eyes were serious as she spoke. "Tony, I'm *serious* too. I am *very* serious when I say this ... I *love you, Tony Dash*, and *only you.* Don't *ever* forget that. *Erase* all doubts. Eradicate *all* insecurities. *You* have me. Baby, I'm *yours.* And yours, *only.*"

Tony looked at his beautiful wife. "You're my queen. I don't know what I *ever* did to deserve such an *extraordinary* woman like *you.* You are *more* than amazing." Tony knew that a woman like Raven came along once in a lifetime.

"Tony Dash, *you* ... are *my* Prince Charming. And speaking of men undressing me with their eyes, you are the *only* man who will *ever* know, what lies *beneath*!" said Raven, throwing back the covers to reveal her naked body.

"Is *all* of this *mine*?" Tony feasted his eyes on Raven.

Raven nodded. "Yes. I ... *am* ... *all* ... *yours*." Raven spoke in-between kisses. "Not just *my* body though. You have the *most* important thing of all, Tony Dash. You have, *my heart*." Raven's eyes never left her husband's as she spoke. She wanted Tony to know that she meant every word.

Tony smiled. Raven had erased his insecurities. He felt her words. Tony knew that Raven would always be his. And he would always be hers. Always!

And that night, as Raven and Tony lie quietly in each other's arms, they both knew in their heart of hearts, that no one, or nothing, would ever come between them. They were joined at the heart.

* * *

The next morning, Raven sat in the tub, enjoying her usual, hot bubble bath. She was looking forward to seeing her parents.

Tony was sound asleep. Raven could see her husband through the glass window, as she relaxed in the tub. She watched him, as he slept like a baby. He's my baby, Raven thought. My big, handsome baby. *My*, Prince Charming.

Raven smiled as she thought of her parents. They were scheduled to arrive at LAX at one o'clock in the afternoon.

* * *

After her bath, Raven went to her office to work on a play that she was writing. As she sat at her computer, her mind went back to the dream that she once had, writing a movie that she and Becky would star in. A lump formed in Raven's throat, as she quickly switched her thoughts to other things.

* * *

Raven sat, writing for hours, before she heard her husband's footsteps.

Tony stood in the doorway, looking very handsome and well-rested. "Good morning, beautiful," said Tony, as he kissed his wife on the lips. "How's the play coming?" Tony had read everything that Raven had written so far, and he was very impressed. His wife never ceased to amaze him. She was truly a woman of many talents.

"Morning, Rip. The play's coming along fine. Would you like breakfast?"

"No, thanks, beautiful. I'm a *simple* man. A bowl of cereal will be just fine. I'm going to shave, shower, brush my pearly-whites, then get dressed. Have you eaten?"

"Yes."

Raven and Tony discussed where they were going to take her parents. They wanted to show them a great time. They knew that when the Kensingtons had come to L.A. when Becky died, it wasn't a good time for anyone. But Raven and Tony were determined to make this time, different.

Raven knew that her parents were really coming to see how she was doing, and that was certainly understandable. Raven knew that if she were a parent, she would do the same.

* * *

Later that day, when they arrived at LAX, Mack went inside of the airport to wait for Charles and Mae Kensington. Raven and Tony waited in the limo. The last thing that Raven wanted to do was have her parents surrounded by all of her screaming fans. She smiled. That would have been right up her little sister's alley. Angie loved the spotlight. Raven was surprised that Angie didn't want to become an actress. Instead, Angie's passions were hair and cosmetics. And she was superb at both.

Raven had already called her mother to let her know that Mack would be there when they got off the plane, and that she and Tony would be waiting outside in the limo for them.

Mae Kensington understood. She agreed with her very famous daughter, running through the airport to escape screaming fans, didn't appeal to her either. "And besides," she'd told her daughter, "your father and I are too *old* for all of *that* running."

Raven had laughed in answer.

As Raven's parents and Mack approached the limo, Raven and Tony got out and gave Charles and Mae a big hug and kiss. They were very happy to see them. Raven's parents were also very happy to see their daughter and son-in-law. And they were especially happy to see their daughter looking exactly as she'd always looked. Raven looked well. Very well.

"Are you'll hungry?" Raven asked her parents.

Charles and Mae nodded.

Everyone was hungry, including Mack, so Tony told their driver to take them to Linq's. Linq's served a variety of delicious dishes, there was something for every kind of taste.

Raven, Tony, and Mack ordered filet mignon. Charles and Mae ordered lasagna. The service at the restaurant was first-class, and the food was superb. Tony left a hefty tip for their waiter.

    * * *

Mack and Tony took the Kensingtons' luggage up to their bedroom. Tony was a man of his word. Charles and Mae's bedroom was a good distance from his and Raven's. Raven laughed to herself, as she followed her father onto the terrace. Charles wanted to speak with Raven. Alone.

Charles gave his daughter another big hug. "How's *my* little girl? I have two, but even though you're older than Angie, you're still Daddy's little girl too. And Raven, you will *always* be." He looked his daughter over. Raven looked fantastic. She didn't look sick at all. She hadn't lost any weight either. Raven was simply unbelievable. Charles was elated by what he saw.

Raven gave her father her undivided attention. Her all-seeing, dark eyes searched his.

    * * *

Raven's father told her that he was very angry with God, since learning that she had cancer. Charles told Raven that he had even stopped going to church. Her father shook his head. "I had so *many* questions for God, Raven. Like *why* ... Why *did* He let *you* get cancer? You're so sweet, loving, giving. Kind. You're so inspirational! I could go on and on. I was very angry. *Still* am. I know that bad things happen to good people, but that was little consolation for me, sweetheart."

Raven sat in silence, as she listened to her father. She had always been a great listener.

"I told God to give *me* the disease instead. I told Him that I would *gladly* trade places with you. You're so young, sweetheart. I've lived, at least *longer* than you. You have so *much* to live for. You have so much *more* to do, Raven." Tears rolled down Charles Kensington's face, as he spoke to the person who he loved, and admired, so dearly. His daughter, Raven. "You're *irreplaceable*, Raven." Her father smiled through his tears. "*No one's quite like you. I love you so much. Never* forget that. Your mother, Trey, Angie, everyone loves you very much. And *that* man out there, my *other* son, Tony, he loves you even *more* than we love you, so I *know* you're in very good hands with him. He's a very *good* man, Raven."

Tears sprung to Raven's eyes.

Her father was silent. He had told her what he wanted to tell her. He had said what he'd come to L.A. to say.

"Oh ... *Daddy*. Will you *listen* to me now?"

Her father nodded.

"God has *no* respect of person. Everything is going to be all right. When I say that, I'm speaking on *faith*. God is *far greater* than *any* disease or illness. If *all* I have is *God*, I have *more* than enough. I don't know what the future holds, Daddy, but I *know*, who *holds* the future. And that's where trust comes in. *Faith*. Please, don't be angry with God, Daddy. I know that we're human. Who knows? I may even get angry with God one day. I've *never* been one to say never, because I don't know what I will or won't do. No one does,

Daddy. When I first found out that I had cancer, I certainly didn't jump for joy. I had many of the same feelings, that anyone who would be told that has. I'm human. But, what separates me from you, or even some of them, is the fact that I'm a human being with *faith*. Faith *removes* fear. I took the cancer, and I gave it to God. Nothing is hidden from Him. God knows what's going to happen, *before* it even happens. God's will is *going* to be done, no matter what. Sometimes, He will, and does, *allow* things to happen. Who knows why? He can *stop* the awful things that happen in this world. He can prevent *anything* from happening, in a heartbeat. He's *God*. But His will, and our will, as humans, are not always the same. God gave us free will. It's normal to associate cancer with death, because it is a deadly disease. Daddy, would it make *any* difference, if I'm killed in a car accident, or while out shopping, or if I were to die in my sleep? I don't think it would matter to most people, how *anyone* that they loved died. They would *still* be just as heartbroken and devastated. A death is a *death*. It doesn't always take the sick to leave this world either. Life is very short. It's also very precious, and should *never* be taken for granted. It shouldn't take cancer, AIDS, or a funeral, for *any* of us, to realize that. People were also dying *way* before September 11, 2001, in *all* kinds of ways, and people will *continue* to die. Be it an illness, plane crash, terrorism, murder, car accident. You can die in your sleep, the list is *endless*. Death is a part of life. It's *guaranteed* to come to *all* of us, one day. That's one thing that we can all be certain of. It's also *another* thing, that *all* of us have in common. We are all, going to leave *this* world. One day. The only two things that we don't know, is *how*, or *when*. For *many* of us, it is *only* when death gets *close*, that *life* gets *important*. Death could be around the corner for *anyone*. For *any* of us. That's why we *need* to live life to the fullest. And that's why we should *never* cease to tell, correction, *show* people, how much we *love* them, and how much they mean to us. It's always been *very* sad to me, how some people, *especially* those who supposedly love you, don't make time for you in *life*, but, they make time for you in *death*."

"When they come to your funeral," said her father.

Raven nodded. "*Exactly*, Daddy. That's why Tony and I always tell each other how much we love each other. But more *importantly*, we *show* each other. And not even my career is more important to me than Tony, or you, or Mommie, or *any* of the people who I love. *Nothing*, means *more* to me, than *God* and *family*. *Nothing*."

Charles Kensington looked in his daughter's eyes. They were beautiful eyes that were full of wisdom. Charles had never seen eyes that were wiser than his oldest daughter's. Never.

"No one, is *untouchable*, nor are we here to stay. You can have *all* of the money in the world, but it *can't* buy you life. Money can buy you the *best* medicine and the *best* doctors, but it *can't* buy you *good* health."

Her father sat, marveling at his daughter's wisdom. He had always been impressed by Raven's wisdom, even when she was a little girl. A woman ahead of her time, thought her father, as he sat listening to Raven.

"Only *One* can give life and good health, and only One, can take life. That's God. He made *all* of us. He is the One who breathes life into *every* man. And because of that, He is the One, and the *only* One, who can heal me, and or, continue to *allow* me to live. You know, Daddy, my BMW is a *superb*, high-end car. It runs like the finely-tuned machine that it is, and that it was designed to be. *However*, if my BMW were to *ever* break down, I wouldn't take it to a Ford, or a Chevy dealership, because they didn't make the car. I would take it to the BMW dealership. I would take it to *its* maker. Because I know that if *anyone* can fix the problem, it would be *BMW*, the *maker*, of the car. I said all of that to say this, with my cancer, I have done the *same* thing. I took the disease and gave it to *my* Maker, the *One* who made *me*, to fix it. To fix me. God made *this* body, so *surely*, He can *fix* it. *Anything*, that's wrong with it, or me. If *anyone* can heal me, He *can*. A man can't fix another man. Sure, we have medicines, hospitals, great doctors, but ultimately, the *final* decision, lies in the hands of One. I took my cancer to the *best* doctor of *all*, the One who has *never* lost a patient. One who *never* makes mistakes. *My* doctor doesn't need X-rays, MRIs, and CT scans. He sees, and knows, *all*. I'll use Tylenol's motto, but change it up just a bit, I take comfort in *God's* strength. I have cancer, Daddy, but it *doesn't* have me. The doctors wanted me to stop doing all of my usual activities, but I didn't. Because stopping me from *living*, isn't going to stop me, from *dying*. The day that I'll *stop* living, is the day that I *stop* breathing."

Charles stopped crying. He smiled at his favorite daughter. She was *still* Raven. The same ol' Raven. Incredibly-wise, witty, and very beautiful. Raven had given her father a lot of food for thought. She made him feel a whole lot better. She had inspired him, immensely.

Charles Kensington laughed. "*Don't* call me, Daddy," he joked. "You have *more* sense than me, girl! You're *my* mother."

Raven laughed in answer. She was glad to see that her father felt better about things. Father and daughter hugged before going to join the others. They found Tony and Mae, sitting in the living room, having a talk of their own. Tony and Mae looked up, as Raven and her father entered the room.

Mae smiled. She could sense that her husband felt much better, after talking with their daughter. Mae didn't feel that she had to talk with Raven. Just looking at her, and seeing how well she looked, was more than enough conviction for her. She hadn't expected Raven to look so well. Mae had seen and known many people who had cancer, and they often looked ill. Many of them had also lost weight, and in some cases, they'd lost a lot of it. Mae smiled to herself, *vintage* Raven, defying the odds. She studied her daughter. Raven was definitely not ordinary. And her mother knew that she'd never been either. There had always been something different, and very special, about their oldest daughter. And this was another thing that validated what Mae Kensington had always known. Raven, was extraordinary.

* * *

The foursome sat in the living room talking and laughing for hours. Afterwards, they went to the movie theater to watch movies. Raven had a number of movies that she knew her parents would love.

When the last movie ended, Tony and Charles volunteered to go to the grocery store to get food for dinner, and to give mother and daughter a chance to be alone to talk.

Tony suggested having a barbecue by the pool. That idea sounded irresistible to all of them.

"Tony and Daddy, please don't get the lettuce and cabbage mixed up!" said Raven.

Everyone laughed hard.

"Lettuce really *does* taste much better with tomatoes than cabbage does."

Tony laughed at his wife. He loved her sense of humor.

"I'm *serious* you two. I'm *not* joking. No pun intended." Raven spoke with a straight face.

Raven and her mother sat out by the pool talking, while their husbands went to buy groceries. Mae told her daughter how happy she was to see her looking as she had always looked. She was the same ol' incredibly-astonishing Raven. The only thing that had changed was the fact that she did have a deadly disease inside of her, but it had not killed her spirit, or her faith.

"You were *always* a fighter. I have always known that. It didn't take cancer for me to know how *strong* you are. You've always been very strong, Raven."

Mae Kensington filled Raven in on the rest of the family, who had been calling Raven regularly, especially since learning of her illness. Trey, Stephanie, and their children, along with Angie and Aunt Ruth, had all come down when they'd first been told of the news. They spent two weeks with Raven and Tony. They all rallied around Raven, with lots of love and support, including Tony's family. Raven and Tony were very grateful for all of the love and support that they had received from family, friends, and fans alike.

Becky's family still couldn't bring themselves to come back to L.A., but they called Raven, regularly, to see how she was doing. And *everyone* knew, beyond a shadow of a doubt, that Rebecca Simms would have been by Raven's side, *every* step of the way.

Mae Kensington told her daughter that she would have told her about her father being angry with God, but she knew that Raven had enough to deal with, without worrying about her father. Mae was very happy that they had come to L.A. It did Charles, and her, a lot of good.

The two women had a nice, long, mother-and-daughter, heart-to-heart talk, before the men returned with their hands filled with bags. It looked like they had gone shopping for an army. The women laughed, as they helped carry the groceries. Mack had left for the day. Tony had given him the rest of the day off.

Everyone donned swimwear, and sat by the pool, while Chef Tony barbecued, and Raven made her famous potato salad, that her father loved.

Everyone was having a very enjoyable time, including Pugs, who ran around the grounds, barking and wagging his tail. Tony turned the radio on, and found his favorite oldies station. He also knew that Raven's parents would like the station.

The foursome sung along with the O'Jays, Ray Charles, the Temptations, Smokey Robinson, Stevie Wonder, Barry Manilow, Otis Redding, Phil Collins, Lionel Richie, the Jackson Five, and Elton John.

Raven's parents slow danced to "My Girl."

"Now *that's* music!" said Charles Kensington. "Music that had *meaning*. Songs that *stirred* the heart and soul! This *stuff* today is *nonsense*, or a lot of it is, anyway. *Nothing* beats the oldies!"

Everyone nodded in agreement.

Tony looked at his wife. "May I have this dance, *beautiful*? I just wanna hold you close and whisper in your ear," he whispered to Raven.

"*Hmmm* ... I don't know. I don't *think* my husband would like that." Raven laughed, as she slow-danced with her husband.

"It *always* feels so good, holding you in my arms. In *my* arms, is where *you* belong, beautiful. I *love* you ..."

"I *love* you too, baby."

"You're in *big* trouble, tonight." Tony whispered in his wife's ear.

"Be a *good* boy, Tony Dash. My parents are *watching*."

Tony laughed. "I'll be on my *best* behavior. For you, *anything*."

    * * *

Raven and Tony took the Kensingtons to both of the R.K. by Design stores, Disneyland, the Grauman Chinese Theatre, Paramount and Universal Studios, and Hollywood's Walk of Fame. And on the Sunday before Raven's parents left, they went to church with Raven and Tony.

On her parents' last day in L.A., Raven stood alongside the car, hugging her parents and crying. She always hated good-byes. Raven hated to see them go. Mae Kensington cried too, while Charles fought back tears.

Charles looked at his daughter. He couldn't stop beaming. His mother had always told him that one could learn from anyone, no matter what their age. His mother was right too. Charles had learned so much from Raven. And he was elated to see her looking, and doing, so very well.

Charles and Mae hugged Raven and Tony again, before leaving to board their plane.

    * * *

On the ride home, Raven sat thinking about her parents' visit. She had enjoyed them immensely. She knew that Tony had too. Her mother told her that the Tunis community was very grateful for all of her and Tony's monetary contributions that they had given to the community.

Helping others, and giving, had always made Raven feel good. It enriched her life *immensely*. She never reserved giving for Christmas only. She did it year-round. Raven knew that giving was something that one should do regularly. And even though she gave money to help many, Raven knew that giving, also meant giving of one's self. She always gave if, or when, God led her to. Like with most things, Raven was very careful and cautious. She would always have the charities thoroughly checked out, first, before donating. She knew that some charities used donations for *other* things, including, placing money into their very own bank accounts. Raven's thoughts were interrupted by her husband.

"'Young, Beautiful and Worth *Billions*. The Most *Powerful* Woman in Show Business.' Whew! The woman on this magazine cover is *beyond* beautiful. She takes *my* breath away."

Raven bent over to get a closer look at the magazine. She laughed when she saw who the woman was.

"You know, sweetheart, she looks *a lot* like *you*," said Tony.

It was she.

* * *

After seven months, and two and a half weeks of chemo and radiation treatments, Raven was elated that it was over. She had never liked taking medicine of any kind. Her hair had started growing back after her chemo treatments ended. She was very happy about that too. But most of all, Raven was thankful to God for her life.

To celebrate, Tony whisked Raven away to an island. Her, island.

"This is a *beautiful* island!" Raven told her husband.

Tony smiled. "For a very *beautiful* woman. It's *yours*, sweetheart! Raven, I bought this island for *you*. It's the *Raven* Island." He pointed to a sign that bore her name.

Tears filled Raven's eyes. "*Tony* ..." was all she could say at the moment. She was speechless.

The island was huge, isolated, and breathtaking. It was surrounded by crystal-clear, blue water. The bluest that Raven had ever seen.

* * *

Tony had a lavish and spacious condo built on the island. The condo had every possible luxury known to man. And although they were alone on the island, a number of servants were just a phone call away. Tony took Raven's hand in his, as he gave her a tour of her island, and the condo.

Raven still couldn't believe it! Her husband was full of surprises. And this was a surprise that she would never forget. She was ecstatic, as she watched her husband with love and admiration.

"I *love* you, Tony Dash," said Raven. She gave him a breath-stealing kiss, that was filled with emotion.

"Wow!" said Tony.

"You *spoil* me so much, sweetheart, but, I'm *not* complaining!"

"Raven, I told you from day *one* that the honeymoon *wouldn't* end. I told *you* that I would *always* spoil you. Money is great, it certainly has its advantages. But I would be just as happy being poor, as long as I was with *you*. It's *not* what I have, or what I can *get*, it's *who* I'm *with*, that makes me *happier* than anyone, and happier than *anything*. Raven, *you*, make me, a *very* rich man."

"*Tony* ... I *love* you so much. *You* make me very happy too. *You*. *Not* the wonderful surprises, but *you*, sweetheart. *Nothing* means more to me than *you* do," said Raven. "*Nothing*, or *no one*."

And she meant it. They both did.

That evening, they dined on the seafood and wine that their chef had prepared for them, earlier that day.

After dinner, they relaxed in the Jacuzzi. Both enjoyed being isolated, and the peace and relaxation that came along with it.

Tony held Raven in his arms that night, as they watched the sunset.

"I *love* watching the sun, set, and *rise*, in *your* eyes." Tony whispered to Raven.

His wife smiled. "Oh, *my Prince Charming*! This is so beautiful! Let's *stay* here *forever*."

"I would *love* to," Tony told Raven, as he kissed and caressed her. "But, you *know* the acting-bug *isn't* out of your system yet."

Raven laughed. "Yes, you're *right*. You know me all *too* well. But one day, my love. *One day ...*"

   * * *

When Raven and Tony arrived back home in L.A., they were elated to hear that Raven had been nominated for another Oscar, for portraying the Paris singer, Lorraine Shears.

Andy had also given her some shocking news. While she and Tony were away, Tessa Winters was killed in a car accident.

Raven was saddened by the news. She never liked Tessa's actions, but she never wished her any ill will.

"When was Tessa's funeral?" Raven asked.

"Two weeks ago." Andy told her. He told Raven that he hadn't attended. He had never liked Tessa. "She was a cruel and heartless woman." Andy told Raven. "She was filled with hate and jealousy. *Lots* of it."

"My heart goes out to her family though. My thoughts and prayers go out to them too." Raven told Andy.

After hanging up with Andy, Raven thought of Tessa. Raven knew all too well how much Tessa hated her, but she still wasn't thrilled to hear that she was dead.

   * * *

When Oscar night arrived, Raven couldn't attend. She was sick with the flu. She watched the Academy Awards from her bed. Regardless of how sick she was, she felt better when she heard that she had won *another* Oscar. Her second one in two years. Tony and Mack were thrilled for her too.

"Unfortunately, Raven Kensington could *not* be here tonight," said the Oscar host, Zenny Martinez, who was a famed comedian. "Her publicist informed me that she's at home with the flu. Raven, get *well* soon! *Congratulations, Ms. Kensington!*" Zenny waved her Oscar at the screen, as if to make Raven see it better, should she be watching. "You know, Raven Kensington is *unbelievable*! She made believers out of *all* of us! She has all of us under *her* spell. I go see her movies, just to *look* at her. You'll have seen her. She is an exquisitely-beautiful woman. Ms. Kensington's the kind of woman that turns a glance, into a stare. And she's *fine* too. Mr. Dash, *please* don't get upset. It's *only* a compliment. You are a *very* lucky man."

Raven and Tony laughed.

Zenny went on, "I never would have thought that I would live to see the day, when a person of color, *especially* a female, would be the *most* powerful woman in *Hollywhite*, I mean, *Hollywood*."

The audience roared with laughter.

"Seriously, who *knew*? *Who* knew? This sister has *taken* over! I repeat, *this* sister has taken over!"

The audience roared with laughter again.

"Congratulations again, Ms. Kensington. And get well soon! We *love* you!"

During the commercial break, Zenny stood, holding Raven Kensington's Oscar. He was a fifty-two year old Hispanic male, who had also experienced a lot of discrimination. And he still did. Zenny was thrilled beyond words, to see a black woman with so much power, and influence, receiving all of the props that she deserved. He knew that Raven hadn't been given any of the massive fame and fortune that she had attained, she had earned it. Every bit of it. She was still the hardest working person in show business, and she'd definitely earned the right to be the international superstar that she was today. He hated that Raven was ill. Zenny was looking forward to meeting her in person. He wanted to give her a big hug and kiss. Who wouldn't want to touch a woman like *that*? Zenny smiled, as he thought of sinful thoughts. Raven Kensington, was *every* man's dream.

* * *

Tears filled Raven's eyes. Winning one Oscar was saying a lot. But winning *two*? In two years' time? Raven was ecstatic!

The superstar thought about Zenny's comments. Raven knew that the comedian's comments, reflected the thoughts of many. Someone was certainly looking out for her. *God*. Raven hoped that she wouldn't be the only person of color, to reach the great heights that she had reached. Raven hoped that all of the great and incredible things that had happened for her, and that were still happening for her, would also happen to many people of her race. She hoped that it would spread like wildfire. God knows that it was long, *long* overdue.

"Congratulations, beautiful wifey," said Tony, who kissed his wife, despite Raven's warning that he could catch the flu.

"I'll just have to catch it." Tony told Raven, as he kissed her again.

Raven shook her head. "Tony Dash, what am I going to do with *you*?"

"Whatever you *want* to do," said Tony. "I'm all *yours*."

Raven laughed. "Yes, *you* are. You certainly *are*."

Raven stayed in bed with the flu for two and a half weeks. And as always, her husband pampered her. Tony also made sure that she followed the doctor's orders.

As soon as she got completely well, Raven started filming her next movie. Raven Kensington was the busiest star in Hollywood. It felt good being able to pick and choose roles. Raven usually chose roles according to substance.

Raven employed many talented black producers, directors, actors, and writers. She also influenced Hollywood to do the same.

On the set of Raven's movies, cast and crew were diverse. There were people of various races and backgrounds. It was how she wanted it to be. And what Raven Kensington wanted, she got.

* * *

Raven continued filming movies back-to-back, for years. She wrote and starred in three plays on Broadway, two of which she had written, and won Tony Awards for. She was also the go-to woman for voice-overs. Everyone loved that eloquent, and incredibly-sultry voice of hers.

* * *

Raven Kensington reigned in Hollywood, for decades. At the age of sixty-seven, she filmed her last movie. Even after she had decided to leave Tinseltown, she still remained a major force. And that alone, spoke volumes.

* * *

Raven flashed her trademark smile, as she relaxed in her Jacuzzi. Her mind went back to all of those *many* years ago, when she had stood in front of the sixth grade class, reading her book report. Raven had made *all* of her dreams, become reality.

Raven Kensington was Hollywood's highest-paid star. She was a billionaire, in her own right. Her resume in Tinseltown was unmatched, by *any* actor, or actress, who had come before her. Raven won a countless number of Oscars, Screen Actors Guild Awards, NAACP Image Awards, People's Choice Awards, and Golden Globe Awards. Raven was also among the elite, when she was awarded the Humanitarian Award, the Honorary Lifetime Achievement Award, and the Peabody Individual Achievement Award. Raven was also a Kennedy Center honoree. She was the youngest person, *ever*, to receive Philadelphia's Marian Anderson Award. Raven also received a star on the Hollywood Walk of Fame. And there were streets named after her, in Beverly Hills and Manhattan.

Raven Kensington had made history in so many ways. But most of all, she loved the fact that she had made, a *difference*. A big one! She opened doors for many people of color, other minorities, and females, of *all* sizes. Hollywood was more diverse than it had ever been, in front of, and behind, the cameras. And there was also a lot more diversity with sizes. The media was now celebrating, like never before, females of *all* shapes, sizes, and colors. Raven had joined African-Americans before her, in showing Hollywood, especially, that a woman didn't have to be white, and rail-thin, to achieve success in Tinseltown.

Raven Kensington made a positive difference in Hollywood, and the world. She was an inspiration and a great role model to millions of people, of all races and walks of life. She was named as one of the 100 Most Influential People of the 21st Century, by Time magazine.

Raven created a countless number of acting and directing programs for minorities. She continued sharing her immense-wealth with people all over the world, including her hometown, where streets were named after her and Becky, the two hometown girls, who had made it big.

Raven flashed her trademark smile. She had kept her promise to her mother, and to herself. She had kept the promise that she had made before she left home, when she was a young, eighteen-year-old woman, leaving for Hollywood. She had kept her morals, values, and integrity. She had never sacrificed, or compromised, herself. She had played the game *her* way, and won! Not only had she *survived* in Hollywood, she had *triumphed*. In a *huge* way. *Most* importantly, Raven Kensington made a *difference, for all those* ...

Tears stung the superstar's dark eyes, as she thought of Becky. Raven still missed her sister, *terribly*. Raven knew in her heart, that she would *always* miss Becky. And despite Raven's unmatched-career, despite her immense-fame and fortune, she would have traded *all* of it, in a heartbeat, to have Becky *alive* again. And *well*. Raven smiled through her tears, as she remembered Becky's words, *"Sis,* you are *going* to be the *biggest* star that has *ever* graced Hollywood!" Becky was right. Raven just wished that Becky was still alive, to share all of it, with her. Raven had never gotten over Becky's death. And she knew that she never would. It was a pain that Raven knew, she would *never*, outlive.

Raven continued to think, as she smiled through her tears. She had accomplished everything, that she had set out to do forty-nine years ago. God had *blessed* her in *countless* ways.

At sixty-seven, Raven was still an incredibly-beautiful woman. She was a timeless-beauty. And unlike so many celebrities in Hollywood, Raven never had plastic surgery. Many were in awe of how young and gorgeous she still looked. But who was like Raven Kensington? She had always been in a class all by herself, and she *still* was.

Hollywood had a number of legends and movie goddesses, but *Raven Kensington*, was *Hollywood's greatest*. Hollywood, the world, had *never* seen *anyone* like her, and many *doubted*, if they *ever* would again.

* * *

After *many* years, the Dashs' marriage, was stronger than ever. Raven and Tony had always worked to maintain a healthy, happy, and strong marriage. They also kept romance alive and well in their marriage. Time had revealed what the two of them had known from the beginning, *they*, were soul mates. Raven and Tony were joined together at the heart.

"A penny for your thoughts," said Tony. He looked at his wife, who was still the most beautiful woman that he had ever laid eyes on. Raven was an ageless-beauty. And even after all of the many years that they had been married, she *still* made his heart race. With her, love, nor desire, had ever waned.

Tony was still strikingly-handsome, and he was as charming as ever. His hair was gray now, as was Raven's, at least mostly. Tony's body was still strong, healthy, and athletic.

Raven smiled. "I was just *thinking*. You know me, I'm *always* thinking, sweetheart."

"*Thinking*? About what? Please *elaborate*, Mrs. Dash." Tony smiled that charming smile of his.

"About *us*. I was also thinking of Mack. Pugs too. Pugs *Dash*." Mack and their dog of many years, had died the same year. "We're so blessed to have each *other*, Tony."

Tony walked over to Raven. "I love you woman with the inquiring mind. You've *always* been a deep thinker. I *still* pinch myself. What did I *ever* do, to *deserve* such an *extraordinary* woman like *you*?"

"What did *we* do to *deserve* each other?" said Raven. "You *are* an *extraordinary* man, Mr. Dash. I've told you *many* times, *don't* sell yourself short."

Tony laughed in answer.

* * *

That night, Tony held Raven in his arms, as they lie looking up at the stars.

"Where did *all* of the time go?" Tony asked his wife. He was happy that God had allowed them to grow old together. It was something that Tony had always prayed, and hoped for.

"Time does fly, *doesn't* it?" said Raven.

"*Especially*, when you're having fun." Tony finished.

Raven looked at her husband. The moonlight shone on his face. She still thought him very handsome. Tony looked younger than he actually was.

Raven and Tony were now a good-looking, elderly couple. And they were still energetic. And very much in love.

* * *

For years, Raven and Tony travelled around the world. They spent a lot of time on the private island that Tony had bought for Raven. They also spent a number of years in Paris, Greenwich, and on their Wyoming ranch, before heading back to Malibu.

* * *

They were in Malibu, when Tony became ill. A now, ninety-four-year-old Raven, was sitting in the living room watching *CNN*, when she heard her husband call her.

"Raven!"

"I'll be right there, sweetheart!" Raven answered.

When Raven went to their bedroom, Tony told her that he wasn't feeling well.

Raven took her husband's temperature.

Tony had a high fever.

Raven told Brunner, one of their servants, to bring the car around quickly, as she helped Tony get dressed.

Brunner drove them to Cedars-Sinai Medical Center. Tony was immediately taken to E.R., where, after checking his temperature and vital signs, he was admitted. Tony had pneumonia.

"Brunner, my niece, Simone, is coming to L.A. I'm going to stay here with Tony. I need you to pick her up at LAX at noon. I'll call Simone and tell her that you will be there to pick her up. You remember Simone, don't you? She calls all the time. She also visits fairly often."

* * *

Brunner nodded. "Yes, ma'am. I remember Simone."

Simone usually visited her aunt and uncle at least once a month. She was Angie's great-granddaughter. Raven and Simone were close.

Raven was going to spend the night at the hospital with Tony. They had never spent one night apart, since getting married so many years ago, and Raven wasn't about to break the cycle now.

* * *

Brunner dropped Simone off at the hospital, and she stayed there all day, with her aunt and uncle. Simone wanted to spend the night at the hospital too, but Raven told her to go home and get some rest. "I'll call you. *Thanks*, sweetheart."

Simone left, reluctantly. She knew better than to argue with her Aunt Raven. She was one woman that you didn't want to argue with.

* * *

Tony remained in the hospital. Seven days passed. Raven would spend the night, then go home to bathe, change clothes, and eat, before heading back to the hospital. It had become routine for her.

Raven kissed her husband tenderly on the lips. "I'll be back, handsome."

"Okay, beautiful," said Tony.

Raven walked out in the hall, where Simone was waiting to drive her home. Raven's mind was on her husband. Sometimes Tony looked like himself, and sometimes, he didn't.

* * *

The staff went into a frenzy. Everyone knew who Raven Kensington and Tony Dash were. They had more than made their marks. The doctor warned them all to be professional. He told them not to ask for autographs. It would be very inappropriate, and heartless, he'd told them, under the circumstances.

* * *

The staff watched Raven in awe. Everyone admired Hollywood's *greatest* legend and movie goddess.

* * *

Dr. Werner went to check on Tony. He didn't think the old man would live much longer. His vital signs weren't good. Pneumonia was always worse for those whose systems were too weak to fight. The old man was having complications. Dr. Werner looked at the one-hundred-and-one-year-old man, with admiration. The old man was weak, but he was fighting hard.

"How are you feeling, Mr. Dash?" Dr. Werner asked. The doctor knew that Tony was weak. And so did Tony. He also saw the look on the doctor's face. Tony knew that the doctor didn't think he was going to make it.

"I've felt better," said Tony.

Dr. Werner made sure that Tony was comfortable, and he gave him plenty of liquids. The doctor gave the old man comforting words, then left the room.

The nurse looked at Tony. "I'll be right back with your medicine, Mr. Dash."

Tony nodded. He knew that he was getting weaker and weaker. His mind was on Raven. *"Please … God … don't take me yet. Please … let me say good-bye … to the love of my life. My beautiful … Raven …"* the old man whispered.

When the nurse came back with his medicine, Tony told her to call his wife. "Please call my wife now. Tell her to come to the hospital. Right away."

The nurse nodded, as she phoned Raven. "Mrs. Dash? This is Marsha Winser, at Cedars-Sinai Medical Center. Your husband wanted me to call you. He wants you to come to the hospital *immediately*."

"I'll be right there," said Raven, hanging up the phone. "Simone, take me to the hospital. We *have* to hurry."

* * *

Tony knew that his life was about to end. He had always prayed and hoped that Raven would outlive him. It would have been *unbearable*, living without her. He knew that she would be devastated by his death, but he also knew his wife's strength. Raven was an incredibly-strong woman. Tony had always admired her strength.

Tony continued to think about his wife. He hadn't been lucky to have Raven as a wife, he had been, *blessed*. Raven Kensington Dash, was an *extraordinary* woman. And even now in his weakest state, just *thinking* of *her*, gave him strength. He could never put into words, just how very much he *loved* her. He loved her so deeply and dearly. Raven was the *only* woman that had *ever* stopped his heart, literally. Tony lies in his hospital bed, remembering, when he'd first laid eyes on Raven. "*Please* ... God ... *Please* ... let me live to say *good-bye* ... to *my baby* ... The love of my life ... *My beautiful* ... *Ra-ven* ..."

* * *

Simone got her aunt to the hospital in record time.

"Wait *here*." Raven told her, as she hurried to Tony's room. Raven wanted to be alone with her husband.

Tony's eyes lit up, as soon as Raven entered the room. At the sight of her, he smiled instantly. Looking at her, had always, brought a smile to his lips. "*There you are* ... *my beautiful* ... *Raven*. I couldn't *leave*, without saying *good-bye* to *you*."

Raven sat by her husband's bed. Tears streamed down her face, as she held Tony's hand. They loved each other so deeply. They had always been like two hearts, that beat, as one. Raven and Tony were connected at the heart, and a connection such as that, would *never* be broken, not even by death.

"Oh ... *Raven* ... I remember when I *first* laid eyes on you. You were, you *are*, *beyond* beautiful. I went *crazy*. You *stirred* things inside of me, that I didn't know were there. I had *never* seen, or met, a woman like you. I have *never* known *anyone* like you, and to *this* day, I *still* haven't. You brought *so* much *love*, *joy*, and *happiness*, to *my* life, for so *many* years. *Many* years. *Seventy-one*, to be *exact*. I may be weak, but my memory is *still* intact." Tony smiled. "Remember how nervous I was when I came to the church, just to get *your* phone number?"

Raven nodded through her tears. She was too overwhelmed with grief to speak.

"No matter how nervous I was, I was *determined*. I *had* to have *you*. A woman like *you*, only comes around, *once*, in a lifetime. I *remember* those times as if they were yesterday. We had so *many* *wonderful*, and *incredible* times, didn't we, beautiful?"

Raven nodded again.

"*In* bed, and *out* of bed."

Raven smiled, thinking of her husband's *insatiable* appetite.

Tony wanted to see her smile, one last time, and she knew it.

"*There* it is ... Just what I was *looking* for. *That* dazzling *smile* ... *That* million-dollar, trademark smile, of *my* baby's." He had always loved Raven's smile. "You know, even if you would have been married, I would've gotten rid of the guy."

Raven smiled again through her tears. Another thing that she and Tony had in common, was their sense of humor.

Tony looked deep into his wife's eyes. He looked at the woman who he loved, more than *anyone*, or *anything*, in the world, *more* than life itself. "Those *mesmerizing*, dark eyes of yours. *X-rays*, as your mother and I always called them. You *are* as wise ... as *you* are beautiful. When I *first* looked into *your* eyes, Raven, I saw *forever*. The *only* thing, that I *ever* wanted to do ... was *please you*."

Raven found her voice. "*Tony* ... *My king*. *My* ... *Prince* *Charming*. *You* have *always* pleased me. *Beyond* words. You made me the *happiest* woman in the world, Tony. You *always* showed me how very much, you *love* me. *You* made me feel like I was the *only* woman in the world. Baby, I *love* you so very much. And I have *always* ... *loved* you, *dearly* and *deeply*. And *I will always love you* ... *Tony Dash* ... *Always* ..." Raven's voice broke.

"I *know* how much you love me, beautiful. My mother is dead and gone now, but she was *right*. She once told me that *you* would mean a great deal to *many* people. She said that you would change the lives of many. But you changed *my* life, *more* than you changed *anyone's*. *More* than your millions of fans, *more* than *all* of the people who love you, and look up to you, *more* than *all* of the poor that you've helped, and that you're *still* helping. You're *such* an inspiration to so *many*, my love. I learned *so* much from *you*. You *are*, *truly*, an *extraordinary* woman, *Mrs. Dash*." Tony smiled before going on. "Raven, you have *always* been so *beautiful*. *Always*, so very *lovely*. And even *now*, that we're in our *golden* years, you've aged so *gracefully*. You're *extremely* beautiful on the inside too, as you've *always* been. My mother also said that we would grow old together, and she was right about that too. *God* has been *so* good to *us*, beautiful. He's been so *very* good to *us*."

Raven nodded again. She was overwhelmed with grief.

"*Oh … beautiful*, I could *never* put into words, how *much* I *love* you. *Never*. The woman, the person, *my* wife. You have *always*, made *every* moment of *my* life, *worth* living. You were *always* … the *best* part of *my* day. And you were *certainly*, the very *best* part, of *my* life. *You* made *every* day, seem like *Christmas*." Tony smiled. "Your *favorite* holiday. I *lived* and *breathed* for *you*, Raven." Tears filled Tony's eyes. He was very weak, but he squeezed Raven's hand, as best he could. He hated to leave her, but he knew that his time, was almost up.

Raven and Tony had never spent one night apart, in all of their many years of marriage. Raven's heart ached, *immensely*. They both knew, this was one journey, that they would *not* be able to take, *together*.

"You and I fit *so* well, *together*," said Tony. "We *stood* the test of time. We *never* took each other for granted. And, we *always*, put each other, *first*. Beautiful, *remember* all of those *many* years ago at the park, what that elderly man told us?" Now, Tony Dash was an elderly man himself. But he had never forgotten what he and Raven were told by the stranger. "That old man was right." Tony didn't wait for Raven to answer, he was getting weaker and weaker. "He told us that, the *only* thing that was *better* than *falling* in love, was *staying*, in love. We did that, *didn't* we, beautiful?"

"*Yes*, my *love*. *We did* that." Raven whispered. There were tears in her voice.

"*You* made it *easy*, to do. I *love* you *more* than life itself, beautiful. I will *always* love you, *Raven. Always* ..."

They shared one last, heartfelt-kiss. As they kissed, they tasted each other's tears.

Tony's eyes reached deep into Raven's. *Everything* that he felt for her, was in his eyes. *All* of the love, admiration, respect, how deeply he cared for *her* ... It pained Tony to see those mesmerizing eyes, that he had looked into for so many years, filled with enormous grief.

"*Our* time, together, is *almost* up, beautiful."

"*Oh ... Tony* ..." Raven kissed his hand. "*Love*, lasts *longer*, than *time. Love* has *no* end, time *does*."

Tony nodded his head in agreement, as he continued to look at the woman, who had always been so full of beauty and wisdom. His eyes rested on the woman, who had brought him *immeasurable-*happiness, for so many years. Tony looked into those wise and beautiful eyes of Raven's. "*Always remember, beautiful, home is where the heart is, and my heart, will always, be with you. I'll be watching* over *you. And I will* be *waiting* in the wings, *for my beautiful angel ... The most beautiful one of all. The love of my life ... Ra-ven. Thank you ... so ver-y much. I will love you ... al-ways ... Ra-ven ... Al-ways ... Ra-ven* ..." Their eyes locked and held. Tony's eyes never left Raven's, as he closed his. *Finally.* Those were Tony Dash's last words.

"*Always ... Tony ... my ... Prince Charming ... Tony Dash. Thank you. Thank you* for *all* of the love, happiness, and joy, that you brought *me*. For *so ... many* years." Raven was overwhelmed with grief. "*Oh ... God!*" she screamed. "*Oh ... God! Please God! Help, me! Help me, God! Oh ... God! Oh ... God* ..."

It was the *darkest* day, of Raven's life.

When Raven cried out, the enormous pain, grief, and devastation, could be heard in her voice. It was the cry of a woman, who had lost someone who had meant *everything* to her, someone who was nearest, and dearest, to her heart.

Simone and the medical staff quickly ran into Tony's room. They knew that Tony had died.

Raven waved them all away, including her niece, Simone, who was reluctant to leave at first. She wanted to be there for her aunt.

"*Please* ..." Raven told them all. "I *want* to be *alone* ... with ... *my husband.*"

"Aunt Raven ..." Simone cried.

"We're very *sorry*, Mrs. Dash," said Dr. Werner. "We are very *sorry* ..."

The old lady nodded, as tears fell from her eyes like heavy rain.

Everyone reluctantly left the room, granting Raven her wish. They wanted to put their arms around the old woman, to comfort her, but the *only* arms Raven wanted around her, were *Tony's*, the arms that had held *her*, for *seventy-one years*.

* * * * *

Chapter 12

Raven sat beside her husband's hospital bed for hours, with his hands in hers. Tony's body was still there, but his spirit had left. Tears continued to fall from the old woman's eyes like heavy rain, as she thought of all the wonderful and unforgettable times that they had shared over the years. *Many* years. Raven smiled through her tears. Theirs was a marriage that was as close to a fairy-tale as any could get. But their marriage was *real*, and so very wonderful! They were so much in love. They loved each other deeply and dearly. And, *unconditionally*.

Tony was right, they had also *stayed* in love. Raven looked at the man lying in the hospital bed. Tony had left his heart, with her.

The old woman grieved heavily for the man, who had always loved and cherished her. The wonderful man who had *always*, treated her like a queen. Raven grieved for everything that Tony was to her. Husband, soul mate, best friend, lover, her biggest fan, her rock, her support system ... He had been so *many* wonderful things to her. For many, many years. Tony Dash, had been her *everything*. He had also walked the walk, all of the way, until God took him. But, before He took him, He had given them many years of marital-bliss. They were *very* blessed.

Raven's thoughts went back to when she had cancer, and she had lost all of her hair. Tony proved that he loved *her*, not her hair. He proved that he loved her *unconditionally*, time and time again.

The old woman found her voice. "*Oh ... my dearest ... Tony ...* What a wonderfully-*amazing* man you were, *my* love." Raven's heart ached like never before.

Raven sat beside Tony's hospital bed for hours, reminiscencing, thinking back. She continued looking at the man, who had made her so very happy for so *many* years. She looked at the man who had loved her *more* than life itself. He was so loving, caring, kind ... *Tony Dash*, was a great man. The *greatest*.

Tony had always made Raven feel very special. He had always made her feel like she was the only woman in the world. He'd always treated her like royalty. He had *never* stopped courting her. Tony Dash was a man who knew a woman's worth. *Truly*. There was never a doubt in Raven's mind, how much Tony loved and appreciated her. He had always cherished her.

"My *dearest* love, my *sweet* Tony, our love will *never* die. I *will* see you again, someday." Raven knew that she was going to miss Tony, *every* single *moment*, of the *rest*, of her days. They had loved each other for so very long. And now, Raven faced the hardest challenge of her life, living, without her *beloved* Tony. Her, *Prince Charming*.

The old lady smiled through her tears. She wouldn't have traded all of the years that they had shared, for *anything* in the world. What she and Tony had was very rare. It was precious, and it was certainly priceless. Raven was grateful that Tony's wish of being able to say good-bye to her, had been granted by God. She also felt comfort knowing that Tony knew how very much she loved him, and how very much she had always loved him. And God knows she *always* knew, how very much, he *loved* her. She and Tony didn't just say that they loved each other, they had always *shown* each other.

"*Oh ... Tony ... my love*. As I told you so long ago, you have my heart, and you *always* will. Not even death can change that. You will *always* be right *here*," said Raven. The old lady placed her hand over her heart. "*Right ... here.*"

The old lady stood up, finally. She looked down at her husband, for one last time. And for the first time in Raven's life, she wished that life were a fairy-tale. If only, for a *moment.* She wished that she could kiss her Prince Charming, and wake him up, bring him *back* to life. But she knew that life wasn't a fairy-tale, and she knew that death was the end of life, at least here on this earth. She and Tony had given their lives and souls to God, so Raven knew where her husband was now. He was no longer sick or weak. He was never going to suffer or die again. The love of her life was now in the *best* of hands.

Raven thanked God. She had so much to thank Him for. Yes, He had taken her husband, and now she was heartbroken and grief-stricken, beyond words. But the wise old lady was ever-so thankful and grateful, for what God had also done. He had put them together. He had also *kept* them together, for many long and happy years. The kind of marriage that she and Tony had was few and far between. Theirs was *truly* a match, made in heaven.

Raven bent down and kissed her husband, tenderly. Then, the old lady, slowly, walked out of the hospital room. Raven's heart, had *never* been so heavy. It felt as if a bowling ball, was on her heart.

* * *

Tony Dash's funeral was private. It was what he had wanted.

Raven made sure that her husband's *Home Going* was a *celebration of his life*.

Although Tony's funeral was private, it was still huge. He was very well-known. Many came to pay their respects. They came to say good-bye to the remarkable man, who was well-loved and admired, and who had done so many incredible things, on and off the football field, and in the business world.

He was the greatest NFL running back, turned billionaire businessman, to *them*, but what Tony Dash was to the old woman who sat on the front row, was priceless, and could never be put into words. What he was to *her*, didn't have *anything* to do with celebrity-status, sports, business deals, or money.

Raven wore a black suit and hat, with a veil, that covered her dark eyes. She listened to all of the countless, wonderful remarks, that were made about her husband. No one knew him, better than she. And Tony had meant far more to her, than he had meant to anyone. No one felt his loss, more than the old lady. But Raven knew that they all meant well. And she appreciated their kind words and support.

Raven didn't speak at her beloved Tony's funeral. The old lady just sat, with an immensely-heavy heart, grief-stricken, as tears streamed down her face, nonstop.

Her niece sat beside her. Simone kept her arm around her aunt. She was there to comfort her "Aunt Raven."

Brunner sat on the other side of Raven. He comforted her too, as he cried, like many in attendance. So many were going to miss Tony Dash. *A lot*. He was just that kind of a man. And what a wonderful man he was!

Raven looked at her husband, for the last time, before his casket was closed. He looked so very handsome. And peaceful. Tony looked like he was asleep. Raven bent down and kissed her husband, for the *last* time. Her voice cracked, as she whispered the words ... "You're in *my* heart, *always* ... I *love* you very much, Tony Dash. *My*

... *Prince Charming*. I will *always* love you ... I'll meet you in the wings, one day. I will *love* you *always* ... *Tony*. *Always* ..."

Simone and Brunner stood on both sides of Raven, giving her the support, that they knew she so badly needed. Simone knew that this was the most difficult time of her aunt's life. She had never seen her aunt so devastated.

Simone looked at her aunt with great love and admiration. She was an extraordinary woman. Her Aunt Raven was a rock to her and for so many others, now it was their turn to be a rock for her. Her aunt's strength was immeasurable. Simone never understood where it came from. She felt that if she had some of her aunt's strength, she would be okay. Simone recalled her aunt telling her that "strength comes in many forms." She had always loved her aunt's wisdom too.

Raven received a massive amount of support from many people in the area, and worldwide. The old lady was showered with flowers, cards, and kind words. She was very grateful, but she knew that God, prayer, and time, would be the *only* soothers.

* * *

Raven was quiet most of the time. It pained her to look at the many photos of Tony. It also pained her to look at the photos of the two of them, together. But Raven refused to remove the photos. She missed Tony so much. Raven would walk into Tony's closet and smell his clothes. His scent was still there. Raven cried most of the time, as she prayed for strength. The kind of strength that only One, could give.

Simone remained with Raven. She had recently gotten divorced. She wanted to talk with her aunt about her own life, but for now, she had to think of her Aunt Raven. She was her priority now. Simone decided that once her aunt started feeling better, then they would talk.

Although Simone was there with her aunt, she also honored her aunt's wishes. Sometimes Raven needed, and wanted, to be left alone.

* * *

Raven would often lie in bed at night, thinking of, and missing Tony, so much. Her heart ached like *never* before. There were no words to describe her heartache. Things were very different, without *him*. Very different. The old lady knew that things would never be the same, again.

Raven hadn't slept by herself since she'd left the Summerwood Apartments, all of those many years ago, when she and Tony had gotten married. Unbelievable, the old woman continued to think. Where had *all* the years gone?

Thinking of the Summerwood Apartments, made her think of Becky. "Oh … *Beck* …" was all that Raven said. She thought of how young Becky was when she died. She'd had her whole life ahead of her. She had missed out on so many wonderful things that life had to offer. Raven continued to think about her other *sister. Rebecca Simms*.

The old lady continued to think. Unlike Becky's short life, Tony's life had been long. God had allowed him to live to be one hundred and one years old. Tony Dash had lived a long, healthy, and happy life. The old lady laughed to herself, it still wasn't long enough for her. Words couldn't express how very much she missed her husband. *Everything*, reminded Raven of Tony. And *nothing*, was the same, without *him*. Nor would it *ever* be.

Raven knew that she had to go on living. And she knew that Tony was still living, and would *always* live, in her heart. Raven always felt her husband's presence. It was as if he were *still* there with her, watching over her. Keeping watch over, *his* beautiful Raven. The old woman smiled through her tears. "Oh … *Tony* … I will *always* love *you*. My king … *my* Prince Charming. *Always* … *Tony* …" Raven whispered through her tears. "*Always!*"

* * *

Because of Tony's celebrity-status, he was featured on the news, often. The media showed countless photos of him. There were pictures of Tony, running with the football, during the days that he had been a superstar running back in college, and in the NFL. The media also showed countless pictures of Raven and Tony. They had even showed some of their wedding pictures. Tears filled Raven's eyes, as she watched Tony. Young, very handsome, dashing ... He was looking down at her, smiling. It was their *wedding* day.

The old lady sat watching. Tears fell, but she told Simone not to change the channel. The photos brought back memories. *Sweet* memories. Memories that she would *never* forget. They were ones that she would *always* cherish.

Raven refused to remove all of the many photos that filled the Malibu home. Removing pictures wouldn't change how much she loved Tony, or how very much, she missed him.

Whenever God took her, they would be together again, with their Father. Raven bought the burial plot right next to Tony's. Raven wanted her and Tony to be *together*, side by side in death, as they had been in life.

Raven visited Tony's grave, frequently. She would sit by his grave and talk to him, for hours. She kept his grave well-maintained, and she also kept pretty flowers on it. She did the same for her mother, father, Angie, Trey, Becky, and *for all those*, whom she loved, and were now gone. They were gone, but *not* forgotten. And the old lady knew, that she too, would be here one day. Because death, was a part of life, for *everyone*.

* * *

Years passed. Simone was still living with her Aunt Raven. They were just as close as they'd always been. They talked often.

Simone loved watching her aunt's movies. She would watch them, repeatedly. She watched "Aunt Raven" in awe. She beamed at the staggeringly-beautiful woman, who sizzled on-screen. She could easily see why her aunt was the *greatest* to *ever* grace Hollywood. She was astonishing!

Raven and Simone would often eat their meals together. And sometimes, Brunner would join them. Raven was also happy to have him around. He was a very nice man. And he had always been. Raven had known him for a long time. He had worked for her and Tony for years. Brunner was one of their best employees. He reminded Raven a lot of Mack.

"Aunt Raven? We're going to the park today, aren't we?" Simone asked. She loved going to the park with her aunt. She had long since known how much her aunt *loved* parks.

The old lady smiled. "Yes. But we're going to a *different* one today."

They went to the very park, where so many memories had been made. On the way to the park, Raven pointed out the Summerwood Apartments to her niece. "That's where your Aunt Becky and I used to live, so *many* years ago."

It was a gorgeous day. Raven and Simone sat on a bench, drinking soft drinks, and admiring the scenery. The old lady's mind went back to the past. As Raven looked around the park, it was as if she could see her and Tony strolling in the park, hand in hand, young, and so much in love. Her dark eyes danced. There were many *great* memories, that the two of them had shared, in this very place.

Simone watched her aunt. It had been a long time since she'd seen her aunt's trademark smile. "Aunt Raven, you're *glowing*!"

The old woman flashed that dazzling, trademark smile of hers. Age, had not changed that. "*Yes*, I am." Raven told her niece about the time when Tony had surprised her with a picnic. "It was the very *first* time that we had come here together. In fact, it was our *second* date."

Simone smiled. Her aunt had always had a photographic memory. Simone told her aunt that she had always wanted a marriage like theirs. Theirs seemed so very special, and they also seemed very happy. "You don't often see marriages like that anymore. Like yours and Uncle Tony's." Simone told her aunt.

Her Aunt Raven agreed. "You're *right* about that, young lady. Many don't stay married for *six* days, let alone sixty-nine years. We were very much in love, and very happy too. Marital-bliss. *Truly*."

"What was your and Uncle Tony's secret for having *such* a happy and solid relationship?" Simone wanted to know.

"Tony and I didn't just invite Jesus to our wedding, we kept *Him* in our *marriage*. The ceremony is *minor*, the *marriage*, is of *utmost* importance. The key ingredients that I have always told you about are very important. Everyone is different. We have always heard that opposites attract, but *similarities*, bond. And bonding is *very* essential. Attraction is *not* enough. Tony and I were very physically attracted to each other, but far greater than that, was the *immensely-* strong, *emotional* connection, bond, that he and I shared. We grew, *together*. We didn't grow apart, as some do. Tony and I also *cherished* each other. That's also very important. The *right* person makes *all* of the difference. Oftentimes, two people marry, and they're not right for each other. It's important that it's the right fit. Never force it, because if you do, it will always come back to haunt you. If it's *right*, you won't have to force anything, *everything*, will come naturally. Tony and I enjoyed each other's company too. We had *a lot* of fun together. Tony *never* stopped courting me. We shared our innermost thoughts and feelings. Your Uncle Tony and I were also *best* friends. And *most* importantly, God, the matchmaker of *all* matchmakers, put us together. He also kept us, *together*."

"Uncle Tony loved you so much, Aunt Raven. He treated you like a *queen*."

The old lady smiled. "Yes, Tony loved me *very* much. And yes, he also treated me as if I were the only woman in the world. He treated me like royalty. And to be candid, young lady, I wouldn't have allowed him to treat me *any* other way."

"Aunt Raven? Did you know that your marriage would last 'til death did you'll apart?"

The timeless-beauty shook her head. "No, young lady, I didn't. *No one* knows that. There are very few things in life that come with guarantees. Death, is the *one* thing, that we can all be certain of."

Simone told her aunt that she wanted to marry again, but she didn't know if that would ever happen. Simone was getting impatient. It had been years since her divorce, and she was ready for a relationship. "Am I going to the *wrong* places, Aunt Raven?" Simone asked.

Raven laughed. "Simone, *don't* go looking for him. The man *finds* the woman. That's *Bible*. If it's God's will that you get married again, in God's *own* time, He will *send* the man, to *you*. God *knows* your name. He *knows* your address. He knows *everything* about you. He made you. So *relax*, and try *not* to think about it. You don't have to run in front of a car, or do *anything* dangerous, or *drastic*. If you're a good catch, you are bound to get caught. Sometimes, things, or *people*, in *this* case, come when we're not looking, when we're not dwelling on it. *Believe* me, he'll find you. And it doesn't matter where you are either. When the right time comes, he *will*, find *you*. God has His time set for you, young lady. He doesn't go by *our* time. God goes by *His* time. Sometimes we may think that we're ready for something, and we really aren't. He is one Father, who knows *best*. He also knows *everything*. So *trust* Him, sweetheart."

"But Aunt Raven, today's times are *different*. Women are pursuing men now. Females are very aggressive today."

The old woman looked at her niece. "Young lady, that's where many of today's problems lie. Human beings are making their own rules, and doing their *own* thing, instead of doing it *God's* way. I will say *again*, that the man, *finds* the woman. God knows all. God is *not*, nor will He *ever* be, out of *style*. Just think, Simone. The Bible has been around for many years, before we were even born. Yet... the Bible is *fulfilling*. Wars and rumors of wars, is that not happening today?"

Simone nodded. Her aunt always made her think.

"When a woman gives birth to a child, she goes through pain. These were *God's* words, so you see, it speaks for itself. God spoke these things, before they even happened. And they are *still* happening. *Now*. *Today*. Just as He said they would. He's the same God, Simone. He *hasn't* changed. Nor has His word changed. He *still* speaks and knows, *all* things. Young lady, man, will *never* be ahead of God. A man is not greater than His maker, sweetheart. We are peons. We humans aren't even in God's league. And as I stated earlier, when humans start doing things *their* way, that's when disaster strikes. Look at the shape the world is in now. I have *never* seen the world in such terrible shape. Never! And it's getting worse and worse every day. It's not getting better. Always listen to *God*, Simone, *not* man. Unlike some human beings, God doesn't think that He knows it all, He *does*, know it all. That's why we need to seek guidance from Him. If *anyone* knows what is best for us, God does."

Simone looked at her aunt. She was so incredibly-wise. "You're right, Aunt Raven. See, that's why I *need* you. You keep me on the *right* track. You also make me think about things that I've never thought of before. I can't say enough about your wisdom and insight. Aunt Raven, I hope these questions aren't stupid."

"No, Simone. There is no such thing as a *stupid* question. Just ask away. You know that I don't mind. As far as I'm concerned, what's stupid, is *not* asking. Especially, if you don't know the answer."

Simone nodded. "Aunt Raven? Losing Uncle Tony was very difficult for you, wasn't it?"

The old lady nodded her head. "Oh, *yes*, sweetheart. It was *extremely* difficult. My heart had *never* ached so immensely. But, *all* things come to an end. We always hate to see good things, or *great* things, come to a close. However, to *everything*, there is an end. Tony and I were like two hearts that beat as one. You can't get any closer to anyone than that. But God was so very good to us. He didn't have to give us seventy-one long, and *joyous* years together, but He did. Not everyone can say that. There are people who lost a spouse after just a few years of marriage. That's why in *all* things, we should give thanks. As Paul said."

"You and Uncle Tony were married for sixty-nine years, right?"

"Yes. We dated for two years, and we were married for sixty-nine years. We were an item, for *seventy-one years*."

"Wow, that's a very *long* time."

The old lady smiled. "It sure is."

"Aunt Raven, what was Aunt Becky like?" Simone had never asked her aunt about Becky. She knew the two women were very close though.

Raven smiled. "Sweetheart, your Aunt Becky was an *incredible* woman. She had a heart of *gold*. Beck was a very *loving* and giving person. She would help you in *any* way that she could. She was beautiful on the outside, and on the inside. I can still see her long, golden-blonde hair, and *those* big, sky-blue eyes of hers. And her big, bright smile."

"The two of you were close, weren't you, Aunt Raven?"

"*Yes*, Simone, we sure were. Beck and I were very close. I couldn't have loved Rebecca Simms more, if we were *blood* sisters. She's in my heart, like all of those who are gone now. They are gone, but they're *not* forgotten. Nor will they *ever* be."

Simone was silent for a few minutes, before she asked her next question. "Do you think that chivalry is dead? Well, in your case, Uncle Tony treated you like royalty. My ex-husband was awful! A lot of men treat women like dirt. There is so much physical, verbal, and mental abuse. I often wonder about what if."

"*Correction*, they're *not* men, they're *males*. There is a *difference* between the two. And sweetheart, it's not what *if*, it's what *is*. *Always* remember that. People will often do what they can get away with doing. Your Uncle Tony *treated* me like a lady, because I *acted* like one. And, again, I would not have allowed him, or anyone else, to treat me *any* other way. Simone, always remember, people can dish whatever they want to out, but you don't have to take it. And if you do take it, then you're sending them a message that it's *okay* for them to treat you that way, and they will often continue treating you badly. And *if* they treat you badly, it's also a sign that they don't care about you either. If you love someone, you're not going to treat them badly, even if they allowed you to. *You*, *teach* people how to treat you."

Simone nodded, as she looked into her aunt's dark eyes. She saw lots of wisdom there. Raven was obviously a woman who had seen, and learned, a whole lot.

"Speaking of my ex-husband, we had a very nasty divorce, Aunt Raven."

Simone was married to a very prominent lawyer who owned his own law firm. She received a seventeen-million-dollar divorce settlement. Simone had also been given their large, tudor-style home in the Hamptons. She would also receive fifty percent of all future profits from her ex-husband's law firm. Simone never had to work again. She was set for life.

Her aunt laughed. "Nasty divorce? *Hmmm* ...You received half of *everything*? Sounds like a *Hollywood* divorce to me!"

Simone laughed. "Aunt Raven, speaking of Hollywood, I've seen all of your movies. You were a *knockout* when you were young! Not that you're not good-looking now. You've aged very gracefully. You know what I mean, Aunt Raven."

The old lady smiled and nodded. "I know what you mean, sweetheart. I'm still in *good* running condition."

The two women laughed.

"I hope that I'm as fortunate. I bet you had the men's hearts racing!"

Raven laughed in answer.

"Aunt Raven ... you are *stunning*. I know you drove the men *crazy*. So many people refer to you as *the* staggeringly-beautiful and *sultry*-movie goddess. What does being *sexy* mean to you?"

"Sexiness, like with *everything* else, comes from *within*. Sexiness isn't found in a dress size. Nor is it found in lack of clothing. Scantily-clad outfits. What's in you, will often show on the outside. It's *not* what you're wearing, or not wearing, that makes one sexy. As I have always shown, you *can* leave things to the imagination, and *still* be sexy. Very sexy. The same thing with class. A person can have on the *most* expensive attire, and not have an *ounce* of class. Clothes don't make the person. Money *doesn't* make the man either. The *person*, makes or breaks the person."

Simone listened to her aunt. She took everything in. She had always loved her aunt's confidence too. And she told her as much. "You were *always* confident, Aunt Raven."

"Yes, *still* am," said the old woman. "Confidence is extremely important, *especially*, *self*-confidence. So is *self*-love."

"Aunt Raven? You never took off your clothes in movies. Was that *your* choice?"

"Yes. It was definitely *my* choice."

"Many actresses show *everything*. What do you think about that?" Simone asked.

"That's certainly *their* choice. But, that was never me. I wasn't one to do that. I remember what my mother told me before I left for Hollywood. She said, 'Be *you*. Be Raven, Raven Kensington.' That's who I was. I would not have been happy being *anyone*, but me. Always be who you are, not what others want you to be. Always be *true* to yourself. I had already decided that if I was going to make it, it would be on *my* terms. And it would be the *right* way. I saw Hollywood's terms and conditions, and they were *appalling*. I have always enjoyed acting, even before I got paid for it. I loved bringing my fans joy. Again, my focus was on being the best *actress*, that ever graced Hollywood, not the best stripper."

Simone laughed hard at her very wise and witty aunt.

Raven went on, "But to each their own, whatever floats your boat. Their choice was, and *is*, their choice, and my choice, was *my* choice."

Simone looked at her aunt with sheer admiration. Aunt Raven always had high standards. Her aunt was a woman who took the high road. Simone smiled, her aunt was a very high-class lady. She was the *classiest*.

"Not only are you immensely-beautiful and classy, you're also a fighter, Aunt Raven. I can't say enough about *that*."

Her aunt smiled. "I've never been one to accept *anything* just because someone said so. Especially, if it was wrong."

"That makes sense. Aunt Raven, why do you think Halle Berry cried so hard when she won an Oscar in 2002?"

"I feel that she cried for all of those wonderfully-talented black actresses who came before her, who should have received that *same* award, but, because of the *color* of their skin, they didn't receive it. I also think that she cried because it took seventy-four years, for a woman of color, to receive that award. It was more than enough to make *anyone* cry. Racism is disgusting, among other things. Grant it, things are better than they used to be, but they are *still* not nearly, where they *need* to be."

Her niece nodded her head in agreement. Simone asked her aunt about her R.K. by Design stores.

Raven told her that she and Tony sold the stores a little before she left Hollywood. The new owner retained the name. The stores were still very profitable.

"Aunt Raven, why didn't you and Uncle Tony *ever* have children? You would have been the *best* mother."

"Aunt Ruth always told me that. A baby changes everything. We were extremely busy with our careers, and if I would have become a mother, I would have devoted all of my time to our child, or children. I refused to have them and let a nanny raise them. Your Uncle Tony and I were both happy with each other, and the way our lives were, so we kept it that way. I don't have any regrets. I don't think he did either."

* * *

The two women continued to talk. Raven gave her niece more advice. "Always, *stop*, and take time out to enjoy life. And *always*, take time out to enjoy the ones you love. Never take life, or people, for granted. I liken it to planting a beautiful garden, and never taking time out to stop and smell the roses. So oftentimes, we don't. And before you know it, life passes us by. You only get one life on this earth. This is it! No one can turn back the hands of time. That's another thing that your Uncle Tony and I had in common, no matter how busy we were, we were *never* too busy, for each other. We *always* took time out to enjoy life, and each other. And despite how successful we became, we never used that as an excuse. Our work, our careers, revolved around our marriage. It wasn't the other way around, like so many are today. Tony, was my life, not acting. Or Hollywood. There are a number of very important things that money, and no amount of success, can buy or replace. Time, and life. They are both priceless, and very special. Life is short, it's precious, and it's a gift from God. No one is here by accident. We all have a purpose. We don't get to choose how, or when, we die, but we *do* get to choose, how we live."

Simone sat, taking in all of her aunt's wisdom. She hung on Raven's every word.

Raven Kensington's mind was still incredibly-sharp, even in her old age. "And oh yes," said Raven, as if it were an afterthought, "remember to *laugh* and have fun. Not everyone has a sense of humor, but it helps a lot to have one. It can help a great deal in life. It certainly helped me."

Simone nodded. "Aunt Raven, do you think if more blacks were in power positions, things would be better for other blacks?"

Raven shook her head no. "Not necessarily. It depends on the person who is in power, not his or her race. Although I would love to see more blacks in the driver's seat. We pay our fares, and we deserve to be in power positions. However, it's not a guarantee that just because a person is the same race as you are, that they're going to help you. I have helped, and I still help, many people of *all* races. And when I was a member of the Academy Awards panel, I would cast my votes for the *best* acting performances. The race of the actor, or actress, was irrelevant to me. And that is the way that it should be, and the way that it should have *always* been. If I couldn't look past an actor's race, I would have removed myself from the panel. I have never asked of anyone, what I wouldn't ask and demand of myself. I believe strongly, in practicing what I preach."

"Regarding the size thing in Hollywood, Aunt Raven, you did more than anyone in that department. No one made the impact that you made. You were the *most* successful actress that *ever* graced Hollywood. *No one* has ever reached the heights that you reached,

Aunt Raven. *No one.* That says a whole lot. I'm so very proud of you!" Simone had always been very proud of her aunt. "You accomplished so much. You made history in so *many* ways."

The old lady nodded. "Yes, sweetheart. But I didn't do all of the many things that I did, to make history. I did them, to make a *difference.* Making a difference, helping people, was *always* very important to me. Still is."

"Did you enjoy writing your autobiography, Aunt Raven?"

"Yes, sweetheart, I certainly did. *Every* life, has a story," said Raven.

Simone started talking about relationships again. "I hope that my second marriage is much better than my first."

"Sweetheart, it can be. I'm sure that there were warning signs, red flags, before you married Lark, weren't there?"

Simone nodded her head yes. "Yes, ma'am, there were. But, I loved him."

"Sweetheart, always take heed to warning signs. They are there for a reason. Oftentimes, we will keep walking towards danger instead of turning around and going the other way. When two people meet, it's very important that they get to know each other. And looks are irrelevant. You see instantly how the other looks. You can see that right away. But the important thing is seeing, and knowing, how the person *is.* It's the things that can't be seen, except with time, that you need to pay close attention to. Time reveals *all* things. *Always* get to know who a person *really* is, before marrying them. You should both get to know each other very well, *before* hand. If a person is right for you, it will feel right. If it doesn't feel right, more than likely that's because it's the wrong person. If it doesn't fit, don't force it, let it go. It's like before we purchase shoes, for example, you know that if the shoe is too tight, or too loose, it's not the right shoe for you. Therefore, it would be very foolish to buy the shoe anyway. The only one that will feel right, is the one that *is* right. You will know it, because again, you will *feel* it. *Especially*, in your heart."

* * *

"I want that perfect man to come along. I want to have that *perfect* marriage, like yours and Uncle Tony's."

The old lady laughed. "No wonder you're still single!"

Simone laughed hard.

"Young lady, if you're waiting on the *perfect* man to come along, you will be waiting forever. Sweetheart, the perfect man, will *never* come along, because he doesn't exist. Human beings are *not* perfect. Therefore, there is no such thing as *the* perfect relationship either. Your Uncle Tony and I had an incredibly-strong, loving, solid, and immensely-happy marriage, but it wasn't perfect, because we weren't perfect."

Simone told her aunt that she thought she could change Lark.

"That's another very common mistake. Very seldom will a leopard change his or her spots. If you're not willing to accept all of their flaws, then by all means, don't move forward. We all have flaws. No one will like everything about anyone, but we must truly accept them, if we are to be happy. If whatever it is bothers you a lot during the courtship, then that's a sign not to go on and marry that person. It's not going to change, after you marry him, that's for sure."

"Aunt Raven, people can change, can't they?"

"Of course they can, sweetheart. But do they? Not always. It's completely up to them. The one and only person that anyone can change, is *self*. We can't change others. That's another big mistake that we often make, thinking that we can change someone."

"Sometimes, doing the right thing can be confusing," said Simone.

"Not if you follow your heart. Listen to your heart. The answer lies in you. The answer lies in all of us. Always, follow your heart. It won't steer you wrong. Your heart, is the *best* compass that you have. The heart, is *much* wiser, than the head."

"Aunt Raven, I was *so* devastated when my marriage ended. At times I wondered how I would go on without Lark. I also allowed Lark to mistreat me for years. He was physically and verbally abusive for many years. I didn't understand why he treated me like that."

"Many people aren't happy to see their marriages end. Most go into marriages thinking that the marriage will last, 'til death do them part. Whenever you lose anyone that you love, you're definitely going to feel it. You will go through a great deal of pain, especially your heart. Cry as often as you need and want to. That's perfectly okay. Everyone goes through pain differently. Do whatever works for *you*, as long as it's not anything that will be harmful to you. Breaking up is a part of life, and we must deal with things, and move on. Never dwell. Although the right choices make all the difference, we are all human, and we will still make mistakes. Everyone makes mistakes. Always learn from them, but don't beat yourself up over them. Learning from your mistakes can make you a wiser, better, stronger person. You can also grow from disruptions. Positive things can come out of not-so-good things that happen to us in life. Some things we have control over, some we don't. I'm a firm believer that time heals all wounds. Or most, anyway."

The old woman paused, thinking of her husband. It had been fifteen years, since Tony's death, and not a day went by, that Raven didn't think of her beloved Tony, *her* Prince Charming.

"As with any wound, it hurts the most in the beginning. Sweetheart, always remember, you were making it before you met Lark; therefore, you *can* make it without him. Life goes on. Simone, one monkey, doesn't stop the show."

Her niece nodded her head in answer.

"And that last statement you made about wondering why Lark treated you badly, that sounds typical. It is *you*, that you should be questioning. We *must* take responsibility for our lives. You should ask yourself *why* you *allowed* him to mistreat you. That's why self-love is very important. Don't give anyone power and control over you, your life, or your happiness. The devil is powerless. We give him the power that he has, and he uses it against us. He certainly doesn't love us, nor does he mean us any good. *Any* power that the devil has, is *given* to him. By us. The same with Lark, or anyone, sweetheart. It's something how we give people, or things, power over us, and they turn around and destroy us with it. Always remember, Simone, *your* happiness, is in *your* hands, not anyone else's. What's to be, is up to you, and *only* you. Again, *you* teach people, how to treat you. I can't emphasize that enough."

Simone listened intently, her aunt's wisdom left her in awe at times. Simone smiled. "I'll remember that. And as always, your wisdom is food for thought. It's priceless food for the heart and soul. Everything that you've told me, Aunt Raven, will be forever stored in my memory bank. Aunt Raven, no matter how incredibly-successful you became, I have never seen you look down on anyone."

"No, I have never done that. Only God sits that high. A person's net worth doesn't have anything to do with their *real* worth. Your bank account doesn't make you bigger, and or better, than anyone else. Nothing does! No one, is better than anyone else. Everyone is a VIP, very important person, in my eyes. In God's eyes too. One didn't have to be a star, to be in my show. I have always loved that song."

Simone looked at her aunt with great love and admiration. "You've helped so many people, and you still help a lot of people, all over the world."

The ageless-beauty nodded. "Being successful in my eyes, meant making *others* successful too. After all," Raven laughed, "you can only buy so many pairs of shoes."

Simone laughed hard.

"It's a lot more to success than material things. It's the things that money can't buy, that bring the *most* joy and happiness. Helping people, and making a difference in the lives of others, is a great feeling! It's *so* enriching. And it doesn't matter who you are, or how much money you have, *someone* helped you along the way. It's so unfortunate that some forget where they came from. They never seem to keep in mind that none of us knows where we're going, or *who* we might need. Sometimes, the ones that you have treated badly, or looked over, may be the very ones that you might have to look at, one day. We never know. It's great to have money. But I've never let money control me, neither did Tony. We were alike in so many ways. I've seen some rich people grip their hands tight. Some never help others, especially those less fortunate. But the one thing about a closed hand, no money goes out, but none comes in either. Your Uncle Tony and I gave a lot. We always gave from our hearts too. God paid us. He blessed Tony and me, again and again. It was as if when we gave, God gave it back to us, tenfold. Tony's many businesses, my R.K. by Design stores, my unmatched-acting career ... It seemed everything that we touched, turned to gold. The world would be a much better place, if we all loved, and helped, one another. In life, it's not what we get, it's what we *give*, that makes *all* the difference."

Simone smiled and nodded. Her aunt's heart and wisdom were immense. "Aunt Raven? What are your thoughts on temptations?"

"We all have them, sweetheart. Even Jesus was tempted. As it says in the Bible, *flee* temptation, don't yield to it. We should never put *anything* in front of us, that we shouldn't have *inside* of us. Be it drugs, sex, gambling, whatever the temptation may be. Temptations differ. Not everyone is tempted by the same thing. Never flirt with temptation. Never flirt with the devil either. If you give the devil an inch, he will take more than a yard, he will become, your ruler."

"Aunt Raven? Is walking away from something a sign of weakness?"

"No, honey, it's not. It's not always walking towards something that shows how strong you are, sometimes it's having the strength, to walk away."

"Aunt Raven, I read your autobiography. You went through *a lot* in Hollywood early on. But you *never* gave up, you kept fighting. You are one *tough* cookie, Aunt Raven!"

The old lady flashed that trademark smile of hers. "It's *hard* to stop a train!"

* * *

Simone laughed. "It sure is, Aunt Raven. It sure is!"

"Never let anyone, or anything, stop you from making your dreams come true. Stick to your guns. *Always, believe in you. Always, resist* the word, *can't.*"

"You gave a lot of time and money to hospice."

"Yes, I did. I really appreciated what hospice did for Daddy, when he was diagnosed with cancer. What they did for him, and our family, was priceless."

"What exactly is hospice, Aunt Raven?"

"I didn't know a lot about hospice either, until Daddy got sick. Hospice is a very *special* concept of care. Hospice provides medical and emotional care, for the terminally-ill, and their families."

"I've heard of Elisabeth Kubler-Ross."

Raven nodded. "Yes. *Remarkable* lady. She was largely responsible for bringing the hospice movement to the United States. A British doctor, Dr. Cicely Saunders, started the hospice movement in the 1960s, near London."

"Aunt Raven, why didn't you think less of me when I told you about all of the horrible things that I've done in my life? They are things that I'm definitely not proud of. I'm also ashamed of some of the things that I've done."

"Sweetheart, I have also done horrible things in my life. There is not anyone living in this world, or in the grave, that has never done horrible or shameful things. Life isn't a game of tag. Just because you've done *it*, it doesn't mean that you *are* it. The great thing about life, is that an experience doesn't define you. Never define who you are, by something that you have done. And never let *people*, define you. There is bad in the best of us, and there is good, in the worst of us. The One who can show you who you *really* are, is God."

"Aunt Raven, you are *incredibly*-wise. You're a great inspiration too. Thank you for *always* being there for me. I don't know what I would do without *you*." Simone gave her aunt a big hug.

* * *

"I'm here for you, sweetheart. And if ever there comes a day when I'm not here, and that day *will* come, my words and actions will always be. And when, or if, you *ever* need guidance, always follow the Son. He will guide you *far* better than anyone. He's the very *best*. Let God be your steering wheel, not just your spare tire."

Simone continued to marvel at her aunt's wisdom. She took everything in. She had always loved the fact that "Aunt Raven" always made things *crystal*-clear. She never left you hanging, there were seldom "yes" or "no" answers with her. She always elaborated to make sure that you understood exactly what she was telling you. That was obviously very important to her.

"The race card? What do you think about whites who say that blacks or other minorities often use the race card, especially in the courtrooms? I don't mean to sound like twenty questions, but I love and trust your wisdom, Aunt Raven."

The old lady smiled. "Not a problem. Asking questions is how we get answers. All of these questions aren't bothering me in the least. If they were, you know me, I would tell you. Now, in answer to your question, as I have said before, and as I have also seen, in all of my many days, race, was usually an issue. Very seldom is it not. Even now. I think that race will always be an issue. To say that blacks bring up race, well, it's hard not to. Many times it's very obvious. There are exceptions when race amazingly may not be an issue, but they are very few, and far between. The majority of the time, race *is* an issue, and nine times out of ten, it will always be. We can even look at the justice system, which is *still* an injustice to blacks. We still see blacks who commit the same crimes as whites, punished more harshly. They often serve longer prison terms. Injustice, discrimination. Words can't describe how horrible those things are. To this day, they still exist. That, my child, is reality. The package that anyone comes in, should be appreciated by them, if by no one else. As African-Americans, we are a race who have suffered and conquered so much, good and bad, for *so* long, and we still do. However, *no* amount of terror that our ancestors experienced in slavery, no injustice of any kind, *nothing*, will *ever* change the fact, that we come from *greatness*."

Simone told her aunt that she often had a fear of failure, and therefore, she was often afraid to take risks.

"We all have fears, but never let your fears overtake you, or cripple you. That's not good, nor is it healthy. Sometimes we have to throw caution to the winds. And remember sweetheart, sometimes the greatest risk, is *not* taking one. We have to *step* out, in order to *find* out. We will never know otherwise."

"True. The kind of cancer that you had was non-Hodgkin lymphoma, wasn't it?"

The old lady nodded. "Yes, sweetheart, it was."

"Didn't Jackie Kennedy have the same kind of cancer?"

"Yes, she did."

"She died about six months after being diagnosed, didn't she?"

"I think so. I do know that God is truly, *amazing*. He allowed me to live countless years after my diagnosis. *All* things, are in His hands. There isn't a day that goes by, that I don't *thank* God for healing me. It's great to have a Father, who can do *anything*."

Simone brought up her ex-husband again. "Aunt Raven, it's very hard for me to forgive Lark. He did so many horrible things to me."

"We *must* forgive, Simone. If we don't forgive others, God won't forgive us. Oftentimes, when it comes to forgiving those who have wronged us, we want to make them pay. We also want them to pay, *now*. Right now, not later. Many of us think that if *we* don't make them pay, they won't get paid. But they will, sweetheart. They *will* get paid. By God. Vengeance, is the Lord's. Believe you me, no one, can do anything, like God can. *No one*."

"It's hard, Aunt Raven. And you're right, I do want him to pay for what he's done to me, now. Right *now*."

"Forgiveness, can sometimes be hard, but it's not impossible. And as a *wise* pastor once told me, *in God's own time*. So, I'll say this to you, sweetheart, Lark will get paid, in God's own time. Not your time, not my time, or anyone else's time. God knows best. And

He knows *all* things. He has His time set for all things. He has His time set for all of us. We will *all* reap what we sow. You're damaging yourself, by not forgiving Lark. The hate that you feel for him is eating you up, not Lark. Let it go. Take it to God, and leave it there. If you do that, you'll be able to forgive your ex-husband. You'll see. You have to let it go, sweetheart. Lark could be getting his due now. Who knows?"

Simone gave her aunt a big hug. "Thanks, Aunt Raven! You have always put things in ways that made me understand very clearly. You've always made me think. I will pray regarding this. When I was little, I used to think that if you went to church, you were a Christian."

The old lady laughed. "There are many *adults* who think the same thing. Going to church, has never, nor will it ever, make *anyone* a Christian. There are a lot of *churchgoers* in this world. *Christianity is not* about *church-membership*. It's also *more* than praying, or saying that you're a Christian. It's in one's *actions*. The evidence, that someone is a Christian, is in their *actions*, sweetheart. It's not in the talk, but as always, it's in the walk. Our actions, the works that we do. How we live seven days a week, 24 hours a day. How we live, what we do, when we think no one's watching. Your actions, will always speak for you. Pretending is useless, because *no one* can fool God. He sees, and knows, *everything* that we do. And say. Nothing, is hidden from Him. There are *many* hypocrites, pretenders, many *actors*." The old lady smiled. "I know a *little* somethin' about *acting*."

Simone laughed. "You certainly do, Aunt Raven!"

Raven thought of Tony. Her beloved Tony, her Prince Charming, was still very much alive in her heart. She loved and missed him immensely. She still visited his grave, often. The old lady smiled, knowing that she would see him again one day. Her *beloved* Tony …

"Aunt Raven, there's that smile again! I don't have to ask *who* you're thinking about."

The old woman laughed.

"Aunt Raven, what's the *key* to understanding?"

"*Listening.* With the heart, and with the eyes. Notice that I didn't say ears."

Simone smiled, as she marveled at her aunt's wisdom. "Whatever happened to Andrew Spellman?"

"Andy, the *point* man, died years ago. He died ten years after I left Hollywood. We were good friends. He believed in me when no one in Hollywood would give me a chance. I was always grateful to him because of that. He was always honest with me too. More than a great agent, Andrew Spellman, was a good man. Tony also liked him."

"Your success in Hollywood is unmatched, Aunt Raven."

"To some, success is measured by money, and material things. Not with me. I have always measured my success, by my *service* to *others*. I measure it by what I can *give*, not by what I can *get*. If you give, you will automatically get."

The two women finally left the park and went home, where they joined Brunner for dinner.

After dinner, everyone watched, *Heartless War*.

The old lady smiled, as she watched her very *first* movie.

When *Heartless War* ended, they watched the *Day's Dawn* episode, when Raven had guest-starred on the show.

Simone laughed when she saw her Aunt Raven and Aunt Becky clowning around in-between takes. The young beauties looked very happy. It was very obvious how close they were.

Raven hadn't seen the tape in years. And even after all of the many years, seeing Becky, still tugged at Raven's heart. There she was, as Raven had always wanted to remember her, with the long, golden-blonde hair, those big, sky-blue eyes, and that big, bright smile.

* * *

That night, Raven couldn't sleep. She went back to the living room and turned on the TV. Everyone else had gone to bed. She decided to watch *CNN*.

"Aunt Raven? I thought I heard the TV. You're never up *this* late. Can't sleep?" Simone asked her aunt.

"No, honey, *Aunt Raven* can't sleep."

Simone sat with her aunt. And as always, Simone asked her aunt more questions. "Aunt Raven? Do you think that America is really a melting pot?"

The old lady shook her head no. "No, sweetheart, I don't. There are some races, nationalities, who refuse to melt. They refuse to mingle and they refuse to associate with anyone who doesn't look like them. I have always made it my business getting to know other cultures. What they're like. If you only want to be around those who look like you, what's the point in that? You already know how you are, and most people already know what their culture is like. I have always made it a necessity to broaden my horizons. Always. It keeps one smart, and keeps one sharp! And as I've said for so many years now, differences should be celebrated, not discriminated, or isolated. *All* kinds of differences, including sizes and shapes. What's important, is to surround yourself with people who *are* like you, *meaning*, good people. People of integrity. People with morals and values. People of character. And notice that I didn't say people who *look* like you. I had the *greatest* friend that anyone could *ever* have in Beck, and we didn't look alike. Nor were we the same race. You don't have to look alike, to *be* alike. How a person looks, is irrelevant. How a person *is*, that's what counts! That's what's *important*."

Simone sat listening, hanging on her wise aunt's every word, as usual. "That's very true, Aunt Raven. How many times do many of us judge people based on looks? *Especially* when we choose our companions. I did that with Lark. He was handsome, but he wasn't a good man."

The timeless-beauty nodded. "Oh, yes. We all know that many

people go for looks, no matter what. Looks can be deceiving. I would rather have a *good* man, instead of a *good-looking* man, who wasn't *any* good. Tony, *my* Prince Charming, was a *very* handsome man. But it wasn't his great looks, nor was it his money, that I fell in love with. I fell in love with, and I loved, the man. The great man that he was. If he wasn't a good man, I wouldn't have given him the time of day. Looks don't buy happiness, nor does money. If that were the case, good-looking couples who are rich, wouldn't get divorced. And they would always be happy."

"Very true. Aunt Raven, what are your thoughts on backstabbers?"

The old lady flashed her trademark smile. "Don't worry about backstabbers, sweetheart. God can turn knives, into *boomerangs*."

Simone continued to marvel at her aunt's wisdom. "I always hope that things turn out how I want them to."

"Most of us do. However, always *pray* that things turn out as they *should*, not, as you want them to." The old lady yawned. "I'm going to call it a night. Good night, sweetheart. I love you. *Always* remember that. And never forget what I have told you. But, more importantly, don't forget what I have *shown* you. Leading by example, is the *only* way to lead."

"You have *always* been a *fine* example, Aunt Raven. The *finest*."

"Thanks, sweetheart." After giving her niece a hug and kiss, Raven walked to her bedroom.

Simone stood, watching her.

"Go to bed and stop watching me."

"Aunt Raven, how did you know that I was watching you?"

Raven laughed. "Because I *know*."

* * *

The next morning, Simone showered, brushed her teeth, then went to make breakfast, as she did every morning.

It was very quiet in the house. Simone went to the living room.

No Aunt Raven.

Simone went to her aunt's bedroom and knocked on the door. "Aunt Raven?"

There was no answer.

"Aunt Raven? *Aunt Raven?*"

After waiting and receiving no answer, Simone opened the door.

Her aunt was still in bed.

"Aunt Raven? Are you sleeping in this morning?" Simone walked over to her aunt's bed.

Raven had a smile on her face. Her eyes were closed.

Simone shook her aunt.

Her aunt didn't stir.

"Aunt Raven?"

Simone shook her aunt gently again. Tears filled her eyes. Her aunt wasn't breathing.

Raven, Kensington, Dash ... was dead. She died quietly in her sleep. She was one hundred and nine years old. The old lady looked very peaceful. That trademark smile of hers, was still there. That's something that not even death, had removed.

"Brunner, call 911! We need an ambulance! Aunt Raven's *not* breathing!" Simone performed mouth-to-mouth resuscitation on her aunt. "Brun-ner! Brun-ner!" Simone screamed at the top of her lungs.

Brunner ran to Raven's bedroom. "An ambulance is on the way! Oh ... my *God ... Mrs. Dash ...*"

A devastated Simone knelt down beside her aunt's bed, screaming, crying, and feeling scared and helpless.

* * *

The ambulance and police arrived in a matter of minutes. The paramedics tried to revive Raven, but there was *nothing*, that they could do.

Raven's body was covered, then transported to Cedars-Sinai Medical Center, where an autopsy was performed immediately.

The police stayed behind to do their routine-questioning, and to complete a report. Simone, Brunner, and the entire staff, told them everything that they knew.

Before leaving, the police thanked everyone for their cooperation, and they told Simone that they were very sorry about her aunt.

The autopsy was ordered immediately, because everyone knew that Raven Kensington was a very rich woman. The police wanted to make sure that there wasn't any foul play involved, in spite of the superstar's age.

* * *

News of Raven Kensington's death, spread like wildfire. Every channel covered her death, and her *enormously*-successful career, that was *unmatched*.

Millions all over the world, mourned her death. People were deeply saddened. Many of the news channels and radio stations played, "Wind Beneath My Wings." The song couldn't have been more appropriate, for the truly-amazing woman, who was a hero, to millions.

"Breaking news story! It is a *very* sad day in Hollywood, and in the entire world. *Raven Kensington*, Hollywood's *greatest* legend, and movie goddess, has died. Ms. Kensington died quietly in her sleep at her home in Malibu this morning. Time of death is unknown. Raven Kensington was one hundred and nine years old ..."

The reporter's voice broke. He had tears in his eyes. He remembered meeting the screen legend once. He had never admired anyone as much as he had admired her.

The reporter went on, while trying hard to maintain professionalism. "*Raven Kensington* was *the* star of all stars. The staggeringly-beautiful, multi-talented, *renowned*-superstar, took stardom to new heights. Raven Kensington was Hollywood's *most* famous star. There was *no one* like her. Ms. Kensington made the world stand up and take notice. The Tunis-born *megastar*, made history *many* times over ..."

Simone turned the TV off.

* * *

Raven Kensington's death was front-page news. Her death was covered in every newspaper and magazine in the country. The media covered the woman, the philanthropist, her unmatched-acting career, and how she became Hollywood's *greatest* legend. The media showed countless photos of Raven.

Many fans camped outside the gates of the Dashs' Malibu estate. Thousands went out and bought every, and anything, with Raven Kensington's name and face on it. Anything, with the superstar's name and face on it, sold like hotcakes.

* * *

The autopsy results came back days later. Raven Kensington died of natural causes.

Raven left Simone over her estate. She knew that she could trust her niece to do everything that she had requested in her will. Raven had also told Simone where all of her important papers were. And Simone knew before even reading her aunt's will and testament, that she was going to be buried right beside her "beloved" Tony. And as always, Raven made everything, *crystal*-clear.

Simone took her aunt's death very hard. Her aunt was her best friend. They had always been close. She could always talk to her aunt about anything. She was also the last known family member that she had. She was going to miss her dearly. The huge, ultra-lavish home wasn't the same without her, nor would it ever be. Raven Kensington was the glue that held everyone, and everything, together. As far as Simone was concerned, the world, wasn't going to be the same without *her* either.

Simone sat, looking at her aunt's beautiful photos. Her aunt had always loved pictures. Simone knew the pictures that her aunt cherished the most, were those of her and Tony. Gosh, they were *so* much in love. I pray and hope that one day, I will have what Aunt

Raven and Uncle Tony had. Simone knew that what they shared was incredibly-special, not to mention rare. Simone smiled through her tears. "Aunt Raven, you will get to be with *your* Prince Charming again." Simone knew that was something her aunt looked forward to.

Simone stared at the huge portrait of her aunt that hung above the fireplace in the formal living room. Her eyes locked on the *exquisitely*-beautiful woman, who smiled back at her. *That* dazzling, trademark, Miss America smile. Simone continued staring at the woman, who was *more*, than amazing.

* * *

Simone thought her aunt acted a little strange during the last few days of her life. She remembered her aunt staying up really late the night before she died. Her aunt had never done that before. Simone couldn't help but wonder if her aunt knew that she was going to die.

Raven had also died smiling. *That* dazzling smile. Her smile was definitely her trademark. And it was the way that she had left the world.

Fans came in droves, placing flowers and cards outside of the Dashs' gates. Simone had never seen so many flowers and cards in her life. Nor had she ever seen so many tears. Raven Kensington was a woman who was truly loved, and adored, by millions, and she was going to be *sorely*-missed.

* * *

Simone dressed her aunt. It was the hardest thing that she had ever done, but she wanted to do it. She dressed her in a very elegant, white dress-suit. Raven had always preferred suits, instead of dresses. Tears fell from Simone's eyes, as she dressed her aunt. Raven's hair was combed as she always liked it. And as always, there wasn't a hair out of place. Hair that was once long and raven-black, was now, long and cotton-white.

* * *

Simone always wondered, like so many, how Raven would look just as impeccable at the end of the day, as she did in the beginning. She was such an incredible woman. *Truly*-incredible. *Amazing. Phenomenal.* Simone had learned a great deal from her Aunt Raven. And she was determined to put that knowledge to *use*.

* * *

Simone released a statement to the media. In her statement, she thanked "everyone" for their love, prayers, and gratitude. She declined interviews. But she wanted all of the many people who had loved and admired her aunt to know, how very much she appreciated everything that they had done. She was very grateful for all of the love and support. Simone wasn't surprised though. Her Aunt Raven was definitely well-loved. She had touched *millions* of lives. In Hollywood, and more importantly, in the world.

"Oh ... Aunt Raven. You were such an *extraordinary* woman! If I am a tenth of the woman that you were, I'll be okay. Tell Uncle Tony hello, and give him my love. He will be waiting in the wings for you, just as he said he would be. I will *always* love you, Aunt Raven ..." Simone's voice cracked. Her aunt would finally be with the love of her life. They would be together, again. Simone smiled through her tears. "Your Prince Charming *awaits*."

* * *

Raven's wake lasted for three days, before the funeral took place. Her casket was heavily guarded. Hundreds of thousands of mourners came to view Raven's body, and pay their respects, to the woman whom many deemed, "their *hero*." At the end of the three days, 850,000 people had viewed Raven Kensington's body.

* * *

Raven Kensington's funeral ... Law enforcement was in full force for security and crowd control. But the L.A.P.D. was not prepared for the *enormous* turnout. They figured the Hollywood legend's funeral would be huge, but they hadn't expected what they saw early on. They immediately called for help from neighboring suburban cities.

Sergeant Miller shook his head. "I've been to many funerals, celebrity-ones included, but I have *never* seen a funeral even close to *this* size."

His partner nodded his head in agreement. He too was amazed. "No kidding! Raven Kensington was obviously very well-loved, and greatly admired."

"Apparently," said the sergeant. "*Very*, well-loved."

Sergeant Miller hadn't been born yet during Raven Kensington's reign in Hollywood, but like so many, he had definitely heard about the "great" Raven Kensington, and all that she had accomplished. All of the great things that he had heard about her, made him a huge fan of hers. She was an outstanding woman in his eyes too. Not to mention a fabulous-looking one. Sergeant Miller smiled. His father had a huge crush on Raven Kensington. As did males all over the world. She was a staggeringly-beautiful and sultry woman.

"We'd better get going!" said the young rookie cop, interrupting his boss's thoughts.

They both continued to shake their heads in amazement at the massive crowd. Streets were lined with cars. Sidewalks were jammed with people. It was as if everyone who lived in Los Angeles was there.

Raven Kensington's funeral was the largest that many in attendance had ever seen. People from all over the world came to pay homage to this extraordinary woman, who did so much, for so many. People from all walks of life were there. The rich and famous, the powerful, the poor, the unknown, the President of the United States and First Lady, the Prime Minister, the Arab king and his wife, the list was endless. There were people of all nationalities too. It seemed as if everyone who was anyone, was there. In Raven Kensington's eyes, *everyone*, was "important." There were no big I's and little u's.

Raven's obituary had a beautiful photo of her, flashing that trademark, Miss America smile, that she was well-known for. *Raven Kensington Dash. Sunrise: March 9, 1994. Sunset: February 27, 2104*, was inscribed beneath the photo.

Raven instructed Simone in her will, not to stop anyone from coming to her funeral. "*Whoever* it is, if they want to come, let them."

And come they did. The streets of Los Angeles had never been so crowded.

Raven's funeral was televised on every major channel. The police worked very hard to control the enormous crowd, that seemed to grow more and more, as time went on. Many had to stand outside, because there wasn't enough room in the enormous church.

This woman had done so much, for so many. The city, the poor, the world ... *They* had all come to say their final farewell, to the very fine and *phenomenal* woman, that Raven Kensington was.

Every reporter known to man was also there, covering Raven Kensington's funeral. A number of reporters estimated correctly, that there were at least two and a half million people, in attendance.

No one had ever seen the L.A. sidewalks and streets so packed with cars and people. Planes flew overhead too. Many people had even started camping outside the church, days before the funeral.

Millions of people had loved and admired Raven Kensington in life, and they were now *honoring* her, in death.

Pastor Brooks presided over the service. Because of the immense-crowd, a select few were allowed to speak.

"Please!"

Simone and Pastor Brooks looked to see where the voice was coming from. They turned to see an elderly lady making her way through the massive crowd.

"Please, I *have* to speak!"

Pastor Brooks looked at Simone. It was up to her. She was in charge.

The old woman seemed adamant. "Please!"

Simone nodded. She did what she knew, her aunt would have wanted her to do. She let the woman speak. Simone looked at the woman, wondering who she was. Whoever she is, thought Simone, she's certainly determined to speak.

The elderly lady was crying hard. Finally, she pulled herself together. She was determined to share her story. She *had* to. "I am ninety-one years old. I first met Ms. Kensington, when I was seven. I was poor then. I lived in Compton with my mother and grandmother. I sat in school one day crying, hoping that *this* superstar, who was my hero, would write me back. There was a part of me that didn't think she would. She didn't write me back either. She did something *far* greater instead. Ms. Kensington came to my house to visit me! Boy, was I shocked! It was totally unexpected. My grandmother was shocked too. The old shack of a house that we lived in, didn't have heat. Well, the central heat wasn't working. The landlord never fixed it. The house was cold. Ms. Kensington called her husband, who fixed our central heat for us. It was a big blessing for us, because it was cold outside, and the little electric heater didn't heat too well. While her husband fixed the heater, Ms. Kensington and I talked." The old lady smiled through her tears, as she found her voice again. She remembered that conversation as if it took place yesterday. "*Many* years have passed since then, but I have *never* forgotten the words of wisdom that she gave me, nor have I *ever* forgotten what she did for me, and my family. Ms. Kensington still wasn't finished. She moved *us* into a brand new home. She also bought us a brand new car. I have *never* known anyone with a heart as big as hers. She was incredibly-beautiful outside, and inside too. My name ... is Layla. *Dr.* Layla Halter-Robbins. I had to speak! I will go to my grave, being *immensely*-grateful, for what *this* incredible woman did for me and my family." Layla looked at Simone with tears in her eyes. "*Thank* you!"

Simone nodded in answer, as tears streamed down her face.

Pastor Brooks stood at the pulpit. Tears were streaming down his face too. He was going to preach. But before that, he had to *adulate* this extraordinary woman. *Raven Kensington Dash.*

The pastor began. "May *all* of the great and wonderful works, that Raven Kensington did, *speak*, for *her*."

"Amen! Amen!" roared the congregation.

"I may ramble. This isn't easy for me." Pastor Brooks prayed silently to gain his composure. "*This* ... is a *very* sad day, for *all* of us. Oftentimes, during funerals, or *Home Goings*, people will stand and say things about the deceased that may not be true. However, in *this* case, in Raven Kensington Dash's case, *everything* that has been said, everything that I am going to say, *is* true. I've known this *extraordinary* woman for thirty years, personally. She was so much, to *so* many." The pastor looked at Simone Kensington. "To the young lady sitting on the front row, she was 'Aunt Raven.' To me, she was my mentor, my best friend. To the world, to all of her *millions* of fans, she was an *international superstar*. Raven Kensington, was Hollywood's *greatest* legend. Notice that I didn't say *one of*. I said, *greatest*. She was *perfection* on-screen. She was the best actress that I had *ever* seen. Ms. Kensington was acting at its very best! She could play any role and play it like no other. Her smile and talent were as well-known as her *staggering*-beauty. She was the young black girl from Tunis, Texas, who made *all* of her dreams, become *reality*. Ms. Kensington soared higher than an eagle. She left *no* stone unturned. She became everything that she was capable of becoming, and then some. And she *always* encouraged others, to do the same. She was a breath of fresh air for Tinseltown. And for the world. The *unconquerable*, Raven Kensington, was a woman who fought hard, to make Hollywood, a Hollywood for *all*. She proved to Hollywood that being different, could mean that you were *better*, and in her case, it meant that you were *the best*. The very best. Raven Kensington helped change the face and size of Hollywood, and society. She was *much* more than an icon, she was an *institution*. She was a star that *never* lost her glow. Never, has

Tinseltown been as diverse in colors, shapes, and sizes, as it is now. *Never.*"

"Amen! Amen!"

"Ms. Kensington's *immeasurable*-success and *incomparable*-talent as an actress, and best-selling author, *paled* in comparison, to who she was as a *person*, as a woman. There were women, then, there was … *Raven Kensington*. Ms. Kensington, was the *definition* of a lady. She raised the bar!"

The massive, grief-stricken crowd nodded their heads in agreement.

"Ms. Kensington was *truly*, the *epitome* of beauty, class, elegance, and integrity. She was the elite of the elite. And that dazzling, trademark, Miss America smile of hers, will *forever* be etched in our hearts and minds. She was the *incomparable* Raven Kensington. A woman ahead of her time, a great philosopher. Very *distinguished*. Unique. Very confident. She was a woman of *immeasurable*-strengths. A scene-stealer on, and off, the set. Raven Kensington was the kind of woman that made one turn and stare. She had *enormous* magnetism and presence. She was the kind of person that even if you had met her once, you would never forget her. She had a very *powerful* effect on people. This *breathtakingly*-beautiful woman was also as tough as nails. She was a mighty, *mighty* warrior. She was very gutsy and strong-willed. And as many of you know, she didn't just fight for herself, she fought for *many* others. And as she often told me, she fought *for all those* ... Ms. Kensington was a *tireless* warrior for justice. She was the best fighter that I've ever known. I certainly would not have wanted to get in the ring with her!"

That comment drew a laugh from the grief-stricken crowd.

"She was a mover and a shaker, if there ever was one. She was unstoppable. After all, it's very hard to stop a train. She was the kind of person that you could give the ball to, and stand back, because you *knew* that she would deliver. Raven Kensington would deliver like no other. She had no respect of person. There were no big I's and little u's with her. She was a woman very comfortable in her own skin. She was *extremely* proud of her heritage. Many often commented on how very beautiful she was, but let us not overlook her *immense*-wisdom. She was as wise, as the ol' owl. Her eyes were not only *mesmerizing*, they were the wisest eyes that I had ever seen. They looked *inside* of you. I will never forget what this great and wise woman told me, when my first wife left me for another man. At first, I told Ms. Kensington that I was finished with love. Then later, I told her that I wanted another companion, but that I didn't have the heart to love again. Ms. Kensington always called me by my last name. She said, 'Brooks, you can't search for love, nor can you hope to love again, if you've lost your heart.' I am now happily-married. Her *immeasurable*-wisdom, helped guide me *many* times over the years. Talking with her, was very *empowering*, and *enlightening*. Ms. Kensington also had a great sense of humor. She was also *intensely*-private. Very *resilient*. Raven Kensington was a leader, not a follower. She made her own trails, she didn't follow paths. And she *always* took the high road." Pastor Brooks paused again, to regain his composure. "She was *my* hero! And borrowing from one of my favorite songs, *she* was the wind beneath *my* wings. We could *all* take *many* pages, out of her book. She was a great role model, mentor, and *huge* inspiration, to all of us. She was a woman who didn't do the *expected*. There were *so* many things that I loved about this *extraordinary* woman. The thing that I loved *most* about her though, was her heart. Ms. Kensington's heart was as big as the state that she was born in. She always said 'heart-work pays off.' And we all know that she did a whole *lot* of heart-work! Her other motto was: 'Just because you can't help everyone, it should *never* stop you, from helping *someone*.' She was right too. She made a *substantial* difference, not only in Hollywood, but *much* more importantly, in the *world*." Pastor Brooks paused again. He looked out at the massive, grief-stricken crowd. "Raven Kensington opened her heart, and her purse, and she gave a lot of her time, to so many people, and to *many* causes. She was the most *generous* philanthropist that I …

have *ever* known. The impact that Ms. Kensington had on others, was *immeasurable*. She cared a *great* deal about humanity. Many people ate, because of *her*. Many lived in nice, decent homes, because of *her*. Many schools were remodeled, and furnished with new books, computers, and other very *important* educational materials, because of ... *her*."

Pastor Brooks knew that the Rebecca Simms Foundation was very near and dear to Raven's heart. He also knew why. The foundation was still going very strong. Thanks to the *generosity* of this great and admirable woman, whom God had now taken.

The pastor continued. "I never understood how she was able to juggle it all, but she did. One hundred and nine years old! God blessed Ms. Kensington with a very *long* life. I think it was because of the kind of person that she was. I liken Raven Kensington to an angel, that God sent to us, for a spell. She couldn't stay forever. None of us can."

Pastor Brooks paused again, before going on. Like so many in attendance, his heart, was very heavy. "It didn't matter *who* you were, she touched you in *some* way. Be it something that she said, something that she did, closed doors that she opened ... She touched you, *somehow*. Ms. Kensington was a woman who set standards for greatness! No matter how tall you were, you looked up to her. Raven Kensington changed hearts, and she changed minds. And although her life has ended, her *countless* contributions, her *enormous* heart, her messages, her actions, her *immense*-wisdom, her beautiful spirit, her *astonishing*-beauty, and *that* dazzling, Miss America, *trademark* smile, will live with us ... *always*! *These* things, will live on!" The pastor smiled through his tears. "As I look out into the massive crowd, I see people of *every* kind of race known to man. I see people from *all* different backgrounds, and from *all* walks of life. Ms. Kensington would have been *ecstatic* to see this picture. It was what she fought so hard for. Unity! *Everyone*, coming together, being together. Because after all, we are *all* God's children. And we are *all*, *His* creations. Ms. Kensington was a woman who brought *unity* in life. And now, even in her death, she brings us all together, again, in *unity*."

Pastor Brooks regained his composure before going on. "And last but not least, it is *not*, how we look in man's eyes, but it's how we *are*, in *God's* eyes, that counts. Ms. Kensington was a God-fearing, Christian woman, so we know whom she's with now. No matter how great we are on this earth, it doesn't end here. We *must* make our choice in life, where we would like to be, in death. And whereas Hollywood, and other things, *are* make-believe, heaven and hell, are very *real*. It was *truly*, the *greatest* honor, to have known, Ms. Kensington. And like many of you, I will *never forget her*. She is *definitely* one legend, that the sun, will *never* set on."

Pastor Brooks looked out at all of the grief-stricken, tear-stained faces. There wasn't a dry eye in the enormous church.

"*This extraordinary* woman, was *not*, an *African-American* treasure, nor was she an *American* treasure, or a *Hollywood* treasure. *Raven Kensington*, was a **world-class treasure**! She was *incredible*. She is *unforgettable*. And she is simply, *irreplaceable*!"

The pastor paused because of outbursts from the massive crowd. Tears continued to fall from his eyes, as he continued. "A person like *her*, comes along, *once*, in a lifetime. There may be copies out there, but there is only *one* original. There will *never* be another, *quite* like *her*. There will *never* be another, **Raven, Kensington, Dash**."

*   *   *   *   *

Dear Readers:

I hope that you enjoyed reading this book, as much as I enjoyed writing it!

Best wishes!

~Michelle Cole